THE MURDER BETWEEN US

M|M ROMANTIC SUSPENSE

TAL BAUER

A NOAH & COLE THRILLER

This novel contains scenes of intense content and mature sexual content.

All rights reserved.

No part of this publication may be reproduced, distributed, or transmitted in any form or by any means, including photocopying, recording, or other electronic or mechanical methods, without the prior written permission of the publisher, Tal Bauer, except in the case of brief quotations embodied in critical reviews and certain other noncommercial uses permitted by copyright law.

Second Edition

10 9 8 7 6 5 4 3 2

Edited by Alicia Z. Ramos

Copyright © 2021 Tal Bauer

Cover Art by Rocking Book Covers © Copyright 2020

Published in 2021 by Tal Bauer

United States of America

1

IT'S VEGAS. This city was built for people to come and shake out all their bad decisions. All their... curiosities.

Noah wove his way through the casino hall, sidestepping for a waitress balancing an overloaded tray in one hand. He smiled. She smiled back.

His friend James spun and watched her walk away, whistling as he stared at her long legs encased in sheer black stockings. Her skirt ended at the tops of her thighs. More than a few guys were breaking their necks to watch as she sashayed down the casino hallway amid the whirs and jangles and frantic chimes pouring out of the rows and rows of slot machines. Even some of the guys at the blackjack tables turned to look at her.

She glanced back and met Noah's gaze again. She winked. A slow smile unfurled over her perfect face.

"Dude!" James grabbed at Noah's arm and almost walked backward into one of the pillars lining the hall. Noah grabbed him with both hands, steadying him before he fell into a crowd of Japanese tourists. "She smiled at you, man. Go back there! C'mon, go on. You definitely have an in!"

Noah shook his head. The rest of their group slowed to a

tipsy halt, forming a loose bubble around Noah and James. They were practically carbon copies of each other: seven guys lurching toward middle age with mostly flat stomachs and most of their hair still on top of their heads. They were all dressed the same, even: khakis and a polo, but some of the guys had left behind their sport coats before dinner. They were the ones wearing the fanny packs around their waists.

"Go on!" James tried to push Noah after the waitress who had simply smiled at him, a gentle flirtation after he'd stepped aside to ease her way.

He wasn't kidding himself. There was no way a woman like her—gorgeous, with a perfect body, and young enough to make him uncomfortable—would ever want him chasing her down.

"I think the night is over," Noah said, spinning James and propelling him toward the elevators. The group laughed and followed, the just-past-drunk, ambling stroll of men at midnight in Las Vegas. "We've got an early morning. C'mon."

James groaned. "Why do they have this conference here?" He threw his head back and trudged toward the elevator bank. "Why can't they have this conference in…" His eyes slid sideways. He grinned. "In Des Moines. Somewhere boring." Noah knuckled his friend's hair as James laughed.

All one thousand of them were there, spread across the tenth through twenty-fifth floors of the hotel. God bless the government and its bulk room discounts. Where should the Federal Bureau of Investigation put the special agents who attended the largest annual FBI conference? All together, like sardines in a can. No one could quite figure out whether the conference was a mini vacation or a horrible tease. Agents had to attend a week's worth of sessions, lectures, and breakout workshops, each of them putting together their own thirty-hour-long conference schedule. Nights were theirs… as long as they badged in every morning on time. More than a few agents overslept each morning, hungover and destroyed from a night out on the town. If an agent was late two days in a row, they were sent home, and from there, it was a short trip to the doghouse—or worse. Maybe the whole conference was a test of character.

Whatever it was, the conference was Noah's week away from home—Des Moines, Iowa—and a chance to reconnect with his friends from the academy. James had been his roommate way back when, and now he was chasing bank robbers in Southern California. Gary was running the white-collar crime squad out of Philly, while Pete and Carl were chasing right-wing terrorists in Seattle.

Everyone else was in a major field office, while Noah had somehow landed in the Des Moines resident agency—a satellite of the larger Omaha field office—and stayed, like a farmhouse dropped by a tornado. He was the assistant special agent in charge of Des Moines now. Technically, that meant he outranked all of his friends. Even if it was only Des Moines.

Everyone had done well. Everyone was at that comfortable point in their careers: close enough to the middle to settle in, far enough from the beginning to have shaken out the kinks and the nerves. Far enough away from retirement for that to still be a distant thing, something relegated to when the knees began to act up and the gray hairs were multiplying.

The elevator doors slid open, and the guys piled in. They leaned against the mirrored walls, laughing about the evening, reminiscing over the dinner they'd spent way too much money on, remembering the women they'd seen out in the casino and on the Strip. Everyone's eyes were glassy. Their shoulders were starting to droop.

Noah's hands shook inside his pants pockets. One foot tapped silently against the carpet. *It's Vegas. You waited all year for this.*

He'd chickened out for the past two nights, heading back to his room when everyone else did and pacing for an hour before watching the neon glow of the Strip from his window. Eventually, he'd turned on CNN and listened to the warble of the news anchors as he face-planted in bed, hoping the drone of their voices would force out the thoughts that kept circling around and around his mind. *Coward. You'll never know. You'll never know if you don't try.*

The elevator started spitting everyone out at the eleventh, fourteenth, and seventeenth floors, until it was just James and him stepping off on the twentieth. Their rooms were across the hall from each other.

James leaned back against his door, key card in one hand, sport coat crumpled in his other. His holster was out and visible now—a violation, but it was midnight, and they were alone. Who was going to write him up?

"I'm telling you, man," James said, in the languid drawl of the inebriated. "You should go back down there. Maybe she's not the one for tonight, but she definitely would be willing to flirt with you if you happened to run into her again. How long has it been since a pretty woman smiled at you?"

Noah's eyes fell to the carpet as he dug his shoe into the wool fibers.

"I know you've been focused on your career, and…" James trailed off with a sigh. "I know it's been a while. That can eat at a man, you know? You deserve to be happy. God, out of all of us, *you* deserve to be happy." James smiled, a lopsided, tipsy grin. Despite wolf whistling at the waitress, James was all set to pour himself into bed and call his wife, whisper sweet nothings to her as she recounted every moment of her day with their three young daughters. James had been texting her throughout dinner, sending her pics of the appetizer and then his entree, and of his ridiculous drink.

James was a man who had certainty. He had the love of a great woman, three amazing daughters, and the satisfaction that came from knowing his place in the world.

Jealousy seared through Noah. Certainty. What a thing to be jealous of. To know yourself and what you wanted.

"Breakfast tomorrow?" James pushed off and shoved his key in the lock. It beeped, and he shouldered open the door before tossing his jacket into the darkness.

"Meet you in the restaurant." Noah nodded, waiting for James to head inside.

His friend, despite seeming to be the inebriated fool, was still a federal agent, and he could still put the clues together. He looked Noah up and down, eyes narrowing as his smile shifted, turned almost salacious. "Tell me 'bout it in the morning," he said, disappearing into his room. "Have fun!"

The door shut. Noah heard the deadbolt turn.

It's Vegas. You're supposed to do this in Vegas. You're supposed to let loose. He tipped his head back. Sighed. *Go down there. Just for a few minutes. Just look.*

Yeah, okay. He could do that. He could look. Looking wasn't anything permanent.

First things first. He pushed into his hotel room and unholstered his gun, locking it in the safe. If he was going to head back out, he might as well freshen up a bit. Change out of the clothes he'd worn all day. In the bottom of his suitcase were a pair of black jeans, snugger than he ever wore in Iowa, and a slim-fit button-down he'd accidentally bought along with the regular ones he preferred. It was way too tight to wear to the office, and he felt ridiculous when he put it on. In the slim cut, he felt like he was playing dress-up as Hollywood's idea of a special agent. But he had to admit the shirt showed off his flat stomach and his broad shoulders, the taper he'd built in high school and college through intramural sports and kept up thanks to turning to the gym whenever his frustrations started to boil.

Might as well run his fingers through his hair, too. And brush his teeth. Should he shave? Why not.

Half an hour later, Noah stared at himself, eyeballing the

tall, dark-haired, shit-scared man in the mirror. He was just a guy. Just a guy going down for a drink. Nothing more. "It's Vegas," he whispered. His fingers curled around the sink's edge. "Let yourself look."

He never had before.

Noah grabbed his wallet and his room key and forced himself to walk out the door. He left his badge and gun behind. He wasn't a federal agent tonight—or at least, not for the next hour. Or, hell, the next ten minutes, if he was truthful with himself about how long his courage was likely to last. He'd rather be back at Quantico than let go of the hotel room door and go down the elevator.

The hallway was empty, not a soul in sight up or down its cavernous length. It was that in-between time for Vegas. Too late for families, too early for the partygoers. All the people who weren't going out were in for the night, and those who were still going were going to last all night.

But not him. No, he was just going to have one drink. One look.

One, two, three steps. Noah shook out his arms, rolled his shoulders. Strode down the hall. He could do this.

HE COULDN'T DO THIS. What had he been thinking?

The casino, if possible, was even more packed than earlier. The floor was brighter, louder. The slots were screaming, electric jangles and digital bells roaring. Neon and strobe lights slammed into him. Men and women, couples and groups, surged. Laughter and shouts rose from the gambling pit, the cocktail tables, the crowds by the slot machines.

He was adrift in a sea of humanity. No one else was alone like he was. Everyone he saw had someone. Friends, a significant other, a partner. Someone they were with. Except him.

The bar was dead ahead, a giant circle of raised marble in

the center of the casino floor. He beelined for it, sliding into an open space and leaning on his elbows. He squeezed his eyes closed. What was he doing? He should go back to his room and turn on CNN. Again.

"Hey, honey!" A slim hand landed on his shoulder. Noah jerked, twisted—

It was the waitress from earlier. Her name tag, pinned low on her breast and drawing the eye to her cleavage, said *Rachel*. She leaned into his side, beaming, and one of her stocking-clad thighs rubbed against his leg. "Uh—" he stammered.

"Ditch your friends?" Her gaze flicked down, taking in his change of clothes. Her eyes seemed to ignite, and her smile, when she looked up, was different. Hungrier. "Hanging around for a bit, sexy?"

Noah swallowed hard. "I… I don't know." He shook his head. He couldn't think. She was too close. Her breasts were pushing against his arm. As gingerly as he could, he shifted away, putting centimeters between his body and hers. "I only came down for one drink."

As quickly as she'd lit up, she became completely uninterested. She shifted away and flicked her hair, sending her long, black tresses over one shoulder. "If you're here for a drink, Philippe will get you one." She caught the bartender's eye and jerked her chin to Noah, then pushed back from the bar top. "Enjoy your night."

"Have a good night, too," Noah tried to say, but he was speaking to her back as she strode away, smiling at new people, taking drink orders effortlessly and batting her eyes at the men with the tallest stacks of chips in front of them at the blackjack tables.

"What'll it be?" a gruff voice barked. Philippe, behind the bar, was six feet of solid muscle. He had long hair pulled back in a ponytail, and his black T-shirt wasn't just tight, it was stretched so thin Noah could almost see the individual fibers struggling to hold on to their atomic bonds. Philippe glowered down at Noah, rubbing his hammer-sized hands in a bar towel.

"Whiskey, please. Jameson on the rocks."

Philippe nodded and poured his drink silently, then slid it across the bar top. "Twenty-four dollars."

Jesus. He didn't know which to be more confused by, the outrageous price or Philippe's hostility. How had he pissed off two people in less than a minute? *You're not in Kansas anymore.* Or Iowa, even. He opened his wallet, thumbed out thirty dollars, and slid the bills to Philippe. Philippe pocketed the cash and walked off.

And then Noah was alone again, sandwiched between two groups of businessmen who had passed tipsy an hour ago and were howling at stories that were being told louder and louder. Elbows jostled him, and a man in a blue sport coat backed into his hip, barely grunting an apology before Noah spread his arms and tried to stake out his territory a bit better. Maybe he should take his drink and go. Walk. Find somewhere else to be. Hell, he could sit in front of a slot machine and get ignored by Rachel and have a better time.

Or he could go back upstairs.

So much for his big try.

Sighing, he slumped forward, head down, fingers twirling his glass on the marble bar top. Ice sloshed and slipped in and out of the amber liquid.

This wasn't him. He wasn't this uneasy, this out of his element. He was forty years old, not fourteen. Too old, maybe, for this. He gave himself a silent toast—*Hey, you tried, have a participation trophy*—and downed the rest of the whiskey.

He caught sight of a man staring at him across the bar. An attractive—*Jesus, he was really handsome*—man. His blond hair shone under the bar's lights, and his head was tilted to the side, just so. A tiny smile played on his lips as if he was laughing at some inside joke he and Noah shared.

Lightning sparked down Noah's arms, electricity zinging beneath his skin.

He froze, whiskey half down his throat, glass to his lips. He nearly inhaled the Jameson, almost ended up spraying whiskey over the backs of the obnoxious sales guys crowding him on his right. His eyes watered, and he set his glass down too quickly, nearly losing it as his hand slipped on the condensation. He couldn't have looked more undignified if he tried. Heart pounding, Noah peered across the bar, trying to spot the blond man again. His breath hitched, caught, as Philippe paced in front of him—

The blond man was gone.

Disappointment knifed through him. He dragged in a slow breath as his fingers clenched around his empty glass. One look. One glimpse. One skip of his heart. Jesus, if this was the reaction he got just from making eye contact with a good-looking guy, then...

Well. It's not like he really wondered anymore. He pretty much knew. But there was a difference between thinking, and wondering, and pretty much knowing and... *really knowing*.

Of course, to know, he'd have to work up enough courage to do something about it, and considering his track record...

It wasn't so bad, being alone.

Besides, that guy was probably looking at someone behind him. One of the sales guys, or, more likely, Rachel. Or any other attractive person, male or female. Who in this casino would pick him out of the crowd, drinking alone at the bar, to smile at?

Well, he'd had his drink, he'd seen a guy who made his heart race, he'd nearly dropped his drink, and now it was time to head back to his room. Noah batted his glass between his palms on the bar top: once, twice, a third time. He nodded. He'd done what he said he would. Time for another year of thinking about it, thinking he might be—

"Can I buy you another one?"

The voice that spoke was honeyed whiskey, amber and gold sliding down his spine and burrowing beneath his skin. Warmth flowed from Noah's chest, slid up his neck, and grabbed the back of his skull. A hard body leaned into him, just like Rachel had, but instead of cleavage and soft curves, a sculpted chest wrapped in a dark suit slid against his side. A knee brushed the back of his.

The impulses to jump and to melt crashed inside Noah, and he did both and neither at the same time. Jerking, he twisted, losing hold of his empty glass in the process. He lunged for it before it slid off the bar top.

The man beside him caught it one-handed, as if Noah had pitched it to him on purpose.

Jesus. Noah flushed from the roots of his hair to his toes. His eyes flicked down, and down, and then up, quickly. It was him. The blond man who had smiled at him was right there, one leg behind Noah's, elbow on the bar top, holding Noah's glass. He was close enough that Noah could feel the heat coming from his skin, see his chest peeking out from beneath the top two buttons of his shirt, undone and open.

He was tall, as tall as Noah, able to look him in the eye as they stood practically inside each other's shadow. Up close, Noah saw a distinct lack of fine lines and crow's-feet, the signs he'd come to recognize in the mirror as he hit the big 4-0 and that he saw creeping onto the faces of his friends. Deep brown eyes, like old leather and cognac, stared back at him. His stomach flip-flopped.

The sales guys behind Noah roared again, laughing at yet another story told too loud. One of them backed into Noah, this time not even bothering to mumble an apology. Noah turned, glowering. "Hey. Back up, please. No need for that."

They were drunk enough to be happy, and the group shifted six inches down the bar. When Noah turned back, the blond was studying him, that hint of a smile back on his lips, as if he was appraising what Noah had just done.

"Sorry." Noah gestured to both the sales guys and his glass —still in the blond's grasp—at the same time. "It's a little crazy here tonight."

"This isn't your normal scene."

"Definitely not." Noah chuckled. "I uh, wasn't planning on coming out tonight."

Noah felt the blond's eyes rake down his body. "I'm glad you did."

He flushed, as if the sun had turned its entire focus on him and him alone. His vision blurred, and there were suddenly two blond hunks in front of him until his eyes snapped back into focus. He coughed, looked down. Ran his finger over a seam in the bar's marble as he fought a slow smile. "When in Vegas." He shrugged.

Silence. He felt studied, like a lab rat. He looked back up and met the blond's gaze. The lights from the bar dipped in and out of his facial features, curving around his angled cheekbones and the square lines of his jaw. Across the bar, he'd been eye-catching. Up close, he was breathtaking. Noah's chest squeezed.

"Is this your first time?" The question was quiet, the man's voice soft. Gentle.

He barked out a quick laugh and looked away, squinting at the bottles of top-shelf liquor. He was going to jump out of his skin. "Is it that obvious?"

"Well, I saw you shoot down the waitress—who, I might add, a hundred other guys would give just about anything to get a smile from. I thought I might have a better chance with you than she did, but… now I'm thinking I might be the first guy who has ever asked to buy you a drink." His eyes peered into Noah's, searching.

Noah swallowed. Lifted his chin. "You are."

"Was my offer unwelcome?"

It was an off-ramp, a way to escape this conversation. Escape the question, escape his own question, escape his search for answers. "No. It was welcome. You're right, though. I've never done this before. I'm not sure what I'm doing."

"What did you come here for?" The man was still staring at Noah. The rest of the bar faded away: the shouts, the jingle of the slots, the electronic chimes and whirs. Even the sales guys and their boisterous, drunken laughter. Everything disappeared except the two of them and the inches that separated them. The heat of the blond's knee where it brushed the back of Noah's.

"I was…" He was what? Coming down here to look at men? How did that sound, when he said it outside the four walls of his hotel room? He sounded like a creep, like someone he would investigate and expect to find a string of sexual complaints behind, maybe some Peeping Tom activity or stalking. It hadn't sounded that ridiculous before. *Let yourself look. Let yourself pretend you're allowed to.*

God knows he'd wanted to.

He'd imagined meeting a man so many times, dreamed it and yearned for it and hungered for it, the skin of his hands itching from wanting to reach out and…

He wanted to know what it was like. Was the reality anything like the wanting?

"I was giving myself permission," he said.

Smiling, the man held out his hand. "My name is Cole." His smile made his whole face light up, turning the strong angles into gentle curves. "If you'd like, I'll buy the next round and we can chat for a while."

He has kind eyes. Whirlpools of warm wood, dark velvet and starlight. Cole's eyes went right through Noah. That clench he'd carried for years was back, a constriction in his chest like his heart couldn't beat right. "I'm Noah." He took Cole's hand. His skin was warm, smooth. His fingers were long. Jesus, he was gorgeous. "I'd love to have a drink with you."

Cole beamed.

2

THEY TALKED about everything and nothing, working through one round and then a second. It was neither of their first times in Vegas, but Cole enjoyed the nightlife while Noah confessed this was his first time out without his friends in all the years he'd been coming. They were both there on business, but Noah didn't elaborate—he didn't want to drag the FBI into tonight, into this moment that didn't seem real—and neither did Cole, following his lead. Cole loved football and hockey, and they argued about the NFL and the division rankings before Cole tried to explain hockey to him. They both hated golf.

The conversation veered back toward the personal, and the reason they were even talking, after the second round. "Are you questioning, curious, or…" Cole's eyebrows flicked up, and he took a sip and waited as Noah stared into his own drink.

"'Or,' I think. I mean, I'm curious, but it's more than that. I think I'm…" *Gay. You think you're gay.* He gestured at nothing with his glass. Shrugged. "And I want to know."

"Is this a recent question?"

Maybe Cole was a psychologist. He seemed to know just

what to ask, and when. "No, not recent. I've been curious since I was a teenager. I shoved it away when I was younger. Coming out in high school twenty years ago, it wasn't totally acceptable." There were things he'd wanted, things he'd imagined in his life, that he thought would be forever off-limits to him if he was gay. So he decided he wasn't, and that was that.

And here he was. "I only started thinking about finding out for sure in the last couple of years."

"And tonight was the night you decided to do so? On a Wednesday in Vegas in the middle of your conference?" Cole was poking fun at him, but there was a serious question hidden there, too.

"I wasn't going to do anything tonight. I thought I'd grab a drink and tell myself… 'Someday.' I don't know, it sounds stupid to say it out loud. Like I was doing a dress rehearsal or something."

"It's not stupid. Everyone has their own process."

He smiled. "This is the only time I can try, or do whatever I'm doing. I can't be like that back home. I thought maybe letting myself feel the attraction I wanted to feel would be something. Some small step."

"Well, I don't think you're lost on a river in Egypt." Cole held out his glass for a small "Cheers." "I'm impressed. I wasn't nearly so calm and collected about my own coming-out."

Noah chuckled. "I am far from calm and collected."

"You look that way from here. Trust me, I've seen plenty of men get drunk, fall into bed with someone they didn't expect to, and then wake up to a colossal panic attack and the kind of psychological crisis that can undo a person if they're not willing to face the questions that come up after such an event. But here you are. You're not running away from your curiosity or trying to hide from it."

"Not anymore. I want to know." What he'd do after he knew… Well.

"How's your experiment going so far?" Cole swirled his drink before taking a sip. His gaze, so warm and serene and kind, sparked. Fires smoldered in its depths as he stared at Noah.

Noah's mouth went dry. He licked his lips. Cole's eyes darted to his tongue, then back to Noah's eyes. Heat pooled in Noah's belly. He shifted, one thigh brushing against Cole's. They were standing so close together. "I'm having a great time."

"Care to keep the night going?" Cole set down his empty drink, and Noah stiffened. "No, sorry. I meant, would you like to come with me? I'm heading out to watch a late-night jazz set. They don't start until one a.m. at this place. It's a tiny hole-in-the-wall, very anti-Vegas. No flashy lights, no slots, no big stage. There's maybe six tables in the whole spot. But it's my favorite, and I guarantee, you'll never hear better live music."

"What kind of jazz?"

"Fusion. The guys playing tonight are a little more bluesy and have a little bit of rock in their sound. If you like the darker, more moody kind of jazz, they're perfect for you."

Noah smiled. "I happen to love blues, and blues rock, and moody jazz."

Cole, again, beamed, turning the full force of his breathtaking smile on Noah. "Let me take you on your first date with a man, Noah." He held out his hand.

Jesus. His breath stuttered, his stomach flip-flopped, and his heart went wild, pounding so hard Cole had to hear it. Hell, he had to *feel* it with how close they were standing. Why were they so close together? When had that happened?

This was way, way more than he had been expecting from tonight. Or had ever imagined would happen. But was it too much? Should he just thank Cole for the drinks and go back to his room? He was stealing this night from his life, and nothing that happened here would mean anything. Not really.

Not when it was back to the FBI office and back to his real life. Why tease himself with something he couldn't have?

Though, if all he had was tonight, why not seize it—and Cole—with both hands?

He took Cole's hand and smiled. "Show me."

THE PARROT ROOM was indeed a hole-in-the-wall, a cramped, crowded, smoky bar. Instead of a stage, there was a corner marked off with duct tape, and six tiny tables lined two walls. The tables were large enough for a couple of drinks, the cushioned bench seats pushed against the wall only large enough for a couple to cuddle close. Four were occupied, couples huddled together in the dim light thrown off from the flickering candles. Long legs, high heels, men's dark pants.

Cole led him to one of the last open tables, settling in while leaving as much room as possible for Noah. Even so, their hips and thighs were pressed together. A server appeared to take their drink orders, and before Noah could argue, Cole had passed her his credit card to open a tab. While they sipped their drinks—whiskey for him, a margarita for Cole—the band finished their warm-ups. The bassist noodled out a slap rhythm as the guitarist riffed, and the drummer stretched after he put in his earbuds. Noah and Cole talked as much as they could, picking up their conversation from the walk over. It was easy to talk to Cole. Easier than Noah had thought it would be to talk to a man he was attracted to. And, whoa, was he attracted to Cole. His pulse was still wild, his palms still sweaty.

The lights dimmed even further, only a single spotlight on the band while the candles flickered on each table.

The music began softly, almost a tease, an unfurling ribbon of sound that curled around the room, weaving in and out of the smoke and shadow. It built like the beat of a heart, rising and falling, becoming faster, harder, quicker, more urgent. Noah fell into the rhythm and the beat, let the notes flow into his bones and into his blood, and it was only when he closed his eyes that he realized he was listening to a musical rendition of lovemaking.

"How did you find this place?" he asked, leaning closer to Cole and speaking into his ear as the band switched to a new song. The applause was loud in the small space. One couple stood to dance, a man holding a woman close, cradling her as she laid her head on his shoulder.

"The best places in Vegas are only ever discovered through word of mouth. I was told about it a few years ago, and every time I come back, I never miss it. Now you know, and you can tell someone, too."

"It's incredible."

"I'm glad you're enjoying it." Cole shifted and rested his arm on the bench seat behind Noah, almost but not quite wrapping him in a one-armed embrace. His fingers danced on Noah's shoulder, one drawing a slow circle from his clavicle to his deltoid and back. "Is this okay?"

A thousand fireworks exploded inside Noah's body. Fire burned where Cole's finger brushed over his shoulder, as if he'd scorched his skin through his shirt. Ice shivered down his sides, then bolts of heat, and then a rush that went straight to his groin. He swayed into Cole and nodded.

Cole's finger kept circling around his shoulder slowly, lazily, as the next song unfurled in the darkness.

Their thighs were pressed against one another, hip to knee. Cole's warmth was permeating Noah. He sat with his hands wrapped around his glass, knuckles white, forearms trembling. What would happen if he reached out and...

As the guitar wailed, notes screaming into the smoky darkness, the sound of longing and secrets and sadness, Noah reached under the table for Cole's leg. His fingers brushed

Cole's suit pants just above the knee and stroked the brushed wool. Cole's finger stuttered and stopped.

Noah laid his hand on Cole's knee and stroked upward, slowly, until his palm rested on the center of Cole's strong, lean thigh. He squeezed, then tapped out the bass line against Cole's inseam.

Cole shifted into Noah ever so slightly. The hand on Noah's shoulder disappeared, then slid up the back of his neck, Cole's long fingers playing in the short strands at the base of Noah's skull. He sighed, melting into Cole's hold. The fingers stayed in his hair, massaging his skull, running softly over his skin.

The music built in waves, filling the darkness and twining with the ribbons of smoke until every molecule of the bar vibrated with passion and purpose. With desire. With a promise of more hanging on the edge of every quivering sound.

By the end of the late-night set, Noah was lost in a heady rush, filled with dark music that strummed on his deepest longings, his most carnal dreams. He was filled, too, with the scent and heat and presence of Cole. Cole, hot beside him, Noah's skin burning where Cole's arm draped across his shoulders and where his fingers had massaged the lines of his neck. He stroked Cole's leg, down to his knee and back up, higher on Cole's thigh than he'd thought he was brave enough for. High enough that he felt the core of Cole's heat. High enough that Cole subtly spread his legs. Adjusted himself.

They applauded as the musicians bowed, toasting as the crowd sent them another round of free drinks. Cole leaned into Noah, lips brushing over the curve of his ear. "My driver is outside."

Driver? What? Before Noah could respond, Cole was on his feet, signing the credit card slip and holding out his hand.

There wasn't even a question about whether he'd go with him. Noah took his outstretched hand. Cole led him out of the Parrot Room, keeping Noah close and their fingers laced together. They spilled out of the cramped bar onto a side street off the Strip where a Cadillac idled, the young driver waiting by the rear passenger door. "Hey hey, Cole! How are you tonight?"

Cole led Noah to the SUV and waited for him to climb in as the driver, dressed in a perfectly tailored suit, held open the door. "We're doing great. How's your night been?"

"No complaints. The evening has been good to me."

The door shut, and Noah settled against the soft leather as Cole pressed their hips and thighs together once more. It was like they were meant to be like this, bodies brushing, pressing, touching. Cole grabbed his hand and twined their fingers again, resting the back of his hand on Noah's knee. "Let's head back, Gregoire."

"You got it." They pulled away and merged into the neon buzz of the Strip. Lights flickered across Cole's features, pink and blue and strobing yellow carving into and out of his eyes, over his cheekbones, and falling from the cliff of his jaw. His pupils shone as he stared at Noah, watching him for the length of the drive.

Which wasn't long. Gregoire pulled into the meandering drive of the Aria, one of the handful of five-star luxury resorts on the Strip, and brought them to the lobby's front door. "Welcome back, Cole," Gregoire said, hopping out of the driver's seat to grab their door.

Noah's eyes darted around the Cadillac SUV, the Aria's entry, and Gregoire, before returning to Cole. What was happening? They'd purposely shied away from personal details, Noah because he didn't want to drag his professional life into this night and Cole because… Because he didn't want to admit he had a private driver and was staying at the Strip's most luxurious address? Who was he?

Dizzy, Noah slid out of the SUV, holding on to Cole's hand for a moment before squeezing and letting go. Cole, ever the gentleman, smiled and fell in step a half second ahead, enough so that he could grab the door for Noah as they made their way into the Aria.

What was he doing here? He looked around at the soaring ceilings and the multistory fountains, wreathed in paper lanterns, that filled the football-field-length lobby. High heels *click-clack*ed, echoing on the marble. The noise in the Aria was more subdued, more dignified, than at the bar and casino in Noah's hotel. Of course, his hotel was nothing but a three-star, where anyone who came to Vegas could stay. At the Aria, you probably needed a credit check just to book a room.

"Can I buy you a nightcap?" Cole beckoned him toward the late-night bar, a cloistered, private enclave that opened onto a patio surrounded by a lagoon bedecked in flickering lanterns. Candles floated on the water's surface, bobbing in the neon lights of the Strip reflected off the Aria's mirrored exterior.

They were alone on the patio. In the silence and the darkness, Cole took Noah's hand again and led him to a table at the water's edge. A server appeared, and Cole ordered a split of champagne. Noah didn't know his champagnes, but what Cole ordered sounded exceptionally French, and it wasn't any label he recognized from the grocery store aisles. He must have fallen into a fairy tale sometime this evening. How else could he explain this night? Cole, and everything that had happened?

Maybe he was asleep. Maybe he'd wake up drooling on himself as CNN droned in the background.

He squeezed Cole's hand until it hurt. Cole squeezed back.

"You're from the Midwest, right?" Cole asked after a moment.

Noah started. "I am. How did you know?"

"I have a weakness for men from the Midwest." Cole winked. "There's something indefinable about midwesterners.

Something very Norman Rockwell. The stereotype, of course, is the hard worker, the show-me, take-no-bullshit uprightness, but it's more than that. I think midwesterners are..." Cole bit his lip. "Genuine. In a way that can be hard to find nowadays."

"Where are you from?" He half expected Cole to say the Aria, that he lived here in the penthouse. Or he was the owner. Stranger things had happened. Never to Noah, but there was a first time for everything.

"I live on the East Coast now, but I was born in Orange County."

Was he an investment banker? Did he work on Wall Street? Or maybe he had a private practice somewhere wealthy, a psychologist's office where he listened to the stay-at-home mothers of Manhattan or Westchester County weave their troubles. Listened to stockbrokers scream into his couch pillows and cautioned them not to jump. He probably made and lost in an afternoon what Noah earned in an entire year. *Vegas. Where you can meet anyone.* "And now you're in the Aria?" Noah imagined a room here for a week was all of his monthly salary.

Cole smiled. "I appreciate the best and finest things in life." His gaze lasered into Noah as he sipped his champagne. Cole's thumb brushed over the back of his hand.

"Do you like older guys?" He squinted, scrunching up his face before glancing at Cole.

"I like you."

Noah swallowed.

"Did you have a good time? And did tonight answer any of your questions?" Cole's thumb kept running over his knuckles. The waterfall at the dark end of the lagoon trickled, its burbles and babbles the backdrop in this corner of Vegas seemingly carved out just for them. Who knew—maybe Cole had paid to keep the bar open for them alone?

"I had a great time." Noah smiled, and he turned his

hand over, grabbing Cole's. It was simple, but it was also heart-stopping and grounding, all at once. He was holding a man's hand. And not just any man. Cole was… He hadn't found the words yet. The way Cole looked at Noah—looked *into* him—and drew him out slowly, until here he was, holding Cole's hand moments away from the neon glow of the Strip.

Cole was someone Noah wanted to spend more time with. Someone he wanted to get to know. Cole was, when he allowed himself to think that far, the kind of man he hoped to one day meet. When he imagined falling for a man, he imagined a smart, sensitive, sophisticated man, someone who could talk football and enjoy a quiet evening of music at the same time. Someone gentle enough not to rush him but who still pushed all of Noah's buttons. He'd thought he was imagining a fairy tale. A fantasy. But, hell, it was his daydream, so he made his fantasy man exactly the way he wanted. Someone who looked at him with kind, gentle eyes, who smiled and laughed and held his hand, and who wanted more of who Noah was.

Why did it feel like he'd gone and met the man of his dreams, on a Wednesday night right here in Las Vegas?

"What about you? Taking out a guy who doesn't know what he's doing can't be that fun. Hardly an exciting night." Noah shrugged, tried to laugh. Cole might be his Prince Charming, or Noah might be projecting a million fantasies onto a mystery man he didn't know anything about, but Noah had to be a charity case to Cole. How much fun was it to play with Noah's shoulder and collarbone for hours?

"I had a fantastic time," Cole said. "And you're wrong. Taking you out tonight was better than every other night I've spent in Vegas."

Noah snorted.

"I'm serious. Thank you for letting me buy you a drink, and for allowing me to take you on your first real date." He held his champagne out for a toast. "Those aren't small things. I'm honored."

"I think I should be thanking you." He sipped his champagne, letting the bubbles float through him, fill his veins. "This was the best date I've been on in years. Maybe ever."

"Only maybe?" Cole arched an eyebrow.

"I took out Casey Peters in eleventh grade. She was a varsity cheerleader, and we made out in the back seat of my dad's Volvo for about two hours." Noah chuckled as Cole tipped his head back and laughed. "I don't think anything has ever beaten that." The rush of hormones, his father's car, the first time another person had touched him, and a thousand fears and hopes and questions surging in his blood. He'd been a rocket with no destination, looping in the sky of his life.

"What position did you play in high school? On the football team."

Noah flushed. "Quarterback. How did you know?"

"Midwestern men. God bless 'em. Nearly everyone plays football, and you have the look of someone who was a leader on the field. Plus, I can imagine you in football pants." Cole winked again, his smile turning wolfish before he finished his champagne. He set the glass down on the table and squeezed Noah's hand. "I have one more question for you."

Noah nodded, gulping half his champagne in one go. Cole's thumb was back, stroking over his skin, leaving lines of fire in the wake of his touch.

"I had a great time tonight. Really, I did. You're a great guy, Noah. There will be a million men out there who crave exactly who you are. I have a feeling you're going to find the answers you're looking for, and you're going to find the man who makes your whole world spin right."

"I'm sensing a but."

"No buts." Cole kissed his knuckles. "If you'd like, we can finish here, and Gregoire will take you back to your hotel. You can remember tonight however you want to: a moment in time, a search for answers. Moonlight and neon and great jazz with decent company." Cole smiled. "Or, if you'd like, I can take you upstairs to my room and try to answer a few more questions for you. I can, hopefully, show you a great time."

Noah's breath hitched. Stuttered to a stop. Cole clenched down on his hand, and Noah squeezed back reflexively. His eyes searched Cole's.

"It's your choice," Cole breathed. "I'm happy to walk you back to the car. To end this here. We've had a great evening together." He turned Noah's hand over, uncurling his fingers before he pressed a kiss to the center of Noah's palm. "But I'd be lying if I didn't tell you I want to be your first kiss, Noah. I imagined kissing you the whole time we were at the Parrot Room. Turning your head, holding your face in my hands..." His breath ghosted across Noah's skin, his palm and his wrist. Now, suddenly, the side of his face. They were so close together again. As if they couldn't stay apart.

What did he want? Did he want to leave now, go back to his room? Face-plant into his bed and listen to CNN until dawn? Replay this moment, this evening, for hours, days, weeks, months? Years, even?

Fear made him still, made his toes curl. What would it mean if he took this further? If he kissed Cole, if Cole kissed him back? If he followed him upstairs?

What would it mean if he left?

What would it mean if he stayed? If he, finally, *knew*.

Noah slid his shaking hand over Cole's cheek, his jaw, up into his hair. His fingers played in his blond strands—short and trim, just the way he liked. He'd always been attracted to the clean lines and features of a military man or a government man, and Cole had that in spades. He was pure Americana, a suntanned surfer and an erudite elite and warm-blooded, big-hearted man. He was everything Noah wanted... and somehow he wanted Noah in return, at least tonight.

Noah tugged. Cole surged forward, both hands rising and

cupping Noah's face. His fingers splayed over Noah's cheeks, thumbs brushing up his cheekbones, over his stubble. Their lips met, dry, champagne-tinged, brushing shyly at first. Then not shyly, and then deeper, until Cole's tongue teased at Noah's mouth. He hissed, parted his lips.

And then they were kissing, drawing each other close. Noah felt like he was falling forward, falling into Cole, spilling over and into Cole, falling out of himself in the places where they were merging. Lips and tongues, arms winding around each other, chests and shoulders pressing, rubbing. There was that heat again, a fire billowing inside of Noah, roaring through his veins and into his cells. A million times he'd imagined this moment, but he'd never imagined the fever, the flutter, the way the world spun and made him dizzy and everything shifted, resettled into a new understanding of reality as the kiss went on and on.

Cole pulled back first, pushing their foreheads together. Noah tried to chase him, kissing his lips and his chin as he held on to Cole's shoulders and the back of his neck with both hands.

"It's your choice," Cole said, panting. His voice was deeper, thicker than it had been a moment before. "Noah…" He dug his forehead into Noah's. Their noses brushed. Breath tangled between them. "God, Noah."

He was sixteen in the back of his father's Volvo again, that same mixture of adrenaline and fear and so much fucking hope, so much want surging through him. He'd never have this moment again, or this man, or this night.

He'd never, ever wanted something as badly as he wanted Cole and the promise of his hotel room upstairs, right now. "Take me upstairs." His voice came out in a growl.

Everything was a blur. Cole grabbed his hands and dragged him off the patio, through the candle-strewn darkness and then across the too-bright lobby. They bypassed the main elevator bank and made for a red-velvet-roped side lobby, a private entrance for the Tower Suites elevators, where an attendant welcomed Cole by name and keyed the elevator for immediate entry. Cole's hand was laced with his, squeezing over and over in time with the beat of Noah's heart. "Have a good night, sirs," the elevator attendant said, closing the doors behind them with a flick of his master key.

Alone. Cole backed him against the mirrored wall as the elevator soared. His hands grasped Noah's hips, and he looked into Noah's eyes before he kissed him again, gently this time. They traded soft, tiny kisses, almost nervous brushes of their lips, as they stared at each other.

Noah grabbed Cole's hips, slid his trembling hands beneath Cole's suit jacket, and followed the line of his belt to the small of his back. He tugged, pulling Cole against him, their bodies finally flush together the way he'd wanted to be all night long. Cole kissed him, captured his lips, devoured Noah as he spread his legs, his hardness suddenly there, digging into Noah's hip.

Noah pulled back with a gasp as the elevator dinged, the doors opening at Cole's floor. Cole guided him out, kissing him every three steps, zigzagging from wall to wall on their meander to his suite. There were only ten rooms on this floor, Noah noticed, a far cry from the two hundred at his hotel.

A door unlocked behind him, and Cole pushed him into a suite, filled with sleek furniture and gold wallpaper illuminated by the lights from the Strip that shone in via the wall of windows wrapping around Cole's corner suite. The Bellagio's fountains were going off again, a golden glow filling the arcing water and scattering prisms across the hotel room walls.

They stood in the muted light, breathing hard, hands stroking, lips meeting and parting, meeting and parting. Cole's hair brushed Noah's forehead. Noah's heart thundered, so hard and loud he thought he might die. *If this is the end, I'll die happy. I'll die knowing.*

"Noah," Cole whispered. His fingers danced up Noah's sides, over his ribs, and rested over his pounding heart.

"Show me," Noah breathed. "Everything."

Cole's eyes flashed. "Do you have any idea," he said, undoing Noah's shirt buttons, "how sexy you are? Especially in this shirt?" He pushed it off Noah's shoulders, dragging it down his biceps and letting it fall to the floor.

A broken laugh escaped Noah before his lungs seized as Cole's lips landed on his collarbone. "I bought it by accident."

"Go buy ten more." Cole's gaze flicked to Noah's face just before he kissed Noah's chest. His teeth bit gently into the swell of Noah's muscle. "The first thing I noticed about you was your shoulders, and your chest. How did you squeeze yourself into that shirt? You have no idea how hot you looked, do you?"

He thought he had looked ridiculous. "The first thing I noticed about you was your eyes," he blurted out. "Even across the bar, you looked... kind."

Cole stilled. A smile unfurled across his face, and his hands pressed into the small of Noah's back, pulling them close together again. "You're a romantic," he breathed.

"Is that a bad thing?" Noah gripped Cole's forearms, stroked up to his elbows, his hard, lean biceps. There wasn't an ounce of fat on Cole, not anywhere. Noah was suddenly all too aware of the soft top layer of his flat abdomen.

"Not at all." Cole kissed him sweetly, his hands gliding up Noah's spine. Noah trembled, almost collapsed as the room spun, colors swirling even when he closed his eyes. The only things tethering Noah to reality were Cole's lips, the taste of his kiss, and the feel of his body pressing against Noah's. Nothing else existed, not now. Nothing beyond the spaces between them and the flutter of Noah's heart.

He'd never been this gone, absolutely gone, with desire for another person. He didn't know it was possible to feel like this, to want something and someone this deeply. He was harder than he'd ever been, and all they were doing was kissing. Cole was still fully dressed.

Time to change that. His shaking fingers worked over Cole's buttons, and as Cole had done to him, he pushed the shirt back over Cole's shoulders and down. Skin met skin, naked chest to naked chest. The room was cool, the air-conditioning running silently, but their bodies were on fire. Goose bumps erupted all over Noah's body, rising beneath Cole's fingertips along his spine and the curve of his lower back. His cock throbbed, aching against Cole's matching hardness.

Cole backed Noah up, slow steps across the suite and into and out of the pools of light on the plush carpet. He kissed Noah with every step—a peck to the lips, each cheek, his chin, his neck, both pulse points—and then nibbled on his collarbone and the swell of his pecs. A hint of stubble grazed Noah's chest. He shuddered, grabbed Cole with both hands and held his face to his chest, dug his fingers into Cole's hair.

Noah felt the mattress behind him and sank backward, holding on to Cole as he went. Cole fell with him, landing on hands and knees above him. He smirked and kissed Noah until Noah forgot his own name, wrapping their fingers together before sliding Noah's hands over his head. "Leave them there," Cole breathed. He bit Noah's lip. "If you can."

And then he began to kiss his way down Noah's chest. Down to his belly button, and then farther. Noah was nothing but raw nerves and anticipation, years and years of dreams and wonderings and imaginings and fantasies and late-night jack-off sessions distilling to this one moment, to Cole staring up at him as he undid Noah's fly, pulled down his zipper, and—

"Jesus!" Noah arched his back and lurched, his hips jerking, thighs falling open as Cole's lips closed around him, wet heat and suction, so much suction, liquefying his bones and turning his muscles to jelly. Cole hummed, almost laughing, and he looked up at Noah as he sank all the way down—

"Cole—" He couldn't hold back, not with Cole doing *that*, looking at him like *that*, as if he'd seen into Noah's brain and had plucked Noah's deepest, dearest want from his mind. It was too much, this perfect man and this perfect moment and the culmination of all his questions and desires and yearnings. "Cole, I'm—"

Cole swallowed, taking him—if possible—deeper, and stared into Noah's panicked gaze.

Noah cursed and exploded, spasming and shaking and coming completely undone beneath Cole's lips and tongue and throat, beneath the hands that stroked up his hips and his ribs and down the small of his back, steadying him as Cole kept swallowing, sucking, drawing out his orgasm as Noah panted, whimpered, gasps and *please* and *fuck* and *God* and *Cole*.

Finally, Cole popped off, smiling. His lips were red and wet, swollen, and he licked them as he grinned. "Good?"

The best I've ever dreamed. Noah surged forward. He had to show Cole, if he could, what that had meant to him, how it had felt, not just physically, but deeper. What it meant to his soul.

They came together in a frenzy, kissing furiously as hands worked over flies and zippers and shoved pants down and socks off, all while never breaking their kiss, never taking their hands off each other. Noah pushed Cole back, straddling him —suddenly naked—on the bed. Hot skin against hot skin, they writhed together, bodies arching and flowing, pressing, pushing, thighs against hips, hands running over backs and sides and down arms, up necks as fingers played through each other's hair. Cole's hard length dug into Noah's hip, and Noah's cock, unbelievably, hardened again. Never, ever in his life had he been this turned on.

He kissed his way down Cole's chest, mirroring Cole's actions. Cole cradled his skull, held him. "You don't have to—"

"I want to." Noah kissed Cole's navel, the tender skin beneath, and buried his nose in the line of soft hair trailing down to Cole's crotch. Cole's scent—his heady, masculine musk, amber and velvet, with a hint of midnight and smoke—made Noah think of sweaty nights, hard muscles, hard cocks, and wailing blues. Notes quivering between curls of shadow, and the feel of Cole's body beneath him. He smelled like all of Noah's unuttered desires, all the dreams he'd wrapped in silence and buried inside himself.

Cole's cock, rock hard, brushed over his lips, hot and wet with a salty smear. He lapped at the head, almost drooling, almost drunk with the force of his desire. He wanted this, wanted Cole, wanted everything.

Cole groaned, curling upward and around Noah as Noah sank as deep as he could go. Fingers tugged on his hair, pulled on his scalp. His world went white-hot, his vision blurring, white noise filling his skull as Cole's cock, his taste, filled every corner of his being. This, this was what he'd wanted forever. A man beneath him. A man moaning for him. A man, hard and wanting, *because* of him.

It felt like seconds before Cole was tugging at him, dragging him off his cock and pulling him upward, pressing their lips together as he shuddered. "Not yet," Cole breathed across Noah's lips. "I don't want to come yet." He rolled with Noah, their bodies coming together as one, pulsing, pushing, grinding until he settled between Noah's spread thighs, their hips aligned, cocks flush together. Noah hooked one leg around Cole's and wound his arms around Cole's neck. Cole's weight surrounded him, enveloped him, pressed him into the mattress.

They kissed until Noah couldn't breathe, rocked until Noah didn't know where he began and Cole ended. He couldn't think, not anymore. All he could do was feel. Feel Cole, feel their bodies, feel the perfect pleasure Cole had unlocked inside him. Feel his heart about to burst, feel his veins and muscles and bones crawling with pleasure, with electric joy, with an answer to his questioning hunger and his yearning in the dark.

It could have been ten minutes or an hour, he couldn't tell. He was racing along exposed nerves, dancing on the knife-edge of pleasure. They were breathing each other's breath, trading kisses and discovering brand-new calculus in the angles of their hips and thrusts and sweat-slick skin sliding on skin. And then Noah was flying, tumbling, screaming Cole's name as he fell, as his stomach burned and he caught fire from the inside, coming just as hard as he had down Cole's throat, this time tangled up in a man's arms like he'd always wanted—no, better, because he was wrapped up in *Cole*.

Cole followed, groaning as he buried his face in Noah's neck and flooded Noah's belly with his come. "Noah," he breathed. "Fuck, Noah…" His fingers curled around Noah's hip, and one hand rose, found Noah's, squeezed. He pulled back far enough for a kiss. His blond hair had fallen forward across his forehead, messy and sweaty and undone. He looked absolutely gorgeous, flushed and orgasmic and gazing at Noah like Noah was special to him, like that had meant something more than just sweat and heat and great orgasms.

Hands down, it was the best sex he'd ever had. And they hadn't even… But still, that *had* to mean something.

It did mean something, at least to Noah. He grinned up at Cole, still trying to catch his breath, his heart still thundering. "You know, I think I might be gay."

Cole threw his head back and laughed.

3

THE HOURS PASSED with their legs and arms tangled together, and they traded kisses in between every other sentence as they talked softly in the neon-lit shadows. Kissing turned to making out, which turned into another slow thrust and grind and then Cole asking him if he wanted to try sixty-nining.

"Absolutely," Noah said, and he whimpered as Cole gently thrust his cock over Noah's tongue, teasing his throat, until Noah grabbed his hips and pulled him down, swallowing Cole as deep as he could go while he exploded in Cole's hot, wet mouth. Cole came soon after, and Noah's eyes rolled back in his head, another mini orgasm washing through him as he lapped at Cole's come and kissed his trembling hip and belly.

Slowly, the light outside shifted, the velvet black of night beginning to lighten, the neon losing hold over the Strip. Persimmon and periwinkle whispered across the horizon, teasing the desert out of the dark.

"What time is it?" Noah whispered.

Cole rolled, checking the bedside clock. "Five," he said, rolling back and kissing Noah's knuckles. "What's your day like today?"

Noah groaned. "I have workshops I have to attend, and I'm supposed to meet my friend for breakfast at our hotel. I'd rather stay here."

Cole grinned. "I'd rather you stayed, too." Another kiss, slow as molasses, and Cole's leg slid up Noah's, his ankle hooking around Noah's knee. There wasn't a part of them that wasn't touching.

A curl of fear dug into Noah's heart. His breath fluttered over Cole's lips. "Is this goodbye?" Was the fairy tale over? Was this his one magical night? If it was, it had been more than he'd ever expected, ever hoped for. He'd be okay with it if this was all he got. He'd remember this forever. He'd remember Cole forever.

Cole gazed at him, those kind eyes searching, always searching, for something inside Noah. "It doesn't have to be. Do you want to meet again tonight?"

"Yes." Noah didn't even breathe before he spoke, before the word burst out of him. "Yes, definitely."

Beaming, Cole kissed the center of his forehead. "Dinner?"

Anything. "Yes. I'll call you?"

"Put my number in your phone?"

Finally, they separated, and Noah dug his cell out from the pocket of his discarded pants, tossed aside on the carpet. "Damn it, my battery's dead."

"My phone is… somewhere." Cole laughed, looking at the mess of clothes on the hotel floor. Their pants, shirts, jackets, socks, and shoes were scattered in every direction. "Here." Cole grabbed a pad of paper from the bedside table and scribbled down his number. "Text me later today?"

Cole had a D.C. area code. Noah folded the paper and slid it into his pocket as he pulled on his jeans. He was sore, his muscles working in ways they hadn't in years. Other parts of himself were aching, too. He hadn't had a three-orgasm night in… maybe ever.

Cole helped him put on his shirt, kissing him with each done button until they were making out again, kissing like they needed to to live, holding on to each other as the sun finally peeked over the horizon and flooded the room in a golden desert glow.

Squinting, Noah blinked hard. "It's been a few years since I've had an all-nighter like this." Most of the time, a late night meant surveillance, squeezed into the back of a van with three other agents and cops, everyone inhaling coffee and donuts and trying to stay awake.

"Me too." Cole smiled. Kissed him again. "I'm not complaining, though."

"Me either."

"I'll see you tonight?"

"Definitely." He'd make up an excuse to ditch the guys. He'd already spent half the week with them. And if James thought he'd met up with someone last night—met up with a woman—he'd be Noah's biggest champion, encouraging him to head out and stay out for the rest of the night.

It took another ten minutes to leave, and another hundred kisses, but eventually Noah left Cole's suite ten minutes before six a.m. He padded down the empty hallway. Giddiness filled him, made his steps light, as he called for the elevator. He was the only one going down.

Had that really happened? Did he... Noah fell back, collapsing against the wall. He could still smell Cole on him, all over him. In the reflection, his hair was mussed. Cole had finger combed it, but he still looked freshly fucked.

Noah stared into his own gaze, and, slowly, his smile grew so large and wide his cheeks ached. Yes, he did.

And he *loved* it. Every moment.

The sun was climbing as he stepped out of the Aria's front doors, out to the sweeping drive and the grand entrance. The valet looked him up and down and offered to call him a cab. Noah shook his head. It was early, and his own hotel was only across the street. The morning air was crisp, and he wanted to soak everything in. Stretch this morning, this moment, out as long as he could. Every step he took, he could smell Cole—feel him, even. It was almost like they were walking together.

Easy. He had to pump the brakes a bit, mentally, emotionally. Possibly even physically. He'd met a man, had a great date with him, gone back to his room and had mind-blowing sex. But there was a lot of ground to cover between sex with a gorgeous, intelligent, kind, funny, fun, interesting man and... whatever lay beyond that.

It wasn't like he was looking for anything beyond that, even. Not right now. Not with his life. He couldn't.

But knowing. Finally. Really *knowing*.

It's Vegas. It's what you're supposed to do here. He had two more nights left. If Cole was open to it, he'd spend them both with him. If not, well, he'd always have the memories of last night. And this beautiful morning. He *knew*, finally.

His own hotel was less impressive than the Aria, the lobby more worn, the walls and carpet drab and starting to show signs of age. There was no private elevator to his floor, and as he waited, Noah tried to stand apart from the gaggle of elderly couples finishing up their early breakfast at the hotel's buffet. He also kept an eye out for anyone he might recognize. It was too early for James to be up and about, but there was a chance some of the other guys could be out for a run. He slid into the elevator silently, hanging back, and, thankfully, his floor was deserted when he arrived.

First things first. Charge up his phone, take a shower, and get ready for the day. At some point, he'd need about a gallon of coffee. Exultation would only take him so far before exhaustion slammed in. For the moment, joy was still pumping through him, and he hummed in the shower as he soaped up, shampooed, and rinsed. His imagination ran wild, and he pictured Cole showering as well, the water running down his lean legs, his strong back, his chiseled abdomen.

Unbelievably, Noah started to harden again, but a quick twist of the water knob cured that. With a shockingly frigid finish to his shower, he climbed out and wrapped a towel around his waist before he shaved.

While brushing his teeth, he padded out to his room, biting his toothbrush as he riffled through his clothes. Khakis and a blue polo, or khakis and a white polo? God, he was midwestern all right. Most people thought the FBI was interesting. He snorted. He was the very definition of boring. *You have no idea how attractive you are.* His eyes closed, and he smiled around his toothbrush.

Buzzing broke through his daydreams, a clattering across the cheap laminate top of the hotel room's dresser. His cell phone was going crazy, finally charged up enough to turn on and start delivering messages and notifications. Jesus, there had to be fifteen, twenty, or more. It wasn't even six thirty in the morning. Was James up, texting him from across the hall? Teasing him about last night?

He swiped his phone on and picked it up. Eight missed calls. Thirteen text messages.

All from Des Moines.

Oh no. His heart sank, dropping to the hollow pit of his stomach as he opened the first text. Then his legs buckled, and he sank to the edge of the mattress, toothbrush and toothpaste forgotten as he read one text, and then the next, and the next.

Five minutes later, Noah had his suitcase packed and was calling down to the front desk to arrange a taxi to the airport. *I'll be on the next flight back,* he texted. *I'm on my way now.*

4

WARM WIND SWEPT across Iowa's green and golden grasses, bending the delicate stalks into rippling waves along the split-rail fence surrounding the property. The farmhouse stood out from the rolling flatlands, the crops stretching in all directions. Copses of gnarled oak and a few cedars and cottonwoods dotted the landscape, breaking up the cornfields and the grasses and, in the distance, grain silos and an old water tower.

The farmhouse had been the pride of the Olson family. Noah remembered listening to Bart detail all the home-improvement projects he was tackling, how he was turning the older property into his dream home. *What I always wanted*, Bart had said. *Peace and quiet.*

Noah's stomach twisted as he ducked beneath the yellow crime scene tape roping off the wraparound porch. The front door was wide open, and a dozen crime scene technicians were crowded inside Bart's house, taking photos and measurements and dusting for fingerprints.

He forced himself to take in the scene in pieces, starting on the outside and sweeping his gaze across the devastation. Broken furniture. Shattered glass from broken picture frames.

Drag marks. Smeared bloody handprints in the hallway leading to the back of the house and the bedrooms. Blood on the carpets. The walls. A thick, wide pool of blood cooling in the center of the living room, surrounding the broken, badly beaten body of Bart Olson, Boone County Sheriff.

Deputy Sheriff Andy Garrett, Bart's third in command, was like a tornado hovering in place, a storm cell whirling inside his stone-hard body. Minute tremors tore through him as he stood at the edge of the crime scene, staring at the body of his former boss. His uniform was pristine, starched and crisp and ironed into exact creases, every button of his long-sleeved shirt fastened. He still wore his uniform hat, a broad, flat-brimmed Stetson, angled down over his eyes as if he could shield his sight. But he hadn't looked away, not once, since Noah had arrived on scene.

"Andy." Noah joined him, glancing down at the notepad Garrett held in his hands. His pen hovered over the page. He'd written down nothing. The paper was blank. "I'm sorry."

Garrett's jaw clenched hard, the muscles in his neck bulging over his high collar. He didn't look at Noah. "It looks like the sheriff surprised the intruder," Garrett spat. "We think he arrived home while the… attack was in progress."

Noah nodded. Bart was almost unrecognizable. His face was caved in, bruised and broken and bloody, and if it weren't for Bart's uniform and his shockingly red hair sticking up from the mess that had been his face, Noah wouldn't have believed the corpse before him was the sheriff.

"There are defensive wounds on his hands and arms," Andy grunted. "He fought."

"There might be DNA under his fingernails. Might be something we can use to identify the killer."

Andy nodded, his lips going thin. He swallowed. His pen tapped on his blank notepad.

Deputy Venneslund appeared at Andy's shoulder. He

looked at Bart and then away, swallowing. He was a sick shade of green, and his eyes were red. No one wanted to find their own like this, beaten so savagely, so brutally. He kept his gaze off of Bart as he joined Noah. "Are you going to catch him this time?"

His words were a punch to Noah's gut. "We've never stopped trying."

"The task force was shut down."

"We ran into dead end after dead end. And there hadn't been an attack since…" He inhaled.

Venneslund turned, a single, lightning-fast movement. One moment he was looking at Andy. The next, he was staring at Noah, his dark eyes unblinking.

"I never stopped looking," Noah breathed.

Andy's lip curled up. It was an ugly, hateful look. He snorted. Venneslund closed his eyes. He exhaled, his hands fisting at his sides.

"I need to see the rest of the scene," Noah said softly. "I need to know if it's him."

"It's him," Venneslund spat.

"I need to see."

Andy's nostrils flared as Venneslund sighed. A moment passed, and then another, Venneslund and Andy sharing a long look. Andy nodded, and Venneslund spun on his heel, gave the sheriff's body a wide berth as he crossed the living room, and led Noah to the hallway that went to the bedrooms at the back of the farmhouse.

Signs of a struggle surrounded them: dents in the drywall, those smeared handprints, blood splatter. Someone had fought for their life in this hallway.

Someone had lost.

As he neared the open door to the last bedroom on the right, Venneslund removed his Stetson and held it against his chest. Camera flashes flickered out of the bedroom door. Soft murmurs spilled into the hall. "In there," Venneslund mumbled. "It's him," he growled as Noah passed. "And you *know* this isn't the first one."

The smell hit Noah as he crossed the threshold. Victims of strangulation always smelled the worst. It was an insult added to injury, a degradation after the fact. The stench of panic leaching out of the victim during their slow, terrible final moments, combined with the body's reflexive last voiding at the time of death, led to a particularly foul residue. It stained the molecules that hung in the room, coated the air in an oily residue that covered the tongue and the back of the throat. The stench of terror, and horror, and death.

It was the stench left behind at each of the Coed Killer's murders.

It hit him hard, and Noah froze just inside the door, dizzy. His eyes closed, and a kaleidoscope of murders flashed behind his eyelids. Pretty young women, college students, every one of them smiling and happy and looking forward to her future, the long years of their lives stretching before them. Each of them dead. Murdered and then thrown away, discarded carelessly, forgotten as soon as their deaths had served the killer's needs.

He's back.

A crime scene tech bumped Noah's shoulder as she squeezed around him, taking another photo of the corpse on the bed. Noah shifted, giving her room, and then stepped closer and leaned over the body of Jessie Olson, Bart Olson's daughter. Her sightless eyes stared at the ceiling, salt lines from dried tears dusting her cold cheeks. Dark, angry bruises dug into her throat, the clear outline of fingers and two palms wreathing her neck. Her head was tilted unnaturally, as if something had come undone inside her. She was lying on her back, sprawled half on the bed, one foot still on the floor and the other dangling off the mattress. Her hands were open, carelessly flung sideways.

Her nightstand was toppled, a lamp on the floor. Noah

looked from the door to Jessie's bed in the corner. He could picture the attack, the killer getting his hands around Jessie's throat and pushing her through the room, throwing her on her bed and squeezing—

He looked away, to Jessie's walls. They were covered in awards, certificates and ribbons and photographs from 4-H and the FFA and Girl Scouts. Jessie had made a name for herself in the local ag scene. She was an accomplished young woman, showing prize animals at the state fair and local shows and collecting awards for years. At last year's holiday party, Bart had bragged about Jessie's straight As in her agricultural science major at Iowa State. Bart had been so happy, just six months ago.

Jessie, too, if the newspaper clipping from three months before tacked to her wall was any indication. Her smile stretched from ear to ear, like Julia Roberts's, so big and wide it was like an Iowa horizon at sunrise. Her long, straw-blonde hair was loose around her round, open face dotted with freckles over her nose from long days in the sun. "Local Sheriff's Daughter Awarded Top Honors," the headline read.

He's back.

Accomplished, beautiful young women, successful in their college and university programs, had always been the Coed Killer's targets.

Noah hung his head. Years before, he'd been tapped to join the joint task force hunting the Coed Killer. Local law enforcement from Des Moines, West Des Moines, and Polk, Dallas, Warren, and Story Counties, along with the FBI—Noah—had trailed after the serial killer for eighteen months. He left no forensics. No footprints. No trail. He appeared out of the shadows, stole a young life, and disappeared without a trace.

The helplessness had nearly suffocated them all, the ache in their souls when they couldn't track the killer beyond the crime scene tape enough to choke on. Noah had never felt so helpless, so worthless. And it wasn't just him. One of the Polk County deputies had hurled his laptop against the wall, four murders in with no leads and after they'd all received another callout to come to the scene of yet another murdered young woman.

The night of Stacy Shepherd's murder at Iowa State University, a young couple, graduate students walking their dog near campus after dark, had been gunned down, shot and killed after neighbors reported the husband, Kyle Carter, had shouted for someone to stop. No one had seen what happened, but neighbors said they'd heard Kyle bellowing, sounds of running, Shelly screaming, and then four gunshots. Their dead bodies were found in the street, their golden retriever running in circles in a neighbor's yard, barking its head off.

Years passed. There were no more killings. A theory developed that Kyle and Shelly had interrupted the Coed Killer escaping after murdering Stacy Shepherd. They'd confronted him slinking through the neighborhood that bordered the Iowa State dorms. Had the killer been injured? There was no indication he'd been wounded, no defensive wounds on Kyle or Shelly. No blood, other than their own. No forensics on the street or in the yards up and down the block. They never found the gun that fired the bullets. There had been nothing other than circumstance. Stacy's body, the neighbor's reports of Kyle confronting someone, running footsteps. And then the Coed Killer's disappearance.

Did being sighted spook him? Had he uprooted or gone to ground?

After all this time, why was he back now?

You know this isn't the first one.

Three months earlier, Kimberly Foster, a sophomore at Faith Baptist, had been killed in her home. Strangled. The police were investigating her boyfriend, an obsessive fellow student at the college, someone she had complained to the dean about several times. She was requesting a restraining order, had it in her purse to file with the court, when she was killed.

What had seemed like the tragic but foreseeable outcome of the dean's inaction and failure to take assertive steps was now cast in a new light. She had been the captain of Faith's women's volleyball team, a team that had swept its division and gone on to dominate the playoffs and win the championship. Her photo had been in the local paper. She'd been interviewed about her leadership, how she led the team through the season. Copies of the articles were on the walls of her stalker's apartment, a printout of her photo in his wallet.

But…

Noah made his way out of Jessie's bedroom and wound through the farmhouse and back out to the porch. Venneslund had joined Andy at his vigil over Bart Olson's corpse, one hand on Andy's shoulder as Andy's jaw clenched and unclenched. Venneslund stared at the ground, shaking his head.

Noah peeled off his blue gloves and shoved them in the pocket of his khakis. His receipt from the cab to the airport that morning was still in the same pocket. *Vegas*. No, he couldn't think about that now. Not anymore. Maybe not ever again. *What happens in Vegas.*

He fished his phone out and dialed his boss, Special Agent in Charge of Des Moines John Hayes. Hayes was three years from retirement, winding down a thirty-five-year career that had started in New York City and was ending in West Des Moines. He'd requested the transfer to the Midwest from Detroit ten years earlier, getting surprised with Des Moines but making the best of it. He'd taken Noah under his wing when Noah was still young and green and trying to find his feet.

"*How's it look, Noah?*" John asked, answering on the first ring.

"It's him. He's back."

John cursed. "*And the Faith Baptist girl? Do you think she's connected?*"

"We have to very seriously consider it. The MO is too similar."

"*Why would he reappear now? After six years? Could this be a copycat?*"

Noah chewed on his bottom lip, staring at the horizon. It felt like the Coed Killer. At least, it did with Jessie, in her bedroom. What happened to Bart… "This feels like him. Jessie, she was—" He swallowed. "She was the same as the others. The exact same. Even things we didn't release to the press." No sexual assault, for one. The Coed Killer never touched the girls, despite what the media lasciviously reported. Noah stared at the cornfield neighboring Bart's property. Thigh high by July was what they said about corn. The golden heads of the stalks were already up to Noah's eyes. It would be a good harvest. "It's him."

"*Damn. Thought he might have gotten hit by a train.*"

"We should be so lucky." They didn't know where he'd been, or why he stopped six years ago, or why he was back now. "We need to examine every murder of a young woman for the past few years. See if we missed anything. Check other jurisdictions, too. If he murders across state lines, we take over primary jurisdiction."

"*We're probably going to take over anyway. The sheriffs from all four counties, along with the chiefs of Des Moines and West Des Moines PD, have asked the FBI to take the lead in restarting the Coed Killer Joint Task Force, if this is definitely his work. No one is comfortable with one of our own being murdered.*" Hayes sighed, ragged and rough. "*We have to stop him this time, Noah.*"

Noah nodded. His breath echoed over the line. "I want to bring in more help this time. Let's call the BAU, see if Quantico can send out a profiler. I want to throw everything at this. We didn't catch him the first time, and now he's back."

"I'll put in the request today and ask them to send someone out as soon as they can. The best profiler they've got."

"Thanks."

"Get the task force back up and running. You run this how you need to. You're going to get him this time. I know it. Let me know what you need."

Noah hung up. He tried to smell the summer wind, the sun-warmed corn stalks and the nitrogen-rich earth. Tried to recapture a single molecule of the happiness he'd touched so fleetingly, and that he'd left behind under neon and desert darkness. The joy he'd brushed—that certainty—seemed so far away, so removed from his life. Were Vegas and Iowa even on the same planet? It didn't feel like it. Whoever he'd been when the sun rose that morning, he was no longer the same man. He couldn't be. Not here, not now.

He sighed, reaching, grasping, for sunlight, for neon, for something.

But all he smelled was death and despair.

5

ANOTHER MONDAY, another flight.

Cole rolled his head against the headrest and stared at the carpet of clouds floating below the wing of the plane. He blinked. Beneath him were all those flyover states. Middle America, those midwestern states. Full of midwestern men.

Damn midwestern men.

His eyes slid closed. Cold sunlight fell on his face as the plane banked gently, turning at the outer marker for the last hundred miles of the flight. God, he flew so much he practically knew the pilots' routines and the routes they flew by heart. Not that he'd ever flown *here* before.

Maybe if Noah had called him, he could have taken a few days and paid him a visit before this assignment. Or after. Or during. He could have seen Noah again, met up with him in whatever city was nearby. *I can't be like that at home.* So Noah was closeted, even though he wanted to know who he was and what he wanted. That was okay. Cole could work with that.

Hell, he'd work with anything if it meant he got to see Noah again.

When was the last time he'd been so captivated by a man? By all of a man? Sure, it was easy to fall for a man's physicality, his appearance. But he would run out of fingers and toes if he tried to count how many men he'd been attracted to who, after he got to know them, made Cole want to run for the hills. There wasn't a way to put a paper bag over someone's personality, and he was finally growing out of his testosterone-fueled-fuck years, where it didn't matter who someone was as long as they had a killer body and *fuck-me* eyes.

Meeting a man like Noah was like finding a diamond buried on an endless beach. He had that bashful, shy attractiveness that drove Cole wild. Noah had no idea, none at all, how sexy he'd looked when he'd come out that night. There was a reason that the waitress had zeroed in on him. And if Cole hadn't made his move, someone else would have. There was no way Noah would have been alone that night.

Had he done something wrong? Had he pushed too hard? He thought Noah had been having a good time. He thought they had been on the same page. How much had Noah drunk? He hadn't been out of control, wasn't even tipsy. Cole never wanted to take advantage of him. He just didn't want the night to end.

It had seemed like Noah didn't want the night to end, either. Especially when they got back to his room and—

God, the way his eyes went wide, went wild. The fire burning inside Noah. How hungry he seemed for Cole.

He wasn't actually hungry for Cole, though, was he? No, he was hungry for the experience, for the novelty. For knowing who he was. Cole was just some guy, muscles and a dick and his first kiss, his first blow job from a man. Cole could have been an escort, for all it ended up mattering.

Damn it, he'd let himself be captivated by Noah. By that midwestern earnestness, that all-American solidity, that bashful, quiet strength wrapped in a gorgeous body. He may have been 'some guy' to Noah, but Noah had gotten under his skin. Clearly.

He'd really wanted that dinner date. He'd really wanted to

hear from Noah again. Maybe it would have all gone sideways and the spell would have been broken. Maybe reality would have crashed in on that second date. But maybe it would have been just as magical as the first. Maybe they would have built on that spark, fanned the flame between them. Maybe there would have been candlelight and nuzzling each other and holding hands until they made out in the booth. Maybe they would have gone back to his room again and explored some more. Maybe he could have shown Noah even more.

And maybe, since he was now on his way to the Midwest, he could have seen Noah again.

If only.

If only Noah had called or texted. If only Cole hadn't sat waiting for hours, staring at his phone screen at the hotel bar as the pit opened up in his stomach and the rejection sank deep. What had he done wrong? How had he spooked Noah?

Were there... other reasons? He'd checked—he always did—for a wedding band. He hadn't seen one. But that didn't mean Noah wasn't married. He'd been emphatic that he couldn't be gay, couldn't be out, back wherever home was for him. Couldn't be gay, in 2021? Why?

"Ladies and gentlemen, we're on our final approach to Des Moines International Airport. Winds are calm and the weather is beautiful, so we anticipate a smooth landing. We'll have you on the ground and at the gate in about ten minutes. Thank you for flying with us, and have a great day in Des Moines, or wherever your final destination may be."

After the pilot spoke, the flight attendants bustled through the cabin, collecting the empty coffee cups and waking the morning nappers to pull up their seats and stow their tray tables. The first flight out of D.C. was always a healthy mix between the people trying to get another three hours of sleep and those who were already overcaffeinated by 5 a.m. and who spent the three hours in the air trying to be the passenger who typed the absolute most on their laptop. Snores and keystrokes, an endless duet.

Cole passed his coffee cup to the flight attendant and tried to smile. He failed. Damn it, this was hardly the first time he'd been rejected. Why was he still upset about it days later?

Well, this was the last time he was going to think about Noah or what might have been, or imagine the night—nights—they could have had. Damn midwestern men. Damn Noah. Would it have been so hard to text him, say thanks but no thanks? That was the polite thing to do. Maybe Noah was secretly an asshole. Or not so secretly.

No more. He was done. He was done with Noah.

He shuffled off the plane with the rest of the early morning crowd, thanking the flight attendant and the pilot and ignoring the not-so-subtle eye fuck from the gay flight attendant in the first-class cabin. He wasn't in the mood for a bathroom quickie. Besides, he was being picked up. No car on this TDY. Which was fine. He could be chauffeured around and pocket the per diem instead of renting a car he really didn't need. Last year, he'd made more in per diem and temporary duty overtime than his base salary.

If he'd had a reason to rent a car, like driving out to see someone…

Enough. You're done.

He thumbed through his phone, checking emails as he headed for the arrival hall. He had his carry-on and his laptop bag, and that was it. He'd learned to travel light. Whatever he needed, he could buy, wherever he ended up.

When he looked up, he spotted a mountain of a man holding a small white sign that read "Dr. Kennedy." He waved.

The giant—easily six foot seven, two hundred and eighty pounds of solid, thick muscle—held out his massive paw. Cole's hand was lost in his grip as he shook, surprisingly gentle. "Dr. Kennedy? Special Agent Jacob Moore." Jacob's voice was exactly as deep as Cole expected, like an organ rumbling in some register that was almost indefinable. He felt his voice in his bones.

Jacob's face seemed like it was carved from clay, but by a child, with his features slightly offset and mismatched. His nose had clearly been broken one too many times, but by whom, Cole was almost scared to ask. "Nice to meet you, Agent Moore."

Jacob waited. One eyebrow quirked up. "Isn't this when you make the joke about me being corn fed, or ask what's in the water here in Iowa?"

"Takes a lot more than corn to have a body like that, and if there's anything in the water in Iowa, it better comply with the EPA." Cole grinned. "I'm sure you've heard all the old jokes a million times by now."

Jacob smiled. His whole face lit up, giving his vaguely Cro-Magnon visage a sunny, almost boyish expression. "Maybe you can hit me with a new joke, then. Something I haven't heard. "

"If I tried to hit you, I'd hurt myself."

Jacob kept smiling. He held out his hand for Cole's suitcase, but instead of wheeling it, he held it in one hand as if it were a purse. "Everyone's expecting you. I'll swing you by your hotel, and then we'll head to the office. Unless you need to make a pit stop?"

"I've been fed and watered on the flight. I'm good to go."

Jacob chuckled again as he led Cole out of the airport and to the black SUV parked at the curb. Jacob waved to the deputy as he stowed Cole's bag.

The hotel the local office had put him in wasn't the worst, but it was a far cry from what Cole would have picked. Then again, he operated on a different budget, thanks to all that TDY pay he pocketed. The room was clean and comfortable, the bathroom serviceable. He dropped his carry-on and grabbed a soda from the lobby, and then they were off.

In the car, Cole pulled out his ID badge and slipped it on.

Des Moines wasn't his office, but he'd still need to badge in and out. Jacob's gaze caught on his lanyard, and he did a double take as he looked Cole up and down. "Are you gay?"

Cole ran his hand down the rainbow lanyard that held his FBI ID and badge. "Yep." Jacob's badge was shoved in the center console, the lanyard faded but still sporting the logo of the Denver Broncos. "You a Broncos fan?"

Jacob sighed, the defeated, agonized sigh of a weary fan. "I am, even when they make it hurt." He looked at Cole as he pulled to a stop at a red light. "You? Who's your team?"

"Chargers."

Jacob squawked. He smashed the door lock, unlocking the car, and pointed at the curb. "Out."

"The Chargers are having a great season. Did you see their win yesterday?"

"Of course I did," Jacob grumbled. "Considering they destroyed my Broncos."

"Man, Herbert's having a good season, isn't he?" Cole rattled off the young quarterback's stats, shaking his head as he whistled.

Jacob glared. "Are you really a Chargers fan?"

"Honestly, more of a 49ers fan, but I couldn't pass up the opportunity."

Laughing, Jacob turned into the parking lot of a nondescript business park, three stories of concrete and dark glass and the obligatory pond with a fountain by the front door. "We're on the third floor."

Cole followed Jacob in, watching as he badged for access to the third floor in the elevator and memorizing the code Jacob rattled off. Jacob made small talk about the 49ers, who were, if possible, having a worse season than the Broncos. The elevator ride was short, and the doors opened to a small lobby and a set of double doors that read "Federal Bureau of Investigation—Des Moines."

An older man held the door open for them both, smiling

at Jacob before holding out his hand to Cole. "Special Agent in Charge John Hayes. You must be Dr. Kennedy. Thank you for coming out here so quickly."

He shook Hayes's hand. "Happy to do whatever I can to help, sir. I read the brief, but I wanted to wait and hear the details from the case agent and the local officers who have handled the bulk of the investigation."

"You're in luck. Downing is leading a briefing right now. Everyone's gathered."

"Did something come in?" Jacob led the way down the corridor toward a conference room along the back wall. Cole spotted a gaggle of men and women sitting around a large table surrounded by whiteboards to the left and right. A tall man with his back to the hallway spoke to the group, gesturing to something projected on the wall.

"Autopsy reports," Hayes said.

Jacob cringed. "Garrett in there?"

Hayes nodded. Jacob shook his head, sadness turning his face gloomy.

Everyone turned when Hayes pushed open the door and led Cole into the conference room. Cole's gaze swept the room, across the table of FBI agents, sheriff's deputies from four counties, and the local Des Moines police. "Everyone," Hayes said, "This is Dr. Kennedy from the FBI's Behavioral Analysis Unit. I asked them to send the best profiler they have, and—" Hayes clapped Cole on the shoulder. It was a paternal move, and kind. He smiled.

Cole's gaze shifted, flicked to the man leading the meeting, the commander of the task force—

Shock rocketed through him.

Equally shocked—and absolutely terrified—eyes bore back into his own. Honey-hazel eyes, eyes he remembered gazing up at him with a dazed, glorious, burning look. Eyes that had seemed to say *I want you. I want this.*

"Dr. Kennedy, this is Assistant Special Agent in Charge

Downing. He's running the task force and taking the lead on the hunt for the Coed Killer."

Assistant special agent in charge. Cole blinked. Tried to swallow. He held out his hand. "Cole," he almost stuttered. "Pleasure to meet you, Agent Downing."

"N-Noah." Noah did stutter, and he dropped Cole's hand like touching him was physically painful. His gaze skittered down to Cole's rainbow lanyard. If possible, he blanched even further. "Thanks for coming, Dr. Kennedy." He looked away, his jaw clenching hard. Cole saw his pulse leap beneath his jaw.

"Please don't let me interrupt." Cole tried to shift backward, blend into the dull paint, hide himself against the doorjamb. Or, better yet, turn around and walk away. Go right back to the airport and then fly back to D.C. and tell his boss that someone else had to take this one. Someone who hadn't slept with the lead agent. Someone who hadn't been ghosted by the lead agent. Fuck, was there a policy on this? What to do if your new boss ghosted you after mind-blowing sex?

He wanted to disappear.

Not as much as Noah wanted to disappear, it seemed. He was as white as a sheet, and his hands trembled as he gripped a pen. He stared at his laptop, fiddling with the keys as he cleared his throat.

"Dr. Kennedy?"

He started, turning. Jacob had pulled out a chair at the end of the table. He nodded to the open seat, then stepped back, leaning against the wall. If Jacob raised his hand, he could palm the ceiling.

Everyone murmured their hellos as Cole made his way to his seat, nodding and smiling to the agents and officers and deputies. It was a somber meeting, and he noticed one of the deputies glaring out the window, not meeting his gaze. Anger pulsed off him, hot and furious. Cole settled into his seat and slid his laptop bag between his legs.

Noah cleared his throat and gestured to the screen on the far wall. He tapped at his laptop again, and the screen saver vanished. Autopsy photos appeared side by side: a young woman, strangled to death, and an older man, beaten beyond recognition. Cole blinked, taking in the savagery of the act, the rage. The hatred.

"Sheriff Bart Olson," Noah said. "And his daughter, Jessie."

Leather creaked as the furious deputy squeezed down on the arms of his chair. His wide shoulders trembled.

"Dr. Chen has completed her autopsy of both victims." The medical examiner's report replaced the graphic photos, complete with wire diagrams documenting the injuries to the dad and daughter. "Just like before, we've got nothing. No DNA under Bart's fingernails or from his defensive wounds. No trace fibers or hairs left at the scene. No DNA from the killer on Jessie. No fingerprints anywhere in the house that aren't accounted for. No fingerprints on either of the victims. This killer covers his tracks very, very well."

A binder appeared in front of Cole, sliding down the table from Noah's direction. Cole looked from the binder to Noah, who wouldn't meet his gaze, and then back to the binder. It was thick, at least four inches, and stuffed with papers divided into sections labeled Victims 1–6. "The original case file," Noah choked out. "Files from each of the first six murders."

He pulled the binder to him and flipped it open. Crime scene photos and autopsy photos assaulted him, followed by reams of reports. He flipped quickly from one autopsy report to the next. "Same MO?"

Noah nodded. He still wouldn't look at Cole. "Same MO. Every time. With the young women, at least. This is the first time he's been interrupted. And—" Noah's lips pressed together.

"And he was angry about being interrupted." The rage was clear. The absolute brutality of the beating Bart Olson had endured said it all. "Was there anything about the Jessie Olson kill he wasn't able to complete? There's no evidence of sexual assault—"

The scowling deputy shoved back from the table and stormed across the conference room. He ripped open the door and marched down the hall, sliding his hands through his hair as his face went purple.

Cole leaned back, watching the deputy when he thought he was alone. The young man faced the wall, almost out of sight, and pitched forward, bracing himself on both elbows as he squeezed his eyes shut.

Hayes appeared, coming out of his office and laying his hand on the deputy's trembling shoulder. He leaned in, speaking softly into his ear. The deputy's expression crumpled. He hung his head. A soundless, broken sob shuddered through him. Hayes guided him into his office and shut the door.

"That's Deputy Garrett," Noah said softly. "Bart Olson was his boss."

"And someone important to him."

Noah nodded. Silence fell over the room, heavy with unspoken words. "No sexual assault. Not in any of the victims," Noah finally said. "We held that back from the press six years ago. Our perp is not a rapist or a necrophiliac. That's not what is motivating him."

"What is?" Cole looked up and met Noah's gaze.

Noah stared back, frozen.

One of the sheriffs down the table leaned forward. He was an older man with a white walrus mustache, a thick head of silver hair, and a strong barrel chest. His name tag said "Clarke." His Stetson sat on the table in front of him, crown down. The band inside was stained with sweat. He worked, and worked hard. No office liaising for this sheriff. "Dr. Kennedy," Sheriff Clarke drawled, "isn't answering that question why you're here?"

Cole smiled. "Yes, sir, it is. I like to gather everyone's

thoughts and opinions first. Everything tells a story. The scene the killer leaves behind. The evidence, either present or absent. The killer's MO. And even the reactions of law enforcement, the thoughts and feelings that arise after the crime. He's leaving a trail behind him, if not through fingerprints and DNA, then through the crime itself. His desires. His fantasies. We'll find that trail, and then we'll find him. No one in this world is an island unto themselves, and no one can keep their secrets forever. Not anymore."

The burly Sheriff Clarke nodded and sat back.

Cole's gaze slid to Noah. He'd gone bone white, again, and hid his hands in the pockets of his khakis.

They fumbled through the rest of the debrief of the Olson autopsies. Cole kept his mouth shut, taking everything in, cross-checking the autopsies against the other six victims and taking notes as Noah spoke. Noah never regained his color, but there were other officers and FBI agents who'd also paled when the photos of the autopsies and crime scene started cycling on the screen.

The meeting broke up around one, and Cole spent the next hour introducing himself to the deputies, sheriffs, and FBI agents on the task force. Jacob hung in the back of the room, answering emails on his phone and keeping an eye on Cole. Noah had vanished.

Finally, the last of the agents left the conference room, leaving Cole and Jacob in what was obviously the task force command center. Cole sagged against the table, hitching his hip over the side as he sat and folded his arms. His gaze roamed the whiteboards: the details of each murder, the details of the victims. The Coed Killer was aptly named. His victim profile was clear. What else could they learn from his victimology?

"I was assigned to help you," Jacob said, throwing himself into one of the chairs. Cole winced, expecting it to flatten beneath the man's massive frame. "Whatever you need, I'm here for."

"Right now," Cole said, sighing as he pinched the bridge of his nose. "I need caffeine and a pizza."

"You don't get that body eating pizza," Jacob said.

"I take it back. Bring me a nice, big, juicy, corn-fed steak. And whatever is in your Iowa water."

Jacob laughed. "C'mon, I'll show you the break room."

He led Cole on the nickel tour, showing him the break room, bathrooms, and the bullpen of cubicles where the eight agents who made up the Des Moines FBI office worked. Some of the spare cubes were filled with deputies and local Des Moines cops, representatives assigned to the task force. Two offices lined the far wall: SAC John Hayes and ASAC Noah Downing.

"Where will I be working?"

"Where do you want to work?"

"In the conference room would be best. I need to get up to speed on this case. That seems to be the center of it all."

"Then that's where you'll be. I'll tell Noah and get the rest of the case files brought to you." Jacob walked him back down the hall. Cole cut into the break room when he spotted a fresh pot of coffee brewing. Jacob followed, leaning in the doorframe. "Were you serious about the pizza?"

"Hell yes. Know any good local spots?"

Jacob grinned. "I'll be back." When he said it, he made Arnold Schwarzenegger seem childish.

Cole reached for a coffee cup and froze.

Noah leaned against the counter, his back to Cole, both hands braced on the countertop. His knuckles were white, as if he were trying to claw his way through the counter, grab on to something he could cling to. His back was rigid, spine taut. His muscles trembled beneath the stretched-tight fabric of his polo. He stared at the wall. Even from behind, Cole could see the pounding of his pulse in the tight line of his neck.

An empty coffee mug sat abandoned by the coffee pot, now done brewing.

Cole hadn't meant to ambush Noah or trap him in the narrow break room. It was a single hallway, one long counter with cupboards, a sink, and a coffee pot crammed in next to the employee fridge. HR notices and office-wide emails were taped to the front, reminders about parking permit renewals and an office picnic.

He'd had a thousand questions he wanted to ask Noah, a thousand variations on *What did I do wrong* and *How did I scare you away* and *Why didn't you call*. Now that Noah was in front of him, an arm's length away, every one of those questions vanished, sucked out of the universe.

An odd kind of anger filled the spaces where they had been. It was formless, shapeless, and it oozed through him like tar. *I didn't know you were FBI*, he wanted to say. He eyed the gun on Noah's hip, identical to his own. Neither of them had been armed that night.

I didn't know you were FBI, either, he imagined Noah saying in return. Neither of them had brought up their personal lives. What they did, where they lived. If they had families. He hated himself for it, but Cole tried to see Noah's left hand, get eyes on his ring finger. Was there a wedding band there today that hadn't been there on Wednesday night? Was that why Noah was so fucking terrified? Was that why he'd been so adamant he couldn't be out at home? In Des Moines, Iowa? In the FBI?

Cole filled his coffee cup and set the pot back on the burner, spinning it so the handle was at a perfect ninety degrees. "I'll be working in the conference room," he said. He spoke to the wall, not to Noah. "I'm going to read through the case file, then start talking to the members of the task force. Who has the most experience? Who has been on the task force the longest?" He was expecting it to be one of the sheriffs, one of the locals. It was usually a local, someone who had jurisdiction and command control but needed the heft of the FBI to support the on-the-ground investigation.

Silence. Nails scratched against the laminate countertop. "Me," Noah choked out. "I've worked the case the longest. I'm the only one left from the original investigation."

New plan, then. He'd talk to everyone else first. Cole nodded, running his tongue over his teeth. "We'll talk later." He pivoted and strode to the doorway. Noah didn't move.

He wanted to come up with something to say. Something cutting. Something scathing. Something witty or wonderful. Something that would hurt like he'd been hurting, and something that would remind Noah of Wednesday night, of what they'd shared.

He kept his mouth shut but let his gaze linger on Noah before heading back to the conference room.

6

THE PIZZA JACOB brought back was delicious. He and Jacob demolished the entire box in under twenty minutes while Cole asked him questions about the case. Jacob had only been in the Des Moines office for three years. He was too new to have been around for the first six killings. But he'd started working with Noah as soon as Bart and Jessie were found, and he'd spent the whole weekend reviewing the case, getting up to speed on the history and the particulars.

Six victims, all young women, all college age, all accomplished in their own individual ways. Each had been featured in the local news. Each was classically beautiful with midwestern charm. They were a mix of blonde and brunette, blue eyes and brown and hazel. Each had been viciously strangled in a secluded location. Corners of college campuses. Apartments when the women were alone. In their car after working late at a restaurant.

The killer was a predator, a stalker, someone who hunted his targets and lay in wait. He was patient. He was careful. He left no forensic trace, other than the bodies of his victims.

The last three murders happened suddenly, a triple event in a single night. Stacy Shepherd's murder broke the pattern the killer had established. Prior to her death, the killer had been as reliable as a clock, hunting his victims every four months. Cole could imagine the buildup inside of the killer: the hunger, the need, the simmering rage beginning to boil until his blood lust seized control of his fantasies and he had to act. What had made Stacy Shepherd unique that night? Why had he broken his own pattern?

And why kill Kyle and Shelly the same night?

And then why disappear for six years.

Until now.

Jessie Olson was exactly his type. She fit the victim profile to a T. And there were no forensics left behind. No trace evidence. No DNA. A ghost's fingerprints were all over her and all over her father.

Noah appeared while he was poring through the case file, hovering like a gargoyle in the doorway as Cole started quizzing Jacob on the Olson murders. Jacob waved Noah in, pushing out a chair for him. "Noah will know more than I do about the Olsons. He was the fed on the scene. We couldn't get involved until the task force was back up, but the sheriffs, they all requested Noah by name. He's the expert on the case." Jacob shrugged and threw Noah a lopsided grin. "I'm filling him in on everything I can, boss."

"I appreciate that," Noah said, his voice careful. Jacob's brow furrowed. Noah wouldn't look at Cole. He stared at his notepad. He didn't have a pen. "You want to know about the Olson murders?"

Cole flipped through the Olson report. His eyes caught on the time of death, the time of discovery. "When did you get to the scene?"

Noah's lips thinned. "About one thirty. Thursday afternoon."

Well, there was one question answered. Noah wasn't even in Vegas Thursday night when they were supposed to meet. Of course, that didn't explain why he hadn't called or texted.

Hey, I've been called back to the office, can't meet you tonight… Maybe we could keep in touch? Maybe—

Cole shook his head. "Was this the first time he's been interrupted during one of his attacks?"

Noah and Jacob shared a look. Cole's gaze bounced between them. He raised his eyebrows.

Noah pulled another case file out from under his notepad and passed it to Cole. "We're not certain about this one. Kimberly Foster, a sophomore at Faith Baptist Bible College north of Des Moines, south of ISU. She was captain of the undefeated volleyball team last season. She was featured in several local newspapers. Young, pretty, accomplished. She was strangled to death in her bedroom."

"Sounds like a fit to our killer's profile so far. What makes you uncertain?"

"She had a stalker. She was filing a restraining order against him. He was a student at Faith, and he'd gotten aggressive with her in the past. The dean of the school tried to downplay it. Said boys will be boys about chasing pretty girls. That it was harmless." Noah shook his head, disgust clear on his face. "She was being stalked and threatened. The school did nothing."

"You think it's the stalker. What's his alibi? Where was he the night she died?"

"He claims he was in his apartment. He lives alone, and no one can verify if he really was there or not. Cell phone records have him in his apartment all night, but it's easy to ditch a cell phone if you need to. We checked his Netflix records, his cell phone records, his ISP data. If he was at home, he was doing nothing all evening. We don't have any activity on his ISP router until almost four in the morning, when he started playing video games. And Kimberly was killed sometime between eleven p.m. and two a.m."

"Physical evidence?"

Noah shook his head. "Nothing. No fingerprints. No

DNA. No trace. Which, if it was this kid, we'd expect there to be a whole heap of physical evidence." Jacob, catty-corner to Noah, nodded. He pursed his lips as Noah gestured his way. "The locals asked Jacob to sweat the kid a bit, put pressure on him during questioning. He didn't budge. Insisted he didn't kill her. In fact, he was sobbing through most of the interrogation. Could barely get a word in through his tears."

"Sounded like he was dying," Jacob said. "He's a little creep, but I'm not sure he killed her. I usually get confessions from the guilty ones."

"I'll bet you do." Cole shot Jacob a smile.

Noah cleared his throat. His fingers tapped a furious rhythm on his notepad. When Cole turned back to Noah, Noah looked away, jaw clenched, nostrils flaring.

"Where was this kid Wednesday night?"

"Same story: in his apartment. Alone. We've requested cell and ISP data again." Noah's shoulders slumped. "I thought he was good for Kimberly's murder. He had the motive, the means, and the opportunity. He'd been to her house before. She was getting ready to serve a restraining order on him."

"That always makes those types go ballistic."

"Exactly. I know he's not the serial killer we're looking for. He would have been fifteen when the murders started, for one. But is he *a* killer? Or is he just a creep, and Kimberly was a victim of our other monster?" Noah jerked his chin at the whiteboards surrounding the room, the tableau of the Coed Killer's work over the past six years and five days.

"Tell me about Kimberly's murder."

Noah launched into a description of the killing and the crime scene, of the forensics and the investigation. Halfway through, he came around to Cole's side of the table and sat beside him, flipping through the photos in the thick case file one by one and pointing out the details. Cole was uncomfortably aware of Noah, of his heat, his closeness. The way he smelled: the cologne he'd worn in Vegas. It had been sharper then, freshly applied for his night out. Now it was thin as the afternoon wound down.

As Noah spoke, he leaned closer as he pointed out parts of the crime scene. Bruises. Blood splatter. The position of the bodies. It was like being beside him at the bar or in the Parrot Room. The pull toward Noah was there again, impossible to resist, as powerful as it had been that night. Cole wanted to lean into him, bury his face in Noah's neck and just breathe. Kiss him again. Taste his skin. Run his nose up his neck, nuzzle the skin behind his ear, whisper his name through the short strands of his hair.

"Kimberly's dad, Frank, was home sick from work that evening. He worked the late shift at the meat processing and packaging plant in Ankeny. They were home alone. Her mom had been out of the picture for a long time. Kimberly was taking care of him. They had a good relationship. Sometime after midnight, the killer cut the phone line to the house and broke into the garage, where he flipped the breakers and cut the power. He made his way into the house through the garage door, which was left unlocked, and strangled Kimberly in her bed. We think he was expecting the house to be empty and didn't expect her father to come check and see what was going on. The killer turned on the father when he walked into Kimberly's bedroom, strangling him with Kimberly's belt. They were both found there the next day."

Cole spread the crime scene photos out. The father, Frank, was not a small man. Nothing like Jacob, but he wasn't someone who would be overpowered easily, even while ill. He'd have to have been surprised. Cole pulled the photo of Kimberly, lying on the autopsy table, closer. Dark, ugly bruises circled her throat. "It takes some strength to strangle a person. Kimberly was an athlete, too. She would have put up a fight."

"If she'd been expecting it. There weren't any defensive wounds on her." Noah seemed pained, looking at the photos.

He slid a picture of the house over the image of Kimberly's corpse.

"The MO fits. So does the lack of evidence left behind. He clearly hunts these women. Follows them. Gets to know their routines. It's possible he expected Frank to be at work that night and was surprised by him."

Noah nodded. "That's what we're thinking."

Cole flipped open the Olson file and pulled out a photo of Bart, beaten to a pulp on his living room floor. "If he was interrupted during Kimberly Foster's murder and then again while killing Jessie Olson, that might explain the savagery and overkill he displayed with Bart. The rage at being interrupted during his ritual. This beating is outside his normal MO. This is not what he does. This—" Cole held up Bart's photo. "Is pure rage."

A chime broke through the thick air. Jacob sheepishly pulled out his phone and silenced the dinging alarm. "Sorry. Noah, I've got to duck out a little early tonight. Brianna's got a ballet recital, and I promised her and Holly I would be there. I've to get the little lady some roses on the way."

Noah smiled, the same smile Cole had seen Wednesday night. His heart lurched. "Things are getting serious between you two, huh?"

Jacob blushed, his whole face going tomato red. Even his ears went dark. He cleared his throat as he straightened his papers and stood. "Brianna's a great little kid. She's cute. And Holly..." He nodded.

He's going to propose to her soon. Cole watched as Jacob pulled up a photo of a beaming brunette and her toddler daughter, the little girl decked out in a tutu and ballet shoes and a sparkling tiara. Their smiling faces were squished together. It was Jacob's lock screen for his phone. *Very soon. I hope he involves Brianna in the proposal.*

Jacob held out his hand to Cole. "I'm sorry I can't take you out to dinner tonight, man."

It was practically FBI law: the guy on temporary duty got taken out by the host office his first night. Sometimes every night, if the personalities really meshed. But the first night, the guy on TDY could be guaranteed great local food and a decent night of entertainment. Cole had been to more dive bars and jazz bars and piano bars and wine bars in more cities than he could remember.

"No problem. Have a great time at the recital. Get pink roses if you can find them. And a single red one for Holly."

Jacob grinned. "Good idea. Thanks, man. See you tomorrow."

He slapped the doorframe on his way out, and then he was gone.

Silence filled the conference room like helium, squeezing out all the oxygen, pressing on Cole until he felt dizzy. He stared at the crime scene photos, rearranging them on the conference table as if sorting them and resorting them would reveal hidden secrets. Noah's gaze burned into the side of his neck. He refused to look back. Not this time.

Noah's chair scooted across the carpet, almost hitting the wall. "I'm going to go see what the others are doing," he mumbled. Then he was gone.

Cole tipped back in his chair and closed his eyes. A whisper of Noah's cologne hit him, and the memories followed, a cascade of smoky jazz and candlelight and Noah's first kiss. His naked joy, his beaming smile as he looked up at Cole at three in the morning, flushed with arousal and wet with their release.

I want to know.

I can't be that at home.

He threw his pen on the table and scrubbed his face with both hands.

Damn midwestern men. Damn them.

FOR THE FIRST time in the five years Cole had been with the FBI, no one from the office was available to take him out to dinner his first night.

No one… except Noah.

Everyone else had something going on. Which made sense. These people had lives, and Cole had been air-dropped into their world almost overnight. They couldn't drop everything and take care of him, not when they had families and lives and commitments.

He tried not to read into the fact that, out of everyone, only Noah had no plans and, apparently, nothing and no one to go home to.

Of course, if that was the case, why was he checking his phone every thirty seconds, compulsively texting and scrolling through whatever he'd just received? He was doing anything rather than watch Cole pack up his notes and the case file.

"Ready?" Cole asked. Noah nodded but said nothing. He marched down the hall, his laptop bag bouncing off his ass, shoulders taut and tense.

Cole couldn't help it. He stared, drinking in Noah's body where it peeked out from beneath the loose layers, the khakis-and-polo uniform of the federal agent. He'd looked far hotter in his slim-fit dress shirt and those sinful skinny jeans, but nothing Noah could wear would make him look ugly. He wasn't a neon light anymore in his G-man outfit, wasn't screaming *Look at me, look at me*! But for Cole, who'd seen what lay beneath, it was easy to remember the slim hips, the broad chest, the scattering of chest hair. The muscular legs, especially when Noah had wrapped his thighs around Cole's waist or slid one calf between Cole's.

Noah led him to an FBI-issued black SUV in the parking lot. They piled in, and Noah clasped the steering wheel with both hands in a white-knuckled death grip. "Where do you want to go?" he asked. His voice was strained, almost strangled. He wouldn't look at Cole.

Did Cole really want to spend the next two hours with someone who obviously couldn't stand him? Who wanted nothing to do with him? It would be better to head to the hotel and get to work.

"Can you just drop me off at my hotel?"

Noah's jaw clenched. His fingers squeezed the leather steering wheel once more. After a long moment, he put the car in gear and backed out.

The hotel was less than a mile away. As they crossed University, Noah pulled into the McDonald's. "Let me at least run you through a drive-through?" he mumbled.

"Sure. Thanks."

He told Noah what he wanted and then checked his phone and his email. Five messages from his boss, four follow-ups from cases he was consulting on across the country. A trial update for a case he'd helped out with two years before. Nothing urgent. He slid his phone back into his jacket as Noah passed him the bag with his burger and fries.

"Nothing for you?"

Noah shook his head as he pulled to the stop sign and signaled to turn left onto Fiftieth. Cars whipped by them. "I can't eat. If I eat, I'll puke."

Cole stared. It took a lot, honestly, to leave him speechless these days. But, damn, that did it. How quickly they had gone from Noah's tender first kiss and their all-night lovemaking to Cole's presence making Noah want to puke.

That formless anger surged back, white-hot and vicious. Cole dropped the McDonald's bag on the console and grabbed his laptop bag. Cars were still passing in front of them. He could see his hotel from here. They were a block away. "I'll walk the rest of the way," he growled, shoving open the SUV door and sliding out.

"Hey!" Noah shouted. "Cole!"

Cole left the door open and started walking. He heard Noah curse. Heard him shift the car into park. He imagined

Noah reaching across the car to drag the passenger door shut. He was already halfway to the hotel.

Fuck Noah. Fuck him and his closet. Fuck him and his secrets. It was 2021. There was no reason to be afraid of coming out.

Unless he was hiding something—something like a wife, or a family, or some other reason why he was going to puke at the sight of Cole and the memory of what they'd done, what they'd been to each other. For one night at least.

Behind him, an engine roared, and he heard tires squeal as Noah raced down the block after him. "Cole, wait!"

Cole shook his head. He didn't look as Noah pulled alongside him and slowed, creeping along at a walking pace. Cars stacked up behind Noah. He cursed again as they honked.

Cole turned into the hotel's driveway, speeding up as he headed for the lobby doors. Noah sped up, too, roaring past Cole and then throwing his SUV in park. He waited, window down, and for a moment Cole considered going the long way around the back of the hotel and coming in from poolside. There was always a backdoor.

"I didn't mean…" Noah hung his head as Cole neared the SUV. "I didn't think I'd ever see you again."

"Clearly. That was obvious Thursday night. Even more so today."

Noah went ghostly pale. His eyes clenched shut as his hands balled on top of the steering wheel. "At least take your food?" He held out the McDonald's bag. It trembled.

Cole snatched it and turned away. The hotel's glass doors slid open.

"I'll pick you up at seven?"

Cole waved over his shoulder and didn't look back. The doors closed behind him, cutting off anything Noah might have said.

7

THE MORNING WAS COOL, the humidity of the previous day pushed back by the night. It would return with a vengeance, according to the weather report. Cole watched the local news in the hotel lobby as he ate a plate of buffet eggs and wilted pancakes. Hayes was on, speaking to the media about the return of the Coed Killer. *We have put all of the FBI's resources into finding this killer*, he said. *The FBI is working closely with the sheriffs and police departments in the area, and we are all committed to catching this monster and ending his streak of terror.*

At 7 a.m. on the dot, Cole headed out to the parking lot. Noah was already there, parked under the hotel's overhang. He leaned against the driver's door of the same black SUV with two paper cups of Starbucks coffee in his hands. He held one out to Cole. "Morning."

"Morning." He took the coffee and walked to the passenger side, climbing in.

A pile of single creamers, clearly from Noah's house, and packets of sugar cluttered the center console. "I didn't know what to get you," Noah said. "Or how you wanted your coffee."

You would have if you'd stuck around. But that wasn't fair. Noah had been called back to Des Moines when the Olsons bodies were found. He didn't have a choice about leaving.

But he did have a choice about calling Cole, or texting. Saying something instead of vanishing. Which he would have done if he'd felt even an ounce of what Cole had felt.

Cole poured every creamer into his coffee, all seven of the individual tubs Noah had grabbed. He frowned. "Do you have any more creamer?"

"How much more do you want?"

"Do you know that gross color everyone painted their homes fifteen years ago? That beige, off-white, cream color?"

A tiny smile curled the corner of Noah's lips. "Sounds like the walls at my house."

Who do you live with in that house? Cole bit down hard on his tongue. He didn't need to know that. He didn't need to know anything about Noah. Not anymore. "Well, that's how I take my coffee."

They pulled away from the hotel in silence. Noah took them past University and turned into a Starbucks, pulling up by the front doors. "Want to fix it?"

"Yeah. Sure." Cole hopped out and headed in. At the cream-and-sugar station, he poured enough half-and-half into his coffee to turn it nearly milk-white. Looking up, he caught Noah's gaze through the window. Noah was watching him, his expression haggard and exhausted. After a moment, Noah turned his head to stare out the driver's side window.

Whatever. He didn't have time for Noah's misery. He was here to do a job. Cole snapped the lid back on his coffee and headed out to Noah's SUV. "Are we going to the crime scenes today?"

Noah nodded as he backed out. "Do you want to go to the office first?"

"No. I want to see the scenes."

Silence. Noah merged onto the I-35 on-ramp and headed north. Des Moines passed them by, and then the suburbs, and then the burbs petered out to rolling fields of wheat and corn, endless miles of crops that stretched from horizon to horizon.

It was amazing how quickly the country arrived out here. In less than twenty minutes, they were turning onto a two-lane road heading straight for the horizon with corn bracketing them on either side. A TV transmission tower rose ahead, reaching so high it seemed to hold up the cloudless blue sky. If Cole drove twenty minutes away from his condo in D.C., he'd still be sitting in traffic in D.C.

"Kimberly and her father lived in Alleman. It's a small farming community north of Ankeny, north of Des Moines. About four hundred people live here." Noah slowed to a stop at a four-way intersection. Farmland spread in every direction. An old farmhouse, possibly built when Iowa was first settled, sagged on its foundation to the right. They turned left, heading toward a small cluster of turn-of-the-century homes on narrow asphalt streets. All the streets led to the county's combined primary, middle, and high school. Athletic fields wrapped around the downtown, and beyond the soccer and football pitches, more corn spread out in wide, wandering fields.

It was the kind of place where flowers were planted around the base of the wooden power poles and every house had an American flag flying. Rocking chairs swayed in the morning breeze on the wraparound porch of each home they passed. Kids roared by their SUV, screaming as they chased each other on bicycles and tricycles. An adult followed on foot, keeping a wary eye on the children and staring down Noah and Cole as they drove by.

"Suspicious people," Cole said.

"The first murder in town will do that." Noah turned again, pulling them out of downtown and onto an unpaved gravel road that wound into the fields. Ahead, an older, tired home squatted amid the corn, paint peeling on one side, the porch railing splintered on the other. A storm cellar hugged the side of the house, and an oak tree scattered shade and dappled sunlight across the front yard. Rose bushes in desperate need of pruning lined the steps leading to the front door. Crime scene tape, faded from the sun, was still taped across the entry.

Noah put the SUV in park. "This is where Kimberly and Frank Foster lived. She went to the county high school back in town. She earned a full-ride scholarship to Faith Baptist College."

"What was her major?"

"Education."

For the first half hour, Cole stood in the yard, taking in the house and its surroundings. The Fosters' home was secluded, private, and set back from not just the county roads but the small town of Alleman itself. The only way in via road was the gravel drive they'd bounced down. Hardly a silent approach, especially late at night and in a car. Had the killer walked in?

How much would a strange car stand out in Alleman?

Was it possible to come at the house through the cornfields? He'd have to look at the satellite photos, the aerial maps. So far, the fields seemed to stretch forever.

The garage was an add-on to the house, not part of the original construction. It had a single swing door, unpowered. Cole pulled on the handle, lifting and raising the door. The springs were well oiled and taken care of. Used frequently. No squeaking or creaking. The killer could easily have gotten in silently.

And from there, he'd gone right through the door and into the house. The door in from the garage was open, handle and frame dusted black with fingerprint powder. Bootied crime scene techs had tracked the same powder through the doorway and onto the wooden planks of the laundry room and kitchen.

"No forced entry. The killer didn't have to break in." Noah followed Cole, almost too close.

"This isn't the type of place where people lock their doors. Or it wasn't." Cole moved from the kitchen to the living room. The killer hadn't spent time in either. He'd been focused. He'd been on a mission.

Down the hallway. There were two bedrooms across from each other. One was Kimberly's, and the other had been turned into a sunny reading room. Books lined the walls, piled in leaning stacks around a pair of worn side chairs. Nothing had been disturbed in there.

Kimberly's room was a different story.

Crime scene techs had been over every inch of the room. Fingerprint powder and luminol were on almost every surface. There were still evidence placards on the floors and indicator stickers on the walls, pointing out smudged shoe prints—unusable, he could tell—and a palm print on the remains of the mirrored door of Kimberly's closet. Her bed had been stripped, the comforter and sheets taken by the police. He'd read the report last night: no forensic evidence recovered. No hairs, no DNA, not even any trace evidence from anyone other than Kimberly.

"He strangled her to death in here. On her bed." Noah nodded as Cole spoke. He stayed by the door, out of Cole's way. "And there were no defensive wounds on her. He surprised her in her sleep." He thought back to the autopsy report, the photos. The viciousness of the bruising around her throat, the vivid near blackness of her neck. "She was dead in less than a minute. She didn't have time to fight back."

"That's what we think. We think he was on her so fast and so violently she couldn't react. He came here and killed her. He didn't waste any time."

"It's not the stalker. If it were him, he'd confront her. There's be an emotional scene. If he attacked her, he'd have strung it out and made a production out of it. He would have made sure she knew she *caused* him to kill her. This, what happened to her here, isn't that."

Noah stayed quiet.

"Where's Frank's bedroom?"

"Other side of the house. He'd fallen asleep on the couch. We found tissues, the remote, and a bottle of beer half finished. The alcohol and the cold medicine he was taking must have made him drowsy."

"If she was killed that quickly, how did he hear what was happening? Especially since he was medicated and drinking. Was any of her furniture knocked over? Did she manage to kick over a lamp? Hit the wall?"

"No. Not that we found." Noah shook his head as he stared at the floor. One hand grasped the doorframe, as if he was steadying himself. "Dads… They feel things, you know? I think he knew something was going on. He came to check—" Noah shrugged as he picked at a smear of fingerprint powder.

Cole blinked. "Setting aside parental superpowers—"

"Not superpowers. Intuition."

"There has to be a reason Frank got up to check on her." Cole spun in a slow circle, taking in Kimberly's bedroom. The size, the shape. The position of the door. He stared at Noah. Noah looked away. "Frank came down the hallway and stood there, right where you are. He was silhouetted by the hall light. Kimberly's room was dark. Frank came in to check on her, and the killer pounced. He was there, behind you, in the corner." He pointed to the corner behind the door, nearest the sliding closet doors. "He had Kimberly's belt, and he wrapped it around Frank's neck from behind. The force of that pulled Frank back. He fell and tried to grab the closet door"—Cole pointed to the smeared palm print, the shattered mirror—"to get back up. But the killer wouldn't let go. Frank was a lot bigger than Kimberly, but not big enough to overpower someone strangling him with a belt from behind in the dark." Cole hesitated. "Was the light on or off when police arrived?"

"On."

Cole nodded slowly. "He was on his knees, struggling to

breathe as the killer strangled him to death, and he died staring at his daughter's corpse. Because the killer turned on the light."

"Jesus," Noah whispered.

"That was his punishment for being there. He wasn't supposed to be home. This killer is highly controlled. He needs total control over his scenes. For that kind of control, he needs isolation. He needs these girls to be alone when he strikes."

"Why didn't the killer leave, then? If he saw Frank was home, why didn't he leave?"

"He didn't know Frank was here. He wasn't supposed to be. He expected him to be at work. And, once the killer had decided that was the night and Kimberly was his victim, there was no changing his mind. He was committed. He had to act." Cole shook his head. "This is a lust murderer."

"There's no sexual assault."

"This isn't a sexual paraphilia that's driving him. Or not overtly. His desires are about domination and control, about the taking of life. He strangles these girls face to face. He watches them die, inches away from their faces. It's the moment of death that he craves. Seeing that. That's why he doesn't draw their deaths out." He frowned. "Did the medical examiner swab for DNA on any of the girls' faces? Their lips, specifically?"

"I'll have to check."

"Frank checking on Kimberly, for whatever reason, shattered the killer's control of the scene. He lashed out. That's why Frank's death was so much more violent than Kimberly's or the other girls'."

"And the same for Bart Olson?"

Cole nodded. "Most likely. I'll need to see the scene to know for sure."

"Are you ready to head there now?"

He spun one more time, taking in bedroom. What had

called Frank to the bedroom? There was something he was missing. What had Frank heard? What had the killer covered up? Was it, as Noah suggested, parental intuition? Even through booze and cold medication?

The Olson home was much like the Fosters'. Rural farmland spread in all directions, cornfields and horizons the only things in sight. The house sported a mishmash of fixer-upper projects Bart had started and partially completed.

"The killer likes his privacy," Cole said, walking around the Olson property. "Both of these locations are isolated. He chose dark, private, secluded places before, but not like this. Here, he can dominate his victims completely. Take control away from them and take his time. What's more powerful than taking control away from someone inside their own house?"

Noah shook his head.

The bloodstains were still fresh, tacky in some places. The carpet in the living room was still wet. Crime scene markers littered the floors and walls.

"Bart had come off shift at five a.m. He was home by five thirty. He'd told the dispatcher he'd take a nap and be back in before noon."

"He was the sheriff of Boone County. Why was he on the graveyard shift?"

Noah made a face, something between a grimace and a scowl. "He was filling in for one of his deputies. His deputy's wife went into labor the day before, and he was still at the hospital with her. Bart took his shifts for two days."

"So Bart Olson was a good guy."

"One of the best. He moved out here to take over Boone County. He was the chief deputy sheriff of Linn County before coming out here. Cedar Rapids," he said, when Cole frowned.

"He traded in the big city for the fields?" Well, what passed for a city in Iowa.

"He wanted the quiet life, he said."

Cole stared at Bart Olson's blood on the living room rug. "All of the Coed Killer's victims were murdered overnight. Between midnight and six a.m., right?"

"That's right."

"Where was Jessie's mom? Jessie was alone in the house."

"Heather Olson. She's a nurse. She works downtown. Night shifts. She was building seniority before requesting a transfer."

"Where is she now?"

"With family back home in Kansas. She couldn't stay here. And she isn't a suspect. We know where she is if we need to talk to her."

"Who knew Jessie was home alone that night, then? Who knew her dad was filling in for someone?"

Noah's jaw clenched. "The killer surveils his victims beforehand. He knows their routines. Where they walk across campus, what time they go to bed or get off work. When they will be alone. The killer had to have been watching Jessie for days and learning everything about her. Even Heather said she'd felt like someone was watching the house. She said Bart mentioned it, too. They thought maybe someone was up to no good in the field. Heather and Bart must have been feeling the killer's surveillance, and the killer must have seen Bart go to work those two nights. He saw his opportunity."

"The killer is methodical. He leaves nothing to chance or opportunity. Control is what he's all about. I don't see him taking a chance on killing Jessie after seeing Bart drive off. What if he was just going to grab milk?"

"In his uniform? In his duty truck?" Noah shook his head. "Anyhow, I didn't say it was left to chance. Deputy Lee posted on Facebook about his daughter's birth, and he thanked Sheriff Olson for covering for him. He tagged the sheriff's department and Bart personally."

"That sounds—"

"It sounds like Iowa. This is the kind of place where the

sheriffs and the police departments tag citizens in photos at football games and throw barbecues and pool parties over the summer for kids and their families. Last year, the sheriff of Madison County tagged people on Facebook to remind them to pay their traffic tickets. Everyone he tagged did, after some ribbing back and forth."

Cole squinted. "Madison County. Like, *The Bridges of Madison County?*"

"Exactly that Madison County."

"The entire internet, then, knew Bart Olson was taking over Deputy Lee's graveyard shift. And for a killer surveilling young, accomplished, college-aged women like Jessie Olson, that was a gift-wrapped piece of information for him."

"No one knew he was back. No one knew Jessie Olson was being watched—"

"I'm not blaming you. Or anyone else." Cole held up his hands. "This guy works hard at not being found. He's good at evading capture." He looked around the living room, at the blood spray and the surfaces where there should be usable forensics. Should be. "You ever wonder about that? About why he's so good at evading capture?"

"We thought, back during the first task force, that he might have law enforcement exposure. If not experience, then a passing knowledge of forensics. Of course, that was when *CSI* was all the rage. He could have watched a lot of TV or read a lot of books."

Cole paced the edge of the living room. "If you were surveilling someone in a place like this, how would you do it? Any stranger's car would stand out, especially in a place like Alleman or out here near Dallas Center. And I bet Bart Olson would notice if someone strange was poking around his property."

"No one in town would bat an eye if a police car was nearby, though."

Cole nodded. "No one would bat an eye at all."

"There are almost six thousand law enforcement officers in the state."

"I'm not saying the killer is a cop," Cole said. "But he is able to convince people he's not a threat. Blend in, even in places where he might normally stand out. He could be pretending to be law enforcement."

Noah turned away, rubbing his forehead. He circled the stain where Bart's body had fallen, kneeling by an evidence marker and a blood splatter along the wood paneling.

Jessie's bedroom was exactly like Kimberly's: stripped bed, fingerprint powder everywhere, crime sign markers scattered like jacks. Cole could almost see the indentation left by her body on the mattress, or the killer's knees as he straddled her and wrapped his hands around her throat. He held up the crime scene photo of Jessie dead on her bed next to the real thing, trying to transpose the two in his mind. He looked back and forth, trying to take everything in. Trying to work backward and understand the killer. Trying to put himself inside the murderer's mind. *What were you thinking when you looked into her eyes and watched her die?*

"Bart came to check on Jessie when he got home—it was the first thing he did. The autopsy photos showed he was still in his uniform. He hadn't had a chance to change. Where was his service weapon?"

"Locked in the safe in his truck. He had a personal sidearm in a safe inside his nightstand and a shotgun in the master closet. Both were right where they were supposed to be."

"He had his guard down," Cole mused. "But he still checked on his daughter at five thirty in the morning."

He stood in the hall, eyes flicking from smeared handprint to smeared handprint along the wall. They were more like blobs on a Rorschach test, nothing but red and violence and despair. "Bart came to check on her, and the killer surprised him just like he did Frank." Cole mimed the attack, slowly pirouetting down the hall, his shoulder almost impacting the dented drywall, his palm ghosting over a smear of blood running from eye to waist level. "They fought in the hall, until the killer got him to the living room. Then he overpowered Bart."

"How was Bart overpowered?" Noah shook his head. "He was a trained law enforcement officer."

"Surprise and rage are an incredible combination. The killer had the advantage. He was fighting for his life, and he knew it. Bart was stumbling in the dark, and he expected to see his sleeping daughter. Not find a killer hiding in her room."

Noah blanched. He seemed, for a moment, like he was going to be sick.

"Bart's life ended here," Cole said back in the living room. He was stating the obvious, but he tried to see it, really see it. Pull the curtain back, reassemble the devastation to visualize the two men wrestling on the ground, throwing each other into the walls, grabbing furniture and picture frames and broken glass as weapons. He zeroed in on a toppled curio cabinet, on the tumbled frames and broken glass and shattered awards. "In Honor of Fifteen Years of Service," one read. "Linn County Sheriff's Department."

"Did they find what the killer used to beat him to death?" he asked.

Noah shook his head.

"It's probably an award." He squatted by the broken cabinet and picked through the remnants. Ten-year service award. Fifteen-year service award. Commendations. Awards for marksmanship. Community service. There was nothing from Boone County. "Shouldn't Bart have something recognizing his election as sheriff here in Boone?"

"There's a star," Noah said. He crouched beside Cole, poking through the broken glass with his pen. "It's a five-pointed sheriff's badge made of crystal. Their name is engraved on it, and the years of their term. Each sheriff who wins election receives one." He shook his head. "It's not here."

"Someone missed it?" Cole's eyebrows shot upward. "Who was in charge of the crime scene?"

"Deputy Andy Garrett." Pain flickered across Noah's face. "He was a mess the day of the murder."

The deputy who had stormed out, who couldn't take looking at the autopsy photos or hearing the gruesome description of what had been done to Bart and Jessie Olson. How much worse had it been to see their bodies in person? Photos were one thing. The visceral experience of seeing the destroyed remains of someone you cared about was something entirely different. "I sympathize with the man. However, if Deputy Garrett wants to catch Bart and Jessie's killer, he has to process the scene correctly. We've got to find the murder weapon."

"Yeah." Noah pushed himself to his feet. "I'll talk to him when we get back."

By the time they were finished at the house, it was past lunch. Noah drove back toward Des Moines and asked if Cole was hungry.

His stomach growled. Noah chuckled. "If you hadn't had pizza yesterday with Jacob, I'd take you to get a taco pizza."

There was a lot to unpack in that sentence. Cole stared at him. "Taco pizza?"

"Yeah. Tacos, but spread out on pizza dough. Ground beef, refried beans, shredded lettuce, tomatoes, shredded cheese, sour cream. Olives, if you want them. It's very Iowan."

"Sounds like it." He watched as Noah smiled. It was there and then gone, as if Noah had enjoyed himself for a single, fractional moment. "Jealous about Jacob's and my pizza eating?"

"No!" Noah's hands squeezed the steering wheel so hard

the leather screamed, and the tires swerved slightly before he corrected. Silence filled the cabin.

Noah signaled and took the next off-ramp. Three quick turns later, they pulled up to a seafood joint in a strip mall. Red-checked tablecloths fluttered on patio tables clustered in front of the restaurant. Red plastic baskets cradled fish and fries.

"Seafood? In the Midwest?"

"Bluff Lake has the best catfish in four states. It's fresh. This is one of Des Moines' hidden treasures." Noah wouldn't look at him as he climbed out of the SUV. He slammed the door shut before Cole could answer.

"Guess we're eating catfish," he mumbled. *Well done pissing Noah off, hotshot.*

Lunch was strained. Noah wouldn't look at him, or talk to him, or acknowledge his existence. He didn't even sit across from Cole, instead scooting to the right so it seemed like they weren't together. Like they just happened to enter at the same time from the same SUV, order together, and sit at opposite ends of the same picnic table. Noah stared at his cell phone the whole time, scrolling through whatever he was reading and poking at the screen like he was texting someone every few minutes.

Cole caught up on emails and called his office to check in. The catfish was surprisingly good, and he endured his boss's teasing about eating fish in the dead center of the Midwest. "Bluff Lake has the best catfish in four states, I was told." His boss laughed at him.

Twenty minutes later, Noah stood and tossed his lunch in the trash. He hadn't eaten a single bite. "Ready?" Noah grumbled. He jiggled his keys as he glared at the parking lot.

"Still going to puke if you eat?"

Noah walked away.

The drive to the first of the original six crime scenes was deathly silent. It almost hurt to breathe the air in the vehicle.

Waves of misery mixed with quiet fury rolled off Noah, pummeling Cole. He stared out his window, counting the cornfields they passed.

None of the first six were as secluded as the recent murders. None were as rural. In fact, the most rural they got was deserted parking lots and the quiet corners of college campuses. One girl was strangled on a walking path circling the Iowa State quad.

Was the killer easing back in after a long hiatus? Was he spooked from his almost capture, if Kyle and Shelly *had* seen him the night Stacy Shepherd was murdered? Had he learned to be more secretive, more cautious?

How was that plan going, after he was interrupted twice? Was that why he showed so much rage? So much fury when his ritual, his private domination, was destroyed?

Where had the Coed Killer been for six years?

Damn it, he needed to talk to Noah about the original investigation. Really talk to him: ask him his thoughts, understand his processes. Hunting a serial killer was a unique experience. The frustration, the feeling of impotence, and the hopelessness that could set in as the victims piled up and the evidence withered… it could make a man go mad.

Memories from the investigation crystallized, hung like ice sculptures in the mind. Noah knew things. He had to.

And Cole had to break the ice that had reformed between them. Damn him and his big mouth. He shouldn't have said what he did about Jacob, and Noah being jealous. Noah had been nothing but clear that he wanted nothing, absolutely *nothing*, to do with what had happened between them.

Cole turned to Noah, still searching for what to say—

Noah's phone rang. He answered it one-handed, not looking at the caller ID. "Agent Downing." A pause. Then, "*What?*" he roared. His face went pale, bone white, and his jaw dropped. "When? What happened?" Someone was answering his questions, and Noah's jaw clenched hard as he swallowed.

He slammed the indicator down and hit the SUV's lights and sirens as he swerved through three lanes of traffic. "I'm on the way."

Cole kept his mouth shut as Noah blew toward downtown Des Moines. He concentrated on staying alive, holding on to the oh-shit bar and clinging to his seat belt. As if that would save him if Noah got them into a head-on collision.

Minutes after the phone call ended, Noah burned rubber as he spun the SUV into the Iowa Methodist emergency room parking lot. He threw the car into park in the first available space and took off, running for the double glass doors marked "Emergency." Cole followed.

He walked in just in time to see Noah badger the front desk attendant, leaning over the counter with wild eyes as he asked, "Katherine Downing? Where is Katherine Downing? She was just brought in—"

"*Dad!*"

Noah spun. Down the hallway, a brunette teenager in a blood-spattered cheerleader uniform came running toward Noah from the curtained-off emergency room bed she'd been waiting in. There was a bandage taped on her forehead, and her right arm was splinted and wrapped in thick gauze, all the way up to the elbow.

"*Katie!*" Noah bellowed.

He raced for her, and they met in the hallway, Katie collapsing against Noah as he wrapped his arms around her and dragged her against his chest, as if he could pull her inside him and keep her safe. He kissed her forehead, rubbed his hands over her hair, cradled her skull and pulled her back just far enough to stare down into her eyes. "Are you okay? Jesus, *are you okay?*"

"I'm okay. I'm okay, Dad," Katie said. She was trembling.

"Trevor was goofing off and accidentally rolled the car. But we were all buckled in—"

"*Accidentally* rolled the car!"

"The glass cut me. But I'm okay." Katie looked like she wanted Noah to tell her she was okay, too. "And so is everyone else. No one was hurt bad, I promise."

"Jesus Christ…" Noah wrapped her in his arms again, rocking with her in the middle of the hallway as he stroked her hair. His shoulders and back shook. Katie clung to him, her fingers squeezing the fabric of his shirt over his ribs. "That's the last time you're driving anywhere with Trevor," Noah growled.

"Yeah." Katie nodded, smearing her tear-stained face against his chest. "Yeah, definitely. He was being so stupid."

"Katie?" A nurse appeared, looking from Katie to Noah and back. "Hello. I'm Rebecca, Katie's nurse. And you are…"

"Noah Downing, her father," Noah said, at the same time Katie said, "My dad. You called him."

Rebecca looked pleasantly surprised. "I didn't realize you'd be here this quickly, Mr. Downing."

"Agent Downing." Katie smiled. "He's in the FBI."

Rebecca smiled. "Agent Downing, let's get you and Katie back to her bed." She started guiding them down the hall. "The doctor will be back to see Katie as soon as she can. I know Dr. Caulfield wanted to get an X-ray of Katie's arm to make sure there's no fracture. We needed to wait for you to sign off before—" The curtain closed around them, and the conversation turned into muffled words and soft murmurs.

Cole stood alone in the hallway, staring at the empty space where Noah and Katie had collided, had wrapped each other up in bear hugs.

Dad. *Dad.*

Oh.

Sighing, Cole trudged to the corner of the waiting room and threw himself into a plastic chair. He rubbed his eyes, his mind replaying Katie's shout—*Dad!*—and Noah's run for her over and over again.

Oh.

Noah is a father. He has a daughter.

And that meant there was a mother, too.

Cole buried his face in his palms and tried to breathe through the pain.

8

AN HOUR LATER, Noah appeared, shuffling down the hall with his shoulders slumped and his head hanging. His hands were shoved in the pockets of his rumpled khakis. He wouldn't meet Cole's gaze as he neared. He stared at the cracked tile floor as he held out the SUV's keys. "Here," he mumbled. "Why don't you drive yourself back to the hotel? You don't need to stay."

"What about you? How will you and Katie get home?"

"Take a taxi or a Lyft. We'll be fine."

"I'm not stranding you here, Noah. Not with your injured daughter. I can wait."

Noah fidgeted. Shifted his weight from foot to foot.

"How is she doing?"

Noah sighed. He pitched forward, almost collapsing into the seat beside Cole. "They took her for an X-ray. They don't think anything's broken, but they always want to be sure with kids. Growth plates and all that. Other than that, she's okay. Some cuts. One needed some superglue." He scrubbed both hands over his face. "I can't believe that asshole rolled his car with other kids in it."

"Trevor?"

"He's on the football team. Wide receiver. All-state last year." He rolled his eyes. "Thinks he's God's gift to football, that he's the only high schooler ever to have a winning record."

Cole smiled.

"Katie's a cheerleader. She's the youngest cocaptain of the varsity squad." Noah, despite himself, smiled. His paternal pride was obvious. "But she's in summer school right now. She had a rough spring. In the morning, she has her remedial pre-calc and history classes. In the afternoon, cheerleading camp. Trevor's in her history class, and he goes to football camp in the afternoon at the same time she does." He blew out a ragged breath, long and slow.

"Uh-oh. Is that a dad's disapproval of his daughter's boyfriend I hear?"

"They are not dating."

Cole raised a single eyebrow.

"They are not. Katie would tell me. And she knows how I feel about Trevor."

"Mm-hmm." For a moment, Cole wanted to laugh. Wanted to commiserate with Noah and poke fun at him over Trevor and Katie and their possible teen romance. But...

The pit that had been opening inside Cole yawned wider. He felt himself start to fall in. "Is, um. Is Katie's mom going to get here soon?" Is that why Noah wanted him to leave? "Should I make myself scarce?"

Agony rocked Noah's features. He rolled forward, his elbows on his knees as he clenched his hands into fists. His pulse pounded in his temples, at his jawline. "I've got to call Lilly," he breathed. "But I don't fucking want to."

Lilly. A name. Cole felt a bullet slam into his gut. Damn it, he never wanted to be that guy. He hated screwing around with married guys, hated the thought of it—

"We're divorced," Noah whispered. "Four years. It's not a good divorce. She lives in Omaha. She's an assistant U.S.

attorney out there. Works with my boss's boss." He snorted. Shook his head. "Katie lived with her for the past four years, but that didn't go well. She wants to live with me full time. She moved out during spring break, and now we're trialing me having primary custody. See if it's a good fit for Katie."

Oh. *'I can't be that at home.'* "This car accident is the last thing you need, huh?"

Noah laughed, high and thin. He shook his head and squeezed his eyes closed. *"I'm* the last thing I need. Maybe the last thing Katie needs. The last thing anyone needs."

Cole frowned.

"I was definitely the last thing Lilly needed. I wasn't what she wanted. I couldn't make her happy."

"Noah…" Cole wanted to reach out. He wanted to touch Noah, squeeze his shoulder, grab his hand, thread their fingers together. Run his own fingers through Noah's soft hair. A brilliant smile filled his memories. Noah, joyous. *You know, I think I'm gay.* "She couldn't make you happy, either, could she? Not really."

Noah's fists clenched. His shoulders trembled.

Fuck it. Cole reached for him, laying his palm on Noah's knee. He squeezed. "Your life isn't complicated at all, is it?" He smiled, trying to lighten the moment. Trying to connect, in some way, with Noah.

Noah let out a single, strangled sob. He turned to Cole and finally looked Cole in the eyes.

Raw, naked hunger burned from Noah—and a longing that seared Cole all the way down to his bones. He couldn't breathe, suddenly trapped in Noah's gaze, in his anguished, desperate yearning. Noah hadn't even looked at him like that in Vegas. Not like Cole was everything Noah had ever wanted, everything he needed. Cole fought for something, anything to say, but his mind had blanked and all he could do was stare back, frozen, his own hunger rising—

Noah jumped to his feet. His hands threaded through his

hair as he paced away. He made it to the edge of the waiting room before he turned back. As if that was a safe distance, and only with a room between them could he look at Cole again.

Cole slid back in his chair. He tried to catch Noah's gaze, see if there was anything in those honey eyes again, see whether what he'd seen was really there or it was just his imagination—

Noah turned his back on Cole.

Now Cole was going to be sick.

A moment later, Noah pulled out his cell phone and walked outside. Cole watched him take a deep breath and make a call. Noah covered his eyes with his hand as he paced the hospital's sidewalk. In less than thirty seconds, he was shouting, trying to talk over whoever was on the other end of the line. He kept getting interrupted, and then interrupted himself.

Less than a minute in, it was over. Noah looked like he wanted to hurl his phone into the parking lot, or onto the highway overpass. He clenched his teeth and turned his face to the sky, silently screaming.

Cole watched him gather himself, physically drag his emotions back together. Watched him try to breathe in and out. Watched him fight off the sobs that were trying to break free. He watched as the sun set, silhouetting Noah against the Des Moines skyline. His breath caught, and he forced himself to look away when Noah finally walked back into the ER.

If he didn't, Noah might see Cole's hunger, the yearning for Noah that he couldn't escape from.

Damn midwestern men.

KATIE WASN'T RELEASED until almost eight p.m., after the radiologist had reviewed her X-ray and pronounced her good to go. No breaks, no hairline fractures. No bone bruise. The scrapes would heal, and she'd be as good as new.

Noah wrapped her in his FBI field jacket and held her close, one arm tight around her shoulders, as they emerged from her curtained gurney and made their way back to the lobby, and to Cole.

"Katie, this is Dr. Kennedy," Noah said stiffly. "He's a profiler and he's helping us with a case."

"The Coed Killer?" Katie peered at him, looking almost lost beneath Noah's jacket.

"Mm-hmm." Cole held out his hand. "You can call me Cole."

She took it gingerly in her bandaged hand as Noah shot him a stern look. "Dr. Kennedy, Katie."

"Were you guys working when…" She sniffed as her voice trailed off. Cole nodded. "I'm sorry, Dad."

Noah kissed her temple. "It's okay. But, no more driving with Trevor. Ever."

"Definitely not." Katie leaned into Noah, her head almost lying on his chest. "It was really scary."

He kissed her forehead, squeezed her tight, and guided her to the door. "Let's go home."

Cole fell into step beside them. Katie blinked, and she looked from Cole to Noah and back. "Is Dr. Kennedy staying with us?"

"No," Noah snapped. "We're going to drop him off at his hotel."

Noah helped Katie into the back seat, buckling her in like she was five years old despite her protestations. *Dad, I'm fine. Really. I can buckle my own seat belt, Dad.* She did take the jacket Noah laid over her like a blanket, snuggling into its warmth and her father's scent. Noah ran his hand over her hair, smiling as she gave him a tired, shaky smile in return.

Cole slid silently into the front seat as Noah climbed behind the wheel.

Noah sighed before he started the car. Met Katie's gaze in the rearview mirror. "You have to call your mother, Katie."

Katie groaned. "I don't want to talk to her."

"You have to call her. She's expecting your call."

Katie groaned again, throwing her head back on the headrest. "*Dad.*"

"You were in a car accident and in the ER, Katie. You need to talk to her about that. She has a right to know how you are. She is your mother."

Grumbling, almost incoherent, from the back seat. Noah's eyebrows rose. "What was that, miss?"

Katie scowled. "Nothing."

"She's your mother, and she loves you." In the passenger mirror, Cole saw Katie roll her eyes as Noah spoke. "You guys are at that age where daughters fight with their mothers over everything—"

"'Cause everything she says is wrong!"

Noah sighed. "Katie. You're going to call her when we get home."

"Can't you tell her I'm sleeping? I need my rest, don't I?"

"Katie."

It was Katie's turn to sigh, full of the long-suffering anguish and put-upon woe that only a teenager can muster. Noah stared at her until she looked away, pouting as she glared out the rear passenger window. Noah put the SUV in gear and headed for the highway.

Silence filled the car. Cole twisted in his seat. "What's your favorite subject in school, Katie?"

Katie wasn't in the mood to be placated. She didn't look at Cole as she grumbled, "I dunno."

"Katie…" The warning in Noah's voice was obvious.

She sighed. "Athletics. 'Cause I get to cheer."

"Ever take a psychology class?"

A spark of interest ignited in her eyes. Cole's breath hitched. For a moment, she looked like a younger, more feminine version of Noah. As if Noah had been put in a dryer and shrunk. The same angle of the head, the same fire in their gazes when they saw something that intrigued them.

"They offer it as an elective at school. I signed up for digital design, though." She studied Cole. "Psychology, that's, like, what you do?"

"I'm a forensic criminal psychologist. I figure out what people did—and, more importantly, why—at crime scenes. Why did someone behave this way or choose to do this instead of that."

"That's cool. That's more interesting than listening to someone complain for an hour."

Cole smiled. "That's therapy. Counseling and clinical psychology. I've never counseled anyone. I don't see patients."

"But you're a doctor."

"Research doctor. You know what a PhD is?"

Katie nodded. "A lot of college. Like, a lot."

He laughed. "You got that right. I got my doctorate in forensic psychology after I published my research on criminal behavior, specifically studying psychopathy."

"Like, crazy serial killers and insane murderers?"

"Some murderers have mental illnesses, yes. Not all of them. I study the crime scenes serial killers leave behind and build profiles based on what that tells me. I can usually tell who is mentally ill and who isn't pretty quickly."

"Like how? What can you see?"

"So, for example, there was a serial killer we were tracking a few years ago. He would murder his victims… really badly." Cole self-edited, reminding himself that Katie was a teenager. And Noah's daughter. "And when we found them, they all had a sock shoved up their behinds."

"Okay," Noah said. "I think this is getting—"

"Dad," Katie protested. "This is cool. Let him finish!"

Cole waited. Noah sighed. He guided the SUV down the off-ramp and signaled to turn right at the stop sign.

He took Noah's silence as tacit, reluctant permission to continue. He watched Noah out of the corner of his gaze as he spoke. "People at the BAU were divided. Was the sock a symbol? Things are so often symbolic with serial killers. Everything represents something. Forensic psychologists are always looking to assign symbolism to anything. *Anything.*" He grinned. Katie did, too. *She looks so much like her father.* His chest tightened. "So," Cole said, forcing himself to continue, "did the sock have another meaning? Or was the killer just weird?"

Katie thought hard, scrunching up her eyes as they passed the McDonald's from the night before. Cole had tossed the food as soon as he'd gotten to his room.

"Could the sock have been some kind of protection? Like a condom? If the killer was using whatever was available—"

"*Katie!*"

"I'm sixteen, Dad! I know what a condom is!"

"Jesus Christ…" Noah's jaw shifted, his teeth grinding. He glared at the hotel, which was coming up fast.

"Lots of people thought it could have been exactly that. Protection for… entry. Or a way to shame the victim. But, as it turned out, the sock was purely practical. A sock put up the butt is an old military skill they used to teach to soldiers: how to take care of a dead body in the field. When someone dies, they often… let go… of their bowels. Everything comes out. Which can get messy." Okay, maybe this wasn't the best topic to discuss with a sixteen-year-old. But Katie was hanging on his every word, as interested as Noah was furious, it seemed.

Oh well. Nothing to do but finish. "And messy is a problem if you're a serial killer who has to move bodies. But hey, put a sock in it and voilà. No mess. No evidence left behind in the trunk of the killer's car. So we knew then we were looking for a veteran, someone who had seen combat and who had helped to prepare fallen comrades to be taken out of the field. That narrowed the search a lot. And it told us he was a careful planner, and that the sock was purposeful."

Noah pulled to a stop, braking with more force than was necessary, outside Cole's hotel.

"That's so cool," Katie said, breathless and awed. "Did you catch him?"

"We did." Cole grinned. "Pretty quickly after we figured that all out."

"That's so cool," she repeated, beaming.

Cole caught Noah's deeply unimpressed look as he slid out of the SUV. Oops. Well, nothing to do about it now.

Katie's window rolled down as he turned away. "Thank you, Cole!" He saw Noah whip around and glare at her. Katie sighed. "Thank you, Dr. Kennedy."

"No problem." He waved to both Katie and Noah. "See you tomorrow, Noah."

"Good night, Dr. Kennedy."

TWO HOURS LATER, Cole's cell phone buzzed. He was buried in the case file, teasing out the patterns beneath the patterns in the first six murders. He didn't hear the first text come in, or the second. The third finally registered. He grabbed his cell from the nightstand and swiped on the screen.

A new number had texted him. 515. Des Moines.

Katie has been talking nonstop for over an hour about forensic criminal psychology. She wants to switch her elective to the psych class now. Anything that gets her excited about school is good, I suppose. So… thanks.

That was very kind of you to talk to her. I appreciate that.

I'm sorry about what happened today. I'm sorry you were stuck in the hospital for so long. I should have given you the keys right away and told you to head out. You didn't need to stay.

Cole exhaled. There were so many things he could say in response. *I was happy to talk to Katie. I liked making her smile. She's so much like you I couldn't breathe.*

I wasn't going to leave you at the hospital with your injured daughter. I wasn't going to leave you... like you left me.

I wish I could help you somehow. I wish you didn't feel so alone and so broken. I wish you were as happy as that night—

You might be exactly what I need.

Instead, he typed, *So you do have my number. I figured you threw it away on your way out the door.*

He didn't get another text message.

9

HE GRIPPED the edges of the sink. Water dripped from his nose, his chin. A droplet quivered as he exhaled, then fell into the sink's blood-tinged water. Red swirls lazed in wide spirals, working slowly toward the drain.

Damn it. Fucking damn it.

They were faster this time. Last time, there were six dead before the FBI and the task force even knew which way was up. And if it weren't for that fucking couple after the ISU one...

Fucking FBI. Fucking feds. Fucking police.

His arms trembled, a wave of rage thundering through him. His hands squeezed the edge of the sink again.

They were useless before, and they were useless now. All they were doing was getting in the way.

Rage—vicious, snarling, cutting fury—tore into him like a beast from the wild. It was the same wrath that had lived inside him for years. A dark craving as deep as his bones, the feel of it so liquid hot he burned from its power, felt his muscles and skin ignite.

He would show them. The fucking girls—

He would make them see. He would show them all.

They would all fucking know.

The need thundered through him, rising inside him like a tsunami, hatred and wrath and blood, waves and waves that nearly drowned him. The need was driving him, pushing him, coursing through him until there was only one voice inside his head, screaming *Do it **kill** do it **kill** do it **kill**—*

The fucking girls. He would fucking show them.

The picture was starting to tear after so long and being handled so many times. He unfolded it, snarling, baring his teeth at the image. She was the reason. She was the why. The why that had the feds running around and around and around themselves, chasing their own shadows.

The whole world was full of girls just like her. Girls whose smiles radiated up from the newspapers, from the articles that bragged their little achievements to the world. Girls with ribbons in their hair and ribbons on their bedroom walls, but it didn't fucking matter who those girls were under all those ribbons. It didn't fucking matter at all.

None of it mattered. They died, their eyes full of terror and their lips soundlessly begging for mercy, for help, for their fathers or the police to come and save them. But no one ever did. Ever.

He raised the photo to his face, as if he could smell her hair one more time. He closed his eyes, imagining the soft strands flowing through his fingers... until they ran into the matted blood that caked the ends of her curls.

There was still so much to do. So much to show.

So many girls just like her.

No one would stop him. No one could.

10

HE COULDN'T DO THIS. He couldn't go through another day of this.

Another day with Cole right there—*right there*—close enough to reach for, to grab, to hold. Another day with Cole's smile and his laugh and those kind, caring eyes.

Of course, everyone else got to see those kind eyes now. Everyone else heard Cole's laugh. Jacob got to see Cole's smile. Hell, even Katie did. Everyone except him.

Instead, Cole looked at Noah the way he gazed at an interesting specimen. Something curious, but ultimately worthless. Something to be figured out and then discarded. He could almost hear Cole's thoughts whenever he felt the burn of his gaze. *What is your malfunction? What parts and pieces don't line up right? How are you this broken?*

Cole watched him. He watched him far too often. Noah could feel Cole's gaze on him. It burned him alive, set him on fire from the inside out.

It would be easier if all he felt was revulsion when Cole looked at him.

But he didn't. He *wanted*. He wanted so much more of the man. Of what Cole had shown him. Of what they'd shared.

Of that night. Jesus, he'd *slept* with Cole. He'd slept with him and had loved every fucking moment of it. And now—

Now he had to act like nothing had ever happened. Like he didn't know Cole. Like he didn't want to turn to him, grab him, kiss him. Like he didn't still want him all the time.

Cole had been fascinating when Noah knew nothing about him, when all they had between them was neon light and jazz and Vegas after hours. But now, seeing him at work, puzzling out the details of each murder. Drawing out the shape and shadow of the killer from the echoes of his crimes. He was brilliant, even more so than Noah had first thought. He had his doctorate. He was...

He was way, way out of Noah's league.

So you do have my number. I figured you threw it away on your way out the door.

Damn it. Noah rested his forehead on the steering wheel while he sat at the red light. Of course Cole was angry. Noah had disappeared. Never texted him. Never called. But what on earth could he have said that wasn't...

Pathetic. He was absolutely pathetic.

A horn blared behind him. The light was green. Noah rolled forward.

Another day of wanting to claw out his heart. Gouge out his eyes. Skin himself and escape himself, escape this life. How was it possible that the one time, the one time in his whole life he'd given himself permission to take what he'd always wanted, the man he met was not only wonderful but suddenly *here*? In his office. In his car. In his life.

Making Katie laugh.

He jerked the wheel to the right and pulled over, earning another honk as he mounted the curb and braked hard. Traffic whizzed by. He was going to puke. Again. He rolled down the window and waited.

All that was left was bile, rancid and rotten, and it burned on the way up. He wiped his wrist over his lips after and sat back, closing his eyes. He wished he'd never gone out that night. That he'd never met Cole. That he'd never tasted Cole's lips, felt the gentle touch of Cole's fingers on his skin. That he'd never, ever experienced the pure joy he'd felt when he and Cole—

He leaned out the window again, gagging.

Pathetic. You're pathetic.

His phone buzzed with an incoming text. He grabbed it. His heart stopped.

Should I call a Lyft to take me to the office?

Damn it, it was 7:10. He was ten minutes late. *No*, he texted back. *Had to drop Katie off. I'm a few minutes away.* He rummaged in the backseat, searching for a water bottle Katie always left behind, rinsed out his mouth, and spat the water out the window.

He was hiding behind Katie for his lateness, but wasn't one of the benefits of having teenagers being able to use them as excuses? Someone had said that once. It was funny then.

Nothing felt funny now. He put the SUV in gear and merged back into traffic. He'd dropped Katie off at her best friend's house that morning before school started, bringing Susan, Evelyn's mom, a cup of coffee and a croissant and an apology. Susan was polite, if distant, and he'd felt the same judgment from her that he'd felt from everyone else: *You want to raise your daughter on your own? You?*

How could he take responsibility for Katie if he couldn't even get her to and from school without a detour to the ER? Lilly's accusations had echoed in his skull all night. He wasn't able to take care of Katie. He wasn't watching out for her. She was getting up to all sorts of things behind his back while he wasn't looking. She'd never ended up in the ER when she lived with Lilly.

He couldn't really argue with her. Which just made him even angrier as the night bled on.

Sometime around four a.m. he'd given up and tried to

retreat to his happy place. His make-believe fantasy, where he was who he wanted to be, and nothing ever went wrong. He had the love of a man, some tall, gorgeous man who never had a face, and Katie lived with them, and she was happy and vibrant and successful. There wasn't any fear in that place.

But his fantasy had turned on him, and the anonymous man he always cast as his partner shifted, changed, and suddenly it was Cole flipping pancakes and brewing coffee, Cole helping Katie with her homework, Cole leaning across the sink to give him a kiss. Cole leaning over him, hands on the mattress beside Noah's face, his naked body sliding over Noah's, his voice whispering Noah's name, saying *I lo—*

He'd hurled himself into the shower and turned the dial to freezing, then stood in the spray for twenty minutes, until all he could hear was his teeth chattering and he couldn't feel the whisper of Cole's hands on him any longer.

He passed McDonald's on the left. His stomach lurched. He nearly had to roll down the window again.

Cole was waiting outside his hotel, dressed in chinos, a slim button-down, and a sport coat. His badge with the rainbow lanyard was tucked into an inner pocket of his coat. Noah could see it sweeping down from his neck. Cole lived out loud, proudly, effortlessly. He'd never once seemed to care about anyone else's opinion of him, not in Vegas and not here in Des Moines. He had certainty in himself, and he had a confidence Noah could only barely comprehend, barely even imagine.

Some of that confidence had to come from his good looks. The man was practically a model. Or at least, he was to Noah. His blond hair was combed just so, a wave that swept back off his face. He had mirrored aviators on, and he looked so handsome it made Noah's chest seize. *I kissed him*, he wanted to scream. *I made that man come. I, I did. One night, he wanted me. Boring, plain me.*

Cole climbed in when he pulled up. Noah held out the

second Starbucks cup silently. He'd needed about a gallon of coffee at his house after his freezing shower, and he'd bought another cup for himself when he picked up Susan and Cole's coffee.

He waited as Cole pried off the lid and inspected his coffee. Noah had spent an agonizingly long time adding cream and stirring it up, trying to find the exact shade of wall-colored beige that would make Cole happy. Did Cole want milk, or cream, or half-and-half? Sugar? White or raw or artificial? He'd done his best and hoped the handful of travel creamers and sugars he had shoved in the center console was enough.

"This is great," Cole said after his first sip. "Creamy with a side of coffee. Thank you."

Noah grunted. Relief roared through him. He bottled it up, revealing nothing. "There's sugar and more cream if you need it."

"I don't."

Silence settled between them again. Noah's bones vibrated. *Say something. This is the first man you ever kissed. This is the man who answered The Question for you. Say something!*

"Katie is a great kid," Cole finally said as they were turning into the FBI parking lot. "A lot like you." He tried to smile. Stared down at his coffee instead. One fingernail played with the lip of the plastic lid. "I'm sorry if I crossed a line last night. Teens, they're always fascinated by criminal profiling. I've done a few high school career fairs, and it's all anyone ever asks about. I thought I might be able to distract her, or at least bring up her mood." Cole shrugged, an uncharacteristic nervousness passing over his features. "But you didn't seem thrilled about it, and I didn't ask if it was all right to share that kind of stuff."

Noah parked the SUV. "She was fascinated. I could have done without knowing she already knew what a condom was, though." He shook his head.

"She's sixteen. Kids these days——"

"She's my *daughter*," Noah snapped. "She's not just one of the kids these days."

Cole pressed his lips together.

"Sorry. I'm not used to her growing up. When the divorce happened, she was still my little girl. Four years and every other weekend, and all of a sudden, she's…"

"She adores you. And she respects you."

Noah snorted.

"She does. She looks up to you. Listens to you. You're doing a great job."

His throat clenched, and his chest went tight, as if a band had squeezed all the way around him. No one had ever told him he was doing a good job with Katie. Not in the months since she'd moved in, or before that, when he was trying to make every other weekend work with pizza and frozen chicken nuggets and trips to the park and museums and water slides. His vision blurred, and he blinked fast behind his sunglasses. One tear slipped free, falling down his cheek. He turned away.

"Noah…" Cole inhaled. "I'm sorry about what I texted you last night. I was angry. I had a hundred things I could have said, and I went with the worst choice. I'm sorry. And I just want to say——"

Noah braced himself. His fingers squeezed so hard on the steering wheel he thought they'd break. *Tear into me. Eviscerate me. Be angry. I deserve it.*

"I had a great time with you," Cole said softly. "That night. I had a *great* time with you. I loved every moment. I was looking forward to seeing you again on Thursday."

Oh, God. This was worse, so much worse. This wasn't what Cole was supposed to say.

"I know we're not supposed to talk about it. And I won't. I won't ever bring it up again. But you need to know I'm not here to hurt you. I'm not here to out you. I promise, I'm not going to do anything to jeopardize your life and how you choose to live it. What happened in Vegas will always be our secret."

Noah tried to breathe. He dragged in a shuddering breath, so broken it sounded like he was dying.

"If you ever decide to come out, you're going to find a guy who will thank his lucky stars every day for you. And you'll be happy, too. I know you will. But you have to make that choice when you're ready." The car door opened. He heard Cole slide out. "I'll see you inside. Thank you for the coffee. It's great."

The car door shut.

Gasping, Noah pitched forward, burying his forehead in the center of his steering wheel as the sobs broke in his chest. *I was happy with you. For one night, I was happy with you.*

It took ten minutes for his breathing to calm down. For his hands to stop shaking. Another ten to clear the redness from his eyes. He couldn't do anything about the way his face had swelled up. Of course, he'd looked like shit to begin with. He'd been up the whole night, and the night before. Well, it wasn't like he was trying to impress anyone.

Finally he made his way inside, badging onto the third floor and heading for his office. The bullpen buzzed, everyone catching up and sipping coffee and trading ideas. The floor was more crowded than usual with the task force, the deputies and police officers on loan from the area departments. He saw Deputies Santos, Nichols, and Holland gesturing to a map of the kill sites and a gaggle of police officers from Des Moines—Salvage, Reynolds, and Estrada—flipping through old crime scene photos. He didn't see Deputy Garrett.

Noah frowned. The day before, John had texted him after Garrett stormed out of the office late in the afternoon. *Noah, I want to talk to you about Garrett. I'm worried about him. Let's meet tomorrow to discuss reassigning him.*

Maybe Garrett needed to sit this investigation out. Let someone else represent Boone County on the task force.

Down the hallway, Cole and Jacob were in the conference room together, talking as they sipped their coffees. Jacob said something, teasing Cole, and Cole tipped his head back and laughed hard.

Jealousy knifed through Noah's gut. He turned away. *You are not the man for him. Cole deserves a man far better than you.*

He pulled out his phone and texted Katie, checking in. *Hope class is going well. I'll pick you up from cheerleading practice at four. Pizza tonight?*

Katie was supposed to be focusing on her pre-calc class, but he got a text back right away. *OK Dad. Can Cole come? I wanna ask about more cases he's been on and killers he's caught. :)*

Noah groaned. *I'm sure he's busy. Aren't you supposed to be doing schoolwork?*

I am, Dad. He got a picture of her math work, taken surreptitiously from her lap with the teacher at the whiteboard.

Focus, pumpkin. You're doing really well with your summer school classes so far.

Well, I WAS focused... :)

He pursed his lips and frowned. *Okay, fair point. Love you, K-Bear.*

ILY too, dad byex

"OKAY. Time to dig into the killer's profile."

Noah nodded. He tapped his pen against his notepad, sitting across from Cole in the conference room. Cole stared at him a beat too long.

"You can find this guy?" Jacob, at the head of the conference table, asked Cole. He was leaning back in the chair, and the metal was groaning out cries of surrender. Eventually, he was going to break every chair in the office.

"I have a pretty good track record."

"You've caught *all* the killers you've profiled?"

Cole nodded. He fiddled with his papers, his pen. "Noah, talk to me about the suspects the original investigation developed."

"There were two main ones we focused on." Noah fingered the two folders in front of him. His eyes darted to the whiteboard at the head of the table, where two groups of headshots stared down at them. Six young women—Kelsey, Ellen, Paige, Lauren, Monica, and Stacy—were grouped together to one side. He could recite their names from memory, draw up each of their faces in his mind. He'd never forget those girls, not as long as he lived.

Kimberly and Jessie were on the other side. Bart Olson's and Frank Foster's photos sat below their daughters'.

"First, Tech Sergeant Alan Prince." Noah flipped open the folder on the left. The suspect's photo was on top, an eight-by-ten of his last promotion board picture. Prince was a large man, burly, with a barrel chest and a square jaw. He looked like he chewed bullets for breakfast. "Air force, based at Offutt Air Force Base in Omaha. It's a two-hour drive from Offutt to the Des Moines metro region. Prince was a pararescueman."

"A medic."

"Yes. The air force combat medic. Pararescue jumpers are elite service members. Air force special operators. They have one of the highest training washout rates in the entire armed forces."

"Sounds like the outline of an American hero. Why is he a suspect?"

"Prince is a local. He's from Des Moines. A string of juvenile offenses followed him all the way to his enlistment. His high school counselors said he was anti-authority, resisted rules and regulations, and chafed at structure and responsibilities."

"Odd that he chose to join the military, then. Were any of the victims associated with Prince?"

"Four of them, through high school parties, friends of friends, and college parties. His name kept coming up, over and over again. We kept running into him."

"Like a bad penny."

"Exactly. We had to dig into him."

"What was his service record like?"

"Excellent. It seems like once Prince found his calling, he put his all into it. He had glowing remarks in all of his EERs, and he was twice awarded for excellence. There was an interesting note in his deployment record, though. Prince volunteered for additional tours of duty overseas, and his commander declined to allow him to go. He said Prince would benefit more from stabilization and that his presence overseas would 'not be beneficial to the overall mission.'"

"That is an intriguing statement. What is his commander trying to say? That Prince was enjoying deployment too much? Where was he? Somewhere someone who desires an orgy of violence would enjoy?"

"We talked to Commander Vasquez. He said Prince was a little too enthusiastic about the mission. We couldn't get him to elaborate. However, we did a deep dive into his service record. Prior to Offutt, he was in Landstuhl, Germany. There were two unsolved strangulation murders in Landstuhl while he was stationed there. One on base and one off."

"Were there other strangulations when Prince wasn't there?"

"They're not the only strangulation deaths Germany has ever seen, or that Landstuhl has ever seen, but these two were very close to what the Coed Killer left behind."

"Close. What was different?"

"Sexual assault in one victim." Cole frowned. "And the other victim was male."

Cole shook his head. "Our killer wouldn't go from no

sexual assault to sexual assault and back again. And it's highly unlikely he'd deviate from his victim profile. He likes to dominate, exterminate. It's easier to do that with young women, unfortunately, than with men. He wouldn't take the risk of attacking a man. If a man fought back at all, it would break the fantasy he creates, his ability to completely and totally dominate and subjugate his victims."

"My gut said the same." Noah almost smiled. "I couldn't put it like that, though."

Cole's cheeks flushed, a dusting of crimson. "What else? There had to be more for Prince to make your short list."

"His GPS put him in Des Moines on five of the six nights of the murders. Those were not the only nights he was in Des Moines. However, he was confirmed as physically present for five of the six."

"That is compelling. Usually where there's smoke, there's fire. And there's a lot of smoke with this guy." Cole plucked Prince's photo from the file and stuck it to a new whiteboard. "Who's next?"

"Dr. Robin Pflueger. Professor of history at Iowa State University. He mostly taught freshmen. Four of the six original victims were in his classes."

Cole's eyebrows arched high. "And the other two?"

"He knew one through church, Lauren O'Neil. She went to Faith Baptist, just like Kimberly Foster. The other, Paige Blanton, went to Simpson College, which is a straight shot down the highway from Iowa State."

Cole stilled. He turned to the map of the Des Moines region taped to the conference room wall. US Highway 69 ran north to south, from Minnesota to the Gulf Coast of Texas, going right through Ames, Iowa—home of Iowa State University—past Des Moines and on to Indianola… home of Simpson College. Colored dots marked the crime scenes, forming a line that ran up and down Highway 69 and clustered on the Iowa State campus. "Have you heard of geographic profiling?"

Noah nodded. "We were working on it six years ago. Somewhat obviously, Iowa State is the center of the cluster."

"And the highway is a feeder. The whole region is a hunting ground for him, but Iowa State is special." He tilted his head, took in the map from a new angle. "Is Iowa State his main hunting ground, or is Iowa State his home turf?"

"If we could answer that—"

"We'd still have a lot of suspects," Cole said. "But it would help immensely in understanding our killer. Was he traveling to the college, lying in wait, plucking victims out of the dark? Or was he living on, or near, campus, surrounded by potential victims? One answer lends itself to one type of criminal psychology. The other, a totally different one."

"He's traveling to victims' homes now. Lying in wait for them there."

Cole nodded. "His MO has evolved. We need to find out why." He took a deep breath, held it. Frowned. "Dr. Pflueger taught at Iowa State. That's significant. What kind of firearms experience did Dr. Pflueger have?"

"He had a Glock nine mil registered to him."

"The same caliber that was used to shoot and kill Kyle and Shelly Carter."

"And, after Kyle and Shelly were killed, Professor Pflueger moved away. He quit his job in the middle of the semester and moved to Washington State."

Cole's eyebrows shot up. "What did he do there?"

"Taught at a community college. He set up in the center of the Green River Killer's old hunting grounds. His library and Amazon accounts show he has a fascination with Gary Ridgway. He's read every book published on the man."

Cole nodded. "Tell me more about Pflueger."

"He was popular. He was liked by over 90 percent of his

students. He had high satisfaction ratings in online surveys. His classes were regularly wait-listed. There were allegations he slept with some of his students, though. Freshmen and sophomores who took his intro classes. Some of them were barely over eighteen, but there's no evidence he was ever involved with minors. There were complaints from parents, but the college's attitude was that it was all consenting adults and private business."

"Were the students in his class when he slept with them?"

"He'd wait until after they were through with his class, according to what we uncovered. He was careful to follow the letter of the college's rules: no professor may sleep with a current student. Current as in, enrolled in their class."

Cole snorted. "Here's to the hairsplitters." Noah grimaced. One day, Katie would grow up. One day. But, Jesus, he needed to talk to her, start preparing her for the world. His heart raced, and he forced her out of his mind, at least for the moment. He couldn't think about his daughter in the middle of this case.

He cleared his throat. "I think he quit because there was a major sexual assault case coming for him. The parents of a freshman were getting ready to sue. They alleged he slept with their daughter after her fall semester. They say that tutoring sessions he offered her were seductions and that as soon as her final grade was in, Dr. Pflueger contacted her and invited her to his house to celebrate. They say he gave their underage daughter alcohol, so much that she passed out. She claims she remembers coming to three times that night, each time in a different sexual situation with Dr. Pflueger, none of which she consented to. She woke up at his house the next morning with no memory of what had happened. Her nightmares, she said, filled in the gaps. By the time she told her parents, there was no hope of recovering forensic evidence."

"A she-said, he-said." Cole frowned. "Was there anything to support her story? Text messages? Emails?"

"There was enough to show Dr. Pflueger crossed major

boundaries. His defense was that she crossed those boundaries with him willingly and he was trying not to break a young woman's heart."

Cole snorted.

"He quit, and the parents settled with the college for an undisclosed sum. The daughter transferred out."

"And Dr. Pflueger? Where is he now?"

"That's the thing. He moved back to Des Moines six months ago."

Cole stared at Noah.

"He's taking care of his mother. She has dementia. His father died while he was living in Washington."

"Let me guess: he didn't come back for his dad's funeral, did he?"

"No."

"Go on."

"He moved in with his mother, in the house he was raised in, in the suburbs north of Des Moines."

"Near Iowa State?"

"Within spitting distance. The campus shadows his bedroom. He's not working right now. He hasn't found a job in Des Moines, or applied for one as far as we can tell. We think he's living off his mother's Social Security. He stays at her house and takes care of her. Trash is piling up in the side yard. There have been neighbor complaints of screaming late at night."

"Screaming?"

"Officers have responded both times. They say they walked through the house. Just him and his mother, who was not well when they visited. One time, she was screaming about being held hostage, but the officers said she wasn't lucid enough to take a complaint from. She didn't know where she was or who she was. I interviewed the officer who responded. He said he felt sorry for the mom, and for Dr. Pflueger."

"Well, he's a piece of work. Sexual indiscretions galore,

meticulous attention to detail to avoid repercussions, signs of broken familial relationships. No contact with his father but devotion to his mother. However, if he's seducing—or raping—his students, why would he strangle but not sexually assault these girls?"

"Look, if I could have arrested either of these men, I would have." Noah tossed his pen on his notepad. "Neither of them is a perfect fit. This killer is a ghost. This was as close as I ever got."

"I understand. I do." Cole seemed to almost reach for Noah but grabbed Dr. Pflueger's folder instead. "The killer is a shadow. He's hidden. He strikes and disappears. He's spent his whole life being invisible and unseen. He's practiced at not being caught. That's not your fault. And, cut yourself a little slack. A majority of FBI agents never go head to head with a serial killer. Homicide isn't the FBI's main beat."

Noah vibrated. The overhead lights cast the shadow of Cole's hand in triplicate. He wanted to touch Cole, but—

"To catch him, we need to get inside his mind," Cole said. "To do that, we have to dive deep into his crime scenes. That's what he's left us. He thinks he's left nothing, but he's actually left behind a great deal. We can unpack his paraphilias and his psychology from everything he's left. We start there until we can tease him out of the shadows."

"What do you mean by paraphilias?" asked Jacob. Noah had nearly forgotten Jacob was with them.

"A criminal's paraphilias are his desires and fantasies. They, by definition, are outside the norm of what we'd consider acceptable or legal. If they weren't outside the boundaries, he'd be able to lead a normal, successful life. Usually, you can see a paraphilia pretty easily. Does the offender target prepubescent victims? Pedophilia. Does the offender desecrate corpses sexually? Necrophilia. What's he doing here?"

Jacob frowned. "He's not sexually assaulting the girls, either before or after death."

"No, he's not. But he's still getting enjoyment out of the killings, or he wouldn't be killing. The killing itself—the moment of his victim's death—is our guy's peak. That's what he's constantly searching for. Each of the crime scenes he leaves behind is the climax of his paraphilias. He spends all his efforts to get to that moment: when his victim dies by his hands. As soon as he identifies and targets one of his victims, he's already imagined how she'll die. Everything from then forward plays out according to the script he's created. Every step he takes is how he brings that script to life."

Jacob's scowl turned dark. He glanced at Noah, then down to his lap, playing with a pen that looked like a twig in his massive hands.

"He's meticulous," Noah said. "That's not obvious from the crime scenes at first glance, but it's true."

Cole nodded. "The scenes appear chaotic, especially the most recent two. But he has complete control over each kill site. He knows their lives inside and out. He knows their routines. He knows when to strike. He knows when they will be alone—or he thought he did. And he's controlled. He doesn't leave any forensic evidence behind. That takes incredible discipline and focus."

"There's also no sign of struggle with the girls," Noah said. "Complete domination, like you said."

"He's in control until he chooses to attack. He surprises them with overwhelming force and violence. The attack itself is short. He wants their death, not their suffering."

"He stalks his victims. Maybe for months."

"And he does it unseen. He blends in. He's nonthreatening. In fact, he might be representative of something people associate with safety. He's stayed completely under everyone's radar for years. Who, or what, could do that?"

Noah's lips thinned.

"During the first investigation, you thought the killer might have law enforcement exposure."

Jacob's head whipped up. He stared at Noah, wide-eyed.

"I kept that close to the vest," Noah said, eyeballing Cole. "I didn't put that out there for the whole task force—of law enforcement officers—to know."

"Smart." Cole smiled. "But we need to think about it again, especially with how the forensic evidence lines up. The absence of forensic evidence is just as important as if we had buckets of DNA and fingerprints. It tells us something about our killer."

"You really think he's a cop?" Jacob asked. His voice had gone thin.

"He *may* be," Cole said carefully. "For certain, he's part of the local community. He's nonthreatening. He appears to be an upstanding citizen. He is someone people would never expect to be a killer. When he's not committing crimes, he's someone's best friend. He's someone's trusted right hand. He gains people's confidence. He's very, very good at not getting caught. And all of these killings are late at night. He has a day job, or at least a day life. It would be noticed if he wasn't somewhere during the workweek."

"He's not a loner," Noah said. "He's got people who care about him. A girlfriend or a wife—"

"Or a boyfriend," Cole said pointedly.

Noah swallowed.

Jacob's eyes ping-ponged between Noah and Cole.

"He will look normal. Completely, utterly normal."

"What causes this?" Noah asked. "What created this monster?"

"There's always a nexus. Always a moment when the psyche carves off. Splits. Sometimes it's physical, like when we see evidence of head trauma in convicted offenders from when they were very young. One serial killer came from a stable, loving, boring family, but when he was two years old, he was knocked in the head by a ball and was unconscious for two minutes. That's all we ever found in his background. He went on to brutally torture and murder over fifty people. That's *not* causation. Head trauma in children doesn't create murderers or predators. But there are many murderers we've caught and convicted who do have this history of childhood physical trauma. In others, there are signs of emotional trauma. Abuse. But again, you can also find the same signs and same challenges in another individual, and they never become an offender. All we can say is that, retrospectively, there is always an index event."

"What's his?"

"Rejection," Jacob rumbled. He stared at the window, at something far beyond the suburban view. "Somewhere, someone hurt him. Some woman, and now he's punishing *all* women. Making them hurt, like he was hurt."

Silence filled the conference room. Noah's pen *tap tap tap*ped on his notepad.

"This is more than that, I think," Cole said slowly. "It's not just revenge. He enjoys what he's doing. He enjoys shredding lives and destroying these women. He's a sadist. He wants their horror. Their final moments become his, and they are filled with pure terror."

"What about Bart and Frank?" Noah asked.

"Interruptions. Disruptions to his fantasy. His afterglow, as it were, was ruined by both men. That may be why there's so much overkill with each of them. His rage was fully unleashed on the fathers. For those moments, when Bart and Frank came to check on their daughters, he was completely out of control. He lost all his discipline. And he absolutely destroyed both men. In Bart's case, he destroyed Bart's identity. Destroying someone's face is a sign of erasure and hatred."

"The Coed Killer killed every four months," Noah said. "And then he disappeared. Now, six years later, he's back. And he's killing more frequently than before. Why?"

"One of two reasons: escalation or disintegration. He's either gaining confidence from these murders and is escalating his kills, or he's coming undone. In that case he's disintegrating, and he's desperately reaching for what he thinks he needs to feel normal again. Killing is his addiction. It's how he calms the urge inside him, which builds up and builds up until he's overcome with the need. After each kill, he has a cooldown period. Those cooldown periods may last anywhere from several months to several years. The memories sustain him through that period and keep his fantasies in check. He can replay, if you will, the last murder instead of needing to commit another. Now, his cooldown period has changed—several times. This change is significant. Are his urges taking over? Is he losing control? Or is he mocking us? Are his pride and confidence urging him on?"

"How will we know?"

"If he's disintegrating, he'll make mistakes. He'll slip up. If he's escalating, things will get worse."

"Great," Jacob rumbled. "That's exactly what we need."

"There's a reason he's killing faster. We have to find it. And there's a reason he's killing now, again. There was something that started this. With each recent murder, of Kimberly and now Jessie, he's rediscovered how *good* he is at what he does: at killing young women, and now their fathers. He's regaining his confidence. He's successful, even when he's interrupted, which has a dual result in both frustrating and angering him and filling him with confidence and pride. Despite being thwarted, look how he succeeded. Even though he wasn't able to enjoy his kill the way he wanted to."

"You're saying we should expect another murder soon?"

"Yes. He will strike again. Sooner than his pattern, whether he's escalating or disintegrating."

Noah's hands fisted on the conference table. "So who is he? How do we find him?"

Cole pulled Noah's notepad across the table toward

himself. He started scribbling as he wrote, making two columns: *Who* and *How*. "He's a mirror of his victims' race: white male. Midtwenties to midthirties, the period when most men who murder are at their peaks. He's educated enough to blend into society and appear unobtrusive. He lives normally, at least from the outside. He has a respectable job and has people's respect. He's nonthreatening, or even safe, for most people. Lots of people know this man." He moved from the *Who* column to the *How* column and started scribbling again. "He hunts in the darkness, late at night. He knows how to move in the dark. How to fade away. Where to hide. He's local, or very familiar with the area, and, he's getting bolder. He's moved from public places—college campuses and parking lots—to homes. He's bold enough to break into someone's house and strike on their home turf. He gains complete control over his victims, murders them, and gets away cleanly."

"An organized killer?" Jacob asked.

"It's not an either-or determination. It's a blend between the two. Our killer is organized in that he has above-average intelligence—he has to, in order to target his victims, hunt them, and plan these murders so meticulously—and he shows signs of control before, during, and after the murders. The fathers, however, are sinkholes of his rage, and that implies disorganization and a major loss of control. However, purely disorganized killers usually are socially and sexually inadequate men who lash out when they are in crisis. They act suddenly, kill abruptly without preplanning or organization, and show no signs of control, utilizing whatever is at the scene. They have no plan, either before or after the killing. There are elements here that are both organized and disorganized."

Jacob frowned. "What's that mean?"

"It means he's more on the organized side of the continuum. But he's motivated by intense rage, and the hunt for victims is a symbolic search for the woman who wounded him so deeply. Through killing these girls, he's able to feel, for the briefest moment, the satisfaction of revenge. But that moment fades, the satisfaction is fleeting, and he has to hunt and kill again."

"We have to stop him," Noah said.

"You already know he's a ghost. He's deliberately normal. He will blend in with everyone else. He might even be attractive," Cole quipped.

"Well, he's not me," Jacob rumbled. "I don't put anyone at ease. Least of all, women. And I've never been accused of being handsome."

Noah tried to smile. "What do we do?"

"Rock his world. Make him feel threatened. Make his world feel small. Make him feel the pressure of the investigation. Make him think we're closing in. Increase his panic. Increase the focus on him. Narrow his safe spaces."

"Another press conference?" John had already held one the night Cole arrived. The press had bubbled nonstop about Jessie and Bart Olson, and they couldn't keep quiet about what had happened and what they suspected. At the least, the FBI had a duty to warn the public, to warn everyone to remain vigilant. Monday night was the first time the FBI had acknowledged they were looking into the Coed Killer again. That they feared he'd struck again. Maybe even twice.

"Yes, another press conference. Keep the pressure on him. Get the public to help you. Get them to keep their eyes open. He's left a trail here. People know this man. Somewhere, someone knows something."

11

AT NOON, Noah stood outside the FBI office, facing a gaggle of local reporters. Damn it, where was John? He was the guy who talked to the press. But when Noah had tried to reach him, he got no answer. Noah wasn't half as personable as John was, nor did he have a quarter of his experience. John could answer a reporter's question and make them feel like a trusted friend, a confidant. Noah was stiff, and he looked every bit the stereotyped G-man, right down to the polo shirt beneath his FBI windbreaker.

Of course, Cole at his side didn't help matters. Noah had only himself to blame for that. Cole had said he'd keep out of the press conference, but Noah insisted he join in. Cole was the one who had put the profile together.

Nearly all the reporters directed their questions to Cole, if not by name, then by giving him all their attention. The female reporters were the most obvious, eyeing Cole up and down before vying for the next question. Each time, Cole deferred to Noah with a gentle smile.

"No, at this time, the FBI is not requesting Des Moines or the surrounding counties implement a curfew. We are asking everyone to remain vigilant and aware of your surroundings and to report anyone suspicious in your neighborhoods. This killer is part of our community. You may know him. You may have seen the signs that he has committed these crimes. We especially want to talk to anyone who knows someone who may have unexplained absences the nights of these murders. Or any unexplained wounds, especially scratches or bruises to the arms. We want to talk to anyone who has noticed someone hanging around or watching you where you work or live. Cars out of place. If you think something is even a little bit weird, call it in. We want to hear from you."

They were going to be swamped with tips. The task force was already assembled upstairs in the bullpen, phones at the ready, for when the lines started to ring after the conference. Most of the tips would be duds, neighbors reporting gossip or trying to cast aspersions. Many would truly think they were helping but would only be reporting garbage collectors or meter readers or gardeners people had never noticed before.

"We are doing everything we can to bring this killer to justice. The families of his victims need justice. We're closing in on this man, and we will catch him, especially with your help. The killer believes he is above the law, but he is not. He will be caught. He will be punished. There is no escape for him."

That last bit was recommended by Cole, after working on the speech to the press for over an hour. How did they address both the public and the killer, speak to two wildly different audiences simultaneously? How could they reassure the public and rattle the killer's cage?

"Why did the FBI call in a profiler now? Why wasn't a profiler called six years go?"

He didn't have an answer to that. *If we had, Cole wouldn't be here now.* But if they had, would they have caught the killer? Would people be alive today if they had done more back then? Would he have been able to stay with Cole in Vegas, explore the desire and yearning that had ignited between them?

Cole slid to his side, smoothly joining him in front of the reporters' microphones. "The FBI is totally committed to catching this killer. There are many, many components that go into a murder investigation, and I promise you, the FBI has always done their utmost." He smiled briefly at Noah. "Special Agent Downing was one of the agents assigned to the task force six years ago, and now he's leading the hunt for the killer. There's nothing that can get by him. There's no place for this man to hide. I promise you that."

Noise, reporters' questions, voices talking over each other. Blood pounding in Noah's ears, his pulse running wild. The world swimming, arching left and right as white seemed to ring his vision. Cole's hand landed on the small of his back. "Thank you, ladies and gentlemen," Noah grunted. "Please contact the joint task force if you have any information that can help us catch this killer." Noah strode away, leading Cole and the representatives of the counties and police departments that made up the task force back into the FBI building.

Deputies and police officers ambled toward the elevators, heading to the office and to staff the phone bank. Jacob had ordered pizza and wings for everyone while Noah spoke to the media. It was going to be a long afternoon—probably a long night—as the phones rang and they waited for the effects of the press conference to shake out. Tomorrow morning, they'd have more leads, and they'd hit the ground running.

Noah stopped Cole as Cole went to follow the others. He had his hands in his pockets, his chinos showcasing his long, strong thighs. His shoulders highlighted the powerful, yet also delicate, V of his body. Everything about him screamed out to Noah. *This is what you want. This is who you want.*

"Would you like to get lunch?" He stared over Cole's

shoulder. If he looked at Cole, he wouldn't be able to breathe. Or speak.

"Didn't Jacob order food for everyone?"

"Yeah, he did." Noah held his breath. "Do you want to get something to eat together?" His gaze flicked to Cole's. "Just us."

Cole stared. Noah squirmed. This was a horrible idea. *So stupid, you're so stupid to ask. He doesn't like you. Pathetic.* "Forget it—"

"Yes. I'd love to go out to lunch with you," Cole said carefully.

Noah couldn't have cared less about what they ate. He took Cole to a bar and grill that served the standard bar fare: burgers, wings, and pub steaks. Cole ordered a chicken sandwich. Noah ordered a burger he knew he wasn't going to eat.

They sat in silence on a sun-drenched patio beneath a spinning fan, the breeze ruffling Cole's blond hair. Reflections of Noah stared back at him from Cole's mirrored aviators. He turned away, shredding a napkin to individual fibers. The silence lengthened, grew heavy, only ESPN's *SportsCenter* droning from the TV in the corner.

Still, the silence wasn't agonizing or accusatory. It seemed expectant, as if Cole was waiting. Waiting for him, like he'd waited Wednesday night when he held Noah's hand and gave him the choice: stay or go. Come with him or go back to his hotel, his life.

It seemed like the same choice was before him now. Open his mouth. Say something. Take a risk. Or say nothing and go back to his life. Go back to what was before Vegas, before Cole.

Before he tasted happiness.

"That reporter's question," Noah started. He cleared his throat. "About why we requested the BAU's help now?"

Cole pushed his sunglasses up onto his head. He waited, watching Noah.

"I, uh. I asked John to request the BAU send someone. Send their best." He took a quick breath, blew it out. Laughed. "I asked that because, on Tuesday, I was at the BAU profiler workshop."

He didn't have to tell Cole what conference he was talking about.

"I wrote that presentation."

"You didn't present it." A woman had, an impressive special agent from the BAU. She was gorgeous, ebony skin and coal-dark eyes, and she'd seized control of that entire ballroom from the first word she spoke. He could still picture her on the dais in her ivory suit, extolling the benefits of BAU profiling. Going through their successful cases. He'd been sold immediately.

"Cassandra is more striking. She gets a far better response than I do."

"She is striking, yes. But so are you." His breath hitched after he spoke.

Cole froze. A furrow appeared between his eyebrows. "I don't know what to say to you. I don't know how to be around you. I'm trying to follow your lead, but you're giving me mixed messages, Noah."

"I know." He stared at his hands. His skin was dry. He ran his knuckles over the tabletop.

"I wish you weren't afraid of me," Cole breathed.

"I'm not afraid of you."

"You're afraid of something. Something to do with me."

"I'm afraid of what you mean."

Cole frowned. Noah shook his head as he reached into his back pocket and pulled out his wallet. Cole didn't quite smother his sigh. He folded his napkin and set his silverware on his plate.

"No, no." Noah waved him off. "That's not… We're not leaving." He pulled a folded piece of paper from his wallet. Once crisp and white, the sheet was now dull. He'd handled it with fingerprint powder on his hands at some point, and it had transferred to the paper, darkening it. He'd rubbed the note every day until Monday, when Cole had walked into the office and back into his life.

He unfolded the paper and smoothed it on the table. Cole's number, scrawled on the Aria's stationery, sat between them. "I never threw it away."

"You never used it, either."

His cheeks burned. Noah pulled out his cell phone and swiped it on. Pulled up his text messages. Found the draft. "I wrote this at the airport Thursday morning. I never sent it." Obviously.

Cole took his phone and read. His lips moved as his eyes bounced over Noah's words.

Cole,

I'm sorry, I've just been recalled back to my office. There's been an emergency. I'm at the airport right now and I won't be able to meet you tonight. Which... I'm really upset about. I had an AMAZING time last night. It doesn't feel real, what happened. I dreamed of meeting a man like you. I realize I'm not experienced, and I don't have any idea what I'm doing, but I was wondering if maybe we could keep in touch? Maybe we could meet again—

The message ended abruptly. He remembered the furious, burning shame he'd felt at pouring his heart out, blubbering about how happy he was, how much that night had meant, and then, the icy deluge of realizing he was *so fucking pathetic.*

Who the hell was he? He was a one-night stand, a pity fuck, and why on earth would someone like Cole want to see him again? Cole could have anyone he wanted. Why would he waste time on Noah? Inexperienced, boring, ridiculous Noah.

He'd been begging for Cole's attention, and his desperation was leaking out of him, rancid and rotten. *Don't make it more than it was,* he'd snarled at himself.

Cole didn't look up for a long time. Long after he'd

finished reading. He kept staring at the screen, not letting the screen saver come on and wipe away Noah's words. His thumb stroked over Noah's aborted last sentence. "Why didn't you send this?" His voice was soft, softer than Noah expected.

He shook his head. "'Cause I was being pathetic. We had a one-night stand." His cheeks burned. "You took pity on me—"

"I did *not*."

"It was just one night, and it couldn't have meant to you what it meant to me. I was being clingy and..." Pathetic. "I wanted you to remember me well, instead of remembering me as a guy who went overboard. I wanted to remember that you liked me. I wanted to remember walking backward out of your room, not able to stop kissing you, not even for a breath—"

Cole looked away. His eyes fixed on the road, on the passing cars. He didn't blink. His jaw clenched. Trembled. "Noah," he finally said, the word agonized and pushed through gritted teeth.

"You've seen my life now," Noah said. "I was being selfish that night. I wanted, for once, for one night, to know what it felt like to be... *me*. And the only thing that has made sense, in a long, long time, was that night and being with you. It's not just that you were a guy or that we had sex. It was that, but it was more. It was *you*. You were everything I had ever dreamed of." His voice went high and thin, strangled. "And I have no idea what to do."

Cole's jaw worked left and right. Finally, he looked back, but he didn't look at Noah. He stared, instead, at the table, where he'd set Noah's phone. The text was still between them, like an indictment. "What do you want to do?"

"I want..." Noah laughed despondently. "I want to rewind time and stop the Olson murders. I want to have stayed in Vegas on Thursday and seen you again. I want to go back and relive Wednesday, and then stop time so we could have—" His voice choked off. "I want to be as happy as I was that night, and Thursday morning, every day. But I can't."

Cole stared at him.

How could Cole know what it was like to be afraid? He was out, and he probably had always been out. He was from California. Had he ever had reason to fear the consequences of being gay? Had he ever felt the terror of knowing he could lose everything if he let himself be himself?

"How can I be the man I want to be with the life that I have?" Noah whispered. "With Katie? With the divorce, and with custody… I've looked, you know. Dads who are gay, they don't get primary custody. Some of them don't even get visitation. It may be 2021, but the courts—" He shook his head.

"I know a few." Cole's voice was gentle. "It's not unheard of. And it's not outlawed. Custody should be determined based on the best interest of the child."

"A lot of courts feel that a gay dad is not in the child's best interest. And this is Iowa. The Midwest isn't California. Or D.C."

"What's your alternative? Push down who you are? Ignore your own needs? Your own happiness?"

Noah shrugged. "Worked for years, didn't it?"

"No, it didn't. Otherwise you wouldn't be this miserable."

"I shouldn't have gone out Wednesday night. Why did I think it was a good idea to know? Now I know exactly what I want, and what I can't have."

Silence.

Damn it, he was going to crack if this went on much longer. He'd wanted to apologize, clear the air. Explain himself. Tell Cole it wasn't him—God, it wasn't him at all. It was Noah. It was how he'd boxed himself in and was living in a straitjacket, and he'd inadvertently pulled Cole into the disaster that was his life, too.

Cole's voice, when it came, was thick. "You said you wanted to keep in touch? In your text message."

"I was being desperate and pathetic—"

"Stop it, Noah. You said you wanted to. Were you telling the truth?"

He met Cole's gaze across the table. Cole's eyes were shining, glazed with fractured diamonds, a million refractions of sunlight quivering in the thin line of wetness hovering behind his eyelashes.

"I've never lied to you. Everything has been the truth. Yes, I daydreamed all the way to the airport that I could keep in touch with you, maybe meet up with you in D.C. or Chicago. Or anywhere. I wanted to see you again. I would have gone anywhere you wanted."

Cole's expression went hard. He looked down.

Noah pressed on. He might as well eviscerate himself fully. Share it all. "I thought if we kept in touch, I could slowly come out. I thought I could get my feet underneath me, and that maybe you could guide me—" His throat closed. No more words came.

"Noah…" His name was a whisper, and it spun away on the lazy drafts of the ceiling fan. Cole chewed his lower lip, rolling it back and forth between his teeth. "I *really* liked you. I mean, I'm not going to lie—" He grinned, looking embarrassed. "At first, I just thought you were smoking hot, and I wanted to pick you up because of that shirt you were wearing. And those pants."

He almost smiled. "At first?"

"But when we started talking and spent time together, it was different. I never wanted the night to end." His words floated inside Noah. "Everything you're saying is what I've been trying to convince myself: It was just a one-night stand. You didn't want anything more. You were just being polite that morning, taking my number. It didn't mean to you what it meant to me."

Noah flinched, like he'd been kicked in the gut.

"I wanted to see you again, too," Cole said.

The fan spun, air currents pushing down on them. Traffic idled past, lines of sedans and SUVs and pickup trucks. Noah counted the cars, feeling the weight of the world bend his spine. Crush his heart. *You ruined everything. You're a coward, and you ruined everything.*

"We still could," Cole whispered. "I would love to see you outside of the office. Outside of this case. We could steal away from everything, be two guys who might fall for each other."

"I could easily fall for you. So easily. In some ways I already have."

"I haven't stopped thinking about you since you walked out that door. Even flying here, I was still thinking about you, missing you. Wondering *What if* and wishing..." Cole shook his head.

"Why do you want anything to do with me? I'm nothing like you, Cole. I'm older than you—"

"Not by much."

"—and I'm boring. I'm the definition of boring—"

"We've got to work on your self-worth issues."

"Okay, Dr. Kennedy—" Noah started to pull back.

"You're a great guy, Noah. Don't you see that? You're not boring. You're a great father. You love Katie, and she loves you back. You're a great agent. I can't tell you how many field offices I go to that run less than half as well as this one, or whose investigations are just piles of shit thrown against the wall."

"We don't have any idea who this guy is—"

"And that's the point. That's *his* point. He does everything he can to not be caught. He may have some kind of law enforcement experience or knowledge driving how meticulous he is with his scenes. But even without that, methodical sadistic serial killers are the hardest offenders to catch. As much work as they put into their fantasies and their kills, they put the same into not getting caught. If it were easy to catch them, there would never be a victim two, or three, and my job wouldn't exist. Catching these guys is excruciating. I promise you, you're not the only agent who has felt like this. It's not *you*. You're not a failure."

Noah held his breath. He could fall into Cole's eyes, get lost inside of the man. "I wasn't a good husband."

"I've known you for a week, and I can already tell that you're the kind of guy who will do the best he can in everything. Who will sacrifice himself and keep going, pushing, always trying. I don't believe you didn't give your all to your marriage, even if, in the end, it wasn't what you needed."

"I tried," he breathed, his gaze cratering to the tabletop. "I tried to be not like this. For Lilly, and for Katie—"

"What about for *you*? What does Noah want to?"

"I want to be me," he said, so quickly it surprised him. He looked at Cole, into Cole. He wanted Cole so Goddamn much. Wanted to be the man Cole wanted in return. "I want last Wednesday."

Cole slid his hand across the table, one finger slightly outstretched, reaching for Noah. Three inches separated them.

Noah slid his hand toward Cole. Their index fingers touched.

Cole beamed. He looked down, hiding his smile as Noah's lungs stopped working. "We can take it slow, like you wanted. You're not the first man to come out later in life. I can be with you through it, if you want me to."

"Cole—"

His phone vibrated, trilling with the ringtone that belonged to his coworkers. Cursing, Noah pulled his phone out of his pocket but kept his fingertip pressed against Cole's. Was John finally returning his call? Where the hell was he? It wasn't like John to not answer his phone.

Jacob's name flashed on the screen. Noah swiped to answer. "Jacob?"

"*Noah.*" Jacob's voice cracked. A sob came over the line. It sounded like granite breaking, or glass being torn in two. "*Fuck, Noah. We need you.*"

12

COLE GAGGED as they stepped into the house. Noah shot him a look. How many crime scenes—murder scenes—had Cole been to?

How horrible must this one be if that was how Cole reacted?

Noah should be feeling something. Anything. Instead, his mind worked like a checklist, cataloging everything in slow motion. As if the world were a film reel set on the slowest speed, individual frames freezing, then moving forward in clunky jerks. His mind was a camera, stilling each terrible image in place, burning the pictures on the backs of his retinas for the rest of his life.

The sights… and the smell. That Coed Killer smell. The stench of terror and destruction. Desperation. Fear. And death. So much death.

His eyes flicked to the kitchen. Blood and brain splattered the cabinets, the refrigerator. Two bloody handprints slid from the granite counter and disappeared behind the island. Melinda was down there, out of sight except for her feet poking out from the edge of the counter. The pool of blood spreading beneath her had reached her shoes. In another hour, it would pass beyond her toes.

He blinked. Cameras flashed. Crime scene techs spoke in low voices in the family room. His radio murmured with an APB announcement. *Be on the lookout for anyone with unexplained blood on their clothes or their body. Contact all area hospitals and urgent care centers for any admissions with unexplained injuries or defensive wounds.* The man who did this and got away wouldn't be walking around looking clean and fresh. Not with what they'd found in the house.

He didn't want to see the rest.

Blood spread like snow angels beneath the two boys in the family room. Melinda had wanted one more child. They'd ended up with twins. He remembered pride mixed with exhaustion on John's face when he told the office. The unique exhausted joy of a parent-to-be when they knew exactly what they were getting into. The boys had grown since Noah had seen them last. Carter was in flag football, the all-city league. He wanted to start tackle more than anything else. Evan was content to build Lego and play his video games.

Evan must have convinced Carter to play with him. Both boys were in front of the TV, controllers still in their hands. They'd fallen backward and forward. One was on his knees when the bullet went into the back of his skull. The loading screen for *Super Mario Odyssey* was still looping, the bright, cheery jingle a horrifying counterpoint to the bits of brain and bone dripping down the screen.

Cole hung close to Noah, breathing shallowly through his mouth. His gloved hand brushed against the back of Noah's. "Are you okay?"

Noah said nothing.

Voices floated up from the basement. There were two sprays of blood on the wall. Two bullet holes smashed into the drywall, blood arching from their centers like gory shooting stars. A long smear fell to the left, toward the basement door.

Bloody handprints led the way down.

The stairs to the basement were dim. Every few seconds, flashes from the techs' cameras would burst in the darkness, spotlighting the streaks and smears going down the walls. The evidence tags fixed to the wall and the handrail.

The basement was a combination man cave and second family lounge. Molly hung out down there, away from her twin brothers, and had her own TV she shared with her dad. John had built a freestanding bar in the corner. How many times had Noah sat there nursing a beer as a football game droned in the background? Now, two tumblers of bourbon sat on the bar top, half full. The bourbon bottle lay on its side.

The TV had been ripped off the wall, the screen shattered. The old, worn, plaid sofa was on its back, cushions scattered. Battery-powered klieg lights stood in the corners, brought in by the police. It was easier to look at the edges. To stare at the destruction, the secondary evidence. The incidentals to what lay in the center of the basement.

Behind him, Cole's breath hitched. He stepped closer to Noah, inside his shadow. His chest brushed Noah's back. Was that Cole trembling, or Noah? He couldn't tell.

Noah closed his eyes. Maybe, when he opened them, he'd wake up in his bedroom, staring at the ceiling. Maybe this was all a nightmare.

It wasn't.

John Hayes's body lay on his front, his arms reaching for his daughter. Molly lay on her back on the shattered remnants of the coffee table, arms and legs spread carelessly. Dark, vicious bruises ringed her neck. Noah could pick out four distinct black marks in the shape of fingers under her jaw. A thumb laid over her carotid. Her head was tilted at that broken-doll angle, her spine and the bones of her neck obviously ripped apart.

John had collapsed somewhere between the foot of the stairs and the center of the basement. He'd crawled through the TV's shattered glass on his hands and knees. Two exit wounds bloomed outward from his middle back. Nine mil, the same caliber that had killed Melinda and his twin boys. He'd been gutshot at the top of the stairs. Stumbled down, bleeding. Desperate.

Desperate to get to his daughter.

A broken barstool lay on its side next to him. Based on the blood covering the legs, the killer had used it to beat John, smashing it over his back and his legs and his head until his skin had split and his skull had caved in. Bits of bone were mashed into his brain. Pieces of skin and gray matter stuck to the remaining legs of the stool. His body lay facedown in an ocean of blood.

If John hadn't drowned in his own blood, the barstool's leg sticking out of his back, staked all the way through him, would have finished the job.

Still, one of John's hands reached for Molly. His fingers almost brushed her painted toenails. The skin of her foot was gray and cold.

"Is this escalation or disintegration?" Noah turned to Cole, trying to blink away the images. Cameras flashed over the bodies, capturing every angle, every aspect of their agony. Light burst on the edges of his vision, carving John and Molly's last moments into the vitreous humor of his eyeballs. Into the gray matter of his own brain.

Cole's sigh burned over his cheek. "I'm not sure. There's elements of both here." Another deep breath. "Extreme violence. Loss of control." He nodded to the destruction. The blood spattering the walls, the furniture. Arcs looped almost to the ceiling. "You see this in serial killers who spiral out of control. Ted Bundy's final victims were extremely brutal kills. He was still methodical enough to gain entry to the sorority and to abduct the teen girl, but the killings themselves were..." He trailed off, watching as the crime scene tech measured the bruises ringing Molly's neck.

"The killer cut the phone lines on his way in. They couldn't call for help on the landline. It's demonstrably slower calling 9-1-1 on a cell phone. The seconds it takes to unlock the device, pull up the phone app…" Noah pushed through the tightness in his throat, the scream that wanted to rise. "There were no signs of forced entry. No signs of a struggle upstairs. The neighbors didn't report any screaming. No one heard gunshots." The bodies hadn't been found until Jacob drove to John's house, searching for their missing boss. "Did they know their killer? Did they invite him in?" Cole turned back to the basement stairs. He frowned at the bloody handprints.

"He didn't take his time with the people upstairs. He wasn't after any of them. Molly was his target," Cole said. "I don't understand the viciousness toward John, though."

Noah's eyes closed. His throat went tight. "John was a father. What do you think he was doing?"

Images crashed through his mind, terrible images. What if it had been him? What if it had been him and Katie? What if the killer cut his phone lines, broke into his house in the middle of the night, and went after her? For a moment, he imagined himself in John's shoes, bleeding from the stomach, trying to hold in his own intestines as he stumbled after his daughter. Listening to her scream, and then not scream as her air was choked off and the killer's hands closed around her—

His eyes wandered the edges of John's blood pool. There was so much blood. John was drowning in it, for God's sake. His face was lost in the puddle. Would they find froth in his lungs? Had he aspirated? Had it filled his throat, slid down his airway, until—

Fuck, now he understood Garrett. He understood that hard-edged glare he'd had looking at Bart's body. Seeing someone you knew, someone you respected, dead. Not just dead, but destroyed.

What were John's final seconds like? His agonized final

breaths? He'd been reaching for his daughter...

Stop. Focus. He turned away from John's corpse and walked to the bar. Tried to breathe through the kaleidoscope of after images burned into his eyeballs.

Evidence tags squatted next to the tumblers on the bar. Fingerprints circled the cut glass, crowding the rim, as if someone had downed shot after shot.

John didn't drink bourbon. He was a gin man. "These could be the killer's prints."

Cole stopped too close to him again. "It would be a major sign of disintegration if he left behind fingerprints."

"Are you saying he's spiraling?"

"He could be. He could also be gaining confidence. He successfully killed Frank and Bart, on top of Kimberly and Jessie. Success breeds confidence, which breeds further success."

"How does killing Bart lead him to *this*?"

"He might be thinking, 'How many can I kill before I get to what I really want?' Molly was still his fixation." Cole turned, taking in the basement. "Everything in this house leads to her."

Even John. Especially John. His hand, reaching for her pink toenails. He'd been staked to the ground to stop him from reaching his daughter. Noah rubbed his palm over the center of his chest. He could almost hear the crunch of bone, of ribs snapping, as the wooden leg went through John's chest.

"This reminds me of BTK and the Otero murders. Rader broke into the Otero home when a majority of the family was there. His fixation was on the young girl, Josephine. He didn't care about the others. He killed them all quickly, then took his time with the young girl. This feels similar. Upstairs, the quick dispatch of the mom and the boys. Even shooting John upstairs. There's no destruction up there. No devastation. But here..."

"Escalation," Noah said softly.

"Tell me about Molly?" Cole slid in front of Noah, blocking his view of Molly and John.

"Molly was John's pride and joy. They'd always been close. Hiking together, hunting, fishing. As she got older, they became even closer. She'd earned a full scholarship to the University of Iowa. She was prelaw. She wanted to come back and intern with the DA's office next summer. She was working as a paralegal this summer."

"An accomplished, beautiful young woman."

"She was in the paper a few months ago, during the spring semester. It was supposed to be a profile of John, but he spent so much time bragging about her and the rest of his family that they pulled in everyone. Molly shone."

"Fits the profile perfectly."

"But how did he get in? How did the killer get into the house without any forced entry, without any surprise? He shot those boys in the back of the head. Shot John in the stomach."

Cole's lips thinned.

"Agent Downing?"

A crime scene tech, a tall Black woman with her long braids pulled back in a high bun, approached. She had her cell phone to her ear. "Sir, I've got an urgent call from the crime lab. They said to tell you they reswabbed for DNA on Jessie Olson's face. They got a hit." She grimaced. "On her lips."

"Who? Who is it?"

She stiffened. "The hit came from the controls, sir."

The controls… Oh, fuck. The controls were donated DNA from law enforcement officers, used to calibrate the machines against known samples. Which meant—

"The match is to Deputy Andy Garrett."

Noah's gaze whipped to the tumbler half full of bourbon. Garrett drank bourbon at the last Christmas party. And at the BBQ over Memorial Day. They'd been here, at John's house. John wasn't just the head of the Des Moines FBI, he'd been practically paternal to all of the law enforcement officers in the region. John and the older sheriffs had been the wise men, smoking their cigars and flipping burgers while the younger agents and officers chased each other with water guns or threw their kids in the pool or had cannonball contests and tried to splash the wives. He could see it all perfectly, that last party: Bart telling him about how great Jessie was doing in college. Garrett standing beside him, listening with rapt attention as Bart hugged Jessie one-armed and kissed her temple.

Garrett, staring at Jessie, a glass of bourbon in his hand.

"Get those glasses fingerprinted," he growled. He grabbed his radio. "All units, be on the lookout for Deputy Andy Garrett, Boone County Sheriff's. Find him, *now*, and bring him to the FBI office."

Silence over the radio for half a minute. Nothing but static and the whiz of white noise, pops and clicks and radio affirmations. Then, *"Sir, we responded to a vehicle fire out on U Ave, up near Dallas Center, about half an hour ago."*

Dallas Center was a small, rural farming community about thirty miles northwest of Des Moines.

Ten miles away from John's home.

"We found a truck burning off the side of the road, almost in a cornfield. Fire department managed to put it out before the field went up. Sir, the license plate says it's Garrett's truck."

Noah looked at Cole. "He could be running."

"Any sign of Garrett?" Noah said into his radio as he headed for the basement stairs, storming out of the blood-choked horror.

Garrett. Andy Garrett. Staring at Bart. Why? Andy Garrett, who'd been so angry, so despondent. Andy Garrett, crying in the hallway. "Was he in the truck?"

"No, sir. No one was in the truck. There are some bloody footprints leading into the field."

"Stay there. Hold a perimeter. I'm going to get a bird in the air. We'll be there in ten minutes."

13

ANDY GARRETT WAS A MESS.

Blood covered his hands and arms, stained his white T-shirt in a tie-dye of gore. He had a cut running down one cheek. Through the blood they'd wiped from his arms for a DNA swab, they'd spotted older cuts, scabs that were healing.

He sat slumped in the single metal chair inside the interrogation room, staring listlessly at the far wall. He'd shown no emotion since the deputies had hauled him out of the cornfield, thrown him facedown in the dirt, cuffed him, and shoved him into the back of Noah's SUV.

Agents were tearing Garrett's life apart, down to the molecules of his existence.

Evidence was being processed as quickly as it could be. The fingerprints on the glasses at John's house had come back: Garrett's and John's.

So were fingerprints on John's basement handrail and on the barstool that had impaled him. On the kitchen counter near Melinda's body.

Garrett's nine-millimeter service pistol was missing. It wasn't on him, and it wasn't in his truck. Melinda, Evan, Carter, and John had been shot with a nine mil.

Cell phone records had been pulled. In the last six months, Garrett had called Jessie Olson over three hundred times. Almost twice a day.

There were no return calls from Jessie to Garrett's number.

"What do you think?" Cole asked Noah. They were side by side in the dark observation room. Usually, they'd be watching the suspect squirm, but Garrett hadn't so much as twitched since he'd been shoved into the chair and had his wrists locked in the shackles binding him to the room's sole table.

Exhaustion made Noah's brain slow, even as his mind was sparking, a thousand thoughts trying to ignite and failing, crushed under the revolving images of John and Molly and Bart and Jessie. "His DNA is on Jessie's lips, and it would have to be put there extremely close to when she died, if not at the moment of her death. And, it looks like he's got a motive, too." Noah sighed. "But why kill Molly and John, and their whole family?"

"The question isn't why. There's never a good answer to why, not with sadists and psychopaths and serial killers."

"How far back does this go, Cole? Garrett is a local. He was here during the first six murders."

"That's not enough to call him a killer."

"He's only been a deputy for two years. What was he doing before that?"

Cole said nothing.

"Kimberly's, Jessie's, and even Molly's murder all have the Coed Killer's signature. They match his MO. The FBI and local law enforcement held back that the victims weren't sexually assaulted. How rare is it to have a strangulation without some form of sexual assault?"

"Rare," Cole said.

"It was the defining feature of the Coed Killer's MO, both with the first six, and again with Kimberly, Jessie, and Molly."

He scrubbed a hand over his face, over the start of a five o'clock shadow. What time was it, even? They'd been going for hours. "Now we have Garrett, who looks like he's good for at least two of the three most recent murders, and they're the exact same MO as the previous six." He blew out a slow breath. Had there been a wolf in their fold for years? All this time? "You wondered right away if the killer had law enforcement experience."

"You thought that, back with the original murders."

"If it is Garrett, he wasn't a sheriff's deputy back then."

"What was he six years ago? Do you know?"

Noah shook his head. "They're still digging into his background and history. We'll know more in a few hours."

Cole checked his watch. "In a few hours, it will be after midnight. No one is going to be much good on this investigation if they don't eat and get some rest."

"We've got to—"

"We've *got* him." Cole reached for Noah. Noah almost sagged into his touch. "*You* got him. He's not going anywhere. Let's do this right."

Noah sighed. "We can't get into his house until morning. Judge Vargas won't sign the warrant until then."

"And you're going to take a run at Garrett tomorrow. Let everyone do this right, without rushing. Let Garrett stew. Give him time to let the demons in his head go wild. He ran. He's close to his own breaking point, and he might bring himself right over the edge without us having to lift a finger. We'll build the case against him. The evidence is coming in."

Noah pinched the bridge of his nose. "I need to call Katie. I told her to go to Evelyn and Susan's to spend the night." He pulled out his phone. Katie had texted him three times, telling him she'd made it home with Evelyn, that she'd done all her homework, and that she loved him. His heart squeezed. He smiled at his phone.

"I'll give you some privacy."

"No, it's okay." He waved Cole back as he dialed. Cole hovered by the door, his hands in his pockets as he stared at the floor.

Katie picked up on the first ring. *"Dad!"*

"Hey K-Bear. Got your texts. How you doing?"

"We're just hanging out. How are you? I saw the news…"

He couldn't speak. "Yeah."

"I'm sorry, Dad."

He'd taken Katie to John's house for BBQs and summer parties and holiday parties for years, from when she was a toddler in frilly dresses all the way up to the divorce, when Lilly had moved away and taken Katie with her. Katie had been able to come to the summer party two years before. He'd hurled her into the pool a few times, and they'd chased each other around John's backyard with Nerf guns. She'd come into the office with Noah over spring break after she'd refused to go back to Omaha and insisted she was living with him, no matter what. She hadn't been enrolled in school in Des Moines, and he didn't even know if she was allowed to stay with him. Lilly could have filed a kidnapping report if she wanted to. John had spent half the day with Katie, entertaining her and mentoring in that way he had, as Noah tried to figure out what to do.

"I want you to stay with Susan and Evelyn tonight, okay?"

"But you caught the guy, right? The news said the FBI arrested the guy who did it. I saw you on TV."

"We think we caught him, but now we have to prove it. We've got a lot of work in front of us. I just want you to be perfectly, perfectly safe, okay? It's the dad in me."

Like the dad in John, who'd stumbled down the stairs after two gutshots and crawled across broken glass to try and save his daughter. Who had reached for her, even after being impaled. Cold fingers reaching for painted pink toes.

"But when can I see you? We didn't have pizza tonight, and you've been working nonstop since last week. Are you coming home tonight? Can

you pick me up if you do?" The plaintive note in her voice nearly broke him right down the center.

"I'm going home, K-Bear, but it will be late. I've got to wrap up some stuff here, and I'm just going to crash hard when I get home. Then I'll be up early and back at the office. It's better for you to stay at Susan's, okay?"

"*Okay.*" She paused. "*It's really cool you caught this guy, Dad. Like, really cool.*"

"I can't take credit for that, K-Bear. A lot of smart people have been working on this. Dr. Kennedy has been a huge help. He's been invaluable." Noah smiled at Cole across the dark observation room.

"*But didn't you ask him to come help? Doesn't that make you smart? Isn't that what you always tell me, that it's smart to ask for help?*"

He laughed. "So you *do* listen to me."

"*Sometimes.*" He could hear her eye roll.

In the low light, Cole's eyes were like stars glittering on a midnight horizon. Dull light bleeding out of the two-way mirror curled around Cole's face, carving his cheekbones and the roundness of his soft smile into existence. There was a name for the look in Cole's eyes, but Noah couldn't say it. He couldn't say what it felt like when Cole's gaze drifted over him. "K-Bear, I'm going to go. Sweet dreams, and I love you. I'll see you tomorrow."

"*Love you, too, Dad.*"

He hung up and pocketed his phone, fiddled with the folder he held. After his press conference—God, had it only been that afternoon?—they'd had almost three hundred tips called in about suspicious neighbors and men lurking in shadows. But, buried in the middle of the calls, one stood out. The transcript was in the folder.

For tomorrow. Cole was right. Noah was running in circles inside his own mind, trying to understand the curve balls and loops of the case. Andy Garrett, now and then. Crime scenes from six years ago were melding with crime scenes from a week ago and from today. John, staked to his basement floor. Stacy Shepherd, flat on her back and strangled, arms and legs spread, loose limbed like Molly had been. That broken-doll tilt to all of their necks, spines snapped, hyoid bones broken. Petechial hemorrhage on gray skin. Salt tracks down the temples.

"All right. I'm calling it a night." He glared at Garrett, still motionless inside of the interrogation room. It was like he wasn't alive. Was he even blinking? "I'll drive you?"

Cole nodded, and they circled around to Noah's office and then to the conference room to pack up. Cole carted the case files with him back and forth to the hotel each night. Noah left his laptop on his desk and turned off the lights. The last thing he saw in his office was a photo of him and Katie tacked to the side of his monitor. She'd been three then, balanced on his shoulders and holding on to his hands as they faced the camera with matching mile-wide grins.

They both sagged into the bucket seats of Noah's SUV, sighing in unison. Cole rolled his neck, rubbed his shoulders. Noah tipped his head back and closed his eyes.

Do it. Ask him. Ask him before you chicken out. Like you always chicken out.

Noah gripped the steering wheel. His thumbs rubbed over the smoothed, worn leather. *I wanted to see you again, too. We still could.* He cleared his throat. "Do you want me to take you back to the hotel?"

Cole arched an eyebrow at him. "You're implying I could go somewhere else?"

"Would you like to come back to my house? I can make you dinner. Well, I can make a decent grilled ham and cheese, and I think I have a bag of Doritos."

Cole laughed. The sound filled Noah, warmed him, and chased away, for the moment, the images of blood and terror. "I'd love a grilled ham and cheese," Cole said. "With you."

Noah shifted the SUV into gear. "I think I only have the butt ends of the loaf left. I haven't been shopping in a while."

"Lucky for you, I happen to *love* butts."

Noah slammed the brakes and whirled on Cole.

Cole grinned.

Shaking his head, Noah started forward again. After they left the parking lot, he reached across the center console and grabbed Cole's hand. He didn't let go for the rest of the drive.

14

IT WAS ridiculous how nervous he was as they pulled up to Noah's house.

He'd been to dozens of men's houses. Dozens of dozens, in fact. This wasn't any different.

Except it was.

And not just for the obvious. Noah didn't live in a high-rise condo overlooking the Potomac, or a K Street walk-up, or a Foggy Bottom Victorian. His house was modest, like Noah was, a quaint square house with a pitched roof, a two-car gable garage, and a porch swing rocking in the midnight breeze. A small floodlight shone on the American flag hanging off his porch. Daisies and roses were planted in beds lining the porch and the walkway. To the right and left, up and down the block, were versions of the same clean-cut Americana: manicured yards and tidy houses and, beyond, fields of corn. The sky overhead was full of stars, sprays and rivers of them.

He'd arrived in a Norman Rockwell painting. But it wasn't just a patina. This was real, and deep. He stood on Noah's driveway and stared at the stars, the horizon-to-horizon spread. The slice of sky from Noah's front yard was wider than he'd ever seen.

Noah appeared at his side. His keys jingled softly as he rolled them through his fingers. "I bought this house because of the views. There's a farmer behind me, and from the back porch, it's nothing but corn and stars."

"Of course there's a farmer behind you." He nudged Noah gently.

Noah grinned. He sobered quickly. Took a deep breath. "Want to come in?"

Cole almost teased him, but that would only be covering up his own nerves, his own panic at what was happening between them. Sure, they'd talked, and Noah had said he wanted to try again. He wanted Cole, wanted to work toward coming out. But saying and doing were totally different things. Meeting in Vegas or Chicago was very different from inviting Cole into his house. Where he lived. Where he couldn't run.

Cole nodded. He didn't trust his voice.

Noah led him up his porch steps.

Inside was neat and tidy, exactly what Cole would expect from an FBI agent—and, more so, from Noah. He smiled at the walls. They were that creamy beige, the color of his coffee. Hardwood floors ran throughout the first floor. The wide, open rooms were decorated in muted mahogany and leather furniture in shades of blue with gold accents. Exposed wood beams crisscrossed the family room and kitchen ceilings like bridge struts.

Mail was piled on the kitchen island next to a stack of high school textbooks. Dishes dried by the sink. A cheerleading bag sat near the stairs, and several pairs of obviously-Katie's shoes were kicked off by the couch. Two coats hung on hooks by the sliding glass back door, which opened to a wide porch overlooking a flat lawn, a squat fence, and, beyond, an endless sea of corn. Cole smothered a smile.

Stairs rose from the living room. Pictures of Katie and Noah lined the wall going up.

"Sorry for the mess." Noah dropped his keys and wallet in

a decorative bowl on the kitchen counter. He eyed Katie's textbooks and the papers sticking out of the pages.

"There's no mess." Cole laid his laptop bag and the case files on the island. "Your house is great."

"It's..." Noah sighed. Katie's MacBook lay on the dining room table, a charge cable snaking across the floor to the outlet. "It's home."

It was quiet and understated, just like Noah was. Masculine, controlled, and warm. His daughter, too, was all over his life here, in his home like she was in his heart. Cole grinned.

"Are you hungry?" Noah moved to the sink to wash his hands. "I promised you a sandwich. I hope Katie didn't finish off the cheese." As he spoke, he glanced down at his hands, his forearms. Water sluiced off his skin, turning black as it hit the sink. Fingerprint powder, dirt from the cornfield, sweat, and a hundred other unmentionables dripped from his skin.

"We should clean up first." Cole moved when Noah didn't, crossing to his side and turning off the water. Noah started. Cole passed him a kitchen towel. When Noah dried his hands, smears of dull rust-red stained the fabric.

They had to get John, and Molly, and the crime scene off of them. Get Garrett off of them. "Why don't you take a shower?" Cole suggested. "I'll wait."

Noah nodded, padding out of the kitchen with the dish towel balled up in his hands. He threw the bloodied in the trash, hesitating as he stared out the back door. "You need a shower, too."

Cole's heartbeat leaped. "I'll go after you."

"Cole."

Cole swallowed. He looked sideways at Noah's fridge, at the photos of Katie cheering, Katie goofing off for the camera, Katie and Noah arm in arm at a high school football game. Looked down. Looked back at Noah. "Are you sure?"

Noah reached for the buttons on his shirt. He started undoing them one by one.

"I—" It was hard to talk while watching Noah shed his shirt, peel it down his arms and fling it over the back of his couch. He remembered doing that. His palms itched, burning with the memory, the feel of Noah's shoulders appearing beneath the slide of fabric as he pushed it down, down— "Are you sure tonight is…" *Are you thinking clearly? After today?* "I don't want you to regret this."

Noah tugged his undershirt off and threw it behind him. The white cotton fluttered and fell on the coffee table, half draped over the edge.

Damn it, Noah was just as gorgeous as he'd remembered. He hadn't embellished a single thing in his memories. He was still broad shouldered and trim waisted, still had a matting of chest hair between his pecs. He had a solidity to him, the shape of a man who liked to be active, who was comfortable with his strength. Those arms had wrapped around Cole, held him tight, squeezed his back—

Noah held out his hand as he undid his belt and left it hanging open.

"I don't want to be a one-night stand again," Cole blurted out. "I don't want to sleep with you and have to pretend it didn't happen. I don't want you to run away again." *I don't want you to throw me away again.* "I want…" He stumbled. Hesitated. "I want this to mean something to you. Because it does to me." Please, please don't let this just be about drowning out the day, drowning out the images, the blood and the terror. Please.

Noah's hand was steady, still reaching for him. "I want you, Cole. I can't… put into words how much I want you."

Cole took a step forward, and then another, never taking his eyes off Noah's. He expected fear, or trepidation, or nervousness. Instead, all he saw was desire. An inferno of it, that spark he'd glimpsed in Vegas igniting into a conflagration. All of Noah, everything about the man, was burning, focused on Cole. Cole could feel the heat as he took Noah's hand.

Noah made quick work of Cole's shirt, unbuttoning it and pushing it down, leaving it on the floor by the kitchen table. His undershirt followed, but before Noah pulled it over his head, he tangled Cole's arms in the fabric, pulling the neckline tight over Cole's eyes. He was trapped, eyes closed, as Noah's palm cradled his cheek.

"Cole," Noah breathed. His words brushed over Cole's lips, his face. "I have thought of you, of this, every single moment since that night." His lips closed over Cole's.

He made a noise—something embarrassing, something like a whimper or a curse or a groan, or all of them mixed into one. He pulled free of Noah's hold on his T-shirt and shed it, then wrapped his arms around Noah. Skin met skin, and Cole shivered. Noah groaned, deepening the kiss as his fingers dug into Cole's shoulders.

"Shower." Cole pressed his cheek against Noah's. He couldn't catch his breath. The room was fuzzy on the edges. "We need to shower."

They made it upstairs hand in hand, bouncing from the stair railing to the wall in between the framed photos to kiss each other breathless. Near the top, Noah rolled his hips against Cole's, and Cole nearly lost it all there. He shivered from his toes to his scalp, grabbing Noah's hips as he groaned. He felt Noah smile against his neck before nibbling on the skin just above his collarbone.

He steered Noah down the hall, past an open door and a messy bedroom, the floor covered in skinny jeans and T-shirts, and to the room at the end of the hall. He was guessing, but when he backed Noah against the closed door, Noah fumbled for the doorknob and pushed it open. They stumbled together into Noah's dark bedroom.

Noah slapped the light switch. A floor lamp in the corner winked on. Noah had a queen bed flanked by two nightstands and a flat-screen TV sat atop a dresser. Clothes tumbled out of a laundry basket doubling as a hamper. A door led to a bathroom, a plug-in nightlight illuminating the tiled space.

It was just bright enough to see a postcard taped to Noah's mirror, still new, still crisp. *Vegas*, it said in huge font, above a nighttime image of the Strip. It was something you'd buy in an airport on your way out of town. Something to remember a place by.

They were naked and in the shower in seconds. He spared half a thought for Noah's excellent water pressure before everything was eclipsed by Noah. Noah in his arms, Noah pressed against him. Noah's warm, wet body sliding against his. His body hair, soaked by the shower, water running in rivulets between his pecs and down to his belly button, caressing his hips before dropping farther, *down*.

He grabbed the soap and ran it over Noah's shoulders and down his arms. Over the trim lines of his back, to his hips, and then up, sweeping the soap and his hands over every inch of that broad chest. Noah's head tipped back, exposing the long arch of his throat and his Adam's apple jutting toward the ceiling. Cole dropped to his knees and ran the soap over each of Noah's legs, between his thighs, up and down his calves. Over his ankles, his feet. Noah's legs were strong, the muscles firm, long lines that said he was a runner.

He soaped his hands and dropped the bar. It skittered away, circling the drain, but he didn't care. He cupped Noah's crotch, hands encircling his hard, heavy cock and his hot sac. Noah groaned, spreading his legs as he reached back, steadying himself on the tile wall.

Cole stroked Noah's cock at the base. His other hand dipped behind Noah's balls, into the cleft of his ass, into the heat at the center of his body. There, yes. He stroked, circled, and pressed—

Noah jerked as if he'd touched a live wire. One hand grabbed Cole, fingers sliding into his hair. He squeezed, almost hard enough to hurt. "Yes," Noah groaned. "More."

Cole gave him more. He had to fumble for the soap again, get more lather, but soon he had Noah's leg up over his shoulder and was working a third finger into Noah's hole as Noah kept up a constant litany of "Yes" and "Fuck" and "God" and "Please" and, the best one, "*Cole.*" Noah's cock was rock hard, purple, sticking straight up. Noah had taken over fisting it, slowly squeezing the base as if he was trying to hold himself back.

Cole kissed the head as he lowered Noah's leg. Noah stared at him when he stood, looking blitzed and drunk, wide-eyed and flushed from way more than just the hot water. Cole grinned and kissed Noah's cheeks, his mouth. Noah panted.

Cole soaped himself and rinsed in less than thirty seconds. His own cock was aching, and a steady stream leaked from his tip. He could barely stand the water hitting him. Noah wasn't much better. He quivered as Cole guided him under the spray, bucked when the water flowed down his back, between his legs.

Cole tried to dry Noah off, tried to be sweet and wrap him in a towel, ruffle Noah's dripping hair. He'd always wanted to take care of someone like that, be sweet and cute and kiss someone on the nose when he was done drying their face.

But Noah wasn't having it, at least not right now. He pushed the towel off, and then Cole's towel, and nearly tackled Cole, pressing him back against the sink counter. Toothpaste and deodorant spun sideways, and Noah's toothbrush clattered into the sink. Cole grabbed him, hauled him close. Felt Noah's heartbeat thundering against his own. Smelled him: the clean scent of the soap and the smell of Noah, warm and wanting.

He kissed Noah until their knees were shaking. Noah was humping him, an unconscious roll of his hips, dragging his cock up and over where Cole's leg joined his body. Little noises fell from Noah's mouth, sighs and gasps and broken moans. His fingers clenched around Cole's shoulders, ran up and buried themselves in Cole's hair.

"Hold on," Cole whispered. He kissed Noah's cheek, his ear, his jawline, and then grabbed Noah's ass. "Jump."

Noah hesitated. His eyes flicked over Cole.

"I've got you," Cole promised.

Noah jumped. Cole grabbed his ass and held on as their bodies pressed even tighter, Noah's cock digging into his belly, his own cock rising and prodding behind Noah's legs. Noah's ankles hooked behind Cole's back. His hands gripped Cole's hair as a smile broke across his face.

"I've got you," Cole whispered again. He was stronger than he looked. And he really wanted this moment.

"You do."

They kissed more slowly as Cole carried Noah to the bedroom, to Noah's bed. He laid him down and crawled on top, never separating. Noah writhed beneath him, bucking and trembling every time Cole rocked down into him. He grabbed Cole and held him tight, keeping their hips, their cocks, pressed together.

Down Cole went, again, this time only kissing Noah's cock once before lifting his legs, draping Noah's thighs over his shoulders. Cole groaned as he grabbed one cheek in each hand, massaging the thick muscle as he pressed his face into Noah's cleft. His tongue pressed against Noah's hole, a firm, wet stroke, before he sucked. Licked. Nibbled. Worked Noah's ass open with his tongue and his lips and his face until Noah was screaming, back arching, toes curling, thighs quaking as he panted Cole's name.

Cole kissed his way back up Noah's body, lying on top of him. Noah bucked into him, writhed, ground his steel-hard cock against Cole's. God, Noah made it difficult to think. "Do you have condoms?"

Noah blinked. He frowned, as if he didn't understand the

words, didn't understand the language Cole was speaking. He blinked again. Groaned. "No," he croaked. "I was married."

"That was over four years ago."

Noah flushed. "I haven't been with anyone since… last Wednesday."

Vegas. Noah hadn't been with anyone since his divorce, aside from Cole. Aside from his first time with a man, when he'd chosen Cole. Jesus. Fire burned him alive for a moment, and he shuddered, his forehead dropping against Noah's as he struggled to breathe. "Are you… Do you want…" He shook his head. He shouldn't. This was his lust running away with him. This was his desire, damn it, all of his desires, slamming into him. He could feel Noah's heat, so fucking close. "I don't have a condom on me," he whispered. He hadn't expected to need one here. Now. Today.

"That's okay." Noah's hands slipped from his hair down to his face. He made Cole look him in the eye. "I want you."

"We shouldn't…"

"You'll never hurt me."

He lurched, as if all of Noah had reached out and seized all of him, dragged him body and soul into Noah. He kissed Noah harder, deeper than he'd kissed him before, trying to merge their molecules as he grabbed Noah's hands and laced their fingers together, pressing them to the bed beside Noah's face. "Do you have lube?" he asked against Noah's lips, kissing him after each word.

"Lotion." Noah nodded toward his nightstand.

That would do. Cole lunged for it, hating every moment he was out of Noah's arms. Returning, he gathered Noah into his hold, covering him, wrapping his arms around Noah's broad shoulders as he kissed him, rocked into him, pressed their chests together. Was that his heartbeat thundering, or Noah's? Or both?

Finally, he pulled back, grabbing the lotion he'd thrown on

the bed, and balanced himself on one hand over Noah. Noah spread his legs and stared into Cole's eyes.

Fuck, the trust in Noah's gaze burned Cole to the core. His arm trembled, and he pitched forward, burying his face in Noah's neck. "Are you sure?" he whispered.

"Surer than I've ever been." Noah pushed him up, kissing him until he was back on his knees. "I want this. I want you. I want you to do this."

"What? What do you want me to do?"

Noah's eyes widened, and he swallowed. Was that fear? Was he still in some way, running? Was this going to end in complete disas—

"I want you to make love to me," Noah whispered. His mouth worked quickly, silent words discarded before they were spoken. "You may not feel like that's what this is, but to me—"

Cole swooped down again, losing the lotion and grabbing Noah. He kissed him, kissed the words right out of his mouth. "Of course that's what this is."

Noah smiled. He was trembling, quivering where Cole's body pressed against his. He hooked one leg over Cole's hip. "Show me," he whispered. "Everything."

Cole's eyes slipped closed, memories of Vegas slamming into this night for a moment. But this was better, so much better. This was here, and now, and Noah knew who he was, and he'd chosen Cole—again—and he wanted Cole. Again. This was something that was going to last beyond the sunrise, beyond tomorrow. When they did this, it was going to mean something. He felt that in his bones.

Noah squirmed and sighed as Cole slid the lotion as deep as he could. He tried to use enough, too much, until he couldn't even hold the bottle even more. Slicking himself was torture. He had to squeeze himself, count to ten, imagine bugs and calculus and statistics to back himself down. Fuck, how was he going to last? How was he going to make this good for Noah?

"Are you ready?" Cole pressed against Noah's ass.

Noah wrapped his hands around Cole's face. "Yes."

The slide, the pressure, and then the heat exploded around him. He gasped, falling forward, his head against Noah's as Noah went taut, jaw clenched hard, muscles straining. Cole froze. "Noah…"

Slowly, Noah unclenched, and his breathing evened out. "More," he said.

"Fuck." He wanted to hold back, take his time, but he couldn't. He slid into Noah, into the very center of him, gasping. Noah bucked and arched against him, his eyes wide, wild, his legs jerking. He gripped Cole's shoulders, stared at him, panting. "I'm sorry, I'm sorry," Cole murmured.

Noah groaned, his eyes rolling back. He was still shuddering against Cole. "So fucking good," he groaned. "Cole, God."

Cole dug his forehead into Noah's, waiting. Waiting for Noah's heart to come back down to earth. For Noah's breath to return. Waiting for his own breath to return, his own heart to stop racing out of control. He could feel all of Noah, from where they were joined to where they were pressed together, chest to chest, face to face. Heart to heart.

"Show me," Noah said again. "Cole, make love to me."

Cole groaned as he pulled back. And thrust in. He kissed Noah, kept kissing him as their bodies found their joined rhythm, the press and pull and push of two people figuring out how to make love. Sweat rose, slicking their movements. Noah pushed Cole back, clambering upward until they were sitting up together, arms wrapped around each other's neck, Noah rocking on Cole's cock with his legs tight around Cole's waist. Cole kissed down Noah's throat, nibbled on his collarbone. He bit down when Noah jerked, his cock spasming against Cole's belly. "Cole…" Noah's hands threaded through Cole's hair.

Cole fell backward, Noah on top of him suddenly, riding

him as he pressed Cole's hands to the mattress over Cole's head. Now it was Cole who was at Noah's mercy. Hadn't it been like that from the first night? He'd thought he was picking up Noah. When had the tables turned? Sometime soon after that, so subtly he hadn't even noticed. Noah had always been in control of him. He'd always craved everything Noah offered, everything about him. He always wanted more.

His eyes were rolling back, and he was going to lose it if Noah kept up that rock and shimmy, sliding down and up, all the way in and out. He was going to completely lose it, but he wasn't ready yet. He pushed Noah back until Noah was lying down again. His cock was still rock hard, and Cole swallowed it in one long suck. Noah screamed, nearly arching off the bed. His hands grabbed the pillows, the bedspread, ripped the sheet from the corner of the mattress. Cole hummed and looked up at Noah. Noah groaned, long and loud.

He sucked him until Noah's thighs were shaking and Noah was speaking in tongues, nothing but broken syllables and gasps as he fisted the bedding. Then Cole rolled Noah onto his belly and slid over his back, kissing up his spine, his neck, into his hair. He kissed his cheek, found Noah's lips as he slid his cock back into Noah's body. Captured his moan in a long kiss.

Noah pushed back, meeting Cole's slow, gentle thrusts as their hands laced together. And then he was pushing back more, harder, rising to his elbows, getting his knees underneath him. Cole rose, his hands sliding down Noah's back, fingernails digging into his skin. Noah groaned. Cole squeezed his ass cheeks, both round, meaty globes. He slapped Noah's ass as Noah started bouncing back, meeting Cole's thrusts with his own.

"Yes," Noah groaned. He grabbed the pillow, white-knuckling it as he buried the side of his face in the blue fabric. "Yes, Cole."

Too much, this was far, far too much. It wasn't real. It was a dream. One of the dozen dreams he'd had since Wednesday, since Vegas. This was everything he'd ever wanted, the kind of sex he'd always imagined. Sweet and slow and hard and dirty and sexy and raw and fucking perfect, all in one, all with one man. His heart was going to explode. He gripped Noah's hips, felt Noah buck back into him again.

Heat built inside him, fire clawing its way toward his center. There was a whirlpool forming inside him, ready to pull him down. *Not yet, not yet. Never, ever end.* He draped over Noah's body, kissed his shoulder blade. Eased out.

Noah rolled over and reached for Cole, dragging him back on top. Cole went, falling to Noah, chest to chest, hips to hips, his cock finding Noah and sliding inside again. Noah breathed out, closing his eyes, and arched his neck.

He kissed Noah's throat, bit down on the skin stretched over his collarbone. Found Noah's hands and squeezed. "I can't hold it much longer."

Noah groaned.

"Do you want me to pull out?"

Noah's legs wrapped around his waist. His ankles crossed, locking Cole in place. Cole grinned. He nuzzled Noah's neck, his jaw, felt stubble scrape his own skin. Kissed his pulse. Noah turned to him, their lips finding each other, kissing like it was what they were meant to do, always meant to kiss each other like this, make love to each other like this, hold each other close until the very end, until Cole couldn't hold on any longer, and he—

He kissed Noah and buried himself deep, whimpering and gasping as he spilled inside Noah. He hadn't come inside another man in… God he couldn't even remember. Whenever it was, it hadn't been as perfect as this, hadn't whited out his vision and sent pleasure clawing down his spine, burning through each and every one of his nerves.

Noah followed, gripping Cole's hands and screaming his name as he arched and shot his own come between their bellies. Heat spread on Cole's skin, and Noah bucked into it, chased it, then shivered and trembled as the sensation became too much. Cole kissed him, never stopping, through every quiver and gasp.

Silence settled over the bedroom. Cole ran his hand through Noah's sweat-soaked hair, down his cheek. He smiled. They were still connected. He felt himself, hot and wet, inside Noah. Felt his come trickle out, onto his skin. "Wow," he whispered.

Noah laid his hand on top of Cole's. He smiled. "You know," he said. "I am *definitely* gay."

Cole laughed.

15

THEY COULDN'T PULL AN ALL-NIGHTER like they had in Vegas. Noah passed out first, nuzzling into Cole's side, his face pressed to Cole's neck and chest. After a few minutes, he was snoring. Cole kissed Noah's forehead and wrapped his arms around him. Their legs were tangled, and it was easy to flick the corner of the comforter over them both. In minutes, Cole joined him, passing out with his head resting on Noah's.

When Cole woke, before the sun rose, Noah was propped on his elbow, staring down at him as he traced mindless lines on Cole's chest.

Cole took his hand and kissed his fingers, then laid their joined hands over his heart. "Good morning."

Would it be a good morning? How would Noah react? What they'd shared had been... How did you act after such an indescribable, earth-shaking night?

"Morning." Noah studied Cole. He curled his fingers over Cole's heart as if he could hold Cole in his palm.

He could, in a way. Cole had definitely fallen too far for Noah—for a man who had walked out on him a week ago. Too far to be called reasonable. But he didn't care. He'd fallen for Noah, and he was going to chase that. Chase that feeling, that hope. Maybe Noah was falling for him, too. Maybe they could fall, and land, together.

"Are you okay?"

Noah nodded. A flush rose on his cheeks, a dusting of burgundy that spread up to his ears and down his chest. "A little sore," he admitted. "But it's a good sore."

"A good sore?" Cole grinned.

"Yeah. A very good sore." Noah leaned in and kissed him. "Last night was…"

Cole forced himself to wait, even as his heart galloped away from him.

"That was the best sex of my entire life," Noah whispered. He gnawed on his lip, worrying it between his teeth. "You blew away all my fantasies. All my dreams. Everything. Gone."

"Happy to." Cole grinned. "So, it was better than Casey Peters in the back of your dad's Volvo when you were sixteen?"

It was Noah's turn to laugh. "Way, way better."

Cole pulled him on top and wrapped both arms around Noah. "I'm glad." He kissed Noah, then kissed him again, and again. "I'm happy to give you the best night of your life anytime."

"Oh yeah?" Noah's grin was incandescent.

"Oh yeah." Cole rocked his hips upward. He was ready to start right away. Judging by what he found, so was Noah.

Noah braced his hands on either side of Cole's face and scooted back. "How about giving me the best morning of my life?"

Cole shifted, grabbed Noah's hips, and pushed up. "Happy to," he grunted as Noah's eyelids fluttered and his head tipped back. "Might be a faster best morning, though."

Noah rocked and twisted, and Cole groaned. Definitely a faster best morning.

THE MORNING SUN illuminated the kitchen, golden light streaming through the back door and the window over the sink. Noah's house glittered in the morning, warm and welcoming. Cole smiled at him over the rim of his coffee cup. Noah still had the cream in his hand, waiting to see if he'd made it milky enough. Cole had held it up to Noah's wall and declared it perfect. And it was.

They were both in their boxers and nothing else, hair sex-mussed and sporting a few hickeys on their chests. Noah looked freshly fucked, which he was, and delicious. Cole wanted to press him against the counter and drop to his knees, but that last orgasm had hurt. They needed to recharge a bit before he made wild, crazy, best-ever love to Noah again. But he would. Soon.

Noah poured his own coffee and joined Cole shoulder to shoulder as they leaned against the kitchen island and watched the sunlight dazzle the top of the cornfield. "It really is gorgeous," Cole said softly. "It's peaceful."

Noah nodded. "That's what I thought, too. I've spent a lot of days out on that porch, trying to think things through. Figure myself out. What I wanted. Ask those big, scary questions."

"Found any answers?" Cole swung his hip gently into Noah's.

Noah turned and kissed him, a chaste, soft press of his warm lips to Cole's. "I think I have."

Cole smiled and kissed him back—

The lock turned a half second before the front door swung open. "*Dad!*" Katie called. "I'm home!"

Noah flew backward, dropping his coffee cup on the kitchen floor. It shattered, hot coffee splattering their feet, their shins. Cole danced away, hissing as Noah froze, eyes wide, staring down the hallway leading to the front door.

Panicked eyes darted to Cole. "Go!" Noah hissed. "Hide!"

Hide where? Katie was ten feet and one corner away, and he was mostly naked, covered in Noah's dried come, with hickeys on his chest—

No time to think. He tore across the living room and thundered up the stairs.

"DAD?" Katie padded down the hallway to the kitchen. "Is someone here? Did something fall?" She frowned, then jerked when she saw him crouching on the floor in just his boxers, wiping up spilled coffee with a dish towel. "Uh, Dad?"

"I didn't know you were coming home. What time is it?" Noah gritted his teeth. The world spun. He couldn't stand. His legs were shaking. Fuck, Cole's come was still leaking out of him. He was still wet. He leaned forward, bracing himself on his palm as his vision went dark on the edges. A sliver of porcelain dug into his flesh.

"It's early. I set my alarm. I wanted to see you before you went back to the office." Katie went to the drawer where he kept their towels and pulled one out. "I thought we could have breakfast. Besides, I need to get my textbooks for class today."

Katie's shoes skittered to a stop. Noah closed his eyes.

"Dad?"

Not now, please, not now, not like this, not like this not like this—

"Is... someone here?"

He stood slowly, using the counter to help him when his legs almost buckled. He left the towel soaking on the floor and leaned against the island.

Katie's eyes went as wide as dinner plates when she finally saw him. Her jaw dropped. She blinked, looked away. She turned crimson. God, he was nearly naked in front of his daughter, with another man all over him.

"Um, should I—" Katie's eyes flicked over the kitchen and

beyond, taking in Noah's shirt on the couch, his tossed-off undershirt. Cole's laptop case.

And then Cole's discarded shirt.

Oh, shit. No no no no no—

Katie's head spun as she whirled on Noah. Her mortification and embarrassment had been replaced with shock, which melted into fury, into rage. Her eyes glittered, daggers flying as she focused on the hickey Cole had left below his collarbone.

"Katie..."

A floorboard creaked overhead, in Noah's bedroom, where Cole must be getting dressed. Katie's eyes whipped up.

Noah buried his face in his hands.

"Dad, who's here?" Katie backed up, sliding down the kitchen counter. Sliding away from him. "Who is here?" She was almost yelling now. Panic sliced over her features, filled her eyes. Her hands gripped the dish towel, practically tearing it in two.

"Katie..." His voice broke. His hands fell to the counter as he roared through his clenched teeth. Spinning, he punched the fridge, once, twice, a third time, until his knuckles split and warm blood flowed over his hand.

Katie screamed. Noah grabbed the fridge before he fell. He pressed his forehead to the stainless steel. There wasn't enough air—Jesus, there wasn't enough oxygen to breathe. He suffocating, he was going to pass out—

Hands grabbed him and guided him down. His vision swam, but as he fell to his ass, a shape formed in front of him. Tall, dressed in chinos and an undershirt. Blond, messy hair. Both hands holding him steady, repeating his name. *Noah. Noah. Noah.*

Cole. Cole was holding on to him. Cole was saying, "Noah. Noah, look at me." Cole was in his kitchen.

Which meant Katie had seen Cole now. His gaze shifted over Cole's shoulder. There she was, standing by the island, both hands covering her mouth as she stared at him.

He'd never wanted to see that look in her eyes. Never.

Noah's eyes slipped closed as he heard her take off, heard her run up the stairs and slam the door to her bedroom so hard the walls shook. Cole's hands squeezed his shoulders. "Noah…"

"You need to leave," he croaked.

The hand stroking his arm stilled. "What?"

"Take my keys and take the car." It was almost impossible to speak, to force the words out through his clenched throat and his broken heart. "I need you to leave. Right now."

Cole inhaled. He dropped his hand from Noah's shoulder. "Um…"

He pushed himself up, the blood on his hand making his grip slick. He stared at Cole, the man he wanted so desperately to love, and raised his chin. "I need to talk to my daughter. *Please*." He wanted to love Cole, but he already did love Katie, and now she was hurting. Hurting because of him.

Cole turned, grabbed the keys from Noah's bowl, and walked to the door.

It closed behind him with a soft, almost silent *snick*.

Noah's legs gave out, and he slid to the kitchen floor again, gasping, screaming into the tile as he squeezed his eyes closed and his heart ripped in two.

16

HE SHOWERED before he spoke to his daughter.

It was one of the most humbling experiences of his life, bracing himself against his shower wall, face buried in his elbow as he scrubbed at his sore asshole with a bar of soap. Another man's come was inside him, covering him, and he needed to talk to his daughter.

His eyes were red and puffy when he saw himself in the mirror as he quickly dried off. He left his hair disheveled. No time. He threw on jeans—gingerly; Jesus, he really was sore—and a T-shirt and headed down the hall to Katie's room.

It was like walking to his own execution. Not even walking into the courtroom when he and Lilly got divorced was as bad. Not half as bad.

"Katie?" He knocked softly. "We have to talk."

Silence.

"Katie, I'm coming in."

She was sitting on her bed, arms and legs crossed, her old teddy bear tight to her chest. Her own eyes were red and puffy, and the sleeves of her sweatshirt, pulled down over her hands, bore long streaks of wetness, as if she'd been rubbing her eyes and nose. Seeing her made his heart break all over again, and he nearly retreated, nearly backed away and fled to Alaska to bury himself in the wild where he could be eaten by a bear and never have to see his daughter's brokenhearted expression turn his way ever again.

But no. He sighed and walked in, trying to look braver than he felt. He pulled out the pink plastic swivel desk chair with the ridiculous shag back that she'd wanted and sat down. They'd gone shopping the weekend it had become semiofficial that she was going to be living with him full time, at least on a trial basis. She needed a new bedroom, something that was hers, something that was home. The more he'd made fun of that chair, the more it seemed she'd had to have it.

He plucked at a long string of neon pink fuzz, twirling it between his fingers. "Katie—"

She whipped her furious gaze his way. Her glare was cutting, just like her mother's. He almost flinched. "Did you ditch me last night so you could have sex?"

"*What?*"

"Did you send me to Evelyn's so you could come home and have sex? Am I cramping your style living here, Dad? Am I butting in on all the sex you could be having?"

"Whoa! Whoa!" He held up his hands, a surrender and a "Back off" all in one. He frowned. "Katie, I did not send you away last night so I could have sex. We were working!"

She snorted.

"We *were* working. This case is very scary. John was—" His throat closed. He looked down, spinning the pink fuzz around and around his index finger. "The killer targets young women. You're younger than the victims, but I'm your father. And, from the very first girl he murdered, all the way until last night, there hasn't been a night that's gone by when I didn't have a spike of fear that you could be—" His throat closed again, and this time, he couldn't breathe. He turned away. His lungs burned. Visions of his nightmares, of Katie dead, Katie strangled, Katie lying with her arms and legs splayed out, that broken-doll twist of her neck—

"Dad…" Katie's plaintive voice finally broke through the white noise. "I'm okay, Dad."

"I'm always afraid for you, K-Bear. Always."

He heard her sniff. "Yeah, well, you must like *him* more than you like me," she groused. "You at least wanted to be with him."

Noah groaned.

"How long have you been keeping this a secret from me?"

"This?"

She flung her hands out, her eyes wide. "*This*, Dad. You! Being gay!"

He flinched. The pink fuzz wrapped around and around until it snapped in half. "Katie, I barely figured it out myself."

She stared. "What, you just woke up yesterday and suddenly decided you were gay?"

"No." He swallowed. "I've… wondered for a while about myself. I had all these thoughts and these feelings, and I…" He shrugged, deflating. "I'm gay. I'm gay, Katie. And I just figured that out for sure recently." He almost laughed. This was never how he thought he'd come out to his daughter. "Last night was the first time I—" His mouth snapped shut.

She blinked. "So, what, you meet Dr. Kennedy and then all of a sudden you're sleeping with him?"

Oh boy. "Cole and I… We really hit it off."

"Dr. Kennedy, Dad." She shot him a look.

He shot one right back. "Cole—Dr. Kennedy—is a great guy. Whatever anger you have, however mad you are, that anger is for me. Not him. He didn't do anything to you, K-Bear."

She crossed her arms again and glared, her face scrunching up like she was desperately, desperately trying not to cry. "He's done something to you!" she snapped. "You didn't use to push me away, or send me away, or not want to spend time with me! You've never chosen anyone instead of me, but now, apparently all you want is him! You don't even want me around anymore!"

"Katie!" He jumped to his feet. The pink monstrosity wheeled away, bouncing off her bedroom wall. "That's not true at all! Jesus, that's not true." He strode to her, sitting on the edge of her bed. "There is nothing and no one in this world that is more important to me, or that I love more, than you. You are my life." He reached for her. Wrapped his big hand around her wet, limp sweatshirt sleeve. "K-Bear, I wasn't going to do anything. I wasn't ever going to try to meet someone, or sleep with someone, or do anything, because I didn't want *this* to happen. I never wanted to upset you. I never wanted to see you look at me like you're looking at me right now. You are *everything* to me, Katherine. My whole entire world, and I was never, ever going to jeopardize that or put anything before you."

Tears were rolling freely down her cheeks, fat, wet, heavy drops that rained from her quivering chin. "Then—" Her voice shook.

"I didn't plan on meeting Cole," he breathed. "It just happened."

She cried, burying her face in her teddy bear. *This is why you should never have tried. This is why you should never have left your hotel room. This is why you should never have wanted to know.*

Eventually, Katie sat back, rubbing her running nose on her sleeve and sinking into the pillows behind her. "Does Mom know?"

He shook his head. "No one knows. No one except me, Cole, and now you."

She took a deep breath. Her hair was braided, one long French braid for cheer practice that ran almost to the center of her back. She pulled the end over her shoulder and chewed on it, gnawing on the loose strands poking out of the hair tie. "Is this why you're always depressed?"

He stared at her, speechless, for a moment. "I was unhappy with myself for a long time," he said slowly. "It's hard to pretend to be someone I'm not, to ignore how I was feeling. What I was wanting. But I've never been unhappy being your dad."

"I wondered about you and Mom." She shrugged, one shoulder rising and falling. "I mean, I saw it. You were miserable. She was angry. It was never happy in that house, you know? I was so relieved when you guys finally split."

"Katie—"

"Dad." She waved him off. "I thought you were sad and unhappy because of Mom being angry all the time. I used to get so mad at her for yelling at you."

"She was angry because she wasn't happy, either. She was married to a man who—" He blanched. "Who couldn't love her the way she deserved. That's not her fault."

Katie said nothing. She turned her hand over in his hold and laid her palm against his.

He squeezed her hand so fucking hard she winced. "I'm sorry, Katie," he whispered. "I'm sorry about this morning. I'm sorry about last night. I was *not* getting rid of you to have sex." Even saying it was shredding him from the inside. *There goes custody when Lilly hears about this.* "After yesterday, and John, and the crime scene—" He stopped. Closed his eyes. "I just wanted a tiny piece of happiness. I was being selfish."

She stared at him, still biting her lower lip.

"I invited him over, and it *wasn't* for sex. That wasn't my intention. I like him, K-Bear, a lot, and I wanted to spend time with him. But things just…"

She rolled her eyes. "Dad, they teach us this in school. Things happen. One thing leads to another." She waved her free hand, gesturing at nothing. "That's why you're supposed to make better choices, blah blah."

"Well, you can think of me as a perfect example of that." He scrubbed his hand over his face as his cheeks burned. Jesus, would the mortification never end? "I'm so embarrassed. I'm so ashamed of myself."

"Why?"

"You caught me having sex—"

"Caught you after you had sex."

"Close enough. I'm your father. You caught me with Cole. I had no idea you were coming home."

"I mean, that was the point." She tugged on her sweatshirt sleeves. "I wanted to surprise you. I thought we could have pancakes." She shrugged. Frowned. "Are you ashamed of being gay? Or of him?"

How the hell was he supposed to answer that? Noah took a breath, tried to speak. Stopped. Exhaled. Tried again. Failed.

Katie stared.

"I'm not ashamed of Cole. I'm not ashamed of how I feel about him, or about being gay. I am ashamed that you found out the way you did. I'd hoped that you'd be in college before you found out."

"That's *bullshit*, Dad!"

"Katie!"

"Really? You're going to get mad at me for cursing? *Today*?" Her head wove back and forth in that way unique to teen girls. He never understood how they did that. "It *is* bullshit, and that pisses me off!" she said, her voice rising. "Why would you want to keep something like this from me?"

"That's not what I was—"

"That's exactly what you were doing! You think I wouldn't want to know? Don't you think I want to see you happy?"

He blinked.

"I thought you were miserable because of the divorce! I thought Mom ripped out your heart and you were so fucking upset you could never get over her!"

"Uh... no. Not at all."

"How could you think you could keep something like this from me for years? Why do you think I wouldn't want to know?"

"I saw your face downstairs, Katie, okay? I saw how you feel about it—"

"I was shocked! That's how kids react when they see their parents having sex. You had hickeys on your chest!"

"Oh, God, don't remind me."

"Did you really think I'd react badly?" Her voice was still raised, almost shrill.

"K-Bear, I'm not sure I'd call this a textbook-perfect reaction."

"I'm not sure I'd call today a textbook-perfect coming-out to your daughter, either, Dad."

He held up his hands again, surrendering. He sighed. "You're not exactly taking this great. And I get it. I'm not blaming you for that. I handled this horribly—"

"I'm upset because you hid this from me! You hid who you are, and you hid how you felt, and you hid who Dr. Kennedy was and what he means to you. You lied to me!"

"Katie, I wasn't trying to lie to you."

"But you still did." She deflated, curling over her teddy bear. "It's like you didn't trust me."

He stared at her. His voice was frozen. His teeth ground together. "I was scared," he whispered. "I thought you wouldn't want anything to do with me anymore if you found out. I... thought I'd never see you again."

It was her turn to go still, to blink at him with wide, tear-soaked eyes. "Dad... did you really think I'd stop loving you?"

He stiffened. It felt like she'd grabbed his heart and yanked it, still beating, from his chest. He clenched his teeth, tried to breathe through the pain. He couldn't say the words. He nodded instead.

"Dad..."

"That's exactly what I was afraid of. I thought you'd hate me when you found out."

"Dad, no." She crawled across her bed, collapsing against him. He pulled her close, burying his face in her hair as she grabbed him around the waist. "Never. Dad…"

The tears came then, for both of them. He sobbed, wailing into her hair as he held her, cradling her like she was six months old instead of sixteen years. She buried her face in his chest and wrapped both arms around his waist, her teddy bear squished between them, her tears soaking his T-shirt. He ran his hand over her hair, pressing snot-and-tear-soaked kisses to her crown, her temple, the sides of her wet face. He apologized, told her he loved her, told her he was so, so sorry.

They ended up sitting side by side, holding hands, Katie's teddy bear balanced on their legs. "I never want to lose you, K-Bear," he said, his voice hoarse. "And I was scared I would. I never wanted to meet anyone because I was too terrified I'd lose you."

"Don't be stupid." She sniffed. "I'm not homophobic or anything. I mean, I know, like, four gay people on the football team alone. And one of the cheerleaders is a lesbian. It's really, *really* not that big a deal anymore. Only you old people act like it's the end of the world to be gay." She rolled her eyes. Squeezed his hand. "I want you to be happy. Don't not do things because of me, God…"

She went quiet. He could see her thinking. "Dr. Kennedy must be pretty special, then? If you weren't meeting anyone 'cause of me, but…"

"Yeah. He's really special, K-Bear. I think… I think I could be happy with him."

She smiled, faintly. "He's kind of cool. I mean, he had that awesome story about catching that serial killer."

"That was gross."

"It was awesome. He's super smart. Smarter than you." She nudged his shoulder.

"He is definitely smarter than I am."

Katie bit her lip. "Could I, like, actually meet him? Get to know him, kinda? If you and he are going to, you know, date, or whatever, then I think I should know him, right?"

He had two equal reactions to her questions, opposite forces trying to tear him apart. He pushed one down as ruthlessly as he could. "You want to give him your seal of approval?" He tried to smile.

"Who else is going to look out for you? I have to give him the big speech, right? The one you're going to give to all my boyfriends? I have to tell him to treat you right or I'll cut him up and bury him in the cornfield."

Noah laughed, and at the same time, his heart, so fragile, so broken already, cracked again. What were he and Cole? Were they dating? What was two perfect nights and a handful of fumbling days?

He focused back on Katie. "*All* your boyfriends? How many boyfriends have you had, miss?"

She gave him another look. "None, Dad. I'm not dating anyone."

"Not even Trevor?"

"Ew, no. Definitely not Trevor. He's an idiot."

"You're right about that. He is an idiot. And an asshole." She shook her head, rolling her eyes and smiling at the same time. He took a deep breath. "This is the day for mortifying and embarrassing conversations, so I'm just going to blunder right into this next topic. K-Bear, have you had sex yet?" He squeezed his eyes closed and scrunched up his face. "If you have, then let's talk about how to be safe—"

"*Da-ad*," she screeched. "Oh my God, no! I have not!"

"Look, I clearly cannot throw stones—"

"Dad! No!" She groaned, exhaling through her clenched teeth as she glared at the ceiling. "Look. What have you been telling me since I was, like, five? 'Make good choices.' Like, every day, since I was old enough to walk. That's what you told me after you let me touch the stove when Mom wasn't home."

"You didn't touch the stove again, did you?"

She glared. "You always told me to make good choices. And I know it must be a total and complete shock to you, but... I've actually *listened* to you. And Mom. I've put a lot of thought into it. And, yeah, half of my friends are having sex—"

"Jesus Christ."

"But I'm not. I'm not ready. And that's my choice." She sliced her hands, once again covered in the cuffs of her sweatshirt, through the air as if to say, "End of."

He pulled her close in a one-armed hug and kissed her hair. "When you think you're ready, will you come to me? I promise not to judge you. I just want to make sure you're safe when you decide it's time. Get you protection. Birth control. Whatever you need. And... maybe talk to you a little bit about it."

She melted into him, laying her head on his shoulder. "Yeah, Dad. I will. But it will be a while. I'm nowhere close to ready. I promise."

He kissed her hair. "How did you grow up so fast? How did you get so wise?"

She groaned. "I'm not that wise, Dad. Pre-calc is still kicking my ass."

"Language, K-Bear."

She pretended to look guilty for a half second. "Can you help me with my homework? And can we eat breakfast? I really did come home to see you. I don't have school today, just cheer. I thought we could spend some time together."

Andy Garrett was cooling his heels in their cell, and Judge Vargas hadn't yet signed the search warrant. There weren't any 9-1-1 calls on his cell phone from the night before or that morning. For now, for a few hours, he could be a dad again. He smiled. "Yeah, K-Bear. Let's go downstairs and make pancakes. And I'll do my best to help you with your pre-calc."

She threw her arms around him, squeezing him too tight. He couldn't breathe, but he didn't say a word, just hugged her back. "I love you, Dad."

"I love you, too, K-Bear. Always."

17

HEY. Can you come back over?

Cole froze, staring at his cell phone. He'd been pacing since he got out of the shower, even as he dressed, buttoning up his shirt and rolling up his cuffs. What the hell was going to happen now? All Noah wanted was to keep his sexuality private, to shield his daughter, to manage his coming-out slowly and steadily. Privately.

And then that daughter had nearly found them both half naked, covered in each other's come, in Noah's kitchen.

He hadn't looked at Katie, but he'd heard her screams, heard the sound of her running away, storming upstairs. And he'd seen Noah's devastated, destroyed expression. The look of a broken man.

Was it fate that kept turning their perfect nights against them? Were they really, truly not meant to be together?

Nothing good is ever easy. Isn't that how the saying went?

Yeah, but how did that cover the man he—well, the man he was falling for's *daughter* crashing their morning afterglow?

He stared at Noah's text. Could the man be any vaguer? Any less informative? Was he bringing the car back to drop off and leave forever? Was he coming back to hang out? Who was he going to find when he got there? Noah from last night? Or Noah who ignored his existence when they met—again— at the Des Moines FBI office?

I need your address, he texted back. He'd been in too much of a fog to write it down when he drove away. How he'd made it back to the hotel was a mystery. He didn't even remember the drive.

Noah texted, and Cole grabbed his laptop bag and the case files and got into Noah's SUV. Ten minutes later, he pulled into Noah's driveway. His phone buzzed. *We're on the back porch.*

What the... Cole stared at his phone, then at Noah's house. Was that a signal that he should join them? Or leave the car and walk away, call a Lyft, disappear—that Noah was so uninterested in seeing him again that he was hiding in the backyard?

Fuck it. Noah could tell him to leave to his face. Again. He slid out of the car and jogged up the porch, tentatively knocking on the front door before testing the knob. It opened, and he slipped inside, calling out, "Hello? Noah?"

The back door was open. "Out here," Noah called. He waved to Cole from the deck, where he was sitting across from Katie at a picnic table. She'd changed into her cheer outfit, and her long hair was pulled up in a high ponytail, the ends catching on the wind and drifting. A textbook was open between them, Katie hunched over a binder as she scribbled away.

Cole walked slowly to the door, staring at Noah, his eyebrows raised.

Noah smiled.

Cole's heart melted as his lungs started to work again. "Hey," he said, smiling back. He shoved his hands in his pockets and leaned against the glass.

Katie turned to him, her brows raised and forehead furrowed, an absolute mirror image of the way her father had looked at him. God, they were so alike, reflections through time. Even the way they sat, elbows spread wide on the tabletop, leaning forward. The sun shining on their coffee-brown strands, glittering mahogany and cherry highlights sparking. The colors of the moment froze in his mind, a perfect snapshot: emerald grass, crystal sky, golden corn. Two faces gazing at him, soft smiles warming their features.

"Hey, Dr. Kennedy." Katie waved, her smile turning shy. Her pencil eraser tapped a fast rhythm on her notebook paper.

Noah scooted over on his side of the picnic bench, making room for Cole. "We're doing Katie's pre-calc homework."

Katie rolled her eyes. "We're *trying* to do pre-calc homework. Neither of us are any good at this stuff, so it's like the blind leading the blind."

"I'm pretty good at math. I did a lot of statistical analyses in grad school. It's been a while since I did any calculus, but I might be able to help."

Katie wordlessly slid her textbook to him and jabbed her finger at one of the problems. It *had* been a while, but the mechanics of it started coming back. "Okay, start here." He slid her binder to him and set up the first step of the equation. "Can you solve this piece?"

She started working, and they went back and forth, breaking the equations down into smaller elements until she started to outpace him, move ahead to the next step without prompting. "You've got it." He grinned.

"Dad, you're fired," Katie said, scribbling formulas. She didn't look up. "Dr. Kennedy is going to help me with all my math from now on."

Noah chuckled. His hand stroked over Cole's lower back, out of sight. "Fine by me. You inherited my genetics in the math department, K-Bear. I'm sorry."

"Mom's not any better." Katie rolled her eyes. "At least you try to help me. She was always too busy."

"Being an AUSA is hard work." Katie didn't seem impressed with Noah's attempts to defend his ex-wife. Cole kept his mouth shut. Noah leaned into him, their shoulders brushing. "Have you eaten?"

Had he eaten? He arched an eyebrow at Noah and shook his head. How could he have eaten after how their morning had ended?

"I'll get you something." Noah rose and disappeared into the kitchen. Through the windows, Cole could see him moving around, grabbing a plate and reaching into the refrigerator.

Katie's pencil stopped scratching over her paper. She turned to him, her focus suddenly transferred from her pre-calc to Cole. She stared, searching, the intensity of her hazel-honey gaze identical to Noah's. As with Noah, Cole was helpless before that look.

"My dad really likes you." Her eyes darted from his face to his chest to his hair and back to his eyes.

"I really like your dad."

She bit her lip. Looked back at her textbook. A breeze curled the page around her fist.

"You know what I've learned about your dad? There is one thing that his whole life revolves around. One thing he loves more than anything else." Brunette strands swept across Katie's eyes. "You." He smiled.

She tried to smile back, looking down as she fiddled with her pencil. "I want him to be happy," she said. Her foot was jiggling, bouncing up and down beneath the table enough to rock the deck. "He hasn't been happy for a while. Not really. I thought I could help him, kinda."

"You're his daughter. Everything about you makes him happy."

She snorted. "Not everything."

"Well, he really doesn't like Trevor."

Katie rolled her eyes, but she was smiling. "Trevor is an idiot."

Cole almost reached for her but stopped. His hand landed on the table. "You make your father very happy. He has been unhappy in some ways, not because of you—"

"Because he wasn't being himself. And he didn't have anyone." She looked away, her jaw jutting forward as she watched the corn sway. "He needs that," she said. "He needs someone to love him."

"You are very observant, Katie."

"Not really. I didn't know my dad was gay."

"He was hiding it. He did everything he could to cover up who he was."

Her gaze turned back to him. "I want my dad to be happy."

He heard what she wasn't saying, saw the words as if they were being beamed out of her eyes. Fear nearly choked her, made her lips quiver. *I don't want to lose my dad.*

"We can make him happy. You already do. Maybe I can a bit, too?" He laid his hand over hers, squeezing once before letting go. "I'd like the chance to try, together with you."

She smiled, very slowly, before turning back to her homework.

Noah appeared, sliding his phone into his pocket as he balanced a cup of coffee and a plate with a grilled ham-and-cheese sandwich. Cole tried to smother a smile as Noah passed him the sandwich and coffee. Noah sat beside Katie, straddling the bench and facing her as he reviewed her homework. Not that he knew what he was reviewing, Cole thought. He was just checking that it looked complete and that all the assigned problems were done. He faked it well, though, nodding seriously as Katie described the way Cole had explained the equations. Katie had perked up as soon as Noah had reappeared, like a flower blooming in sunlight.

Noah beamed at his daughter as she snapped the textbook closed. "Great job, K-Bear."

"Dr. Kennedy helped a lot." She smiled at him. He tried to smile back, around his mouthful of sandwich. "Thanks."

"I'm proud of you." Noah kissed her hair.

Cole recognized the shift in Noah's gaze, his eyes tightening, the darkness descending. He waited as Noah pressed his lips together. "The warrant's been signed," Noah said, speaking to both Katie and Cole. "The team is starting the search of his house right now."

Katie sagged. "So you have to go to work?"

"Yeah. We have to go to work. I don't know how long we'll be."

She shrugged. "I've got cheer in a few hours. I won't be done until six."

"Well, I'll make sure I'm done at six, too." Noah reached for her and took her hand. "Dinner tonight? To make up for last night"

"Which part of last night?" Katie grinned. "Or… this morning?"

Noah flushed, turning a color that matched his shirt, something deep and dark that reminded Cole of red wine. Or spilled blood. "Katie."

"Just teasing you, Dad. Yeah, dinner sounds good." She grabbed her book and binder and stood. "Can you drop me off at the school on your way in? I'll hang out at the library until cheer starts."

They trooped out to Noah's SUV after Cole shoved the rest of the sandwich down his throat and chugged his creamy coffee. Katie packed her cheer bag and backpack, and Noah carried the case files for Cole. It was domestic, and quaint, and paternal, and Cole had no idea how to feel as they drove to the high school and parked in front to let Katie out. He rolled down his window and waved to her. "Have a good afternoon, Katie."

"Thanks, Dr. Kennedy."

Noah had climbed out of the SUV and stood by the engine, flipping his keys in one hand. He had that scrunched-up look to his face, partially hidden by his sunglasses. Katie joined him, a mirror image, all the way down to the furrow of their noses and the angle of their heads.

"I know it's not cool at your age to hug your parent in public," Noah said softly. "But I could use a hug today, K-Bear."

"Dad." She wrapped him up in a huge hug, both arms around his shoulders, knuckles almost white where she gripped him. He squeezed back, his face in her ponytail. *Thank you*, Cole saw Noah whisper.

Katie pulled back, rearranging her cheer skirt and leggings, hugging her textbook to her chest. "Love you."

"Love you, K-Bear. See you tonight."

18

THE DETRITUS of Andy Garrett's life was laid out on the conference room table.

Photos taken during the search of his townhome showed a life coming unglued. He'd punched his bathroom mirror out at some point. Pieces of glass covered the master bathroom. Blood stains swirled like high-water marks in his sink. A pile of empty liquor bottles squatted in the corner of his living room. His sheets were covered in bloodstains, some fresher than others. Dirt from his boots matched the Olson cornfield and yard. Dried corn husks and wisps of corn silk were scattered in his living room and near his front door, like he'd tracked it in and hadn't cared.

A picture of Jessie was taped to one of the shards of Garrett's bathroom mirror. Jessie, smiling for the camera, a close-up, a selfie. The flash was too bright, and she was washed out, but it was her. Very much alive.

There was another photo of a girl, a different one, torn up and shoved in the back of Andy's nightstand. When the detectives taped it back together, they were staring at a picture of Monica Venneslund, the fifth of the Coed Killer's victims.

What they hadn't found was the missing crystal sheriff's

star, the weapon that had most likely killed Bart. And they hadn't found Garrett's service weapon, though they found about six hundred nine-millimeter rounds packed into the top shelf of his closet.

The manila folder with the report from the tip line sat beside the call logs. Noah flipped it open. A transcript from one of the calls was printed on FBI letterhead.

Hey, I'm with the Boone County Sheriff's, it read. *I want to stay anonymous. If this is nothing, I don't want to cause something. But if it's something... Well, I saw Sheriff Olson and Deputy Garrett have a big fight last week. They were out past Luther, pulled over near the river on 270th. I saw Garrett shouting at the sheriff. He was real mad. Real mad. And Sheriff Olson came over and shoved him, hard. He fell on his ass and stayed there, glaring at the sheriff. Sheriff Olson walked away from him and got back in his truck, and the next thing I saw was the sheriff speeding away, back to Luther. I filed that under not my business, but, well. Thought you should know.*

Next in line, after the transcript, was Garrett's military service record. His DD 214 with his honorable discharge. Four-year simple enlistment in the Marines, basic rifleman. Nothing distinguishing about his service. Nothing detrimental. He was a solid marine, according to the record. He'd enlisted a week after Kyle and Shelly were shot and killed in Ames.

It was what happened before his enlistment that commanded Noah's attention.

He'd never known Garrett had attended Iowa State for two years. Or that he'd studied criminal justice, earning straight Bs for his entire time at the college. Even all the way through the first six murders.

Their names were imprinted on the inside of Noah's skull.
Kelsey Cohen. Iowa State.
Ellen Kemp. Iowa State.
Paige Blanton. Simpson College.
Lauren O'Neil. Faith Baptist.
Monica Venneslund. Iowa State.

Stacy Shepherd. Iowa State.

And now, three more.

Kimberly Foster. Faith Baptist.

Jessie Olson. Iowa State.

Molly Hayes. University of Iowa.

And their fathers and families.

The University of Iowa didn't fit with the Coed Killer's pattern of sticking to Highway 69 and the Des Moines colleges. The University of Iowa was halfway across the state, between Cedar Rapids and Davenport. But Molly was living at home for the summer, with John and the rest of the family. And Garrett knew her, knew John, knew where they lived. She'd also been in the news, like all the other victims. If Garrett had wanted to kill a family, was it inconceivable he could have picked John Hayes's?

Noah rubbed his hand over his eyes as Cole came up behind him. "What do you think?" Noah asked.

"Pretty damning evidence," Cole said softly.

"But no murder weapon," Jacob said.

The whole task force was with them. Sheriff Clarke was leading a team of two Des Moines police officers on a timeline reconstruction of Andy's Iowa State classes, while Deputy Holland, Deputy Santos, and Deputy Nichols were cross-referencing each of the six original victims' classes with Garrett's. Professor Pflueger appeared in the overlap more than once.

The only county not represented on the task force, for the moment, was Boone. Garrett was still in his holding cell, and his backup…

Deputy Venneslund was still in Noah's office.

"Venneslund?" Cole had asked Noah in private, after Deputy Venneslund met them, stiff and uncomfortable and pale, at the elevator that morning. "Monica Venneslund's *father?*"

"Yes. He was the one who did the welfare check at Monica's apartment when she didn't show up for her classes. Finding her like that almost broke him. It did break his wife—and ended their marriage. She's gone, moved to California. Last anyone heard, she was drinking at the end of Huntington Pier, hoping the waves would take her away. John helped him stay on his feet. And we're lucky he did. Venneslund's a great guy. Great deputy. I've worked with him a dozen times, and I'll work with him any day." He'd flinched. "Except today."

Deputy Venneslund had followed the two of them into Noah's office before his stoic facade slipped. He sank into one of the chairs crowded in front of Noah's desk, heaving great gasps as he clenched his Stetson, almost crushing the brim. "I heard," he'd managed to choke out, "they found Monica's photo in Andy's apartment?"

Noah had crouched in front of him. He'd grabbed Venneslund's wrists, steadied the man. "We're going to figure out what's going on. We're going to get answers from Garrett about everything. About Bart, and Jessie, and what he had in his apartment. And if he was responsible, in any way, for anything that happened back then."

Venneslund had sat back, his eyes glazing over as he retreated into the past. He stared at nothing, at the memories he kept on a loop in the back of his mind. "All this time," he'd whispered. "I *trained* Andy. I was his training partner."

"Why don't you stay here? I know Boone County sent you as the task force rep, and I know you've wanted to be involved in getting justice for Monica, but…"

"Noah, you've got to keep me away from that room." He'd nodded to the conference room and the bustle of agents and deputies and police officers hauling in boxes of evidence taken from Garrett's townhome. "Keep me away from him. If he hurt my little girl…"

There was a particular agony that erupted when you watched a man break. It was something wholly alien, an excruciating horror reflected when you witnessed a man fracture on the fault lines of his soul. Noah had felt it six years ago, watching as Deputy Venneslund was escorted out of the morgue, and he felt the echoes of it again in his office as Venneslund curled over his knees and tried to choke back his sobs.

"Stay here," Noah had said again, squeezing his shoulder. "As long as you need. Then go home."

"Promise me, Noah. Promise me you'll find out if that son of a bitch did it."

"I promise."

Venneslund had held his gaze, tears like waves rocking in his eyes, and nodded.

Now it was time to try to put the pieces together.

Who was Andy Garrett?

GARRETT WAS in almost the same position they'd left him in the night before. His head hung as he slumped forward, staring at the floor. He'd been changed out of his dirt-caked jeans, blood-spattered T-shirt, and plaid overshirt and into a jumpsuit. His hair, usually trim and neat, was wild, sticking up in every direction. But it was his eyes that seared Noah, the empty holes where his soul used to be.

He stared at Garrett, then flicked his gaze to the one-way mirror. Cole was in the observation room, along with half the task force. Checking Garrett's answers, if he gave any, against the facts they'd compiled. Would Garrett lie? Would he try to evade the truth?

What was the truth?

"Hello, Andy," Noah said. "How are you doing today?"

Garrett didn't budge. One finger twitched on the steel table. He stared beyond Noah, beyond the plain wall of the interrogation room.

Noah set down three items: Garrett's call records, all his

calls to Jessie Olson highlighted across the pages and pages of billing; an evidence photo taken of Jessie's picture on the shard of mirror glass; and the results of the DNA swab from Jessie Olson's lips. He tapped the last. "Can you tell me why your DNA is on Jessie Olson?"

Garrett's Adam's apple rose. His chin trembled. "Because I kissed her," he rumbled. His voice was like a freight train barreling through midnight.

"You kissed her. When?"

"That night," he whispered.

"That night. The night she died?"

Garrett nodded. His eyes closed. He looked down. His expression cracked, and he clenched and squeezed and seemed to wipe himself thin as the tears started to come, tiny, snuffling sounds that seemed like breaking glass.

"Did you kiss her when you strangled her? Is that when you—"

"No!" Garrett roared, suddenly not crying but raging, bellowing at Noah and lunging forward as far as his shackles would allow. "No! *I didn't kill her!*"

Noah blinked. Behind Garrett, Cole and Jacob appeared at the door, ready to burst in. He shook his head, a tiny movement. Cole scowled.

"When did you see Jessie that night?"

Garrett slumped back, the rage vanishing as quickly as it had appeared. "Just after midnight. I stopped by during my shift. I knew her dad wasn't home, and neither was her mom."

"Her dad. Sheriff Bart Olson." Garrett's jaw clenched. He nodded. "Why did you want to see Jessie without her dad around?"

Silence.

"Did Jessie want to see you that night?"

Garrett frowned. "Of course she did. We were dating."

Noah's eyebrows shot straight up. "You were dating? Wow.

That's news to me. News to everyone, I think. When did that start?"

Shrugging, Garrett shifted. Looked away. "Couple months ago. Maybe six. We met at that BBQ, the one your boss threw."

It was Noah's turn to be silent. He waited, counting down from one hundred until his throat unclenched. "Special Agent John Hayes. My boss. One of my close friends."

"Yeah. Him." Garrett's eyes skittered away from Noah's.

One thing at a time. Noah took a deep breath. Thought of Katie. Thought of Cole.

"Is that why you've been calling Jessie nonstop for months?" He pushed the call records forward, flipping through the pages for Garrett. Nearly all of his calls were to Jessie. The rest were calls for pizza and Chinese delivery, calls to the Boone County switchboard, and two calls to a sex chat line.

"That was our system."

"Your system?"

"Yeah. See, Jessie's dad didn't want us talking, so we developed a system. He kept an eye on her phone and her calls out, so she couldn't call me. But I could call her, especially if I didn't let it ring past one ring. So that's what I did. She'd get to see that I called, that I was thinking of her." He smiled again.

"That sounds a little bit creepy, Andy. It kind of sounds like you were stalking her."

Storm clouds reappeared on Garrett's face. He scowled at Noah, leaning forward, hands clenched into fists. "We had a system," he growled. "She couldn't call me, but she was a computer whiz, you know? Her minor was in computer science. She wanted to get into IT services for ag business, revolutionize the industry and the way they use computers. Smart stuff. Way smarter than I could understand."

Noah's gaze flicked to the one-way mirror. Was any of that

true? He didn't know what Jessie Olson's minor at Iowa State was.

Garrett kept going. "She had a little website set up. Just her and me used it. The system was, I would call her, let her know I was thinking of her, and she would post on the website. Messages to me. Things like that."

"What kind of messages?"

"Things like she was thinking of me. That she loved me. That she wanted to see me."

"She loved you?"

"Yes. And I loved her."

Noah nodded. "Was this how you arranged to see her the night she was murdered?"

Scowling, Garrett nodded. He said nothing.

"You see," Noah said, exhaling, "the thing is, we haven't found any website Jessie made. We haven't found any evidence of any website you guys could exchange messages on. We've been through her laptop and her dad's computer, and there's nothing. Nothing at all that backs up your story. We went to the site you gave us, and there's nothing."

Garrett shrugged. "She used her phone. And it was set to disappear. We were trying not to be found out."

They hadn't recovered Jessie's phone. It wasn't with Jessie when she died, in her bedroom, in the house, or in the yard. Or in a five-hundred-yard perimeter of the Olson home. And it hadn't sent out a ping or a GPS signal since five thirty the morning Jessie and Bart were murdered, when it suddenly went dead inside their home.

Garrett knew they didn't have her phone.

Either he was telling the truth, or—

"Tell me about you and Bart Olson."

Another dark glare as Garrett looked beyond Noah.

"Tell me about the fight you had outside Luther, by the Des Moines river."

"He didn't want me anywhere around Jessie. He thought I

wasn't good enough for her. I wasn't a college graduate, or anything like that."

"But you did go to college, at least a little bit. Didn't Bart know about that?"

Garrett set his jaw and glowered at the wall.

"You must be pretty mad at Bart, huh? Getting in the way of you and Jessie?"

Silence.

"Jessie wasn't a child. And she wasn't shy. Why didn't she tell her dad she was dating you and that it was her choice?"

"We talked about that." Garrett fidgeted. Sadness crawled over his features. His shoulders slumped. "She said her dad needed more time. That he needed to get to know me, the real me, before she said anything to him. But I wanted to tell him. I didn't like lying to him. Shit, I wanted her to move in with me."

The real Andy Garrett. Noah nodded. Who was the real Andy Garrett. "Why do you have corn husks and dirt in your apartment from the fields around the Olson farmhouse?"

"We'd meet out there. I'd park on the highway and hike in. It's not as easy as they make it look in the movies, you know. I'd always get cut up." He showed his arms, the scabs and scars that crisscrossed his forearms. "But it didn't matter. We had a little place, some old clearing the farmer had cut out of his field. Think he used to park a tractor there. We found rusty parts."

"She'd meet you in this clearing?"

Garrett nodded.

"Can you show me on a map where it is?"

Again, Garrett nodded.

Noah sat back, studying Garrett. "Andy." He pulled another folder out of the stack in front of him, plucking an evidence photo from within. He laid it down on top of Jessie's photo. "Why are your fingerprints on a glass of bourbon found at John Hayes's house?"

Garrett's eyes went wide. He paled, the color draining from his face like ink bleeding out of paper. His chest rose and fell.

"Why are your fingerprints on the kitchen counter in John Hayes's home? Next to Melinda Hayes's body?" He laid down another photo, the yellow evidence marker stark and glaring in the center of the frame. "And why are your fingerprints on the barstool that was used to kill John Hayes?" Noah clenched his jaw. His molars scraped against one another. He laid another photo down: John's service photo. Despite the admonition to look serious, like a tough G-man, John had smiled. He tapped the photo. "My friend, John Hayes."

Garrett's mouth had fallen open. His eyes flicked from the photo of the bourbon glass to the countertop to the broken barstool. The photo had been taken when it was still impaling John. He shook his head. Squeezed his eyes closed. "No, no..."

"No what, Andy?"

"*I didn't kill him!*" Garrett roared. He surged forward, nearly lunging across the table. His shackles strained, the chain whining against the bolt in the center of the table. He reached for Noah, hands outstretched, fingers curled like claws, like he wanted to grab Noah and squeeze, and squeeze—

The door burst open. Cole and Jacob barreled in, grabbing Garrett and slamming him back down into his seat. Cole stood with Noah, turning to face the corner, as Jacob roared at Andy, pinning him to the chair as he put the fear of God into him, told him to sit down and shut the fuck up.

"You okay?" Cole breathed.

"Yeah. Not the first time a suspect has come at me." Noah inhaled, exhaled. "I'm good."

Cole studied him. Noah felt his gaze trace over his profile, wander from his hair to his lips, lingering there, before roaming further south. He cast Cole a quick, sidelong glance. "Here? Now?" he murmured.

"Can't help it." A flush rose on Cole's cheeks. "You have me head over heels."

He smiled, briefly, and cleared his throat. Straightened his cuffs as Cole excused himself and Jacob finished bellowing into Garrett's face. He filed out after Cole, waiting for Noah's nod before he shut the door again.

Garrett slumped in the chair, his face twisted and sour. He shot pure poison at Noah. "I am a sheriff's deputy. I know what you're doing."

"You *were* a sheriff's deputy." Noah sat again. "Now, you're a suspect."

"I didn't kill them!" Andy shouted.

"Who? Who didn't you kill?"

"Jessie! Bart! John! The boys! Any of them!"

"Why are your prints all over the crime scene?"

"I was there last night."

"There? Where?"

"At his house."

"At John's house? John Hayes's house?"

"Yeah. He told me to come over."

"He told you to—" Noah clamped his mouth shut. "You couldn't even remember his name five minutes ago. Now you're telling me John had you over to his house last night."

"He did. He saw how I was after Jessie was killed, and after the autopsy came back. I couldn't look at that stuff. Jesus, I loved her!" He curled forward, burying his head in his cuffed hands.

Noah, I want to talk to you about Deputy Garrett. I'm worried about him. Let's meet tomorrow to discuss reassigning him. Noah closed his eyes. They'd never had that meeting. "What did you do at John's house?"

"Nothing. Just talked to him some. Mostly he sat with me. Let me…" He took a shuddering, deep breath. Gnawed on the corner of his lip. "He gave me something to drink in his bar downstairs. I sat on one of the barstools. When I left, I gave his wife a hug and thanked her for feeding me. She warmed up some leftovers for me. I was in the kitchen when she did."

Noah nodded. Convenient. A nice, tidy explanation for why his prints were at the scene and in all the pertinent places. The kind of explanation a cop would give. "And the blood on your shirt when we arrested you? We're testing it now. Whose will we find?"

"Mine." Garrett shook his head. "I cut myself when I punched out my mirror. As you know." He nodded to the evidence photos layered on the table. "And when I crashed my truck."

"Why did you crash your truck? And set it on fire?"

"I didn't set it on fire. Fucking hoses leaked. Fire started after the crash. I was already in the corn by the time it went up."

"Why did you punch out your mirror?" Noah pulled the photo of Jessie on the shattered glass back on top of the evidence pile. "I thought you loved her."

Garrett looked away.

"Tell me about Kimberly Foster. How did you meet her?"

Garrett frowned. "I've never met Kimberly in my life."

"Andy. Tell me about Kimberly."

Andy shook his head. He looked away.

Noah waited. He looked at the one-way mirror. He could almost picture Cole nodding at him.

He pulled out another photo from his stack and laid it in front of Andy. "Then tell me about Monica Venneslund."

Garrett froze. His eyes darted over Monica's photo. She was beautiful, Iowan sunshine and a big midwestern smile. Freckles danced over her nose and cheeks, and her blonde hair was pulled into two braids that framed her face. A locket hung in the hollow of her throat.

Garrett shook his head.

"You had a torn-up photo of her in your nightstand."

He kept shaking his head.

"You were at Iowa State together." No reaction. "Why do you have her photo, Andy? What did she mean to you?"

Nothing.

"Why did you tear up Monica's picture?"

Garrett's eyes squeezed closed. He rocked back and forth, breathing in rapid puffs of air.

"Where were you the night Monica died six years ago? Did you have anything to do with her death?"

"Oh, God, stop," Garrett pleaded. "Stop, stop, stop."

"Stop what? Stop what, Andy?"

"This was all back then. It was all back then. It was all supposed to stay back then."

"What was? What was supposed to stay back then?"

Was it true? Was Andy Garrett the killer they'd been looking for all along?

"Did something happen, Andy?" *There has to be a reason this is happening now. Why did the murders start back up?* Cole's voice, in his head. Noah leaned forward. "Did something happen with Jessie, Andy, that made you think of what it was like back then? Back with Monica and Stacy and Kelsey and Paige and Ellen? Did something happen that made you remember how it felt to show those girls who you were? Who was really in charge?"

Garrett stared at him. Emotions tried to flicker in and out of the black centers of Garrett's eyes. Tears built in the corners. "I loved her," Garrett whispered. "I didn't mean—"

"Didn't mean what, Andy? Didn't mean what? Didn't mean to kill her? Kill Jessie? Or kill Monica?"

The tears streaked down Garrett's face, splashing from his jawline to his scabbed and scarred forearms.

"Didn't mean what, Andy?"

But Garrett wasn't saying anything else. The tears fell, but he didn't say a word. One minute turned into five, and then into ten. Then twenty. Sighing, Noah sat back. He nodded to the one-way mirror.

Cole, Deputy Holland, and Jacob entered. They pulled Garrett up and reshackled his hands behind his back. "Back to the holding cell?"

Noah nodded. "We've got another twenty-four hours before we have to charge him. That's plenty of time for him to come to his senses and start talking to us." Noah tried to find Garrett's gaze, tried to catch his eyes. "Talk to me, Andy. Tell me what happened. Explain it to me."

Everyone waited, but Garrett just let the tears continue to fall. They soaked the jumpsuit the West Des Moines police had brought for him. His feet dragged as they led him out, back down the hall to the holding cell.

Noah sagged against the back wall as Cole crossed to his side. "Pretty clear case of disintegration," Cole said.

Noah ran his hands through his hair, replaying Garrett's words, his reactions. His tears. His final words. "'I didn't mean to.' What do you think he means?"

"I think it's self-explanatory. Especially since he didn't say that until you brought up Monica. I think it's looking like he murdered women when he was a college student, something made him run, and now, something has triggered him to murder again. Jessie Olson plays a part in all this, somehow. John Hayes, too."

"But Kimberly?" Noah frowned. "He didn't have the same reaction to her."

"Kimberly has always been the unknown. You didn't think she was a Coed Killer victim at first."

"I didn't know the killer was active when she was murdered. Her killing fits the profile, and the MO, perfectly."

"The profile is only a guide, and the killer is ultimately in charge of the MO. We need to go over Kimberly's murder again. Check everything. You thought it was her stalker."

"You thought it wasn't."

Cole shoved his hands in his pants. "I have been wrong before. Occasionally. Once or twice."

"Once or twice." It wasn't appropriate to flirt, or joke, not in an interrogation room where a man had nearly confessed to being the serial killer Noah had hunted for almost a decade. It wasn't appropriate to lean into Cole, slide his shoulder along the wall until their hands were hidden, or squeeze Cole's fingers, just briefly. Just once. But he did.

"Sir."

Noah jerked away, standing straight as Sheriff Clarke strode into the interrogation room. His team of Des Moines police officers flanked him, a young man and woman, each with their hands braced on their duty belts. "Agent Downing, we've got something I think you should see." He held out a folder, flipped open to a report.

A report that showed a young Andrew Garrett White of Sioux Falls, South Dakota, with a juvenile arrest record that stretched back to his preteen years. Petty theft, criminal mischief, Peeping Tom complaints. Stalking.

"How was this missed on his background check?" Noah asked.

"He dropped off his last name. He was going by his mother's maiden name, not his stepfather's. His stepfather adopted him when he was four, but there was some kind of paperwork issue with getting Andy's name officially changed. That let him slip through the cracks, and he took advantage of that when he needed to run." Sheriff Clarke flipped to the next page for Noah. "Which he needed to do when he was seventeen."

He was looking at a newspaper report from Vermillion, South Dakota, a city of ten thousand near the South Dakota–Nebraska state line, two miles from Interstate 29. *Coed Slain*, the headline read. *Brittany Dodge, of Junction City, South Dakota, was found Sunday morning on the quad of the University of South Dakota campus.*

"Guess who was a freshman at University of South Dakota then?" The sheriff handed Noah a copy of Andy Garrett White's University of South Dakota ID card. "He transferred to Iowa State the next spring semester."

Noah scanned Andy's high school transcript and his admission record to the University of South Dakota. High school JROTC. Fishing club. Wrestling. Good grades: As and one or two Bs.

"God damn it." He forced himself not to ball up the report, fling the folder against the wall. "Thanks, Sheriff. This is good work."

Sheriff Clarke tipped his head, nodded to Cole, and strode out.

"How did I miss this, Cole? What else did I miss six years ago? How did Garrett slip through my fingers?"

"That's not the question to ask." Cole reached for him. His hand brushed over Noah's. "How did Garrett cover this up so well he was able to join the Marines? And then join the Boone County Sheriff's Office? Work with Monica Venneslund's father? Was joining the sheriff's a way for Garrett to feel superior? Was he trying to revictimize his victims' families? Was this all about power to him?"

Noah frowned. "I got the feeling he really wanted to leave the past buried. That's when he broke down, when we brought up Monica and the others."

"Then why did he start killing again? Why now, if he wanted to leave it all behind him?" Cole paced away from him.

"Didn't you say there's no answer to why?" Noah's gaze slid down Cole's long legs. "What if he was killing the whole time he was in the Marines? What if he never truly stopped?"

Cole leaned against the far wall. "I'll work with Sheriff Clarke and his team and dig into Garrett's past. I'll work up a new profile on him, all the way back to his childhood. You'll have more to work with for the next time you go at him."

Noah nodded. "Jacob and I will work on the physical evidence. Find out what happened at each crime scene, especially Jessie's and at John's house. We know he was there. We can put him with the victims on both nights of the murders."

"We need to look at Kimberly again." Cole frowned. "There's still a lot of unanswered questions here, and a lot of them start with Kimberly and her father."

19

ANDY GARRETT FIT Cole's profile like a key sliding into a lock.

White male, early thirties. Above-average intelligence. Garrett had been on the honor roll in high school and had qualified for a scholarship to the University of South Dakota. He'd transferred to Iowa State with an even better scholarship award thanks to his grades.

"Why did he transfer? Why was he on the move?" Noah stared at Garrett's photo, tacked to the center of the whiteboard, as if he could pull the man's secrets from the still image.

The pictures of the six murdered girls surrounded Garrett, each waiting for Noah and the task force to draw the direct line intersecting Garrett with their lives. On a separate whiteboard, Garrett's photo sat in the center of a two-pronged, partially constructed web, the branches running from him to Jessie Olson and Molly Hayes. Beneath Garrett's photo lay Kimberly's and a stretch of unbroken white space, unmarred or unblemished by any connecting lines.

"Escaping from what he'd done? Running from law

enforcement?" Sheriff Clarke jerked his chin at Garrett's photo as he crossed his arms. "Criminals always run."

"Except," Noah said, his hand coming down on a small stack of old manila folders, "South Dakota wasn't investigating him. They had no idea who had killed Brittany Dodge. His name doesn't appear anywhere in the investigation files. Not once. He had no reason to run."

"That doesn't mean he didn't. And he wouldn't have known if they were on to him or not, necessarily," Sheriff Clarke's task force teammate, Officer Estrada, said.

"Holy shit." Jacob, buried in stacks and stacks of files at the end of the conference table, spoke up. He was the best man Noah had ever met for plowing through records. Jacob could demolish a warehouse full of bankers boxes in a single day. When the records from Iowa State and University of South Dakota arrived, Jacob hadn't even asked. He'd grabbed the first box and settled in at the conference table, cup of coffee at his elbow and a deep furrow on his brow.

"What is it?" Noah asked. Jacob stood, grabbing a dry-erase marker and a printout from the folder he'd been reading.

Jacob drew a thick line between Garrett and Monica Venneslund. He taped the printout below the connecting line. "Monica attended a seminar at USD the fall semester when Garrett was there. It was a criminology seminar, put on by the honors society. Forensic Advancements of the Past Decade. Guess who helped organize it?"

"Garrett." Cole, at the other end of the conference table, said. His face was pinched, his eyes tired, but to Noah, he still looked like perfection.

Jacob tapped the whiteboard, the printout. "And he signed her in personally. This is how they met."

"There's the connection, finally." They hadn't found anything that connected Monica to Garrett other than the torn-up photo in his apartment. No common classes, nothing other than that they were both students at Iowa State. But now this. "That's what brought him to Iowa State. He must have transferred to follow her," Noah said.

"He had her in his sights the whole time." Sheriff Clarke shook his head, disgusted.

"The other girls—they were, what, practice?" Noah arched his eyebrows, questioning, at Cole. "Why kill four girls before Monica?"

"Displacement." Cole leaned back, stretching. Noah's eyes wandered down, over Cole's chest and the taut fabric. His gaze snapped back up. What was he doing? "She was his fixation," Cole said. "Everything built up inside of him, focused on her. His fantasies, his dreams, his aspirations. He probably built an elaborate fantasy world that the two of them inhabited."

"Sick fuck," Jacob grunted. "He was obsessed."

Cole nodded. "Obsession is a hallmark of the psychopathic serial killer. It operates in cyclical phases. Early on, the need builds inside them, and no matter how much the killer tries to displace that need through fantasy or other outlets—sexual sadism, masturbation, cruelty to animals—the need continues to build until he feels he's going to explode. Then he hunts, captures, and kills his victim. Immediately, he discovers the compulsion he felt, that need, is both assuaged and left unfulfilled. Fantasy never matches reality, after all."

Except with you. Cole was everything Noah dreamed of. More, in fact. Beyond a kind and handsome man—someone who showed him the ropes, as it were, with patience and benevolence—he was intelligent, and funny, and so damn sexy Noah could barely control himself. Jesus, was he in a cycle, too? Cycling through his need for Cole, from the buildup to the need for consummation and then the simultaneously crushing and exhilarating afterglow? Questions ravaged him: Where would they go from here? When could he kiss Cole again?

Noah swallowed hard and shook his head. *Focus.*

"Four girls lost their lives because he was obsessed with Monica." Cole rose and headed for the whiteboard. "Each was a prelude, a preview of his fantasy with her."

"Did he want to murder her, or did he want to be with her?" Officer Estrada frowned.

"He wanted to capture her and make her his. In his mind, capturing her meant being together forever. I'm sure he had fantasies that they would be blissfully happy and in love for all time. She represented a vision of a life he could never have. He may have tried to bring that fantasy into reality one night, and she wasn't having it. To him, Monica was everything. To her, he was a stranger, a creep, a threat appearing in the middle of the night."

"We always wondered why the first five murders were like clockwork. Almost every four months, another killing. Then Monica, then within a week Stacy Shepherd, and Kyle and Shelly Carter that same night. A triple event. We thought it was something about Stacy. Thought there was something that had drawn him to her, that he had been so fixated on her he couldn't *not* break his own pattern." Noah's gaze flicked between the timeline of the crimes and the timeline they'd reconstructed out of the wreckage of Garrett's life. He'd enlisted in the Marines right after Kyle and Shelly's murders.

"Stacy Shepherd isn't the key to the killer's psychology. It's Monica Venneslund. Garrett came apart after Monica rebuffed him and he was forced to kill her—in his own twisted reasoning. Stacy was in the wrong place at the wrong time when she intersected with Garrett." Cole stopped at the second whiteboard. He tapped Jessie Olson's photo. "Jessie Olson had to have meant the same thing to him today as Monica did back then. These two are incredibly similar."

Same midwestern look, same blonde, blue-eyed, sun-dappled features. Same spirit, same will. Same strength bursting from the photos. Both young college girls with bright futures and everything to live for, until Garrett had taken that away.

"And, after Jessie's murder, there was another multiple homicide almost immediately. Another disintegration," Cole said.

Noah turned to Sheriff Clarke. "Sheriff, did your guys get out to Bart's fields? Did they find anything to back up what Andy claimed?"

Sheriff Clarke grimaced. "They did. And, tell you the truth, not sure what to make of his stories. We found the clearing he mentioned. Looks like someplace a tractor might have been parked once, and cleared out the crops for a few cycles. We didn't find any evidence it was a secret love nest for the two of them. No sign Jessie Olson had ever been out there. We did find a few discarded condoms. We brought them to the lab to be tested."

"Love nest for one?" Jacob asked.

"That's what I'm thinking," Sheriff Clarke rumbled.

"We still need to connect Andy to the rest of the girls. Four were Iowa State students, like him. What was the overlap? Did he see them on the quad? See them walking to class? What about the other two? And what happened the night Monica died?" Noah moved to Cole's side. "What happened now, six years later, that made him kill again? Was Jessie his new obsession? What was Kimberly Foster to Garrett?" Noah braced himself against the back of a chair, squeezing the stuffed leather. "We're booking Garrett in the morning. Let's build this case right and find the answers that will bring these girls justice." Exhaustion throbbed in his bones. His eyeballs felt like they were unmoored in his skull. "Good work today. We'll call it an evening, and I'll see everyone bright and early tomorrow."

Nods all around, and the soft chatter of the group breaking up, going their separate ways. Jacob lingered, still reading through files, but even he was starting to fade. Sheriff

Clarke and Officer Estrada talked about the South Dakota records and how Garrett could have evaded the authorities there. Their voices penetrated Noah's mind as he stared at the two whiteboards.

Why didn't I see you six years ago?

Garrett's Iowa State ID stared back at him.

He was the perfect predator. Unobtrusive, forgettable. He had next to no connection to these girls. No complaints against him by anyone at Iowa State. He'd learned to hide whatever had driven him through childhood and his teen years. Now he was a deputy, respected by the community, looked at as a man everyone could trust.

How did I work with you for two years and never know?

"It's how they operate." Cole, as if he'd read Noah's mind, slipped in behind him. His voice was soft, pitched for Noah's ears alone. "Predators. Sociopaths. Garrett stalked Monica Venneslund for almost two years, and the only one who knew was him. Now here he is, inside the sheriff's department, the same one investigating his own crimes… and again, no one knew but him."

HE DITCHED Cole and Jacob in the conference room and hid in his office, staring at his phone as he leaned against his desk. Was this smart? He didn't know.

Hey K-Bear, he texted. *How's practice?*

Good. We're done for today, she texted back almost instantly. *We still on for dinner?*

Absolutely. Do you know where you want to go?

She picked one of her old favorites, a place he and Lilly used to take her when she was still in pigtails. She used to eat chicken nuggets and mac and cheese there. Now it was steak and salmon and summer salad. Where had the time gone?

K-Bear, I have a question for you. Tell me the truth, okay?

Kay…

Do you want Cole to come to dinner with us tonight? I was thinking you and he could talk. Get to know each other, like you asked? But if you don't want to, that's fine. I want to spend time with YOU, K-Bear. I'm not trying to change that, or replace you, or push you away. I just thought maybe you'd want to get to know him…

God, he sounded desperate, even over text. Sighing, he crossed his arms and stared out the window, watching the sun start to lower over the suburbs bleeding away from West Des Moines.

Yeah, Dad. Bring him.

Are you sure? Doubt roared in. His chest, his lungs, ached. His stomach flipped over.

Maybe he shouldn't have asked. Katie had been so upset, so certain he was pushing her away in favor of Cole, and what was he doing now? This was supposed to be *their* dinner. Stupid, he was stupid. This wasn't smart at all. Of course she wouldn't tell him not to bring Cole. She was too nice to do that. *Never mind. Let's keep it you and me. I'm sorry.*

Dad, stop. You told me to tell you the truth. I did. I DO want to get to know him. Getting to know him more means I get to know YOU more.

Another text, almost immediately. *Don't push me out of your life. Please.*

You'll never be pushed out of my life, K-Bear. Ever. I swear.

Okay then it's decided. Both of you pick me up? The library closes in twenty minutes.

He checked his watch. With traffic, he could get there in thirty, if they left now. *You sure? Really?*

Stop acting like a teen girl, Dad. :)

He laughed. *Thanks. You know, I'm the luckiest dad in the whole world. I have you.* His throat clenched.

I'm gonna remember this the next time you tell me to pick up my shoes and put away my bag for the seventy zillionth time. Free pass for life on putting away my shoes for finding your dad with his BF?? She sent a smiley with a halo over its head.

Fat chance, missy. Chores are chores. Learning responsibility is important.

Eye-roll emoji. *Maybe put the lessons on responsibility on hold for 24 hours after I catch you with a hickey…*

He flushed. *Be there in thirty minutes, K-Bear.*

Love you Daddy.

He sent her a heart emoji as he left this office. Cole was in the conference room, working one end of the table while Jacob kept up his grind through the files at the other.

"Jacob, go home." Noah slouched in the doorframe, shoulder against the wood. "Go see Holly and Brianna. That will all be here in the morning."

"I can go another hour or two. It's no problem. I feel like I'm close to finding more connections."

"Yeah, that's what the gamblers in Vegas say. They're always close."

Cole coughed. Noah flushed. *Vegas on the mind. Always on the mind.*

Jacob grinned. He stretched, his huge arms rising over his head and nearly hitting the lights, even though he was seated. "You have a good time in Vegas? I never asked when you got back, with everything. I know it was cut short, but you had most of the week there."

"Conference was good."

Jacob's eyes glittered. "See any… sights?"

"You ever been to the conference?" Jacob shook his head. "They make you scan in every morning. If you're late, or hungover, they send you home. It's not really a conference where you can see the sights."

"You didn't have any fun in Vegas? Not even a little bit?" Jacob held out his fingers showing an inch's width.

Cole was staring at his own files, the spread-out papers on the three most recent crime scenes. He didn't look up. His ears and the back of his neck were burgundy.

"I had one really good night," Noah admitted. "Best I ever had, in fact."

Jacob reared back. He beamed, his arms thrown over his head like he'd just made a touchdown. "Excellent!"

Cole looked up at Noah. Surprise warred with adoration on his face.

Jacob's gaze slid from Noah to Cole.

"Got plans for dinner?" Noah asked Cole.

It took Cole a moment to answer. He cleared his throat, blinked. "Pizza in my hotel room, probably."

Jacob should have jumped in, insisted on taking Cole out since he couldn't do it that first night. But Jacob was oddly silent. "Come eat dinner with me, then," Noah said.

Cole's eyebrows shot up. "I thought you had plans with your daughter."

Jacob's gaze slid from Cole to Noah.

"Join us." Noah smiled. His hands were in his pockets, hiding how much they were shaking. Jacob wasn't stupid. And neither was he. He knew what he was doing. He'd have come out to John first, but—

And this wasn't really coming out. He wasn't saying the words. He wasn't asking Cole out on a date or kissing him in public, for Christ's sake. If he woke up in a panic, he could always explain this away. Dismiss this moment as stress and no sleep and the intoxication of Cole and everything he'd ever wanted within reach. Fantasies building up. Fantasies tumbling down. He shook his head.

"Are you sure?" Cole asked softly. Sure about dinner. Sure about what he was doing.

Jacob's eyes lasered into him.

"Yeah. She'd love to hear more of your stories. She's really interested in you." Something released inside of him, a clench he'd held on to for years and years. He exhaled. The ache that had always been there and had shifted into agony around Cole was ebbing.

"Okay. Sure, yeah. I'd love to." Cole was babbling, standing and trying to close his files and not trip over himself. He was flustered. Cole was never flustered. Noah smothered a grin as his heart soared.

"Hey, Cole?" Jacob asked. "You ever been to the Vegas conference?"

"Uh… yeah." Cole wouldn't meet Jacob's eyes. "Yeah, I have. I present there sometimes. BAU, you know." He almost tripped as he slipped his bag over his head and across his shoulder and tried to push in his chair. "We always have a workshop there about what we do. How we can help investigations."

"It's a good presentation." Noah nodded. "It's why I asked John to call in the BAU." He met Jacob's gaze.

Jacob laced his meaty fingers behind his massive head. A tiny, teasing smile played over his misshapen face. The chair screamed in protest as he leaned all the way back.

Cole smiled, nearly ran into the wall, and scooted out of the conference room. Jacob's eyes glittered.

Noah leaned inside. "Go home, Jacob."

"Have a good night, Noah."

HIS NERVES CAME ROARING BACK on the drive to Katie's high school. What if this was a terrible idea? What if Cole and Katie didn't get along? What if Katie ended up hating Cole?

Well, then… He glanced sidelong at Cole. It was too painful to think… and it was pointless to propel himself into the future and imagine either the best or the worst outcome. The world and everything in it—all the choices he had to make, all the actions and reactions, the interactions of the people he cared about most—was a murky, hazy mist, like fog in front of his SUV.

The night was clear, and he focused on the pavement ahead of him. Dinner. The next few hours. That was what was important right now.

Cole fidgeted as he pulled off the highway, playing with the strap of his laptop bag. He'd been quiet on the drive, staring out the window, and that was a whole new set of worries for Noah to chew on. Did Cole not want to go to dinner? Was he being polite, especially in front of Jacob? Was this dinner something Noah was pushing on Katie and Cole both? Had he misread everything again?

Fantasies building, fantasies tumbling.

Katie was waiting on the brick half wall surrounding the flagpole, dressed in her cheer outfit with her leggings on beneath the skirt and her warm-up jacket open on top. Her hair was still done up with ribbons in blue and gold, the school's colors. She'd reapplied her makeup, too. Usually, when he picked her up after practice, her eyes were scrubbed clean, no liner or eyeshadow left, not after sweating in the summer sun. He eyed her as she bounded into the back seat, sloughing her cheer bag and backpack before leaning forward and giving him an over-the-seat hug. "Hey, Dad. Hey, Dr. Kennedy."

"Hey, K-Bear." He kissed her cheek.

"Hi, Katie." Cole half twisted in his seat. His smile was almost shy. Was he…

Noah watched Katie sit back and pull her seat belt on. She smiled back at Cole. It was weak, tentative. Hesitant.

His daughter had never been tentative in her life.

Noah's stomach sank.

───

WHATEVER HE'D BEEN afraid of, he was an absolute idiot.

Katie was snorting, covering her face with both hands as she tried to stop laughing. Cole was three different shades of red at the same time, and he passed Katie his napkin to wipe up the water she'd snorted half across the table. Beneath the table, Cole squeezed Noah's hand.

Noah squeezed back and laced their fingers together.

Dinner had started stilted and awkward, Katie too quiet and Cole so nervous he dropped his silverware. Noah had ordered a double whiskey on the rocks as soon as they sat down. Cole ordered water.

Fifteen minutes later, Cole was deep in the middle of a story from the BAU, Katie was hanging on his every word, and Noah was holding his breath, watching the two most important people in his world try to navigate each other's edges.

Somehow, Cole's story got Katie talking about cheerleading, and the football team, and the personalities of the teenagers she knew. Cole pretended to diagnose each of her friends, then her teachers, but begged off tagging Noah with some fantastical nonsensical diagnosis. The conversation continued as their dinner arrived, moving from friends to classes to books (Cole hated the assigned high school English curriculum, same as Katie) to movies (they both were beyond tired of superhero movies, and Katie was so done with the boys always wanting to take girls out to the thirty-thousandth sequel of the Unfunny Guy Squad with the hot chick sidekick) to music, and then to TikTok and Snapchat. Noah became a sidekick to dinner himself, letting the conversation roll over and into him, listening to Katie share things with Cole she'd never even mentioned to her father.

As the waiter cleared away their plates, his phone vibrated in his pocket. One-handed, he pulled it out under the table and checked the incoming text.

Jacob. *Dinner go okay?*

It's still going. I'm the third wheel.

That's what Holly says about me and Brianna sometimes. :)

Noah smiled.

He finally asked for the check when he caught Katie smothering her third yawn. She was half draped on the table, head propped on her sweatshirt-covered hand, elbow right where her lasagna had been as she listened to Cole describe yet another twisted murder investigation. Katie's eyes were sparkling, dancing in the low lights of the restaurant as she gazed at Cole.

"*Da*-ad," she complained as he signed the bill. "It's still early. We don't need to leave yet, do we?"

"It's after ten, K-Bear. We've been here for three hours." He squeezed Cole's hand again, still out of sight under the table.

"So?" She waved her sweatshirt-covered hand at the space between them and where both of their arms disappeared beneath the table. "I mean, you guys look like you're having fun. And you don't have to hide from me, you know? Not after—"

"Thank you, miss," Noah said quickly, cutting her off as he snapped closed the receipt book. "Ready to go?"

She made a face but hauled herself out of the booth. He wrapped one arm around her as they walked to the parking lot, kissing the top of her head, and she leaned into him, forgetting, for today at least, that it wasn't cool to be seen hugging her dad in public. Cole stayed at their side, his hands shoved in his pockets. He smiled as he walked, staring at some point in front of them as if he were looking at memories or dreams, imaginings playing out in his mind.

This could be our life.

It hit Noah so suddenly, so strongly, he almost doubled over. Like a gunshot, or a gut punch, or a slap to the face. *This could be our life, the three of us.* This could be how his nights went, once or twice a week. This could be the contentment he felt, the warm, full-bodied peace that settled like a blanket on his bones. This could be Katie, leaning into him, cheerful in a way she hadn't been in months—years, even. The two of them close, no secrets between them. Cole, making both of them laugh, smile so much both of their faces ached, making both of them *happy*.

He hissed, his heart aching. Katie turned her face up to frown at him. He pasted a smile on and helped her into the back seat as Cole climbed into the front. "I'll drive you back to the hotel?"

Cole nodded. When they pulled out of the parking lot and into the darkness of the streets, he slid his hand across the center console and rested his fingertips against Noah's leg. Noah laid his hand over Cole's.

In the rearview mirror, he saw Katie smile as she stared out the window.

They made it to the hotel too quickly. He should have detoured to Nebraska. Anything to keep the hum of the tires, the warmth of Cole's hand, and the peace radiating from the back seat going. But he pulled up to the hotel's front doors and shifted into park.

Cole's eyes met his in the half light thrown into the SUV by the parking lot's sodium lamps. They were still holding hands on his thigh. He'd started stroking the back of Cole's hand with his thumb during the drive, tracing Cole's slender metacarpals and the bounding of his pulse. "I'll pick you up in the morning?"

Nodding, Cole brought their hands to his lips, pressing a slow kiss to his knuckles as he held Noah's gaze. Katie was watching from the back seat, seeing everything: Cole's lips touch his skin, Noah's hitched breath, the way his fingers curled around Cole's hand and refused to let go. This was more than Cole kissing him good night. This was the three of them, this moment. Cole and his desire, Noah and his yearning, Katie witnessing it all—

"You guys can kiss in front of me, you know." Only a teenager could sound so unimpressed and thrilled at the same time. "It's fine. Really."

Noah threw Katie a dirty look as Cole chuckled, the tender moment vanishing. He grabbed his laptop bag and the case files and slid out of the SUV. "Night, Katie!"

"Night, Dr. Kennedy!" She leaned forward, half into the front seat, and waved at Cole. "See you tomorrow!"

Together, they waited for Cole to walk into the hotel. As the glass doors slid open, he turned, waving to them both again, grinning. Noah smiled. Katie beamed.

She turned that smile on him as Cole disappeared into the lobby, still half in the front seat. "I like him," she said, letting her ponytail fall over her shoulder as she tilted her head. "Seal of approval, Dad."

He pushed on the center of her forehead. "Seat belt, miss." She flopped back, arms and legs going every which way as she sighed and flounced and rolled her eyes, still with that huge smile on her face. He waited until he heard the seat belt click, watching in the rearview mirror. "So, what's the homework situation tonight?"

She groaned. "More pre-calc due at the end of the week. Why so much math?"

"Well, it is summer school for the pre-calc class you failed."

She made a face and crossed her arms. "Can I just wait for Dr. Kennedy to help me tomorrow? He was way better than you."

"Thanks, K-Bear. I appreciate that." He smiled at her reflection as she blew him a kiss. "Why do you think you'll see him tomorrow?"

She stared, her hands spreading wide, gesturing first to Noah, then the empty passenger seat as her stare called him an idiot in a thousand different dialects of sixteen. "Dad, really?"

"We'll see what we can do tonight, okay? If we can't figure it out, we'll call in reinforcements. How's that?"

"When's he coming over tomorrow?"

HOMEWORK WAS A DISASTER. Katie was too hyper, too unfocused, bouncing from math problems to suddenly talking about Cole and one of the stories he'd shared at dinner. She pulled up the cases he'd mentioned on her phone, reading news headlines from the investigations, the arrests, and the trials as Noah tried to work through the third pre-calc problem.

"Look! He testified!" Katie shoved her phone between Noah's face and the textbook, waggling it until his eyes refocused on the picture of Cole walking into the courtroom with FBI agents from the Boston office. Noah closed his eyes as she pulled her phone back and quoted from the article.

He'd never admit it to Katie, but he hated math, too. It was one of the benefits of being an adult, he'd thought. No more homework. No more worrying about grades. Sighing, he drifted as Katie gushed over Cole, his testimony, and the gruesome facts of the Boston Ripper case two years before, declaring the case disgusting and Cole's testimony awesome in the same sentence.

Two years ago, he'd been living out of a suitcase in a one-bedroom apartment, trying to figure out life after divorce. Katie visited him every other weekend, and he'd give her the bedroom and sleep on the couch. They ate a lot of microwave dinners and Kraft mac and cheese that year. And Cole had been catching the Boston Ripper, appearing on CNN and testifying in court.

Katie had had a million questions when they got home, everything from how old Cole was to what would happen next. When was Noah going to tell everyone he was gay? Would Cole be at the games with him when school started in the fall? If she was on the homecoming court, would both of them escort her out on the football field? Was Cole going to move in with them? If they got married, would Cole take his name, become Dr. Cole Downing? They could all have the same name if he did. They could be a family, she said.

He'd tried to distract her, had begged her to focus on her homework. He didn't have answers for her, not a single one. She didn't seem to mind, breezing from one question to the next, never waiting for his reply. No, she moved happily to cyberstalking Cole, searching for his cases, his Facebook—*He won't have one, K-Bear. You never know, Dad!*—his Instagram, Snapchat, and TikTok, and anything and everything else.

It was useless to persist in this pretense of homework. He had been the only one working for the past half hour. He tossed the pencil in the textbook and scrubbed his hands over his face.

God, what if she found a picture of him with another man? What if she found his Snapchat and it was inappropriate? What if she found his Instagram and there were lots and lots of men? Cole had become so huge in her mind so quickly, almost as large as he'd become in Noah's mind. There was something about apples and trees in that thought, wasn't there?

Katie's excitement tempered him, cautioned him, in a way his own fantasies hadn't. It was one thing for him to daydream and imagine, but it was entirely another to build up Katie's hopes and dreams. If Noah broke his own heart with his exuberance, his desire to risk it all on Cole and hope for the best, that was his choice.

Breaking Katie's heart was unacceptable.

He was her father. Wasn't he supposed to set a better example than this? Show her temperance and caution and wise decision-making? Show her how to navigate the white waters of wanting and hoping, and how, oh-so-rarely, everything coalesced into one perfect thread of emotion and intention. How to navigate dreams that came true, and even dreams that didn't come true.

Snippets of the evening roared back, of Katie and Cole

with their heads together at dinner, laughing, talking a mile a minute while Cole's fingers remained laced with his own beneath the table. How did he bring two people who shared his life together?

Did Cole share his life? No, not really. Not at all like Katie did. She *was* his life, an inextricable part of his existence, his past and his future and his days and his nights forever. Cole could join their life, could become part of their existence… if he wanted to.

But… how? Katie's questions thundered through him, each one a drumbeat building a migraine inside his skull. What did happen from here?

Cole lived in D.C. He lived in Des Moines. He wasn't going to move, not with Katie in high school, on the cheer squad and with her friends. He wasn't going to take her away from all that.

Did he even know what Cole wanted? They'd had one conversation yesterday at lunch, fumbling through Noah's aborted text and his fantasies of seeing Cole at little gay rendezvous in the Midwest. It was one thing to meet Cole in Chicago and pretend to be out. It was one thing to give Jacob enough clues to put the pieces together.

It was something else entirely to commit to a relationship —long distance, in person, or something in between—with a man.

What would he tell Lilly? How would she react to this? Jesus, how would she react to him taking Katie to dinner with Cole? He could hear her now, her fine-tuned legal brain ready to shred him. *You took our daughter to meet your one-night stand, Noah? How is that in her best interests? In four years, I've never introduced Katie to any man I have dated, casually or seriously.*

"Dad, are you listening?" Katie waved her phone in his face again. There was Cole, this time posing for what looked like his official FBI photo. She'd pulled up his doctoral research paper somehow and was flicking through the table of contents, reading each chapter heading aloud to him.

How would Lilly react to him coming out? *Well, that answers a few questions I always had about our marriage, Noah.*

Do you really think it's appropriate to be dating men while Katie lives with you?

Lilly, or her voice in his head, wasn't wrong. What if Cole didn't want anything more than whatever this was? A fling in Des Moines, a few nights a year meeting up in hotel rooms. How would Katie take that? How did he begin to explain whatever *that* was? *We're not really dating, and no, he won't be coming to your games, and no, he won't be changing his name to match ours. He just fucks me once a quarter when he's nearby.*

Jesus.

What if Katie got her heart broken? What if the fantasy she had built up in twenty-four hours came crashing down? Would she want him to date again? Or would she reject any future man he might meet? Was Cole setting an impossible standard that no future man could ever meet, for either him or Katie?

Dread slid through him, dark and poisonous. Dread, and panic, and a building certainty that he'd made a gigantic mistake. Maybe an unforgivable one.

His phone rang, clattering on the tabletop. Katie went still, staring at the screen.

Cole.

Katie beamed. She stood, taking her phone and her shoes but leaving her textbook, and headed for the stairs. "Tell him I say hi!" she called over her shoulder. "And that he needs to come help with pre-calc, 'cause you suck at it, Dad."

He almost let the call roll over to voicemail. His heart was pounding, about to break every one of his ribs. At the last moment, he swiped to answer and pulled the phone to his ear. "Hello?"

"*Hey, gorgeous.*"

He closed his eyes. Agony knifed through him. He *wanted*, he wanted so, so *badly*. But…

Noah slipped to the patio, the automatic lights coming on as he shut the glass door softly behind him. "Hey."

There was a beat of silence. "*You okay? Is Katie okay?*"

"She's…" He sighed. "She's got homework, but she doesn't want to do it. She's not focused enough."

"I feel like I'm responsible for that."

You have no idea. "Partly. I'm more to blame. Dinner was my idea, after all."

"*Noah, Katie is wonderful. She's absolutely wonderful. She's just like you. Dinner was…*" Cole's voice trailed off. "*If I say perfect, will you make fun of me?*"

"It was hardly perfect. She snorted water across the table."

Cole laughed. "*That's what* made *it perfect. She's great. You have every reason to be proud of her. You're a great father, and she's a great, great kid.*"

The knife in his belly twisted again. He doubled over, almost fell onto picnic table's bench seat. His jaw clenched. His molars scraped back and forth.

"*I had such a great time,*" Cole breathed. "*Noah, I had a* really *great time.*"

He couldn't speak. He couldn't get his tongue to move, his vocal cords to vibrate.

"*Noah?*"

"I'm here." He sounded like he was being strangled. He heaved in a wet, ragged rush of air.

"*What's wrong?*"

Damn it. Damn it, damn it. His vision blurred, and he dug his thumb into the wood of the picnic table. He sniffed, tried to blink. Tears landed on the back of his hand. "It's just… Cole, I think I made a mistake tonight."

"*What?*"

"It's Katie. She had a great time, too, Cole."

Cole exhaled. "*Thank God. I was nervous about dinner, when you* asked. I wanted her to have a good time. I... really wanted her to like me."

He tried to laugh. "No danger there. She's head over heels for you." *Like me.* He squeezed his eyes closed again.

"*Then... why do you think you made a mistake?*"

His foot bounced in a manic rhythm. "What are we doing, Cole?" Noah whispered. "What are we? What is this?"

Cole let out a soft, surprised puff of air. Noah heard the crackle over the line. He said nothing.

That's what I was afraid of. Noah swallowed the sob he wanted to scream. "Katie has a million questions now. Questions about us. What we're doing together. What happens next. She wanted to know if you were going to move in with us."

Silence.

"She wanted to know if you were going to be there at her games this fall. My God, Cole, she has so many hopes already. She's built up this future in her mind, and—"

"*Noah*—"

"She did *exactly* what I did. She jumped in with both feet, before everything was figured out, and..."

"*And what?*"

"All that does is lead to hurt."

"*What are you saying?*" Cole's voice was careful, measured. "*I can't read your mind, Noah.*"

"I'm saying I don't see how this can go anywhere. You live in D.C. I live here. Neither of us can move. I'm saying it's not fair to Katie to introduce her to you and give her all these hopes for a happy family life again, when all we are is—" He stopped.

"*Is what?*" Cole's voice was challenging.

"What we are." His lips thinned. "Fuck buddies, right?"

Silence. Hard, cold silence.

"I'm saying that I made a mistake tonight. I leaped without looking. I introduced Katie to you, and now I've gotten her hopes up for something that won't happen. I'm not even... I'm not even sure if I'm ready to really come out."

"*I thought you wanted me to help you. I said I'd be there for you through that. I mean, I thought you were basically telling Jacob tonight.*"

He sighed. "Cole..."

"*This is not really a conversation, is it?*" Cole's breath shook. "*This is you telling me what you've already decided. Did you want to talk about this at all? Or did you want to decide the future, our future, again? Without any input from me.*"

"That's not fair—"

"*No, what you're doing isn't fair! You're telling me we're just fuck buddies? That there's nothing here, that this isn't going anywhere? Do I get a say in that? Do I get to tell you how I feel, or are we playing the game where only how Noah feels matters?*"

"Cole—"

"*Fuck buddies? Really?*" Cole made a noise, something between a snort and a chuckle, dark and ugly. "*If you were just a fuck buddy, I wouldn't have bothered wanting to reconnect with you. If all you were was a piece of ass from Vegas, I wouldn't have bothered with any of this,*" he snarled. "*I can pluck a fuck buddy from thin air! I'm not interested in another fuck buddy! Maybe you are. Maybe that's what you want, what you've wanted all along. Which, fine. You know what? Better to find out now, before this really did go somewhere I was hoping it might. I really, really should have taken a hint from Vegas.*"

"Cole—"

"*Did you just want to scratch your last itch? Were you looking for one final gay fling before you slammed your closet door shut?*"

"I have to think about Katie."

"*It may shock you, but I was thinking about her, too. Do you think so little of me that you think I'd toy with her? Do you think I'd be so careless with your daughter? If you were in my shoes, would you have met someone's daughter if you didn't care about them? If you just wanted them as a fuck buddy?*"

It was his turn to be silent. He couldn't see, not anymore. The world was salt water and agony, tears and a thousand splinters as he dug his thumb into the wood over and over. "I'm sorry."

"*So that's it? You've decided. This is the end, because you say there's no future. Because you can't imagine I'd have already thought about this, already looked at flying between D.C. and Des Moines, already imagined how I could figure out how to prioritize what I wanted in my own life. Because you can't imagine I'd want to put you, and Katie, first. Because you think you know best, you know everything, huh?*"

"Cole—"

"*Damn it, Noah.*" Cole sniffed, the first time Noah had heard anything other than anger—raging, quaking anger—from him since Noah had started this awful conversation. "*I never wanted to say goodbye to you.*" Cole's voice shook. "*Not in Vegas. And not here. I wanted—*"

"What? What do you want?"

"*I guess it doesn't matter anymore, does it?*"

Cole hung up. The line went dead.

Noah dropped the phone and buried his head in his arms, and, finally, let the sobs pour out of him.

20

FUCK THIS HOTEL. Fuck this government-rate hotel with no lobby bar or room service. No way to get drunk when he Goddamn needed it.

He should have seen this coming. Damn it, he should have seen this coming from miles away. From fucking Vegas, in fact.

Noah had already run once. He made up his mind about Cole, about what would happen with them, between them, without any input from Cole, back in the Vegas airport.

And here he was doing it again.

This time, after Cole had gone and fallen that much harder, that much more, for him.

He'd started to imagine *what if.* And how to get to *what if.* There was a nonstop flight from D.C. to Des Moines. He could request to not travel as much. He was one of a handful of single guys in the BAU, and he'd wanted to travel often to rack up the extra pay. But he didn't have to. He could have a more stable, more predictable schedule. Something that lent itself to reliability and long distance. And to *what if.*

But fuck those plans, apparently. Not plans, really. Daydreams. Fantasies. Things that weren't to be.

Damn midwestern men.

He grabbed his workout clothes and changed, heading down to the closet-sized gym for a brutal session that left him jelly-legged and covered in sweat. The anger ebbed but left behind the pain. Moments from dinner—laughing with Katie, holding Cole's hand—played in his mind. Memories from the days before: Noah smiling while he was driving, chuckling at something Cole said, or kissing him as they stood side by side in his kitchen and watching the golden morning sunlight dance on the heads of corn peeking over Noah's fence. Helping Katie with her math homework while Noah watched.

Damn it, he'd wanted to try.

He showered back in his room and paced. He was still too keyed up, still wound too tightly. Too much whiplash, waking up with everything he wanted within reach only for it all to be snatched away before the end of the night.

Enough. He wasn't going to change Noah or change Noah's mind. What was done was done. Noah had had two chances, which was more than he gave anyone.

He dragged the case files across his bed and flipped them open. Instead of sleep, he'd tear through the files, figure out what had drawn Garrett to Kimberly Foster, to Jessie Olson, and to Molly Hayes. Why those three? Why, now, the leap to law enforcement families with Jessie and Molly? Was Garrett hoping to be caught after all this time?

Why had he annihilated Molly's entire family?

He spread the photos of the Hayes crime scene over the bed, separating the upstairs and downstairs crime scenes. Swift execution upstairs and then brutal torture in the basement. What John had gone through to get to his daughter.

His stomach twisted. Nausea rose, nearly sent him to the bathroom. John reached for Molly's painted toenails—so close, and yet he'd never touched her. Never saved her.

If that were Noah and Katie—

He barely made it to the bathroom before he hurled, vomiting the Italian dinner he'd shared with Noah and Katie.

He heaved until it seemed like everything he'd ever eaten was out of his system, then lay his clammy forehead on the toilet seat. *Don't think like that. You can never think like that.*

Distance. Objectivity. Katie might be close to the profile, but she was too young. She was in high school, not college. And she hadn't been written up in the local papers, had she? Surely Noah would have bragged about that. Would have had the article framed in his office. Surely it would have come up if Katie were anywhere close to the victim profile Garrett targeted.

She wasn't in Garrett's victimology, but that didn't stop Cole from picturing Noah in place of John, Katie in place of Molly, when he closed his eyes.

Damn it. He forced the bile down. Distance. Objectivity.
Don't think about Noah. Or Katie.

He brushed his teeth, then padded back to the bedroom and flipped the crime scene photos from the basement over. *Don't think about it.*

Instead, he pulled out Kimberly's case file and flipped through the autopsy and the scene reports, then pulled out the photos. Kimberly, strangled on her bed, silently. Nothing disturbed. No marks on the wall, no lamps toppled over. Across the room, her broken closet mirror, the corner behind the door where her father was strangled with her belt.

Why did Frank come back to check on her? What made him rise from his sickbed on the couch and cross the house, at midnight, after cold medicine and a beer, to check on his daughter?

Parental intuition? Noah wouldn't put the SUV into drive until Katie had her seat belt on.

Was that it? The bond between parent and child, the total responsibility for another life that a parent takes on? The way a child's life is laid into your hands, and every moment of every day from then on is spent caring for that child. Keeping them alive, yes, but also nurturing their soul. Growing their mind. Shaping their life.

Like Noah with Katie, and how good he was—

Groaning, Cole flopped backward, dropping the photos as he pressed the heels of his palms against his closed eyes.

He'd thought about parenthood maybe three times, ever, before this week. He'd noticed a hot young father on the National Mall once. Had thought, *Do I want to have a baby?* And decided no.

And that was it. That's all he could scrape out of his memories.

Now he was mired in a case defined by murdered daughters and the shattered fathers left behind. John's hand reaching for Molly's toes, never reaching her. Deputy Venneslund, carrying on after finding his daughter dead. Six agonizing years—and then realizing his colleague, his coworker, was responsible. Bart, fighting his way to Jessie's bedroom, trying to save her. What had he thought, coming face to face with his own deputy and Jessie's corpse?

Why did Garrett risk being caught by Bart?

Escalation. The thrill of a secondary kill. The rush, the elation he'd felt after getting away with killing Frank. He could take another life, beyond Kimberly, beyond Jessie, and get away with it. He could take Bart's life. The intoxication, the frenzied need of that, must have been intoxicating.

Or was it purely revenge, rage, lashing out at Bart, the man he thought kept him and Jessie apart?

But why did he decide to attack Jessie? Why had he decided to finally attack Monica, for that matter? How did the object of Garret's fixation become his target?

Garrett had reinvented himself after Monica, after Stacy Shepherd and Kyle and Shelly Carter, like he had when he fled the University of South Dakota. Was there a new target in the Marines he'd somehow fixated on? The closest Marine Corps base was over a thousand miles away from Des Moines.

No, it wasn't a change of target or a new fixation. Garrett had truly fled.

They'd have to pull his Marine Corps records, see where there were unsolved murders on or near the bases he'd been assigned to. There had to be at least one. Garrett didn't stop murdering six years ago and then suddenly pick up again with Kimberly and Frank.

But why did Frank come back to check on Kimberly? Cole held the photo in front of his face, trying to see through the celluloid as if he could see through time. Noah would check on Katie. He would check on her if he was feeling parental, or if he was missing her. Or if he called out to her and she didn't respond. If he heard a threat.

Cole blinked. He turned the photo. Stared.

There was a lot of broken glass on the ground. The shattered mirror. Large, silvered panes of glass reflecting the camera flash in a thousand directions. If Frank had punched the mirror, scrabbling against it as he tried to fight Garrett off, the shards would have rained down on and around him as he struggled. Would have fallen largely intact, in big sheets, as they had broken.

Why were there shards that seemed smaller? As if they'd been ground down, stepped on, multiple times? As if... as if Frank had ground his heels against the broken glass while he struggled and fought for his life. As if the glass was already broken when he walked into the room.

As if he'd come to check on Kimberly *because* he heard the glass break. As if he'd been lured into her bedroom.

It wasn't an interruption.

Cole grabbed the case files, flipping through and pulling out the Olson photos. Jessie, dead in her bed. Blood smears in the hallway, handprints. Bart's prints. The fingerprint smears pointed both left and right, as if there had been a brawl. As if Bart had confronted Garrett in Jessie's bedroom and discovered the murder had just taken place, and the two had fought and struggled and almost died in that hallway.

The question wasn't *Why did you risk being caught by Bart?*

No, it was *Why did you wait for Bart to come home?*

To show Bart what he had done. To show him to his face.

He laid out the hallway photos again, his heart pounding, his hands shaking. Five thirty, Bart arrives home. He walks in. They'd all thought Bart had gone to check on Jessie right away, found her body, fought his way to the living room, and suffered his final beating there. But what if that was the wrong way around?

Bart walks in. Garrett, hidden in the darkness, springs forward, beating Bart with the crystal sheriff's award. He incapacitates Bart, cracks his skull, breaks his fingers, his jaw. Broken, bleeding, in agony, Bart tries to scream for help, but Garrett drags him by the hair down the hallway. Bart tries to stop, puts his hands out—there, there, and there—but he's dragged on, all the way to Jessie's door. Bart knows, he knows what he'll see, and he tried to fight it, but—

But Garrett wanted to show him. He wanted to show Bart what he'd done to his daughter. He made him see it, made him feel his daughter's death, see her corpse laid out on her bed.

And then he dragged him back to the living room—handprints there and there, the other direction—and finished Bart off. Beat him until his face caved in and his skull collapsed, until there was nothing left of him except his bruised body and his uniform shirt.

Rage. Incomprehensible, unquenchable rage. But not the rage of being interrupted, the psychopath's overreaction to an intrusion on his fantasy. No, these fathers were *part* of his fantasy. Showing them. Making them see. Making Frank and Bart see what he'd done to their daughters.

And, Jesus, John Hayes. Fingers reaching for painted toes but never making it. The swiftness of the execution upstairs, the mom and the twin boys gunned down with such efficiency. The slowness, the agony of John's wounds. Gut shots, when Garrett had just cleanly executed two boys and their mother.

He'd wanted John to follow him.

Stumbling downstairs. Blood on the handrail. The walls. The floor, where John fell. Hands and knees, crawling across the basement, across the shattered glass, the TV Garrett had ripped off the wall and thrown in his path, struggling to get to—

Cole's breath came hard and fast as he upended the case files and flipped through the first six, checking, and then checking again just to be sure. Yes, that was the difference. Fuck, he'd missed this, totally missed it. The first six girls were murdered alone. In secluded public spaces where Garrett could dominate them in the darkness.

Kimberly, Jessie, and Molly were murdered at home. With their fathers.

Daughters and fathers.

The new victimology was wrong. It wasn't just young, successful college-age girls any longer. It was them *and* their fathers. Their fathers had to witness. They had to feel it, feel the loss.

What was the reason? Why had Garrett changed his focus? Why was he so fixated on these fathers? What united them? Bart Olson, a sheriff, Garrett's sheriff. John Hayes, the head of the FBI office. Frank Foster, a meat packer in a warehouse.

He grabbed his laptop and booted it up, logged in, and searched every database he had access to for information on Frank Foster. Something, there had to be something in Frank's background that tied him to Bart and John.

Frank had put in six years at the warehouse. He was a widower. Kimberly was his only daughter. So far, nothing—

There. There it was. Ten years ago, Detective Frank Foster had been fired from the St. Louis Police Department.

They were all cops.

Daughters of law enforcement fathers.

Which meant—

His phone rang, jarring him out of the black hole he'd fallen into. He grabbed for the phone, missed, and grabbed it again. It fell off the edge of the bed before he swiped it on and answered breathlessly, "Noah?"

"*Cole? It's Jacob. You okay?*"

Cole sank to his knees, straightening the case files, trying to create order out of the chaos he'd strewn across the bed. "Yeah. I'm okay. I was digging into the files. I found out a lot more—Jesus, a lot more about who Garrett was targeting. His victimology, it changed. I don't know why yet, but there has to be a reason." He was babbling, almost incoherent, his voice shaking as he grabbed papers and photos.

"*His victimology changed?*"

"Yeah. It's not just the daughters. He was targeting their fathers. Frank Foster used to be a cop. He had it in for the LEO dads, and he was punishing them by killing their daughters."

"*Fuck,*" Jacob growled. "*Cole, that's a problem. A big fucking problem—*"

"We have to find out why his victimology changed. What motivated this. God, I need to draw up questions for Noah for his interview tomorrow—"

"*Cole, listen to me, damn it!*"

"What?" He stilled. Papers fluttered past his knee. His hand clenched around the photo of John Hayes staked to the ground in his basement, reaching for his daughter.

"*Andy Garrett.*" Jacob exhaled. Cursed again. A radio sputtered static in the background. A siren *whoop-whoop*ed. "*He escaped. About two, maybe three hours ago. We're still trying to figure out when, and what happened.*"

"He *what*? How is that possible?"

"*Officer Fuller was guarding him in the holding cell. I couldn't sleep, so I went back to the office to go through more files. I went to check on Garrett, but Fuller was dead and the cell door was unlocked. Garrett somehow got him close enough to strangle him through the bars."*

"Fuck!" Cole threw his phone on the bed and grabbed his jeans and a T-shirt from his suitcase. He hopped on one foot, tugging on his shoes. Grabbed his gun and his holster and slid them on his belt. "What are you doing now?"

"We've got the entire metro area and the surrounding ten counties on alert. Roadblocks are going up. Every car is being stopped. Birds are in the air. We're searching for him with everything and everyone. Everyone is getting called in right now." Jacob's voice was tinny through the speakerphone.

"Good. Have you reached Noah yet?"

A pause. *"I thought he might be with you,"* Jacob said carefully. *"I couldn't reach him when I called him."*

Law enforcement fathers and their daughters. A hand reaching for painted toes, but never making it.

"He's not with me!" Cole shouted. "Jesus Christ, get a unit to Noah's house! Now!" He hung up on Jacob and dialed Noah as he burst out of his hotel room, bouncing down the three flights of stairs and hurling himself through the lobby for the front desk.

Ring. Ring. Ring. No answer. He dialed again. Nothing. Again.

"*FBI!*" Cole bellowed at the empty night desk. He pounded on the little silver bell. Where the fuck was the attendant? "FBI! Get out here, *now!*"

A petrified teenager, a pimple-covered, gangly boy, all arms and legs concealed in baggy clothes, emerged from the back room, his hands over his head. "I swear, it was only a little pot! I swear!"

"Do you have a car?" He held up his badge and FBI credentials.

The teenager frowned. "Y-yeah…"

"Give me the keys. I need it. Now!"

"Dude, my parents will kill me—"

"Give me the Goddamn keys!" Cole roared. "I need your fucking car, right now!"

"Okay, okay!" The teen fumbled for his keys, dropping them when he pulled them out of his pants. "Can you, like, call my parents about this? They're going to be really pissed."

"Have them call the local FBI office," he shouted over his shoulder as he ran out the front door. He mashed the beeper on the kid's remote, swinging in every direction of the parking lot until a beat-up Isuzu Trooper, more rust than hunter green, flashed its lights.

He drove by memory, his arms, his hands, his legs shaking. His teeth chattered as he tried to call Noah again. No answer.

Overhead, a helicopter circled the air space above the West Des Moines FBI office, making passes over the neighborhoods, the highway, the side streets. Sirens wailed in the distance. Andy Garrett at large. Andy Garrett hunting again.

Hunting daughters and their fathers.

He pounded the steering wheel when Noah didn't pick up for the tenth time. Was he ignoring his phone? Was he ignoring Cole because of their argument? "Damn it, Noah, pick up!" he roared into Noah's voicemail. "Answer your Goddamn phone! Please!"

The houses in Noah's neighborhood were dark, everyone asleep now that it was past midnight. How had it gotten so late? Weren't they just at dinner? Hadn't he just kissed Noah's fingers?

He took the turn onto Noah's street on two wheels, skidding across the pavement and burning rubber as he floored it down the block. His headlights illuminated the front of Noah's house, the porch, the manicured flower beds, the dark windows. No lights, no signs of life.

Cole drove right up onto the lawn, flung the door open, and crouched in the flower beds as he pulled his gun. Rose thorns tore at his jeans. He squashed daisies beneath his boots.

He froze, listening. Sirens in the distance. Helicopter rotors far away. His own breathing, hard and fast, matching his pounding pulse. He forced himself to take a slower breath. Swallowed his heart. Closed his eyes.

Sobbing. Muffled, high-pitched sobbing coming from inside.

Katie.

If Katie was crying, where the *fuck* was Noah?

Fear seized him, harder, faster, deeper than he'd ever felt before. Its claws tore into his quick, shredded his soul, dug into the marrow of his bones.

Noah would never let anything happen to Katie. He'd die first.

John, staked to his basement floor, his hand reaching for painted toenails—

Cole ran. He vaulted the porch, stacking alongside the front door. *Listen.*

Sobbing: the same high-pitched, frightened cry, muffled. Something covering her mouth?

No sign or sound from Noah. *Noah—Jesus, Noah, hang on. Katie, hang on. I'm coming.*

He tried the knob. The door pushed open soundlessly. Unlocked.

Why would Noah leave his front door unlocked? He didn't. He hadn't, not when Cole had been there. Katie came in with a key. Noah had deadbolted the door behind him. And he wouldn't have opened the door for Garrett—

He pushed inside, crouching in the darkness as he flattened himself against the wall in the front hallway. The sobbing was clearer now. Katie, definitely Katie. Terror bled through her, washed her sobs in pure, unadulterated horror. A man's voice was speaking. Not Noah. Not anyone Cole recognized.

Not Andy Garrett.

Someone else.

A different victimology. A different killer, perfectly mimicking the first.

Who?

The voice tickled at him, at the edges of his mind, his subconscious still trying to put puzzle pieces together as he crept forward.

He was ten steps and one corner away from the kitchen. Katie was sobbing, crying, pleading. Crying out for Noah.

There. Another scream, a wail. A muffled shriek, ripped from a ragged, torn throat. The sound roared over Katie's. *Noah.*

"Isn't it awful?" the stranger's voice growled. It was a man. Someone twisted, poisoned, ruined to the core. "Isn't it fucking *awful?* Seeing your daughter in agony? Seeing her suffering? Hurts, doesn't it? Down deep, where you can never get the pain out."

Another scream. Katie sobbed, crying, "Dad! Dad!" The wailing, the muffled roaring, rose. Cole edged a step closer. Around the corner was the kitchen. He'd have no cover as soon as he turned. He'd be exposed, silhouetted thanks to the moonlight coming through the sliding glass door and shining down the hallway while this man had Noah and Katie in the kitchen. This man had every advantage.

"Imagine," the man growled again, "finding her dead."

He found her dead. Are you kidding me? He remembered—

The deputy trying to catch his breath in Noah's office. Noah telling him to take his time. Explaining to Cole that he'd been the one to find his own daughter, Monica, Garrett's obsession.

Venneslund. Deputy Venneslund. Monica Venneslund.

Rage directed at law enforcement fathers. Making them suffer, making them see their daughters dead and dying.

Fathers who had failed to save his daughter or catch her killer.

Revenge, the most classic motive of all.

Who could mimic a serial killer's crimes better than a victim, or the loved one of a victim? Someone who had experienced the killer, who had seen, had felt, his handiwork.

"Dad!" Katie sobbed. "Dad, *please!*"

A muffled scream. An impotent, raging, agonized bellow. *Noah, I'm here.* He edged closer, far enough to peek around the corner.

Katie stood on one of Noah's kitchen chairs in her pajamas, a rope wrapped around her neck and tied off on the exposed ceiling beam. Venneslund stood beside the chair, one boot on the edge of the seat, ready to push it out from under her. She'd hang if he did, strangle and suffocate in under a minute. But the drop wouldn't break her neck. No, she would die slowly, horrifically.

And Noah would have a front-row seat. He was on the ground, his arms over his head, both of his palms stabbed through with knives, pinning him to the wall behind him. Another knife went through his right wrist. Blood ran in rivers down both arms, soaking his T-shirt, his boxers. His thigh was bleeding, a small pool of blood growing beneath his leg. They'd been in bed. Venneslund must have knocked, asked to come in. Noah had trusted him, of course.

And then Noah had been shot. Subdued.

Katie's cheerleading leggings were tied around Noah's mouth, gagging him. He still screamed, still roared, still tried to fight his way free. Tears ran down his face. His eyes were red, swollen and anguished and trying to tell his daughter *I love you love you love you love you—*

Venneslund cocked his gun and aimed it at Katie's temple. "You're getting a little rambunctious, Noah. Calm it down, now."

Noah stilled, still screaming through his gag but no longer trying to escape from the knives pinning him to the wall.

"I'm trying to perfect this," Venneslund said. "At first, it was enough for Frank to find his daughter like I did. Dead.

Cold. *Gone.* To give him the horror that I felt. Let him die with that feeling in the center of him, so that was the last thing he knew: that she was dead and he had failed. But then I wanted more with Bart, and with John, and now you. Especially you, Noah. I want you all to feel a fraction of what I've felt, *every day*, every *single* day, for these six years! Seeing it. Reliving it. Over and over and over again." He gritted his teeth. Grabbed the back of Katie's shirt and nearly shoved her off the seat.

Katie screamed. He shoved his gun against her back.

Noah roared. Fresh tears poured from his eyes.

"You will watch her die," Venneslund hissed. "And you will know—*know*, Noah!—that you couldn't save her. You failed her, just like you failed *my daughter!*"

Venneslund pulled his gun back. He shifted his weight, pushed with his foot. The chair beneath Katie started to slide. Noah screamed, shrieking and bellowing as Venneslund turned the gun on him, aiming for the center of Noah's forehead.

Cole burst from around the corner. He had one shot, one chance. If he missed Venneslund, he'd hit Katie. Then he'd have to take cover while Katie dangled, strangling on Venneslund's noose. Venneslund would undoubtedly kill Noah, too. He had one chance—

Cole fired as Venneslund shoved the chair out from beneath Katie.

The shot boomed through Noah's kitchen. Sparks erupted, igniting the midnight gloom enough for Cole to see Katie's toes dancing, searching for the chair, and to see a black hole open in the center of Venneslund's forehead where Cole's bullet slammed into his skull.

He was across the kitchen before Venneslund's body hit the ground. He holstered his weapon and grabbed Katie's legs, holding her up as she struggled to breathe. Her eyes were already rolling back. He got slack in the rope, but they had to get her down now, now, now.

But he couldn't let her go, and the chair was out of reach.

"Noah!" he shouted. "Noah, I need you to get to us!"

He saw it happen but still couldn't believe it. Noah's gaze locked on his. A thousand emotions burned through him: gratitude and relief and panic and joy and agony and love and fear, terror, horror. He held Cole's stare, took a breath, his red-rimmed eyes clenching, squeezing, tears running down his face in waterfalls as he screamed into his gag—

Noah pulled his hand over the knife, dragging his stabbed palm deeper onto the blade, through the blade, over the handle, until he tore his left hand free. Blood ran down his arms, a torrent of it, too much, much too much. He didn't seem to notice. Noah ripped the two knives out of his right hand and wrist, tore his gag off, and scrambled across the kitchen.

He was screaming, still, his voice raw and broken, screaming Katie's name, screaming Cole's name, screaming and cursing and crying as he used one of the knives that had held him to the wall to cut his daughter down. She collapsed into Cole's arms, who collapsed into Noah's arms, and both of them pulled Venneslund's noose from around her throat. She wasn't breathing. Fuck, she wasn't breathing, wasn't making any noise—

Katie's eyes popped open as she inhaled, gasping, and looked from Noah to Cole and then back to her dad. Her tied hands reached for Noah, grabbing his blood-soaked T-shirt and pulling him to her as she tried to scream, tried to say *Dad Dad Dad*, but her voice was broken and her throat was black and blue.

But she was breathing, and crying, and she held Noah as Noah held her, and held Cole, and Cole held on to both of them, rocking on Noah's kitchen floor as his tears joined their own.

Noah's broken, bloody left hand grabbed him, drew him closer, until the three of them were one, bodies pressed into one mass, tears falling on each other's faces, screams and sobs inhaled and exhaled together. "I love you," Noah breathed. "I love you, I love you, I love you."

Cole kissed Noah's tear-soaked face and then kissed Katie's temple.

"*Police! FBI!*" Ten pairs of boots thundered into the front hallway, holding at the same point Cole had. Jacob, bless the man—and he'd brought reinforcements.

"In the kitchen!" Cole called. "Officer down! Noah's wounded, and so is Katie!" He glanced at Venneslund's body, bleeding all over the kitchen floor. "We're all clear in here. The killer is down. It wasn't Garrett."

21

IT SEEMED as if every law enforcement officer and first responder in Des Moines descended on Noah's house.

Cop cars, sheriff cars, FBI cars, fire trucks, and ambulances lined both sides of the block. Helicopters roared overhead—some from news channels getting the scoop, but mostly law enforcement agencies. The special agent in charge of the Omaha office, Samuel Bray, had flown in that evening planning to meet with Noah after they'd booked Garrett. He showed up at the crime scene, too, listening quietly from the back as Jacob—now the officer in charge of the biggest investigation in Des Moines' history—briefed the assembled group.

Katie and Noah were in the back of an ambulance, bundled in blankets, getting an initial assessment and treatment from the paramedics. Both of Noah's hands were packed and wrapped, and his right arm was in a sling. Katie had an IV going, fluids and sedatives helping to calm her down as she lay on the gurney, her neck wreathed in a cervical collar. Venneslund's gunshot had gone through the meat of Noah's thigh, and the paramedics had wrapped his leg in a dressing and bound up the wound, but said it looked like a clean through and through Noah's outer muscle.

Noah hadn't let Cole leave his side. He'd grabbed Cole's hand as they were escorted from the house, fingertips hooked on fingertips, and pulled him close. Noah's blood was still smeared all over Cole's palm, had dried in the crevices of his nails and fingerprints as he hovered beside their ambulance.

"We're clear to transport," one of the paramedics said to both Noah and the driver. "Let me tell the OIC. We're taking you downtown to Methodist. The trauma center."

Noah nodded, gaze flicking to Cole's. He reached for him again, his bandaged hand like a bear paw. Only the ends of his fingers were visible. Still, he hooked them around Cole's hand and tried to tug him closer. "Will you come to the hospital?" Noah's voice was still broken, his vocal cords shredded.

"Of course." Cole stepped closer, practically inside Noah's spread knees. He hesitated, then raised his hand to cup Noah's face and cheek. Salt trails scratched over his palm. Noah gazed up at him. He leaned into Cole's touch and closed his eyes.

Jacob arrived, radioed over by the paramedic, with Bray on his heels. "What's up?"

"We're taking them downtown. They're being admitted to Methodist trauma."

"Okay." Jacob reached for Noah's shoulder, squeezing gently. "Hang in there, buddy."

Opening his eyes, Noah nodded. He was still leaning against Cole, holding on to him with his bandaged hand. "Thanks," he croaked.

Jacob stepped back. Cole helped Noah to his feet. Noah swayed, almost fell into him, and Cole steadied him with his arms around Noah's waist. Noah looked him dead in the eyes.

He pressed his forehead to Cole's. Rubbed his nose against Cole's, then his cheek. Kissed him in front of Jacob, Bray, and the entire community of Des Moines law enforcement. And probably three different news helicopters circling overhead.

"Noah," Cole whispered. He nuzzled Noah back and

wrapped his hand around Noah's waist. "You've been through hell tonight. You need time to think—"

"No, I don't. I've already thought, and thought, and thought," Noah croaked. "I need *you*. That's what I need."

"You have me," Cole breathed. "You and Katie both. You both have me."

Finally, Noah smiled. He kissed Cole again, and then again, until the paramedic cleared his throat and gestured for Noah to hurry it up. "Come to the hospital?"

Cole steadied him as Noah clambered into the ambulance. He let go when Noah settled onto the edge of Katie's gurney. "I'll be there as soon as I can." He reached for Katie, squeezing her hand as her eyes drifted closed and she leaned into Noah.

Then the paramedics asked him to step back, and the doors slammed shut, and Noah's ambulance took off down the street, red-and-blues flashing over the yards and faces of Noah's entire neighborhood, everyone out on their yards now, watching.

Jacob appeared at his side, his expression unreadable in the flashing lights. He peered at Cole as if sizing him up, taking his measure. Then he held out his hand, pumping Cole's when he took it. "You're a hero."

Cole shook his head. He wasn't. He'd missed so much. He'd barely been in time.

"We found Andy Garrett," Jacob said, turning and glaring down the street. His hands landed on his hips, and his face turned fearsome, glowering. "I sent a unit out to the Olson fields, to that clearing he talked about. He was there, right in the center. He'd blown a hole through his skull, and he was holding a picture of himself and Jessie. They looked close. Like maybe they *were* dating. He'd written a note, too. It said, 'I'm sorry.'"

"When Venneslund heard Garrett escaped, he must have seized the opportunity to attack Noah and Katie. He could pin their murders on Garrett, again. He's been hiding under Garrett's profile. We never even saw him."

Jacob nodded. "Yeah… that's what we think, too. God damn it, he was right there. They both were. This whole time."

Bray appeared, hanging up his cell phone as he held out his hand to Cole. "Dr. Kennedy, I've heard a lot about you. Pleased to make your acquaintance. I'm on the way to the hospital. Would you like a ride?"

IT TOOK over two hours for Cole and Bray to find Noah and Katie in the massive Iowa Methodist complex in downtown Des Moines. They'd both been admitted through the emergency department, Katie to pediatrics and Noah to adult trauma, but, knowing Noah, he was with Katie and wouldn't be leaving. He and Bray were still shuttled between three different wings before Bray put his foot down, pulled his badge, and ordered they be brought to the nurses' station in pediatric critical care.

Noah met them there, bedraggled, bandaged, limping, and dressed in a set of surgeon's scrubs. His hair stuck up in all directions, his hands had been rebandaged, and his right arm was in a much more serious-looking sling.

"Sir," he said to Bray. "Thank you for coming."

Bray gripped him by both shoulders. "Of course. How are you? How is Katie?"

"She's going to be okay. No broken bones, no fractures. They had her in about every imaging machine there is, checking X-rays and CT and MRI to make sure her spine and throat were all right. She's good." Noah's lips quirked upward, a tiny grin aimed at Cole. "Cole saved her. He saved us both."

Bray's hand landed on Cole's shoulder. He felt the warm

squeeze, the gentle reassurance. "And you, Noah? Are *you* okay?"

Noah ran a hand over his face, dragged his fingers through his hair. He turned and looked back at Katie's room, sighing. "Not right now, I'm not. All this—" He waved at his arm, held up his hand, only his fingertips peeking out of the heavy bandages. "Will heal. I'll be fine, they said, after some rehab on my right arm. But…" His haunted eyes met Cole's. "I don't think I'll be able to close my eyes for a while, or forget what happened there."

Cole reached for him. Noah reached back, stepping into Cole's hold and resting his forehead on Cole's shoulder. His breath was warm on Cole's neck. Cole ran his hand up and down Noah's back, over his trembling muscles.

"Did Lilly make it here yet?" Bray asked softly.

Noah nodded. "Yeah. She's with Katie."

Cole's stomach clenched. He kept rubbing Noah's back. Noah didn't pull away.

"I'm going to go say a few words to her." Bray gripped Noah's shoulder again, gave them both a reassuring smile, and then headed for Katie's room.

Noah exhaled as Bray's shoes squeaked on the tile floor. "Lilly is here."

"Of course she is. She's Katie's mother." She'd probably set a land speed record crossing Iowa after she'd gotten the call. State troopers might have picked her up, even. That would have been the safest option.

"She's an assistant U.S. attorney in Omaha. She works with Bray all the time." Noah's lips quirked up again, this time against Cole's neck. "And now Bray is my boss. If I end up keeping John's job."

"The tiny world of federal law enforcement." Cole held on to Noah even as Noah straightened. They were a breath apart, Noah still standing inside the loose circle of Cole's arms, their foreheads, their messy strands of hair brushing against each other.

Through the window to Katie's room, he saw Bray hugging a tall, slender brunette dressed in dark leggings and an oversized sweatshirt. Her hair was pulled back in a ponytail, and her face, delicate and fine boned, almost elfin, was splotchy and tear-stained. Lilly. Noah's ex-wife.

Katie lay in the hospital bed, a padded cervical collar around her neck and the blankets pulled up over her waist. She wore a teddy bear hospital gown, and her dark hair was spread out over the pillow. An IV line ran into the back of her hand. She was asleep.

"Do you want me to leave?"

Noah shook his head. "No. Definitely not. I want you to stay all night, if you can."

"Of course I can."

"And…" Noah took a slow, deep breath. "I want to make this work." He took Cole's hand, pressed it to his chest, over his heart. "This. *Us.* Whatever this is between us. I don't want to hide from it anymore. I don't want to be afraid of it. I almost lost…" The haunted, terrified sheen passed over Noah's eyes again before he blinked fast and squeezed Cole's hand. "I almost lost everything. Katie… And I almost lost the chance to build a life with you. I don't want to spend another moment without you, if you still want me, after what I said and did."

Cole pulled Noah into his arms. Noah folded into him, almost collapsing, his injured arms between them. Cole kissed his cheek, his temple, his hair. "Of course I want you."

"I know I can be difficult," Noah said. "I want to apologize in advance for that." Cole chuckled. "And I'm sorry for saying we were only fuck buddies. We've always been more than that. Even from the first night in Vegas."

"I know." Cole kissed him again, ran his hands over

Noah's back. "I fell hard for you, Noah. Right from the beginning."

Noah pulled back, just enough to look Cole in the eyes. "You saved me," he whispered. "You *saved* me."

Cole kissed him on the lips, in front of the nurses' station, the doctors and orderlies in the halls, in front of Katie's window and Lilly and Bray inside her room. In front of *everyone*.

Noah kissed him back. And smiled.

Bray and Lilly slipped out of Katie's room when Noah and Cole came back, Bray saying something about taking Lilly to the cafeteria and putting food in her. Noah clambered onto Katie's bed, taking her in his arms and holding her, fitting back into the depression he'd already made in the mattress and pillow behind his daughter. Cole dragged one of the visitor chairs to the bedside, facing Noah with Katie between them. Noah held out his hand. Cole took the bandaged fingers in his own. Kissed the tips, and then set their hands down on Katie's blankets.

Exhaustion seemed to tear through them both simultaneously, adrenaline leaching out of their last nerves now that they were together again, and safe, and finally able to be still. Cole's eyelids were boulders, dropping hard until he jerked himself awake again and again. Noah, too, seemed to try to stay awake, but it was a losing battle, and he fell asleep with his cheek pillowed on Katie's head and his hand resting on Cole's upturned palm.

Cole lay his head down beside their hands. Right before he fell asleep, he felt a smaller, unbandaged hand lay across the back of his head. *Katie*. He smiled.

HE WOKE BEFORE THE SUN, his back, his legs, his shoulders screaming. He bit his lip as he untwisted himself, standing and rolling his shoulders, trying to unkink muscles that had seized overnight. Across Katie's hospital room, Lilly slept on the couch, curled up under a hospital blanket. Noah and Katie were in the bed, Noah still holding her in his protective embrace. They both were snoring.

He ducked out to the hall and tried to walk off the stiffness, checking his phone as he rolled his neck. It wasn't even six yet, and he had three missed calls from his boss. Not good. He called him directly, skipping the voicemail.

"*Kennedy, thank God,*" his boss said, instead of hello. "*How soon can you get out to Boston? There's an emergency hearing on the Ripper case, and they need you there ASAP. Today.*"

"Sir, I…" He turned back toward Katie's room, down the long hallway painted in bright, cheerful pediatric colors. "I'm not finished here yet."

"*They need you in Boston. They could lose the hearing without your testimony, and that could set the Ripper up on a path to getting out. You need to be there.*"

Damn it. He squeezed his eyes shut. He didn't want to go. Fuck, he did not want to leave, ever. But he'd known he would have to. Wasn't that why he had been looking at flights? At long distance? At coming back to Des Moines as often as he could?

He just hadn't thought long distance would start so soon, so suddenly.

"Yeah, I can get there today," he croaked. "I'll book a flight as soon as we hang up."

"*Excellent. Then get back down here. We've got things piling up, and I need my best.*"

"Sir, when I get back, we need to talk."

"*Shit. What about?*"

"I need to pull way back, sir. I can't keep this up. This pace, this much travel. I need to get my feet underneath me, have more stability. We have to start farming out these travel gigs to some of the others. Snyder and Ramos and Dominguez."

His boss sighed, a long, crackling exhale. *"We'll talk, Kennedy. If cases need the best, there's only one agent I can send, you know? Like Des Moines. They asked for my best, and look what happened. You caught the guy. Actually, you caught them both."*

"It wasn't all me, sir."

"It wasn't not you, either." A pause. *"Get to Boston. Then come home. We'll talk."* The line cut.

Cole paced for another five minutes before calling to book his flight. Nine thirty out of Des Moines, connecting in Chicago. He had to get back to his hotel, check out, get to the airport. He had to say goodbye to Noah and to Katie.

They were still asleep when he tiptoed back in. Lilly was gone, the couch empty, her purse still on the floor. Cole stood at Katie's bedside and watched them both sleep.

Each of their inhales, each of their exhales made his heart shatter, then reform larger, fuller than a moment before… and then shatter again. He could watch them sleep for hours. Keep watch over them all day. And longer. Maybe for the rest of his life.

He kissed Katie's hair, the top of her head, and then kissed Noah on his forehead, his cheek. Brushed his lips over Noah's, wanting to deepen the moment but holding back. There was a pad of paper and a cheap pen at Katie's bedside. He wrote them both a note, explaining he'd been called to an emergency in Boston but would be back in a few days. He drew a big heart, then a terrible drawing of the two of them in bed together. *XO, Cole.* He left the notepad on the bed, where he'd laid his head and where Noah couldn't miss it.

Walking out of the room was excruciating. Every step felt like he was being stabbed. He had to walk backward, keep them in his sights. *I'm coming back. I'll see you in a few days. I promise.*

He had to move fast when he hit the hallway. If he didn't,

he'd call his boss, resign immediately. Or just break down and sob, fall to his knees in the corridor and let it all out—all the fear, the nerves, the terror, the anxiety that had shredded him. *I don't want to leave.*

"Dr. Kennedy!"

A woman's voice. He froze.

"Dr. Kennedy." Footsteps. She stopped behind him.

He turned and came face to face with Lilly Downing. "Ma'am." He tried to smile.

So did she. It looked more like a rictus of pain. Dark circles marred her porcelain skin, furrows beneath her red-rimmed eyes. She was beautiful nonetheless, delicate and strong at the same time. She stood her ground and lifted her chin, looking him in the eye as she swallowed. They sized each other up, holding each other's stare for a long, long moment.

"Where are you going?" she asked.

"I've been called to an emergency. I have to get to the airport." He almost snorted. That was how Noah left him the first time. Was there something poetic about this? No, it just sucked. It just purely sucked.

Lilly nodded. She went quiet, studying him. There were two cups of coffee in her hand. "Thank you," she finally breathed, "for saving their lives." She held out one of the coffee cups. "I was bringing this back for you. I don't know how you take your coffee, though." She reached into her hoodie's pocket when he took the cup she held out. "Do you take cream?" She offered him a fistful of creamers.

He laughed softly, remembering coffee-cream walls and Noah's smile, how Noah had taken him back to Starbucks to get his coffee just right, even when they wanted to be anywhere but near each other. Or they'd wanted each other too much, and the closeness had physically hurt. His life was being redefined by Noah in a thousand ways, memories of him and Katie attaching themselves to everything, from the banal to the beautiful. "I do. More than is probably wise." He took every creamer she offered. "Thank you."

"Are you coming back?"

"Yes. Definitely. As soon as I can." How did he tell Noah's ex-wife he was going to be dating Noah? That they were going to long-distance it, figure it all out? That he and Noah were going to be joining their lives, and that he'd hopefully become a part of Katie's life, too? It wasn't just Noah he was falling for. Falling for Noah meant a package deal, meant walking into a life that was already formed. Formed and waiting for a missing puzzle piece to complete the picture. Could he be that missing piece?

She nodded. Chewed her lip. Stepped back. "They'll be waiting for you when you do."

22

BOSTON WAS A HEADACHE. His boss even more so.

They agreed to a modified travel schedule, Cole flying anywhere work needed him Monday through Friday, with Cole picking up the cost of travel from wherever he was to Des Moines for the weekends. He'd be living out of a suitcase, and he'd barely ever see his condo in D.C., but he could be with Noah and Katie every weekend... as long everything went according to plan.

He took three weeks' vacation and spent every day with them, starting as soon as they were released from the hospital. Noah had booked a furnished apartment from the hospital, and Cole helped move them into the two-bedroom corporate suite in downtown Des Moines, shuttling bags of clothes from Noah's house so the two of them didn't have to go back there. Black fingerprint powder still covered the downstairs. Bloodstains coated the floor, ran down the walls where Noah had been stabbed. Splinters rose off roughened wood on the overhead beam where Katie's noose had been tied.

For three weeks, he and Noah spent every day together. Driving Katie to summer school and cheer practice. Falling into bed and making love. Talking, endlessly talking, sharing memories and thoughts and dreams and fears and heartaches and hopes. He went with Noah when his rehab appointments started and helped him with the exercises to regain the strength in his right arm.

He held Noah through the midnight hours when Noah would wake in a cold sweat, screaming. Screaming Katie's name, screaming Cole's name. Screaming in terror. Screaming in heartbreak. They'd make love after, often, Noah chasing away the fear with Cole's love until he was smiling again, gazing at Cole like Cole was the rising sun banishing his nightmares.

He took them both to their counseling appointments—at first every afternoon, then tapering to three times, then two times a week. He waited in the lobby for them, holding out his arms for the hugs they both gave him when they came out. The drives home were quiet, him holding Noah's hand in a death grip as tears rained down Noah's face.

Cole began cooking for them when he found out Noah's kitchen skills extended to Hamburger Helper, pancakes from a mix, grilled ham and cheese, and microwaved dinners. Cole made eggplant parmesan from scratch in the cramped kitchen, chicken enchiladas, homemade pizza. Fried chicken and grilled salmon.

Katie fired her father from cooking and told Cole he couldn't leave.

He helped Katie with her homework, the three of them in the kitchen together after dinner. He'd sit at the table and work through each math problem with her, explaining it one way and then another when she groaned and said she still didn't get it. Noah would watch as he washed the dishes, joining them and pressing kisses to their heads when he was finished. His hands would be warm and smell like soap when he threaded their fingers together. Katie always seemed to magically get better at her homework after Noah joined them. They let it slide, and the evenings became almost a ritual:

Noah held his hand after finishing the dishes as Katie hummed pop songs to herself and finished her problems.

One night they watched a movie, Noah on one side of him and Katie on the other. Halfway through, both of them fell asleep, leaning on him until he wrapped an arm around each. He didn't move for eleven hours, letting the movie turn to infomercials as he listened to them breathe. Neither had a nightmare that night. He kissed their hair every hour and let his tears fall silently. *Never end. Never let this moment end.*

Jacob called with updates on the investigation, even though Noah was on medical leave. Frank had lost his job in St. Louis for botching an investigation so badly the offender, a suspected killer, was able to beat the charges. He killed three more people before he was arrested and convicted. Bart Olson had fled Cedar Rapids and the seemingly automatic election to Linn County sheriff after he, too, had overseen an investigation that had gone sideways, allowing a man accused of being a serial predator to remain on the streets for an additional five years, until he killed a girl and was finally put away.

It wasn't hard to see Venneslund's pattern after that. His victimology had been carefully concealed inside Garrett's original one. Officers of the law who had failed, or who he perceived as having failed. Who needed to be punished. Who needed to have their daughters—daughters just like Monica—ripped out of their lives so they could feel an ounce of his own endless anguish and agony. Why he'd started killing so suddenly, no one knew. Not yet. Venneslund's apartment was practically bare, save for the second bedroom that had been set up like a shrine to his daughter. Had he simply cracked? Had he nurtured his rage until it boiled over into a fantasy? Years of wanting to make others pay turning, one day, into plans for revenge?

There was no sign Venneslund knew about Garrett, or vice versa. They weren't working together.

Neither Katie nor Noah handled Cole's leaving again well

at all. Katie was sullen and grumpy in the morning, and she'd picked a fight with Noah over her shoes being left out, eaten half a pancake Cole cooked, and then was quiet the whole drive to school. But she'd hugged Cole until he thought his ribs would snap, and she made him put his phone number in her phone so she could call him and ask for his help when her dad "sucks, as usual."

Noah held him and held him in the airport lobby, his strangled, smothered whimpers falling into Cole's ear. He hid his face beneath the rim of his ball cap until Cole tipped up his chin. "I'll be back," he said. "I already have my ticket."

"I know." Noah took his hand. Squeezed. His grip strength was coming back. "I just don't want to be without you, even for one day. I'm a greedy man."

"Call me," Cole said. "I don't care what time it is. Call me when you have nightmares. I'm here for you."

Noah nodded. He stared at Cole. Fidgeted. Blinked fast. Cole waited. Noah was not a man to be rushed, ever. If he was working up to something, he'd take his time, maybe even a geological epoch—

"I love you," Noah blurted out. "I love you, Cole."

In front of God and the Des Moines International Airport. Cole's jaw dropped, but he recovered quickly, hauling Noah into his arms and squeezing him tight. "I love you, too," he breathed. "I love you, too, Noah. More than you can possibly know."

He cried as the plane took off, and he didn't stop until they were over Ohio. He kept turning on his cell phone, staring at the picture of Noah he'd made his phone background. *I love you.*

He had to cancel his next weekend trip to Des Moines when his boss sent him on an emergency flight to Los Angeles. And then the weekend after that, when he was in Boise on a domestic terrorism emergency negotiation.

Instead of being together, he called Noah and Katie every

chance he could. They ate dinner—takeout—via video call, and he listened to Katie's long diatribes about summer school, her pre-calc homework, cheerleading practice, and the idiot football players. Later, he and Noah stayed on the phone until they almost fell asleep, talking quietly as the hours bled away. Noah was back at work, no longer the acting special agent in charge of Des Moines but now officially the new SAC. And while Cole was being worked to the bone, Noah and his team were enjoying a lull in crime in the Des Moines metro area. It was nice, Noah said, to have time to breathe.

The day before Katie's school started, Cole got a video message from Jacob. Cole was in Atlanta, helping the local police department, and he ducked out to the stairwell to watch.

The video opened on Jacob, Noah, and Katie out at lunch, eating on a patio somewhere sunny and bright. Noah was flushed and embarrassed, Katie was laughing and hanging on to his shoulders, and Jacob held the camera, ducking his face into the frame. "Hey, Cole! Just wanted to give you a shout-out. I've been hearing so much about you recently—Cole this and Cole that and Cole is wonderful and Cole is everything I ever wanted and Cole is perfect, blah blah—but you haven't come in to see me! Hardly what I call perfect and wonderful! What gives, man? Next time you're in town, come on down to the office. I still need to take you out. You gotta need a break from this guy." He jerked his thumb at Noah, rolling his eyes exaggeratedly. "So come say hi, man."

"Come baaack," Katie called to the screen. "We miss you!"

Through it all, Noah was staring at the camera lens, embarrassed and blushing and trying to hide his smile behind his hands, but there was so much love in his gaze that it made Cole's heart ache.

"Oh, I almost forgot." Jacob pulled a small envelope out

of his pocket. He passed it to Noah and winked at the camera. "I got you something. A congrats on your promotion."

Noah ripped open the envelope, and a rainbow lanyard, identical to the one Cole wore, tumbled into his palm. Katie laughed. Noah's blush got impossibly darker. Jacob beamed, mugging for the camera. "Now you guys can match!" He reached across the table, his massive bear paw gripping the back of Noah's neck for a moment. The camera went wonky, then straightened. "Seriously, Cole, can't wait to see you again. Don't be a stranger." Katie waved manically in the background. Noah kept staring at him, fingering the rainbow lanyard, a thousand watts of love pouring from his eyes.

The video ended.

In the stairwell of the Atlanta police department, all alone, Cole fell to his knees and wept.

HE MADE it to Katie's first football game to watch her cheer but almost fell asleep in the stands. Noah prodded him awake, let him sleep on the drive home, and then made breakfast Saturday morning. Instead of the French toast Cole usually made, he cobbled together microwave cinnamon buns. Katie barely noticed the difference, keeping up a running commentary about all the things Cole had missed, every minute detail of her life at school since the year had begun. Noah held his hand through the entire monologue and kissed him when Katie disappeared to shower. "You're a trooper."

He wanted to go back to sleep, pull Noah into bed with him, wake up sometime in the afternoon and make love to him, then go back to sleep again. But Katie had made plans for them all to go roller skating, so he saddled up and off they went. Noah held his hand around the rink, and later, after Katie finally went to bed, he seduced Cole in the best, most delicious way.

Hours later, Cole's toes were still curled, and he was trying to remember how to breathe as Noah pressed his warm lips to Cole's cheek and smiled. "Good?"

"Good? I can barely remember my own name."

"Mm, so I need to work harder. Get you to forget even that."

"I may die." He rolled over, pulling Noah close. He nuzzled his face, kissed his nose. "I love you."

"I love you." Noah lost his playful edge, suddenly going serious. "I do want to be good for you. You're more experienced than I am, and I don't want you to get bored—"

Cole rolled Noah to his back, straddling him and capturing him in his arms. Their faces were microns apart, lips touching. "Never," Cole breathed. "Never, ever, ever. You're perfect for me. Exactly as you are. You're everything I want, Noah. I *mean* that."

Noah made a face. "I've complicated your life. By a lot. I have a lot of baggage." He still called Cole two or three nights a week, coming down from a nightmare. "And I have a very needy daughter. I think she wants to steal you away from me."

Cole laughed. "I never thought I could make someone that happy just by showing up."

"I've never seen her like this. She's so happy, Cole." Noah ran his hands through Cole's hair, fingers massaging Cole's scalp. "I've never been this happy in my life."

"Neither have I." He kissed Noah slowly, and then not slowly, and even though Noah had just rocked his world to the core, he rose to the occasion and they made love once more, until Noah was screaming his name into the pillow and Cole was draped over his back, cursing and praying and kissing Noah's shoulder blades as he told Noah he loved him, over and over again.

IF HE'D NEVER BEEN this happy, he'd also never been this exhausted. Traveling across the country was wearing him down, as was the weekly anxiety about whether or not he'd make his Friday flight to Des Moines. And even if he did, what was the point if he was so exhausted he could barely stay awake while he was there?

Something had to change.

He stood in the middle of his nearly abandoned D.C. condo, folding his laundry as his microwave warmed up a frozen dinner. He looked left, to his empty, cold bedroom. He looked right, at his empty, cold office. There were no shoes thrown haphazardly on the ground, no bobby pins scattered on the carpet or the countertops. No textbooks or homework worksheets on the edge of the kitchen table. No shirts that weren't his in the wash. No scent of Noah on his pillowcases or sheets.

Monday, he called SAC Bray from the Omaha office. Bray called back Tuesday morning, said he was in D.C. at headquarters, and asked Cole to meet him for dinner downtown.

"So you want to put in a transfer request?" Bray's eyebrows rose as he sipped his bourbon. The restaurant lights were dim, and piano music played softly. Lobbyists and government employees at a higher pay grade than Cole's dined here.

He straightened his silverware and spun his wine glass. "Yes, sir. I understand there's an opening in the Des Moines office." Everyone had moved up. Noah was the new head honcho, one of the women who hadn't been on the task force was the new ASAC, and Jacob was third in charge. The rest of the four agents rounded out the office. There was an open spot for a field agent still waiting to be filled, two and a half months later.

"Des Moines is not an easy office to staff. Not a lot of people requesting to be sent there. We usually pull from the academy, send someone brand new out there to cut their teeth for three years. By the time they're able to transfer, they've got the experience to be effective in the big cities. I'm not sure I've ever had someone request to move from a city out to a rural office. Certainly not someone like you, a senior agent in the BAU."

"I want to go, sir."

Bray sipped his bourbon. He studied Cole. "I don't doubt you want to. My concern is, how *long* will you want to be there?" His head tipped to the side. "It's not like I can transfer you out of there quickly. You request this transfer, officially, and you might be looking at Des Moines as your home. Permanently. For better or for worse."

Your home. Permanently. His heart pounded. His hand trembled as he took a gulp of his wine. "That's exactly what I want, sir. I want to move to Des Moines, and I want to stay there. I'm done with this commuting garbage. I want to stay in the FBI, too. I know I have a lot to offer the Bureau, and I like what I do. But, more than all of that, I want to move to Des Moines. So I'd like to request this transfer, officially, and if it's not approved, I'll resign and move there anyway. Permanently."

Slowly, Bray smiled. "You've thought about this."

"I have. I'm certain."

"There are a few things we'll have to iron out. You'll have to report to me, at least for your evaluations and reviews. Your SAC in Des Moines can assign you cases and manage the day to day, of course, unless I start hearing complaints of favoritism. I've known Noah Downing for a long time, though, and I don't see that happening."

His heart was going to burst from his chest. Cole nodded. He didn't trust himself to speak. "However it needs to be, I'm fine with it."

"Have you talked to your boss yet?"

Cole shook his head. "This shouldn't be a surprise to him.

I've been flying to Des Moines every weekend I can, when he hasn't sent me ping-ponging across the country."

"I'll talk to him tomorrow. Put in your official transfer request first thing, and we'll see how fast we can get this going. I might have to tell your boss you'll be resigning if you don't get approved."

"Do it. I'm serious. I know where I want to be, and why."

Bray's eyes sparkled. "Now," he said, leaning forward. "Like I said, I've known Downing for a long time. You do this, you move out there?" Bray shook his head. "Might as well go buy a ring and take him down to the church."

They ate steaks and talked about cases that were ongoing in the Omaha area of operations. Omaha covered all of Nebraska and Iowa through the main office and the eight smaller offices, like Des Moines. Cole floated through the meal, one thought repeating on a loop in his mind. *I'm moving to Des Moines. I'm moving to Noah. We're going to be together. We're going to be a family.*

Bray had told him to put in his transfer request first thing in the morning. He did it as soon as he got back to his condo. Within ten minutes, his boss texted him, a single statement: *Damn it.* He didn't reply.

Just after noon on Wednesday, Bray called him at his desk at the BAU. "*I've got agreements on the transfer, and I'm walking it through headquarters myself. No one has ever seen someone like you request to go to Iowa before.*" He chuckled. "*I told them you had excellent reasons that were all your own and left it at that.*"

"Thank you." He didn't know what else to say. There was a file open on his desk, gruesome murder scene photos. He didn't see a thing. "Thank you. I can't explain how much this means to me."

"*I think I understand. When do you want to start?*"

"How soon can I?"

"*How soon can you be out there?*"

"Day after tomorrow."

"*Well, then, I'll fill in the date on the paperwork and let you start your handover now. See you in Iowa, Dr. Kennedy.*"

FRIDAY MORNING, he badged into the Des Moines office at 9:05 a.m., just after Noah's morning briefing had begun. He bounced on his toes in the elevator, fiddled with the strap of his laptop bag. He had his rainbow lanyard around his neck, ID and badge out, and he entered through the back door of the office, behind the conference room.

Inside, the whole office was attending Noah's morning meeting, sitting around the table with their mugs of coffee. Cole knocked and waited in the open doorway.

Noah turned. Saw him. Froze.

Noah, too, was wearing his rainbow lanyard, his badge tucked into his shirt pocket but the rainbow on full display.

Jacob was the first on his feet, beaming, hand out to shake Cole's as he exclaimed, "What are you doing here, man?"

He shook Jacob's hand and pulled out his transfer papers from his suit jacket. "I've got orders to report to the SAC in Des Moines." He held out the papers to Noah.

Noah's jaw dropped. He took the papers like he was in a dream, a marionette on strings. Jacob leaned over his shoulder, reading along with him. *Dr. Cole Kennedy transferred to Des Moines Resident Agency on this day. Reporting relationship to SAC Bray, Omaha FO. Duties assigned by local SAC of RA Des Moines.*

"Welcome to the team!" Jacob boomed. He came around Noah and pulled Cole into a bruising hug, more a wrestling maneuver than an act of affection. Cole tried to hug him back. It was like trying to hug an oak tree.

The rest of the office started to clap, welcoming him back as Noah stared. A slow smile formed on Noah's face, growing larger and larger until Cole thought Noah was going to explode.

They hugged, and the clapping grew louder, mixed with small cheers and Jacob's happy whooping. "I can't believe you did this," Noah whispered. "I can't believe you're really here."

"I should have done it sooner. But I'm here now." He pulled back, stepped away. He wanted to tell Noah everything, tell him all the hopes and dreams he'd built on the flight out. He was going to put his condo on the market. They could use that money to buy a new house for the three of them, get out of the cramped apartment. Sell Noah's house for cash, quick —just get rid of it and all the horrible memories it contained. Start fresh in a new house with a back porch and a view of cornfields and the setting sun and an ocean of stars from horizon to horizon.

That was for later. Now, he was the newest agent in the Des Moines office, and it was time to do his job. He took a seat at the conference room table, the same one he'd sat in when he first arrived, across from Noah. This time, Noah was beaming at him.

Later, when they picked Katie up from school, she ran to Cole and leaped into his arms, asking what he was doing there, that she thought he wasn't supposed to get in until way later. When Cole told her he was moving to Des Moines, that he'd transferred as of that morning and that he wasn't ever leaving, she screamed, leaped into his arms again, and hugged him until he couldn't breathe.

Noah wrapped his arms around them both and kissed Cole over the top of Katie's head.

23
THREE MONTHS LATER

FOOTSTEPS THUNDERED UP THE STAIRS. "*Da-ad*! Have you seen my jacket? I need the team jacket for the game!"

"Where did you last see it?" Noah hollered after Katie.

"If I knew that…" Katie shouted. She sounded like she was in the loft. "I wouldn't be asking!" A pause. Noah arched an eyebrow at Cole. Cole shook his head, smiling as he washed out the spaghetti sauce pan.

"Found it!" Katie shouted. "I got it, I got it!"

Honking sounded in the driveway. Footsteps again, this time thundering downstairs. Katie appeared, team jacket over one arm and cheer bag over the other, dressed in her winter cheer outfit, her hair in a French braid and tied off with ribbons. Cole had helped do her hair while Noah, in a change of pace, had helped her with her chemistry homework.

After school, they'd had just enough time to throw together dinner, help Katie with an hour of homework, and then get her ready for the semifinal championship football game that night. Winter was knocking on Des Moines' door, and though there hadn't been any snow yet, the temperatures were dipping into the low forties and flirting with the thirties.

Another honk from the driveway. Noah glared out the front door. "That isn't Trevor, is it?"

"No, Dad. Trevor is an idiot. That's Pria." Katie threw an arm around Noah's neck and gave him a kiss on the cheek. "See you at the game?"

"Of course, K-Bear." Noah kissed her back and opened the door. Cold air blew into their house. "Hurry, hurry."

"Okay, okay! See you guys later!" Katie jogged out to Pria's car, throwing herself into the back seat as Noah shut the door and sighed.

Cole wiped his hands, laughing. For the first time in what felt like days, there was silence in the house. "I can hear myself think."

"I can't think." Noah grinned. He pushed off the door and headed for Cole, who was leaning against the entrance to the kitchen. His arms wrapped round Cole's waist, and his grin turned sexy, mischievous, as he leaned in for a kiss. "I don't want to think, either."

The door flew open. "Sorry! Sorry!" Katie shouted.

"Pom-poms," Noah said, his lips moving against Cole's. "Or her water bottle."

"I put both in her bag," Cole murmured. "Cell phone."

Katie grabbed her phone, hidden under her chemistry textbook, from the dining room table and ran back out the front door, slamming it behind her again.

They laughed as they kissed, and kissed again, and Noah's arms wrapped around Cole's neck as Cole grabbed Noah's ass and squeezed.

There wasn't time for more than a quick make-out session in the kitchen, not if they wanted to be on time to the game and get a parking spot somewhere within the Des Moines area code. Cole threw the clothes from the washer to the dryer as Noah put away the dishes, and then they were off, bundled up in hoodies with Katie's school mascot across the front, thick jackets, beanies, and gloves. They held hands walking into the stands and to their seats, just off the fifty-yard line in the first section, close to where Katie and her squad cheered. Katie saw them arrive and waved. Her friends joined in, waving and shouting hellos to them both.

The game was close, and exciting, and cold. Their breath fogged in front of their faces, and when they weren't jumping to their feet to scream and cheer with the crowd, they were huddled together, arms around each other, faces buried in their jackets. After one touchdown, they kissed, hugged, and clapped with the crowd. Through it all, Katie cheered with her squad, tumbling in the end zone and flipping for each point the team put on the board, and then rising to the top of her squad's pyramid before flipping backward and landing safely, caught by her squad mates.

"I hate when she does that one," Noah mumbled, looking away. "I can't watch it."

"You know she does it even more now that she knows you don't like it."

Noah shook his head and grumbled, smothering his grin.

After the game, they met Katie and her friends outside the athletic center. Everyone was still amped from the excitement, from the win, from the cold air and the Friday night lights and the crisp, fresh freedom of a winter weekend. The team was heading to the championship game out in Cedar Rapids in two weeks to play for the state title.

"Dad, we want to go grab pizza. Is that okay?" The tip of Katie's braid swung as she walked and talked. Katie wasn't driving yet, and none of the friends with her after the game were, either. Noah and Cole were the chauffeurs for this late-night crew.

Noah looked at him. He looked at Noah. "Sure," Noah said. "Where are we taking you guys?"

They conferred, as teen girls do, and delivered their decision as they piled into Noah's SUV. The back was filled with loud voices, high-pitched giggles, *Oh my God*s and *No way*s for the whole drive. Cole held Noah's hand, smiling as they drove past the buildings of downtown, glittering against the ink-dark sky.

At the restaurant, the girls ordered a breakfast pizza, while Noah and Cole got cheese sticks. They sat apart from Katie and her friends, close enough to keep an eye on them without being accused of hovering. Raising a teen, Cole had discovered, was a delicate balancing act between trying to keep them safe and not crossing the line into a full-on parental surveillance state.

More friends arrived, summoned by text message, including girls on the squad who could drive. Another pizza was ordered. The girls seemed to settle in, in no hurry to leave.

Eventually, Katie wandered over, all smiles and flushed cheeks and laughing, happy eyes. "Hey, Dad, Evelyn invited me to spend the night at her house with Christina and Emily. And yes, her parents are home. Cool?"

"When will you be back tomorrow?"

She shrugged. "Noon?"

Noah looked at Cole. Cole looked back at him, smiling. "Sure. Just remember we need to finish your chemistry and work on your English paper. And when I say we..."

"You mean me." She rolled her eyes and smiled at the same time. "Can we get a Christmas tree tomorrow, too?"

"As soon as you finish your homework."

She grinned. "Okay." She bent down and kissed Noah's cheek, then kissed Cole's, too. "See you guys tomorrow!"

Katie went back to her friends, and Noah and Cole slid out of the booth, tossing their trash and heading for the door. Cole waved to Katie as Noah held open the door, and he caught the end of a high-pitched group giggle and Emily saying, "Oh my God, do you know what they're going to be doing while you spend the night?" and Katie replying, "Stop.

Those are my dads. You don't make fun of anyone else's parents, so don't make fun of mine."

In the parking lot, Cole pulled Noah to him and crowded him against the SUV door. Noah grinned, his gloved hands wrapping around Cole's neck. They were surrounded by cars liveried in the high school's colors, painted with football players' jersey numbers and "#1" and "Go Team" across the windows. Noah's breath puffed in Cole's face right before Cole leaned in, kissing him softly.

"Is this what you imagined at all?" Noah asked. His nose was red from the cold, but his eyes were shining as bright as the stars overhead. "Did you ever think this would be what your life became?"

I wanted this so badly I ached for it. I dreamed of this future every night. You remade my entire life, and I cannot imagine any other world, any other possible existence, other than being here with you and Katie. Cole smiled. "It's perfect," he said, and kissed Noah's nose.

"Maybe you'll want to stick around?"

"Maybe."

Noah grinned. He kissed Cole, this time not sweetly, not softly. This kiss was hungry, and wanting, and hot. Cole backed him against the door, dragged their hips together, ground against him as he looped his thumbs through Noah's belt loops, skirting his concealed holster.

Noah didn't know it, but Cole had already figured out the sticking around bit. There was a box hidden in his sock drawer, waiting to be wrapped and put under the tree. Inside was a pair of rings, each with three stones laid in a center channel: his birthstone, Noah's birthstone, and Katie's birthstone, all together. He imagined Noah's face when he flipped open the lid, when Cole dropped to one knee and took his hand, kissed his ring finger, and whispered, "Can I marry you, Noah?"

Can I join your life until the end? Can I join you and Katie, and can we make this family we've created last forever?

He thought he knew Noah's answer already. He hoped, at least.

And he thought he knew how Katie would react, too. In fact, he'd gotten her a necklace, a matching pendant with their three birthstones set inside a delicate circle on a golden chain.

He'd even called Lilly last week, giving her a heads-up on his intentions. *"Cole, you hardly need my permission or my blessing,"* Lilly had said. *"But you have them nonetheless. You make them both very happy."*

Noah broke the kiss, pulling back and smiling. "Take me home, Dr. Kennedy. Take me to bed." He kissed Cole again. "Show me how much you love me. Show me everything."

EXCERPT FROM THE GRAVE BETWEEN US

Please enjoy this excerpt from
The Grave Between Us
A Noah & Cole Thriller, Book 2
available at Amazon and on Kindle Unlimited.

Prologue

Cole scraped at the dark soil, fingers sliding through the dirt. His breath fogged in front of his face, puffs that kept time with the frantic, terrified pants he couldn't hold in. Mist hung between the thick tree trunks, wet, frigid claws that scratched down his spine. "Please, please…" he whimpered. "Please, no."

His fingertips hit cold skin. He stilled, breath sliding from him like the blade of a knife.

His trembling hand brushed the loose earth away from the man's face. He knew this face, knew it better than he knew his own. Dirt was clumped in the corners of the eyes and stuck to the cheekbones in long, slender lines, clinging to tear tracks. The blue lips were parted, the tip of the tongue jutting outward.

Cole held his breath and pushed two fingers into the man's mouth. He knew what he'd find.

There. Pinching, he drew back. His vision blurred as he stared at the folded paper crane.

He screamed as he fell forward, crumpling the crane in his fist as rested his cheek against Noah's cold lips. How many times had Noah lain against him, and he'd felt the rise and fall of Noah's chest or his warm exhales against his face or his hair? Now, Noah was still, and nothing was coming out of his lips ever again.

Bugling honks broke through the woods. He turned his head and gazed right. Nestled in the fog was a lake, as still as a mirror, almost black beneath the leaden fog. Cranes crossed the surface, flying in a V, their silent wings slicing the heavy forest air. He opened his palm and stared at the paper crane he'd crushed.

He turned back to Noah. Cradled Noah's cold cheek in his palm. Wiped the dirt away from Noah's tearstained temples. He pressed his lips to Noah's, his tears falling on Noah's frigid skin as he wished, with everything he had, that Noah would kiss him back, that his arms would rise out of his shallow grave and wrap around Cole, hold on to him like he used to.

Nothing.

"I'm so sorry," Cole whispered against Noah's death-pale skin. "It's my fault—"

Cole's eyes burst open as he sucked in a short, sharp breath. He was flat on his back, staring at the ceiling, at the slow circles the ceiling fan carved through the midnight stillness. He reached to the right, groping between the bedsheets and across the mattress for his lover.

Noah snorted as Cole grabbed his hip. He reached for

Cole in his sleep, tangling their fingers together and tugging Cole toward him. Cole went, rolling and melting into Noah's back, burying his face in the short strands of hair behind Noah's ear. His heart was galloping, beating so hard he thought he'd wake Noah.

Noah murmured some nonsense and kissed Cole's hand. A moment later, he snored, boneless in Cole's trembling hold.

Cole waited, counting the seconds and then the minutes as he stared at their bedroom wall, not blinking. If he blinked, if he closed his eyes for even a moment, he'd see the grave again. The woods. The lake.

He lifted his hand, staring at his palm. He could still feel the paper crane tickling his skin.

Chapter One

It happened by accident. One of life's coincidences, where inertia and circumstance connect people who are meant to be together. It had begun years before, when he'd first met Cole in a stifling interrogation room.

At the time, Cole's visits had been the only bright spots in the dreary monotony of Ian's incarceration. He'd stared at his cell walls day in and day out and felt them closing in. Not even replaying each of his kills in the darkness behind his eyelids had made his heart flutter. What was the point of fantasy if he could never wrap his hands around another man's neck? Never feel the life fade away, see the panic in another man's eyes spike and then dissipate, like mist burning off under the sun?

Then Cole had appeared. Agent Kennedy. So young he still seemed to fluoresce neon green. Ian wanted to crawl across the room and pin Cole back, knock him to the ground and kneel on his chest, get his hands in Cole's hair and his nose and his lips on Cole's skin, on the delicate, paper-thin flutter of flesh between jawbone and neck. He wanted to smell Cole, inhale the essence of him. The smell of his fear, beneath the soap and the deodorant and the laundry detergent. The smell the dogs tracked.

Young, eager Cole Kennedy, working on his doctorate, newly out of Quantico. So motivated to crack the mind of the FBI's most intriguing serial murderer.

How many months had they spent together? Days and nights lost their meaning, and Cole's eyes became the sun and the moon Ian's world orbited around. Cole's voice, replaying in his mind, his memories changing until Cole was whispering in Ian's ears, saying the things Ian wanted to hear more than anything else. Things Cole would never say. At least, not willingly. What would Cole feel like under him? He'd wondered, so many, many times.

The only drawback to his escape eight years ago was that it ended his days with Cole.

Six months ago, he'd landed in Iowa. New hunting grounds, where he could pick and pluck the men he needed, the perfect ones, when he felt that buzz in his fingers, the hum in his veins. That hunger, a desperate, howling need, the kind he quenched when he had his hands wrapped around a throat and felt a body struggling beneath him.

Suddenly—like a lightning strike—there Cole was again.

It had been a perfect January Saturday, the air crisp and brittle, the taste of fresh snow from the night before on his tongue. He'd been at the base lodge at Seven Oaks, a postage-stamp-sized ski and snowboard hillside north of Des Moines. To others, he appeared to be people watching, maybe waiting on a wife or a child to finish their day frolicking in the snow.

He'd been hunting, actually. Watching the herds move on and off the ski lifts, careen down the snowy hillsides.

He let his eyes linger on the single men. Alone. Isolated.

Ledges State Park was due south, a perfect place to take a man and a car. Ditch the car and take the life. Only the right man, though.

Ian heard Cole's voice before he saw him.

He'd never forget that voice. It still echoed in all his empty places.

He searched the crowds, scanning and discarding faces left and right, until he found the tall blond man helping a young woman on a snowboard to her feet. He was laughing, and so was a dark-haired man, older than Cole, standing beside him and helping the girl up as well. They both had their hands on her elbows, steadying her. Both had smiles stretching their ruddy cheeks. Both were laughing.

There was something about the way they stood. Angled together, as if they'd just broken apart to catch the girl. They'd been holding hands. He was sure of it.

The girl's long brunette hair was braided in pigtails, the ends poking out from beneath a knit beanie. She was squawking, grasping the two men with both hands as her snowboard slid out beneath her. She was sixteen, maybe. He'd never been good at guessing young girls' ages. He didn't have experience looking their way, letting his eyes travel over their features. For a man like him, any girl under twenty might as well have been fifteen or eleven.

Was she Cole's daughter? No. It had only been eight years since he'd seen Cole. Cole had been young and single back then. Painfully single, if the hours he showed up at the prison were any indication. No boyfriend or husband to go home to, no child he had to tuck in at night, whisper "Sweet dreams" to as he kissed her brow.

She was the older man's child, then.

Older man. About the same age as Ian, now. Jealousy slid up his spine. He hissed, almost crumpling his paper coffee cup.

Tell me, do you like your men a little bit older, Cole?

Eight years where he hadn't seen hide nor hair of Cole, and on a bright, sunny day, Cole reappeared in his life. Happy, laughing, and with an older man and a young girl. He'd made himself a *family.*

Ian watched as they steadied the girl and led her back to the bunny slope. She turned around and waved as she stood on the moving carpet that took her up the gentle hill. Cole sagged into the older man, who threw an arm around Cole's shoulders and buried his face in the crook of Cole's neck. They were laughing again.

So happy. So fucking happy together.

Ian watched the girl bobble down the hill, arms straight out, teetering left and right until she reached the bottom. She was heading straight for Cole and the other man, and she clearly had no idea how to stop. She screamed and then pitched backward, landing on her ass in a puff of snow at their feet. And the routine of helping her up began again.

So fucking happy.

He'd waited for an hour, watching—*cravingyearningscreamingraging***needing**—until a man coming off the cross-country ski trails stopped at the base area. Ian's gaze lasered to the man, taking him in micron by micron. He felt the quickening, the heat curling through his blood. He followed the skier into the parking lot, ditching his coffee cup on the way and making a show of looking for his keys. The man glanced at him and then away as he strapped his skis to the roof of his car.

It took nothing at all to come up behind him, to subdue him and bring him down silently. To push him into the back seat of his own car, restrain his hands and legs in plastic ties as he lay unconscious on the cold bench seat. Ian was out of the parking lot and driving the man's car south, to Ledges, in under a minute.

It was all wrong.

He'd started the day needing to scratch that itch. He'd needed his moment, his hit, his rush, and instead had found the last thing—the last man—he'd ever expected. The skier was supposed to plug the chasm that had opened inside him when he saw Cole, like shoving chicken bones down a drain to block the deluge.

The man didn't sound like Cole. He didn't whimper the way Cole would if Ian were thrusting inside him. He'd had time to imagine how Cole would sound, unfurl the fantasy in his mind, all those days and nights over the past eight years.

Ian fell into the past and into the darkness as he growled, as he thrust. The darkness of a grave, water spilling over the muddy sides, soaking dead skin and swirling in eddies inside open eyes and mouths. His mind kept flashing back to Cole. Haughty, arrogant Cole. Delicious, delectable Cole. The way he'd smelled, the brief taste he'd managed to steal *that day* by the lake.

Cole laughing. Cole smiling. Cole holding hands with that dark-haired older man. Cole across the interrogation table from him, hungry eyes searching inside Ian, trying to unlock all his secrets. Both of Cole's hands moving over that pencil, over wood and #2 graphite. A young man's nerves, encased in steel but betrayed by his fingers.

Memories shook his world, made the center of the sun tremble. Snow puffed around the man's face, screams rising as Ian squeezed tighter. The universe narrowed, focused down to the rush and the tremble of the man beneath him, a fish dying on Ian's line. He whispered Cole's name into the skier's hair, and everything went white, his mind going nova as heat emptied from him—and for an instant, the hunger poured out of him while the man thrashed and weakened and then, finally, went still.

Ian breathed him in, nose buried in the sweaty hair at the nape of the skier's neck.

Cole.

Wrong, all wrong. That wasn't the scent he'd held on to for eight years. That wasn't Cole beneath him.

His rush left as fast as it came, darkness and disgust sliding on its heels. Not what he'd wanted. Not even close. He sighed, pushing off the back of the man's still head.

There was no substitute for Cole. He'd been a fool to believe that.

What would it be like to take Cole? What would Cole's fear taste like? Not his youthful nerves. True fear. The slick heat of terror. The stink of it. Ian could almost imagine it, but the true essence eluded him, a shape in darkness or a shadow at midnight. There was nothing he could compare to Cole.

So many different layers to fear. So many different permutations. Different vectors that led straight to the quick. He'd poked at Cole's psyche all those years ago, had tried to stir those primal fears inside his young mind.

Back then, Cole had so much less to lose.

A teen girl. A dark-haired man. So much fucking happiness.

Ian closed his eyes and imagined Cole spread in front of him. Tied down. Pleading. Terror soaking him. Would he cry? Maybe. If Ian was good enough, he could taste Cole's salt.

He stirred, his erection rising again. This time he held his breath so the skier's wrong scent couldn't invade his mind, ruin the fantasy. This time, behind his eyelids, it was Cole beneath him. He savored the moment, running his touch up and down the cooling form. And when he came, he breathed Cole's name, shuddering as he pushed his forehead between the man's still, cold shoulder blades.

He gave himself another minute, letting the aftershocks quake through him, before he pulled back and tucked himself away. He sat on the skier's legs as he pulled out a square of paper from his jacket pocket. After so many years, he could fold these birds in seconds.

Ian grabbed the skier's hair and lifted his face out of the snow. His mouth was open, frozen in a scream, and it was easy to tuck the crane inside his cold lips, deep into the dark hollow. He pushed the jaw closed after. Rigor would take care of the rest.

Now, it was time to get to the grave.

Chapter Two

The conference room chair creaked as Special Agent Jacob Moore leaned all the way back. Cole was still waiting for one of the chairs in the FBI office to break apart cartoon-style under his weight. Jacob was larger than an NFL linebacker. Cole had never met a bigger man.

Jacob wiped his mouth and tossed his napkin on his sandwich wrapper. "I think Holly and I are going to move in together."

Noah, midchew, raised both his eyebrows at Jacob. He smiled and swallowed. "That's great. You guys going to get a new place, or are you moving in with her?"

"I'll move in with them. Brianna's settled in there. No need to upend a little kid's life moving."

"Yeah, but." Cole winked. "What about all the construction Holly will need to do? Making all her doorways taller?"

Jacob threw his napkin at Cole. Cole ducked and polished off his sandwich, grinning as Jacob shook his head.

The three of them were finishing lunch, sandwiches from one of Jacob's favorite delis, in the same room where, eight months earlier, Cole had come face to face with the man who'd captivated him in Vegas and then ghosted him: Special Agent Noah Downing.

He hadn't known about the agent part in Vegas. He hadn't been thinking about the FBI that night. He'd been too dazzled by Noah, too enthralled. His heart had gotten away from him sometime between buying Noah a drink and listening to him explain how he wanted to know if what he'd been craving meant that he was gay. Noah had questions, and Cole helped him find answers, all night long. Cole had thought, in the morning, that they were at the beginning of something.

The next evening, Cole spent four hours in the hotel bar, waiting for a call, or a text, or a smoke signal, or a bike messenger, or something, anything, from Noah. But Noah never contacted him.

One week later, he'd walked into this conference room, and there Noah was, leading the investigation into the serial murderer case Cole had been assigned from the FBI's Behavioral Analysis Unit.

They had a few more stumbles, a few false starts, but by the time they'd put the Coed Killer down, Cole was ready to make Noah—and Noah's teenage daughter, Katie—his number one priority. Three months later, he put in a transfer request and moved to Des Moines. They bought a house together, figured out how to live day in and day out together, raising Noah's teenage daughter as they filled in the blanks on their love story.

Cole's gaze drifted to Noah's ring finger and the wide band set with three birthstones. It still stunned him sometimes. He hadn't been looking for a man to spend forever with, but he'd met Noah, and that was that. How quickly he'd imagined a future filled with Noah, and with Katie. How quickly that imagined future became a necessity to him. Noah was the love of his life.

And his boss, now. Since the transfer, he technically worked under Noah, though there were some processes in place to avoid running afoul of fraternization rules.

"Cole, what time are you heading out today?" It was Noah's turn to lean back. Stretch. Sip from his soda as his foot reached out under the table and brushed against Cole's.

"About three. That will give me enough time to beat traffic and get to the school." He was picking up Katie as soon as school let out. Normally, she stayed after for cheer practice, but today, she and Cole had a date at the mall. The winter formal was around the corner, and Katie wanted to go dress shopping.

Noah nodded. "I'll be on the regional call after two thirty." The weekly video call with Sam Bray, the Special Agent in Charge of the Omaha office, and all the other agents in charge of the satellite resident agencies, the smaller field offices scattered across Omaha's area of operations.

"I'll sneak in for a goodbye kiss."

Noah's cheeks flushed, and Cole winked at him. Noah was still getting used to living his life out and proud, but he was doing pretty damn well, considering. Unconditional support from his friends and colleagues helped. Jacob had given Noah the rainbow lanyard Noah wore his ID badge on every day, a match to Cole's own lanyard. Katie already called Cole her stepfather. And even Lilly, Noah's ex-wife, seemed to support them. Maybe Noah's coming out had answered a few questions Lilly had always had, closed a few doors on fears and resentments that had lived deep inside her.

"Jacob, can we review the testimony for tomorrow?" Noah bagged up his and Cole's trash.

"Sure," Jacob rumbled. "I need the refresh."

"This for the deposition?" Cole asked. "The soybean thing?"

"Yes, the illegal soybean blends." Noah shook his head. "A big change of pace for you, I imagine. From profiling serial killers to agricultural crimes?"

"I have had enough serial killers for one lifetime." Cole meant his comment to be lighthearted, as much as a comment about murderers could be. His throat seized, though, and he had to force his next words out. "Especially ones in Des Moines."

Noah's smile turned soft. His foot hooked around the back of Cole's calf. "Well, you're in luck. For the most part, it's nice and slow around this here part of the country. The only thing Jacob and I were in danger from during this case was boredom. Do you have any idea how tedious it is to investigate eight warehouses and eighty tractor trailers for illegal oat and soy blending? I'm glad the USDA kicked in a handful of agents, or we'd still be searching."

"Not me," Jacob said. "I'd have gone headfirst into one of those bean silos, just to make it stop."

The clench in Cole's chest relaxed, and he managed a laugh. "I like your risk levels to be about as dangerous as paper cuts."

"Tedium will get me long before I bleed out from a paper cut." Noah stretched as he stood. "Ready to dive back into soybeans, Jacob?"

"Lead the way, boss."

Jacob detoured to his cubicle to grab his padfolio and files as Cole walked Noah back to his office. They lingered briefly in the doorway. They kept things PDA-free at the office, for the most part, but anyone who took a long look at them together could read their body language, Cole thought.

"We'll probably grab dinner at the mall," Cole said. "Do you want me to bring you something?"

"No, take your time. Katie's been looking forward to this. I think she wants some one-on-one time with you, and I don't want you guys to have to rush home. I'll pick up drive-through on my way out of here."

"All right. I'll text you on our way home."

Noah nodded. "Don't forget my goodbye kiss later."

Cole tugged on the end of Noah's tie, grinning. "Wouldn't dream of it, lover."

"Oh my God." Katie's voice rose behind the curtain. Cole's eyebrows arched. He stilled, pocketing his phone as his toes bounced to the beat of the hip-hop blasting over the store's speakers. He and Katie were the only ones in the changing room area, which he was thankful for. The attendant had given him a long look as Katie led him to the back, their arms laden down with dresses.

"Wait there," Katie had told him, pointing to a chair. "I'll model for you."

The attendant seemed ready to set up post and keep an eagle eye on Cole, as if he were planning dastardly deeds in the changing alcove. He'd sat down, casually letting his jacket catch behind his FBI shield, at the same time Katie said, loudly, "It's okay if my stepdad waits here for me, right?"

They were left alone after that.

He'd waited through four rounds of gowns so far. Long, to-the-floor slinky things, sequined puffballs, glittery trumpets. Each one had been too something. Too much, too little, too over the top, according to Katie. He'd followed her lead, patiently agreeing with each of her assessments. Nothing had been quite right yet. Nothing had felt like Katie.

She sounded excited about this one, though.

Katie flung the curtain back and struck a pose, beaming. A strapless, thigh-high, glittery dress hugged her body, clinging like a second skin. The jaw-dropping look was marred by her messy bun and freshly scrubbed face, as well as her slouched gray socks, still on her feet after she'd kicked off her combat boots and jeans. Those incongruous details were reminders that Katie was only sixteen. Too young, in Cole's mind, to wear that kind of dress.

But Katie clearly loved it. She spun, arms over her head. "Isn't it amazing?"

"It's a bold dress." His chest ached. He hadn't even been in Katie's life for a full year, and he was already feeling nostalgic for the summer, when she'd been just a tad bit younger. "But if we go home with that dress, Noah will fall over and die of a heart attack. And then he'll come back from the dead to lock you in your room and murder me."

Katie laughed. "It looks that good, huh?"

He nodded. "I guarantee you, your dad is not ready to see you in that."

She grinned again, running her hands down her hips. Her shoulders twisted as she gazed at her reflection in the changing room's mirror. "Okay, but that's Dad. What do *you* think?"

Cole rose, leaving his cell phone behind on the chair, and stood behind her. Their eyes met in the mirror. "Here's what I think," he said softly. "You're a beautiful girl, Katie, and you're going to be a beautiful woman. Nothing you wear will ever change that."

Katie bit her lip. One foot rose, curling around the calf of her other leg and pushing on the gray sock.

"A dress like this commands attention. I would personally rather see you wear something like this when you're older. It takes a little bit of life experience to learn how to deal with that kind of attention."

Katie was still gnawing on her lip. Her gaze had turned questioning, and she peered at Cole for a long moment. "You were on that murder case with the teenagers killed after prom, right?"

Katie, thanks to Google, knew about his work with the BAU. Or, at least, the cases that had been made public. That was only a fraction of what he'd done. The very tip of the iceberg.

"Two couples, after prom. They weren't murdered because of what they were wearing, though. They were murdered because they intersected with the path of a killer."

He still remembered the crime scene photos. Long

brunette hair splayed out in the surf, the high tide's foamy reach playing peekaboo with the two girls' disheveled curls. Sand clung to their faces where they'd been held down and smothered. Red fingernails dug furrows around their bodies, formed by their desperate scratches to escape. The boys had been killed first, and their tuxedo-clad bodies were still rolling in the waves when the police arrived, tumbling up and down like driftwood. The killer had taken his time with the two girls. Pieces of their dresses were scattered around them, glitter and sequins and satin flitting across the gray beach.

They'd only wanted to sneak a bottle of champagne on the moonlit beach after their prom, and they'd had no idea there was a predator living in his car in the parking lot.

There were times when Cole's memories turned on him, and instead of seeing one of the brunette girls on the sand, or in their body bags, or on the antiseptic steel drawer inside the morgue, he saw Katie. Katie, still as death, the same boneless slump she had when she was sleeping on the couch. Katie, her hair slicked back after a shower like the girls' hair had been slicked back before the autopsies, their corpses freshly washed.

He breathed out slowly, trying to will his galloping heart to slow. Heat crawled up his arms. A flush shivered down his spine. He tried to smile at Katie in the mirror.

Distance used to be so easy. He'd felt for the victims, and their families, in a sympathetic way. Shaken his head, thinking of their sorrow. Waited, biting his tongue and pressing pause on his questions, mentally counting seconds as victims' family members choked through their sobs, curling in on themselves as if they could stop their hearts from shattering while they faced the future with the person they loved ripped from their lives.

His fingernails bit into his palms as he tried to imagine a future without Katie or Noah. If they were there one moment and gone the next, and all he had to cling to for the rest of his life was a text about homework or *Don't forget to grab milk on the way home.* His guts twisted, tried to rise and strangle his heart.

Katie held his stare. He could see her mind spinning, see her putting pieces together. She'd embraced his world, or as much as she could at sixteen. Her psychology class was her favorite, she said, and she'd asked for psych books and true-crime novels for Christmas. Sometimes she'd blurt out questions about a serial killer or an unsolved murder in the middle of driving to school in the morning. Most days, he was torn between pride and terror for her. She was tiptoeing around the edges of shadows, trying to hold a candle against the darkness. There were things he knew that lived inside that darkness, things he never wanted her to find.

"I had another idea for the dance," Katie said, breaking eye contact in the mirror. She riffled through the bulging hangers clinging to the hooks on the wall and tugged free an airy, knee-length ditzy floral dress with a high neck and long sleeves, decorated with tea-stained lace and little buttons. It was almost *Little House on the Prairie*, but the cut was modern, and he could already tell it would look great on her. "What do you think about cowboy boots with this?"

"I think you might need a hat as well. It's cute. Let's see it on."

She grinned and shooed him out, and he went back to his chair. His heart was still pounding. He let out a shaky breath as he swiped on his phone and texted Noah. *Hey you. Home safe?* He waited, his fingers tapping on the edge of the case, counting the microseconds it took for Noah to reply.

Still at the office. :(Leaving soon. Having fun?

His eyes closed. All good. No threat. He took another breath, and then one more. Typed, *Yeah, we are. Hopefully getting close to a decision. Then dinner.*

Great. I don't know if I'm excited or dreading to see what she picks out. He sent an emoji, a yellow face with spirals for eyes.

LOL. I think you'll survive. ;)

I think I still have an Easter dress from when she was five. Big lace bib, puffy sleeves. I think she had on leggings too. How about that?

"I like this!" Katie called from behind the curtain. "It's fierce."

He tucked his phone away as Katie pulled back the curtain and struck another pose, tilting her head to the side, smiling. The dress fit perfectly, and it was sweet and light and charming, dreamy and romantic, wispy and fun. Everything that Katie herself was. "I love it," he said. "It suits you. That gets my vote for sure."

She beamed. Spun in a circle and ran her hands over the delicate fabric as it flared around her. "What do you think Dad will say?"

"He will love it." And, after he told Katie so, Noah would probably hide his misty eyes from her, pretend to do the dishes or wipe down the counters or fold laundry so she couldn't see his wobbling bottom lip.

"Awesome." She bounced on the balls of her feet. "You do know this means we need to go get boots now, right?"

Cole laughed.

Boots acquired—one tawny pair of midcalf cowboy boots, detailed with delicate white stitching—they headed for the food court, and Katie made a beeline for the Panda Express station. They both ordered orange chicken and honey walnut shrimp, then wove through the tables until Cole picked a booth in the corner, his back to the wall, with sightlines to each of the exits and entrances. Katie plopped into her seat and sucked lemonade through her straw, as graceless as a baby giraffe. He shook his head. How she was co-captain of the cheerleading squad, he sometimes couldn't understand.

"When are we going shopping for the wedding?" Katie asked, shoveling chow mein into her mouth. "Have you guys decided on a theme? Do you know what color dress I'll be wearing? I'm going to be in it, right?"

Cole froze, his chopsticks hovering in front of him, one shrimp sliding for freedom. It plopped back in the middle of his chow mein as he blinked. "We haven't really talked much about wedding plans yet."

"Really?" Katie said around a mouthful of food. She frowned. "'Cause Dad is *always* looking at wedding stuff. Like, always."

"He's what?"

"I needed to look something up, and my laptop was all the way on the table..." Depending on where Katie was, that could be an unimaginable distance of a few feet. "And Dad's iPad was right there, so I grabbed it. He had all these tabs open. Like, a dozen or more. Pictures of gay weddings, articles about planning gay weddings. He even had Pinterest open. I didn't even know Dad knew what Pinterest was."

Cole stared at his plate, poking at his orange chicken as he tried to control his face. Was he smiling? Frowning? He wasn't sure. His cheeks ached, and he spun the ring he wore on his left ring finger with his thumb. *Noah...*

He'd tried to ask Noah about his thoughts on their wedding twice. The first time, Noah had looked like a deer about to be run over by a semi, freezing for a full twenty seconds until Cole changed the topic, asking Noah to help with dinner and then teaching him how to panfry the notoriously difficult eggplant. Noah had a second drink that night after dinner, but he'd also made love to Cole with a fevered intensity that had Cole desperately trying to muffle his groans, his gasps that were practically shouts. Lord, he'd hoped Katie had her earphones in that night.

The second time, he asked Noah what he was imagining. Something indoors or out? Large or small? Church ceremony or at-home laid-back style? Noah had said he didn't know as he unloaded the dishwasher, and then he went to the garage to check the oil in his car, or organize his tool bench, or sort through boxes they had thrown out there after the move. He was, somehow, busy and unavailable to talk for the next eight hours.

For three days, Cole had glanced at Noah's ring finger every chance he could, checking to see if Noah was still wearing his engagement band. Was his avoidance a sign? Was he going to hand Cole his ring back? *Sorry, it just got too real.* But, no, the ring stayed on. Cole actually caught Noah playing with it, spinning the ring around and around as he stared off into space, his hands held in front of his heart.

"I'll have to ask him what he's found."

"Shouldn't you guys be doing that together?"

"You know your dad sometimes keeps his thoughts to himself for a while."

Katie snorted. She rolled her eyes and popped a piece of chicken into her mouth. "Mm-hmm," she hummed as she chewed. "Well, what do *you* want for your wedding?"

He shrugged. Twirled chow mein around his chopsticks. "I'm not sure. A year ago, I never imagined I'd get married. It wasn't something I ever thought much about."

"I can see it perfectly. You guys in tuxes, white roses in an arch over your heads. Everyone is there, and everyone's crying, because you guys are so disgustingly happy. Dad's definitely crying." She grinned. "I've got an indoor and an outdoor version. Want to hear both?"

Cole's gaze caught on a man sitting alone across the food court, staring their way as he sucked on the straw in his Sbarro cup. Open-front plaid overshirt, cargo pants, a stained football shirt: the uniform of a hundred thousand middle-aged men from the Midwest. Nothing remarkable about him at all.

Except he was staring at Katie. His eyes lingered on her profile, traced the ski-jump curve of her nose. Followed the wisps of hair that slipped free from the knot on top of her head. He hadn't blinked in the past twenty-three seconds.

Cole's heart jackhammered, his knuckles going white as he gripped his chopsticks. He eyeball fucked the man, boring his own stare into the man's skull. *Look at me, asshole. Look at me. Don't look at her.*

The man's eyes skittered sideways, landing on Cole for a half second before moving on. He stood, grabbed his empty food tray, and headed for the trash cans.

Cole let his breath out slowly. There was a roar in his ears, like the crashing of waves against a pebble beach. Katie's voice broke through the receding noise, coming at him like he was underwater. He snapped his gaze back as she twisted, staring over her shoulder at the empty table where the man had been.

"What is it?" she asked. "Did you see something?"

"No." He forced a smile to his face. "No, sorry. I'm sorry. I got distracted."

Her arched eyebrow called him a liar. But she didn't press, and she let him pick at his food as his hand trembled.

There was knowledge he wished he didn't have inside his brain. He'd amassed a library of facts, statistics, case studies, and biographies, all dedicated to the evil people were capable of inflicting on others. He'd dedicated his life to trying to understand how a man went from laying eyes on someone to deciding to wrap his hands around their neck. How the switch flipped in a man's mind as his gaze traveled the lines of another person's body. What he thought as his eyes drank in the pretty face of a stranger and a vision of her death bloomed like virus cells growing under a microscope slide. And everything that came after. What pliers did to flesh. The definition of piquerism. What skin looked like from the inside.

He was haunted by the things he knew.

Dirt sliding through his fingers, cold fog sliding into his lungs. A paper crane in the center of his palm—

"Tell me about your wedding plans." He tried to smile at Katie. "What are you imagining?"

"Okay, so..."

Grab your copy of The Grave Between Us today! Available at Amazon and on Kindle Unlimited.

It was just one moment.
It was just one mistake.

For years, men have been disappearing. A father in North Carolina. A boater in California. A hiker in Arkansas. And more, scattered across the United States. The FBI knows who's responsible: a serial killer they caught, a man they sent young profiler Cole Kennedy to interrogate. But then the killer escaped, leaving the FBI in chaos and Cole's psyche in tatters.

Eight years later, Cole's life has changed. He's found the man of his dreams, and he's moved to Iowa to be with Special Agent Noah Downing, leaving the FBI's Behavioral Analysis Unit and the murderers behind.

Or so he thought.

An attack on the backroads of Iowa shatters the FBI, and in the aftermath, they uncover the signature of the last man they expect: the killer who got away. Now he's hunting Noah, and the BAU descends on Des Moines, sending Cole back on the psychological chase.

To catch the only man who has ever beaten him, Cole will have to delve inside the killer's mind. It's a place he barely survived before, and the deeper he goes, the more horrors await. And though Noah is ordered to back off the investigation, he won't leave Cole to face this darkness alone.

If Cole has any hope of saving the man he loves, he must unravel the killer's twisted profile and follow his trail of death… even when it leads him into the marrow of his worst nightmares.

ALSO BY TAL BAUER

The Noah & Cole Thrillers:
The Murder Between Us
The Grave Between Us

The Sean & Jonathan Mysteries:
The Night Of

MM Sports Romance:
The Jock

The Executive Office Series:
Enemies of the State
Interlude
Enemy of My Enemy
Enemy Within
Interlude: Cavatina

The Executive Power Series:
Ascendent
Stars

The D.C. Novels:
Hush
Whisper

Stand Alone Novels

Hell and Gone: Gay Western Romantic Suspense
A Time to Rise: Gay Paranormal Romantic Suspense
Splintered: Gay Paranormal Romantic Suspense
Soul on Fire: Gay Romantic Suspense
His First Time: Gay Erotic Short Stories

STAY IN TOUCH!

To never miss a release, sale, or special, sign up for my newsletter!

If you liked this novel, please leave a rating and/or a review. Thank you!

You can find my other novels here!

Follow me on Facebook,
and visit my Facebook reader's group!
Follow me on Instagram!
Follow me on BookBub!

Check out my website at www.talbauerwrites.com

Who is Tal?

Tal Bauer writes breathtaking, heartfelt, and often action-packed gay romance novels. His characters are head over heels for each other, and fight against all of the odds for their happy ending. Nothing stands in the way of love. Tal is best known for his romantic suspense novels, including the *Executive Office* series, *The Night Of*, *The Jock*, and the Noah & Cole thrillers, including *The Murder Between Us* and *The Grave Between Us*.

facebook.com/talbauerauthor
instagram.com/talbauerwrites
amazon.com/author/talbauer
bookbub.com/authors/tal-bauer

ACKNOWLEDGMENTS

Thank you to Maria, Loretta, Lindsey, and Charlotte for their incredible help with this novel.

Printed in Great Britain
by Amazon